Hugh Vaughan has published - *A Bump on the Road* - a book of short stories emanating from the innocent years before secondary school, and the growing out of it. A Bump on the Road reflects an observant child in Ireland attempting to understand the world around him. The reader is taken on a gamut of emotions in this rich and amusing journey of growing up in Ireland.

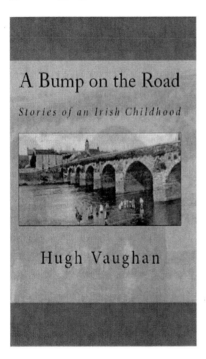

'Vaughan is one of the most eloquent Irish writers to emerge in recent years.' Irish Emigrant.

Contact: hugh@hughmvaughan.com
             http://www.hughmvaughan.com

Cillefoyle Park

'What are you doing up there? I am ready to go shopping.'

'I'm watching two youngsters up to no good. They are back in the fire station's garden again. I'll be right down.'

'Make sure you close the door. You left it open and all the heat from the house has escaped into the tower!'

'Sorry, Marie, I'll be right down. Just waiting to see what those two are up to.'

Harry O'Donnell heard the door below bang shut. He was in his tower surveying the surrounding streets in late December. The mid-afternoon curdled sky cast a violet twilight over the city as he watched the two young men at the end of his street. The streetscape beyond Cillefoyle Park fell to the River Foyle. People scurried about doing last minute Christmas shopping, rugged up against the damp raw wind. Solemn car drivers faced the streaming traffic.

Harry watched as his friend and neighbour, Dermot Lavery left his flat for work and walked down towards the Northland Road, towards the two suspicious figures. Harry adjusted his binoculars, and tried to identify them. He was sure he had taught one of them a few years ago. One was busy in the fire station's garden. The other stood across the road, looking about, nonchalantly, hands in his pockets. A smile rose on his face when he saw Dermot approaching. The one in the garden stood by the bench and bent down for a second. After a moment's disappearance, he resurfaced, holding a brown package. He crossed over to his companion, zigzagging through the traffic, forcing the cars to brake to avoid hitting him. He gave the parcel to the other guy who put it underneath his zipped, black jacket. They talked a moment, looked up at Dermot, laughed and then went south towards the city.

The wooden seat overlooked a grassy patch in the station's garden and down the hill towards Clarence Avenue. The seat was used by nomadic older men or over-laden women collapsing under the weight of shopping bags and children. Harry suspected it had more clandestine uses.

Dermot wore his customary fashionable clothes: jet-black Wrangler jeans, with a slight flare, a Ben Sherman button-down checked shirt under a blue Wrangler denim jacket and a pair of well-worn highly-polished leather brogues. Some people said he was vain, Harry felt it was an undeserved opinion. Yet, his unblemished face was youthful and pale for his twenty-seven years – he looked more like an

6

eighteen year old, without the pimples. He maintained some facial growth to balance his seraphic features. Startling diamond blue eyes and his high cheek bones were bequeathed by his dandyish father, but the smattering of insipid freckles and pouting full lips belonged to his mother. Where his thick wind-combed mat of unruly black hair came from, no one knew – perhaps it had skipped a generation. He was a dapper slim figure – six feet plus, fitted snappish clothes, a handsome individual about town. Everyone said so. On closer inspection, his glacial eyes caught people's attention, a disquieting gaze; its intensity unnerved anyone that took time to look. Few looked for very long.

Dermot Meets Trouble

Dermot never felt comfortable walking the Northland Road. He was going to see a fellow socialist who lived at the city end of it. The route passed a huge stone wall bordering the estate of Dill House, the local big house, at one time. It always unnerved him – a lonely stretch of the road that made him feel vulnerable, especially late at night on his way home after a night on the town or after work. Sometimes it couldn't be avoided. The site proposed for a new university was behind the forbidding stone wall. Dermot, his colleagues, local politicians and business groups were at the forefront of lobbying for the university status of Magee College, an established higher education institute since the mid-eighteen hundreds that was situated at the northern end of the wall. A garden nursery occupied the other end.

Dermot looked down the road towards the city when he reached the junction. He preferred to walk down Lawrence Hill, towards the river and then along the Strand Road to the city. Lawrence Hill was a steep thoroughfare, going and coming, but it also had cordial childhood memories of playing street soccer when he stayed with his cousin, Liam.

The nursery's entrance, solid and ancient, was at the city side of the wall with a magnificent arch. The protective crown provided occasional refuge from the elements for Dermot and other Derry natives. An ornamental boot scraper took sentinel place at the gate lodge on its left with a window of lead light set in a similar arch adding a pleasing attribute to the gaunt fortification.

To his consternation, he thought he had spotted Brendan and Mick at the junction earlier. Unhappily they were in front of him, waiting. An aura of pallor hung over them, soon to engulf Dermot. They were the school yard bullies and his nemesis. Sometimes they drank at his work – The Inishmore Bar. Their agitated behaviour, constantly glancing over their shoulders, gave Dermot the impression they were in the middle of something. He couldn't avoid them as he strode towards the two – hiding his abhorrence with his head held high and an unyielding expression in contrast to their smiles as big as the proverbial Cheshire cat's.

Strangely, there was little traffic on this dreary afternoon, even though the schools were finished. The black jacketed young man called to him:

'What about ye, Dermot? Great to see ya!'

'Where are you off to, boys?'

'Oh, just doing a wee job. Why don't you come with us?'

'No thanks, lads. Off to work. Your uncle Cathal wouldn't be too happy if I was late.'

Their contempt for Dermot was obvious in their patronising smirks. Their contempt for themselves was let loose on the unfortunate barman. Mick's uncle Cathal was Dermot's boss and Dermot used his name in the conversation to remind them of the connection. Cathal was always remonstrating with the two. With their palpable anxiety and false bonhomie, Dermot knew something was amiss and wanted to get away.

Harry had mentioned that he had seen two men loitering in the fire station's garden several times. It must have been Brendan and Mick. Dermot could see Mick had stuffed something under his zipped jacket. Brendan and Mick had picked it up from the drop location behind the bench in the fire station's little garden. Behind the seat were bricks covering a secret space draped in protective ivy.

'Now Dermot you wouldn't want to annoy us today. We are busy boys.'

'Well, sure then I'll be on my way, lads.'

Mick tapped the front of his jacket and anyone could see something was inside. It was obvious they wanted Dermot to ask what it was, what they were doing. Dermot didn't care and wanted to get away as soon as possible from their mindless bravado. Mick had the eyes of a battered boxer, and kept looking about, his eyes darting up and down the road, probably looking for any security forces.

'Oh shit! Look up there. We had better get going.'

Mick exclaimed as he nudged Brendan. As they had stood talking, an army patrol had gathered at the top of Lawrence Hill, and it was walking towards them. Momentarily Dermot considered returning home to avoid being caught with the two boys, but that action too might draw the army's attention – the soldiers may have seen them talking. They were caught in no man's land in the middle of the dreaded stone wall. The boys became more nervous.

Dermot commanded:

'Let's walk.'

'Who the fuck are you to give orders?'

Dermot marched on. If they could make it to the sanctuary of the nursery entrance at the end of the wall, they could vanish from view. However, he also saw some movement at the bottom of Asylum Road, almost opposite the archway. The patrol was behind them and someone was in front. It was as depressing as a Sunday afternoon in Ballymena, the centre of Bible Belt Northern Ireland. Was it a trap set up by the security forces for Brendan and Mick? Had Dermot unwittingly walked into it?

Someone was in front of them, pressed into a privet hedge, yet something was familiar about the figure. Being Derry, everyone was familiar. Dermot strode on, as fast as he could, without drawing attention, keeping an eye on the hedge, his breathing jagged. Brendan, whose legs reminded Dermot of a bandy-legged sailor, and Mick tried to keep up with Dermot.

Dermot was sure he caught the blurred sight of another pair of legs. A little head peered fleetingly over the leaves. Were there two people hiding in the thicket? Mick also noticed and nodded to his companions. Both acknowledged with slight twist to their heads, a familiar Derry mannerism. Mick bent down as if to scratch his shin and ran his finger over the handle of the gun taped to his leg. It was unloaded. Whoever may be waiting for him did not know that. The army patrol was advancing behind them. They had no choice, but to go forward and face the uncertainty of what lay ahead.

They made it to the arch, relaxed a little and stepped underneath, hidden from view. No one was around the nursery's entrance. Dermot bent forward to use the eighteenth century iron boot scraper, balanced his shoe on its edge and fiddled with his lace, as if tying it while watching the patrol's progress.

Suddenly a siren screamed. He jolted erect and saw a couple of kids in the hedge opposite peer out. He relaxed a little. The fire station at the top of Lawrence Hill sped into action. The doors opened and the brigade pulled out, lights flashing. As the engine passed them they saw the firemen inside the cab struggling into their uniforms. The patrol stopped and watched the firemen too. This allowed the three of them time to cross the street and get out of sight – their eyes fixed on the activity in the hedge in front. Two kids jumped out and ran off up Asylum Road.

Half way up Asylum Road, Brendan laughed:

'I nearly shit myself. I was as scared as a turkey at Christmas. What do we do now, Mick?'

Before Mick could answer Dermot said as he turned to leave them:

'See you later, boys. Actually, I don't want to see you two again. I am off to work.'

'Dermot, you're coming with us.'

Mick ordered, trying to be assertive, but his trembling voice reflected his panic.

'You know Mick, you have a great future behind you. No, lads, I am going through Brooke Park, if the side gate is open. You two are going wherever, just stay well away from me. Yous are up to something and I don't want any part of it. So fuck off!'

Dermot strode off from the troublesome comrades – Brendan and Mick were immature young men. But the pair were dangerous lumps of nuisance, not only for Dermot, but also as members of the Irish Republican Army, the IRA. They were only fit to be foot soldiers, if that. Probably useful at times, providing they did what they were told and were under constant supervision.

Mick fancied himself; his high opinion of himself was beyond a joke – it was toxic. Mick being Cathal's nephew seemed to have some sort of kudos. After this escapade, Dermot had no doubts about them.

Mick grabbed Dermot by the arm. This was still a dangerous situation. Dermot turned quickly and pushed both of them into a nearby garden, out of possible sight of the patrol and anyone watching.

'Do you not see them down there? They could come up here any time. This is not the time nor the place to play silly buggers.'

'Never mind them, you are coming with us.'

Mick wanted to show who was boss, throw his weight around and show the power he had in the gun – he wanted to frighten Dermot; he wanted to tear slices off him. Everything about Dermot he despised: his educated tone, his dapper clothes, his good looks, his friendship with his uncle and his socialist ideas. Mick bent down, pulled the Smith and Wesson from his ankle and stuck it into Dermot's groin. His face contorted as if he was smelling shit in the sun.

Without a moment's hesitation Dermot's knee was into Mick's groin and he pulled Brendan's hair so that his face met the same knee. Both fell onto the ground, and Dermot retrieved the gun, but felt something heavy under Mick's jacket. It felt like another gun. The gun that Mick pulled on Dermot was empty and he threw it into a hedge out of sight and for Mick to retrieve after he had left them.

'You bastard, pulling a gun on me. So that's why you were hobbling, the gun was taped to your leg. This is dumb shit. God, you guys never learn. It's often a person's mouth that breaks his nose. I'll be telling Cathal about this. Go! Get lost.'

'Ah, me balls. Jesus Christ. I'll fuckin' kill you.'

'Fuck off and leave me alone.'

Dermot left the two goblins of stupidity. Mick called after him, issuing all sorts of expletives and death sentences. Brendan said nothing. They then realised they were drawing attention to themselves so got up and hobbled across the street and up the hill towards Rosemount.

Dermot walked across a side street towards Brooke Park, still watching for any sign of the army patrol or the two jokers he left lying in the garden. 'Póg mo thóin' was the last thing he heard, but he wasn't too sure if Brendan had found new confidence and yelled it at him. When he looked back they had gone. Dermot thought 'up yours too mate' as he hurried away, thinking Northland Road was definitely a place to avoid. He spotted Frank leaning against a wall, his old childhood friend, also to be avoided, so he did.

When he took a side street to avoid Frank he spotted Mick and Brendan and decided to follow them. He crossed back into a lane and saw them shuffle up some side streets, getting away from any attention they might have caused. They entered a lane backing onto Brooke Park. Mick handed Brendan the parcel, who opened it and then placed the two guns into the brown wrapping. Brendan carefully rolled the paper around the weapons. Mick staged for Brendan as he climbed over the wall with the package and appeared a few minutes later on the wall and dropped into the lane again.

Dermot positioned himself behind a fat oak tree as they came down the lane past him. He heard Mick speak:

'Jesus, I'll kill that bastard one of these days.'

'I'll kill for a drink, right now.'

'Naw, Brendan. If we arrive back with drink on our breaths we will be dead meat. A drink of Club orange and a Kit-Kat may do us. There's a telephone in the shop up here. Then we'll see Cathal and tell him the craic. We need to get our story straight.'

They moved off and Dermot couldn't hear any further conversation, but thought he needed to speak to Cathal before them. He went up to the garden gate where the guns were hidden and where the 'drop' was. He pushed the gate open after it jammed a bit. There was no need for Brendan to mount the wall. Inside, the gardener grew mountainous vegetables. It was full of all sorts – spud bags, pots, cloches, and a water drum sat in the middle of it.

Dermot closed the gate and walked towards Brooke Park side entrance. He went to work.

Inishmore Bar

The Inishmore in Bishop Street, a single-fronted bar, unchanged in decades, but nicely maintained. Dermot walked in, the bar was unattended. The lounge room's door was closed at the rear. An old fellow sat perched on a stool to his right, glancing half-cocked at the television high up in the corner. The old fellow twisted his head slightly, nodded and returned to watching the television. Dermot greeted him:

'Howdy John.'

'Aye. What bout ye?'

'Grand.'

'Frank was in looking for you.'

'Oh!'

John rarely spoke, an agelast of distinction – he wasn't a regular source of optimism and joy so Dermot didn't look for any further conversation. A door closest to the bar led to a narrow hall, a storeroom and office on the left and the rear heavy dirty brown door with its many locks. He looked outside, into the back yard. To the right was an urinal, against a cemented wall, often painted, but now flaking and the gutter ran into a drain. A pipe ran along the wall, above the urinal connected to a cistern for the lavatory. It's chipped brown door open, toilet roll scattered around the bowl. A stale acidic smell hung about. His first job, when he started his shift would be clean up the place with a bucket of bleach. Above, a standalone iron roof provided shelter for all the toilets. Few ventured out there, only through necessity. Few women frequented the pub – it was a 'man's pub'.

The cellar door was open in the yard, its flap doors upright, a short ladder leading down into the blackness. Grabbing its side, he called down. Surprisingly, the cellar was huge for the size of the pub. He was aware of others inside, a stale odour of musty clothes and a hoppy aroma rose from the airless bunker below. A faint but nostalgic smell of oil unsettled him, reminding him of the little cans of oil used on his bike's chain as a child.

'Cathal, are you there?'

'I'll be up in a minute'

'No problem. I'll start my shift.'

'Hold on.'

Dermot heard shuffling down below – he sensed danger and recoiled in defence. A light came on and he saw Cathal and somebody else – maybe his nephew. Someone sat on a bench under the ladder. The two boys couldn't have got to the pub any faster than Dermot. The well-worn ladder and concrete passage way led into the dank space and on either side, sloping into various shades of gloom, was the residue of pub life: beer barrels, broken chairs and tables, numerous drink advertisements decrepit with damp and age, and rusty tools and pipes.

Cathal had a few papers in his hand when he climbed the ladder, and ignored Dermot for a few minutes, fiddling with them.

'I suppose you're going to tell me about those buck eejits, my nephew and his chum? How they safely got you out of harm's way.'

'That's right, only for them I would be up against the wall in Castlereagh Barracks having a power shower up my ass.'

'Well, you know what that crowd thinks up there, we Bog Irish live in the mire and need a shower now and again.'

'Did they tell you they pulled a gun on me too?'

'To defend themselves? Sounds like a different version of a story. I would be surprised if it wasn't. I'll have word with those boys, Dermot. Leave it to me. I'll have a chat with the right people. They have their uses, I'm sure. Just get overexcited, become even dumber. Stay away from them. I'll take care of it. Seriously, Dermot avoid them.'

'Suppose being family and all that. They drink here sometimes. Cathal, I can't avoid them.'

'Sure, it's a wee town. We are all family. I'll tell them to drink elsewhere. You are family and like one big happy family we fight like geese.'

Dermot explained what happened and knew Cathal was genuine in his sentiments to deal with the situation. Dermot was a lifelong friend and Cathal's family had lived beside Dermot's Granny, but Dermot was not family and still seen as a bit of a wild-card.

Cathal was wary of Dermot's intelligence and politics and how he kept his own counsel. Dermot was a strong willed person, as Cathal called him. Not weak like many he knew – it wasn't the first time that Cathal accused him of holding out, commenting 'still waters run deep'. Dermot was a free thinker, a socialist. Cathal wasn't. They weren't quite on the same side, but nevertheless he trusted Dermot.

Cathal was from a staunch Republican family, all involved in some way. Although Cathal was a business man, he was the head of Sinn Fein and closely connected to the Boys, the IRA. Dermot worked well with Cathal, though he couldn't say Cathal was a member of the IRA.

Most of the pub clientele were supporters or some were even members. Perhaps funds were laundered through the business. It was a question of keeping his mouth shut – as they said in Derry – whatever you say, say nothing.

The run-in with his nephew was tricky. Was it a run-in with the IRA? Was it seen as a challenge to the IRA? Cathal had told Dermot not to worry and he knew Cathal had inordinate influence over his nephew and Brendan, but he also knew that Cathal's brother, Conor, was serving time after he was shot and arrested by the army. Conor had been attempting to retrieve guns at an arms dump behind Creggan on the Donegal border. He was lucky to be alive.

A Special Air Services unit, the SAS, a specialist unit of the British Army for covert reconnaissance and counter-terrorism, operated at times in the area. The soldiers lay in wait, camping overnight in the fields, waiting. Locals – farmers and hunters with legally held guns – sometimes hunted for birds, foxes or rabbits in that area and had reported seeing men in distant fields, suddenly appearing and disappearing. Many suspected the army – the SAS.

The belief of the Republicans and many in the community was that the SAS operated a 'Shoot to Kill Policy'. It was known that the SAS and the British Army camped out, hoping to catch the IRA moving weapons, training or planning an operation. They caught Conor red-handed. Luckily for him a local farmer and his family appeared with his sheep when he was arrested, otherwise he might not have survived.

As Cathal was leaving the pub later in the evening, he called Dermot over.

'I got a phone call about them, from you know who. I have sorted it. Just ignore those two, don't get in their way.'

'That's easier said than done. They seem to make a habit of getting in my way, like today. Somebody needs to control them. Mind you, it'll be like putting that stripy toothpaste back in its tube.'

'Funny! My advice Dermot is to forget all about what happened today. Don't overstep the mark, ignore them. Don't let them provoke you, Dermot. Any problems? Come to me. It will never be mentioned by Brendan or Mick again. They too were told to forget it. Stay away from them.'

'I will if they will. You know, sometimes the way to deal with stupidity is get angry with those that are.'

'Don't worry. They have been dealt with. You stay out of it. I'll tell them to stay away. We all have respect for you. Happy families again! Are we? Conor is getting out soon and he wants to become more political, even a peace campaigner. God forbid. Maybe you could mentor him. Talk to him. Educate him.'

'Yes, Cathal.'

'Okay, okay. Let's wait and see. I see from your face that you want to stay out of it. Have a drop on the house to calm your wee nerves.'

Cathal grabbed Dermot around the neck and kissed him on his cheek. Jesus wept, Bondi Beach here I come, murmured Dermot to himself.

Dermot's Liaison

'Dermot, will I see you soon?'

'Yeah, I will be working for the remainder of the holiday so not going too far. Let me know when I can come over.'

'See you, take care in the snow.'

'Sure, Pauline, you know I love this weather. Love the icy-watery stuff dripping down my face. It's peaceful. The streets are empty. The people are all curled up by the telly. It's cleansing. You feel alive. You think this is winter! You should visit Edinburgh.'

Pauline Laughlin stood watching as Dermot Lavery strode off down the virgin snowy path. The unfathomable Dermot Lavery. God, he says the daftest things, always the best of craic, always in good mood. Was he always joking? Pauline was never too sure, but sure of his sensual gravity. She watched a moment longer from the bedroom, as he crossed the sloping street outside Cillefoyle Park and disappeared into the shower of sleet, a white sprinkling on his shoulders already. He was going to the pub, even though it was shut, some stocktaking or something. Pauline knew not to query his behaviour – a stony countenance and a slight furrowed brow was his invariable reaction to her questions.

Pauline switched off the light and was about to close the curtains, but instead opened the window and extended her hand into the falling snowflakes, each melting on impact. Dermot was right, it was cleansing and vital. She felt the cool water through her fingers and patted her brow with them, trying to feel as alive as Dermot. No, it didn't work; it was just too bloody arctic. Only madmen and Dermot would go out on a night like that. She remembered her childhood diversion of sticking her foot out of bed and waiting until it got tinglingly cold. Then she pulled it into the warmth under the blankets and curled up, wrapped around her sister like spoons.

Was the affair with Dermot just an escape from her claustrophobic domesticity? Did she really love home and home making? She loved her husband and her kids. She was just bored and he was boring. But it wasn't fair to her husband and children. She knew that. Was it too close to home having an affair with a neighbour? She knew the answer to that too. Dermot was one hundred per cent trust worthy, but there was a chance of getting caught by a nosey neighbour like Harry O'Donnell in his tower. She knew she was the weak link in the duo.

She glanced down after Dermot and checked her neighbour's tower. A brightening glow of a cigarette or a cigar caught her attention. Sure enough, Harry was in his tower. She stepped back into the warmth of her bedroom, closing the heavy window and pulled the bulky olive-braided curtains over the window, a remnant of past lives, of winter draughts. She hated them – the curtains, the old house, and the penetrating draughts. It gnawed at her despite the fact she had created a thoroughly modern feel throughout her home. It wasn't enough. She wanted a modern home, a contemporary home. A new bungalow out the Culmore Road was her heart's desire, where all the quality people lived. This draughty monolith was old-fashioned but Sean, her husband, loved it for the very reasons she hated it.

Pauline wanted to get rid of the original front door and its jaded curtain and install a new modern double glazed plastic variety with windows to match. She had read in one of her weekly magazines about double glazing and the insulation it provided. They were used in Germany where winters were much colder. 'PVC', she muttered. 'Yes, I want all new PVC windows and doors in my house'.

She sang it as she skipped down the stairs. Unfortunately, her husband Sean thought differently, a stick-in-the-mud sort of guy – if it ain't broken, don't fix it. Installing the central heating was a major step into the twentieth century for him. He'll never change. I married an old stick-in-the-mud sort of guy. A bore, I am stuck in the mud of Cillefoyle Park. Her mind spun in resentment of her domestic life.

The living room was her pride and joy, recently decorated. It was the result of ploughing through her copious weekly issues of the home decorating magazines – Pauline's bible in modern lifestyle. She was stuck in the furthest city in the north west of Europe. Stuck! Stuck! She craved the passion of the cities of the world – New York, London, Paris. This is what she was missing. Although Sean liked the idea of a modern comfortable home, he was more than happy to leave the decoration up to his wife. It would occupy her – a hobby. He knew she had the moods of a banshee but thought she would settle. The upholstered leatherette bar in the living room corner was Sean's input, fully stocked, of course. Blue Nun was a favourite. She hated the bar until she saw it in a James Bond film on television. Bond was mixing his own cocktail. Even though they rarely had dinner parties - they didn't have the same friends – Pauline liked the idea that they could have them. She planned them in her head, but they never materialised. Yet both thought of themselves as a thoroughly modern couple.

She walked over to her new record player, a Christmas present from Sean, and ran her finger over its cover. Already a covering of coal dust had settled on it. She hated the open coal fire too. Songs of Ireland and something by the Beatles were her only two LPs, purchased by Sean. Collecting the latest records in the charts would be a new hobby. Jazz was for sophisticated people. Pauline found a new project for the New Year – music. Perhaps she'd have a musical dinner party displaying her new-found knowledge of music, of jazz.

Sean and the kids were at his mother's in Ballykelly and staying overnight – having consumed another Christmas dinner with plenty of liquid refreshments during and after. Sean enjoyed being fussed over by his mother and Pauline was glad she didn't have to witness the two of them playing doting mother and loyal son. She feigned a migraine as an excuse for not going with the family to the in-laws. Her mother-in-law was a better cook than Pauline and was forever offering advice. It would have been an evening of little nudges and morsels of cooking tips. Another escape. 'I'll give you the recipe for that, Pauline. Sean would love it'; letting Pauline know she was a better cook.

Pauline agreed, she was, always great food with freely available booze. She adored the children. Pauline and her mother-in-law just couldn't rub along together. She loved the soap opera; Coronation Street but Pauline hated it – all those tiny houses. Surprisingly for a God-fearing country woman she enjoyed a drink herself, but thought her daughter-in-law was a light-headed townie. The townie usually disappeared into a fog of wine when visiting. Lately her absence from family visits to the in-laws had not been commented upon. Sean seemed to accept the situation. Always a man to ease the path of peace, just accepted it – they all could relax.

Pauline and Sean had socialised extensively before the children were born. Even when Sam was born, they could always get a baby sitter, but now with three, life was too busy and their relationship wilted. Neither partner making any real effort. Sean didn't want to go out to the pubs or socialise anymore. He was married to the job – working as a manager at Du Pont, a sprawling American chemical complex – people like Sean became known as Derry Yanks. Sean seemed to like the status quo. He had a wife at home, the kids looked after and a lovely home. He was quite possessive of his achievements. His sexual demands were few. Pauline didn't complain, Sean's money was regular and plentiful and she had Dermot, at least for now. Du Pont kept the fox away from many a door in Derry.

Pauline felt deflated – her normal reaction after Dermot's departure. The meshing of guilt and shame, but it soon extinguished. Thoughts of previous extra-marital entanglements swept through her head – nothing as serious or as dangerous as Dermot. She sat in front of the fire, a smoking slack heap – a black covering so fine that it almost smothered it, tiny purple-orange and red sparks emitting from its base. The ebony seductress in the picture above the white and pink tiled fireplace dominated the living room. The swirling orange circles on the wall paper harmonised with the expensive orange fireside mat. A huge brown corded suite filled most of the room, its multi-coloured cushions in disarray on the mat. The television animated in the corner, barely audible. She glanced at the television on her way to the kitchen for her cup of coffee and saw an advertisement for Kenneth McKellar – a Scottish New Year's Eve institution. Her mother-in-law wouldn't miss it. Digging a nail into her hand, she breathed deeply. Pauline needed coffee.

Rusty, their golden retriever lay under the table at the far end of the recently installed kitchen. His head moved slightly in tandem with his tail when he saw Pauline. Yellow tiles flowed between the kitchen mahogany units – each tile a mass of octangular patterns in jade. The room's piece de la resistance – a breakfast bar in matching colour, attached to the cupboards, commanding the centre of the room. The cupboard door under the sink was still open. She walked over to the tap to fill the kettle, peered underneath into the open cupboard and found the wrench still inside.

Dermot had come over earlier in the evening. Pauline's excuse, as if she needed one, was the leak under the sink. The sink trap probably needed tightening again. Dermot had climbed under to adjust it and she was standing beside him, trying to see what he was doing. Within seconds he had his hand up her skirt, fumbling with her knickers and biting at her clothes. Pauline was on his face sucking and licking for all her worth.

Rusty thought it was great fun and jumped into the fray. 'Back to your bed,' snapped Dermot. 'Bed,' both said in unison, giggling like two kids.

Rusty, disappointed, head down, returned to his usual location.

Pauline grabbed Dermot by the ear as he was kneeling, acting like a dog about to perform a trick and claim his reward. He scarpered on all fours into the living room and onto the orange fireside mat. Dermot's erection bulged in his jeans. Pauline tossed her knickers aside

21

and unbuttoned Dermot's trousers. She pulled them and his underpants down to his boots, while he was nuzzling at her crotch.

'I need to get my boots off.'

'Nope, no time.'

They aligned themselves as he thrust deep inside, her legs splayed, one of them feeling the heat from the fire. He drove down into her with an unexpected force, his legs coupled at the bottom. With the hard floor under her back Pauline felt his thrusts more than usual. For some reason, his coming was also an unexpected force and both moaned in rhythm to his pelvic thrusts. It was a coming worth waiting for, short and sweet.

Both relaxed, Dermot on top, squashing Pauline, before being pushed onto his side. As they lay awhile by the fire light Pauline queried:

'That was quick?'

'That, my dear, was your Christmas present! No point in messing about.'

'Have you been abstaining or what? That was some powerful shooting. I could feel the pumping of it and you came so quickly. Anyway I want a David Cassidy LP for my new record player. Or is it David Essex?'

'Well, you know what a man and his tools are like. That wrench and your legs were much too much for me.'

Pauline rolled her eyes and cleaned herself with her knickers, and was gone upstairs in a jiffy. What am I doing? Always the same – guilt! It was good fun but these quickies made her worry. Oh, if people knew me, knew me really. Pauline, you are an idiot. Once again Pauline knew she had to bury these thoughts and just be more careful. Dermot was good like that, dependable, non-demanding, knew the score. He didn't want any trouble. It was their secret. No one will know. I trust Dermot. He trusts me. He is such a cold fish, at times. Forget about it. No one knows. Just beware. Pauline liked this subterfuge, so did Dermot. He's a real bloke but a gentleman bloke, unlike some other locals. Well read – knows his history. If only he would lighten up a bit. Pauline's thoughts swirled around as before. Enough. Enough. She tried to stop thinking about the mess, but the thought of the kids brought a knot to her stomach.

She had gone into her bedroom and looked outside, still snowing. The cool air came off the window was fresh between her legs. A David Cassidy song popped into her head. She tried to remember the song.

22

Oh come on. What is it? Pauline was thinking hard, burying into her recent memories of the last few days on the radio. The tune was in her head – Daydreamer. Dat. Da. Da.

'Cos I was living in a world of make believe.

But now you're gone.

I'm just a daydreamer.

I'm...walking in the rain'

She repeated it over and over again, priming her memory to get the lyrics firmly into her head.

After cleaning herself in the bathroom she put on a clean pair of pants. Her bed was made up, but she noticed one of her husband's hairs on his pillow. She ran her finger over the edge of the bedside table, and then dug her fingernail into her palm.

Dermot was left to his own devices. He only had a spotlessly clean hanky and didn't want to use that so hobbled his way to the kitchen, his trousers still around his ankles for some kitchen roll. After cleaning himself and dressing he returned to the living room. He was about to pick up the cushions and noticed he had dribbled over the mat and returned to the kitchen for more kitchen roll. He wiped as best he could and tossed the paper onto the fire.

A drink was needed. He switched on the bar light and helped himself to a Gin and Tonic when Pauline returned, all neat and hair brushed. She didn't look at him:

'Making yourself at home? I'll have one of those, thanks.'

They sat on the sofa with an upholstered sigh, the light from the television flickering shadows on the wall, looked at the fire and enjoyed the quiet, jigging flames. Dermot spoke first:

'I guess I should make tracks.'

'Literally.'

'What?'

'Making tracks, literally, you will be tonight, in all that snow.'

Dermot smiled, pecked her on her cheek and was by the kitchen door putting on his coat before Pauline had drained her gin and tonic.

They kissed at the back door, lingering rather than passionate.

'What a night, do you need to go out?'

'I don't mind at all, actually I am looking forward to it, walking through the streets of Derry on my own.'

After she left him at the back door she went up to her bedroom to watch him. Pauline detected his usual toughness – a resolve. His youthful face and his empathetic character hid something deeper. This was not a man to betray, thought Pauline. He was an ideal barman though – friendly, good listener but talkative and tough, when necessary. Why was he going to the bar? Nobody would be out visiting any bar on a night like that.

Back in the Tower

Harry was on his first tipple of Bushmills whiskey – a further endearment to his already melancholic inner glow. It was the satisfying result of the seasonal abundance of food and drink. Harry had relinquished his fireside comfort after a sleepy embrace with his wife and climbed up to the chilly tower. He sucked on a fat cigar of indeterminate origin – a Christmas gift from his son, Niall. It was a clear and dazzling vista that lay before him. The resolute figure of Dermot down below stamped his solitary presence into the crisp-topped layer of unblemished snow, but as Harry knew, little was unusual about Dermot. His indistinct silhouette turned in the street, stood a moment and looked up towards the park, before resuming his trek down towards Northland Road, leaving imprints in the snow. His stride was unworried by the brittle surface. Perhaps, thought Harry, he had a good pair of snow-crunching boots.

Cillefoyle Park had a communal garden, unseen in a canopy of white. To his right sat two similar houses, not quite as grand, but still solid red brick double-fronted homes, each with a different porch. The furthest, the Laughlin's, had bay windows and had installed windows in their porch. Their exterior light casted a yellow fuzz on the snow. Harry pulled in his cigar from the outside of the open window and lowered it unseen into the well of the tower. Although he was a familiar figure in the tower, it was best not to be seen too often. His astute wife constantly warned him he would be regarded as a nosy neighbour given his propensity to use binoculars on his frequent visits to his tower.

Dermot turned right into the Northland Road, the route taking him past Saint Eugene's Cathedral, and through the Bogside, on his way to his work in the Inishmore Bar. It was opposite the demolished jail on Bishop Street, where only a tower built in 1791 remained. It was a holiday night and coupled with the dangerous weather, it was a strange night to walk, but Harry thought no more about it, after all it was Dermot. He would avoid Lawrence Hill, a street so steep that Harry avoided it under normal circumstances, but it would be a treacherous endurance going up or down, even for Dermot. Harry could barely see the roof of the fire station on the Northland Road. Its little garden, indistinguishable even from Harry's elevated position, was smothered in white, including the bench enjoyed by all sorts of passing pedestrians. The visits by two young men over the last year interested Harry. Dermot stepped into the obscured garden, looked around, swept the snow off the back of the bench with his hand, bent down, disappearing from Harry's view for a few seconds. He reappeared and returned to the main thoroughfare for his trip south to the city. Harry reminded himself to visit the garden to investigate his new-found interest.

Harry felt the heat in his cheeks. Blushing with festive tolerance and aided with copious red wine he followed the determined gait of the barman below. Harry loved Christmas. His native city gleamed like a scene from A Christmas Carol, a book he reread every year – Dickens's famous book of redemption. The Foyle River flowed in the reflected glory of the moonlit night.

Derry, a luminous divided city in the North West of Ireland, bordering the windswept majestic beauty of county Donegal. Separated naturally by the fast flowing River Foyle – Protestants on one side, Catholics on the other. Each group had their own name for the city. The official British name was Londonderry, favoured by the Protestant and Unionist sections of the community. The Maiden City, so called because its historic medieval walls, defended by the Protestants were never breached by the famous siege of 1690. Those Protestant descendants within the walls and without who settled in the north of Ireland many centuries ago called the city 'Londonderry'. The native-born Gaelic Irish – the Catholics – know the city as Doire or Derry. Yet many citizens call it the city of Derry, when referring to everyday happenings, especially when the context was removed from political overtones.

This was the historic city of Derry/Londonderry, heavily burdened with a bloody past. That night, as Harry looked out and Dermot tramped his way to work, it looked like something from a Disney cartoon – the virgin snow obliterating the dark veil of its depressing churning history.

Harry sipped his nectar from a Derry Crystal glass, cut in the town. His chest heaved and his melancholy surprised him, binoculars hanging from his neck, saying to himself 'nothing is open today', as Dermot disappeared from view.

Derry was a white delight – a picture-perfect Christmas card scene. The saccharine village, snow-covered, frost-encrusted trees and windows, the tinsel-embroidered glowing Christmas tree, the river translucent in the moonlight, resplendent under a sea of stars. Like many of the Christmas cards displayed on the piano downstairs and throughout the homes of Ireland and Great Britain.

This city was a village really, and mentally a remote satellite of the British Empire. The second city of Northern Ireland, removed from the source of power and wealth, the capital, Belfast. Even further, geographically removed from Dublin, the capital of Southern Ireland, and further even from their thoughts, unless some politician reminded the Irish Government of the turmoil of its fellow islanders in the 'Black North'.

He opened the window again and hooked the latch as a draught of icy air invigorated his cigar and himself. Stirrings of snow blew in. Harry drew on the biting breeze and it felt good. The past days occupied in pleasantries and busyness, spilling shopping crowds and jostling get-to-togethers, family and friends, hovering children and fleeting presents. Another Christmas! In his tower above Cillefoyle Park and the surrounding streets, his blurred vision of the sight below, stuffed again with turkey and roast spuds, wine and whiskey, why, even the nutty Brussels sprouts were appetising. It was basically the same meal he had had the day before at his mother-in-law's. The decent bottle of red predisposed his emotional state, a congenial evening in his own home.

Harry had spent the winter festival engrossed in its merriment in every way possible, even decorated his classroom. He enthusiastically helped organise the school carol service, bombarded any hint of cynicism from the pupils or staff with his various renditions of Christmas carols – convoluted into some familiar elongated sing-along. Staff were bemused at his noteworthy antics, never having experienced him with an interest in such matters and most thankful when the principal, Brother O'Regan, declined his offer of mounting a Christmas play. Harry had said to him:

'I can do 'A Christmas Carol'. The kids and parents would love it!'

'Much too late in the school term to organise it. The staff, boys and parents needed more warning for such a time-consuming event.' The principal replied, relieved at having thought of an excuse so quickly.

Even his wife, Marie and their children noticed, in mystified awe, Harry's enthusiasm for Christmas. Once again he was so grateful to his great-grandfather, Samuel O'Donnell, for building the house in Cillefoyle Park, notable for its glass tower. He relished the tower. He savoured it in all seasons. The capricious weather bashed its panes, threatened to break through, but never did. It was his childhood home, where inside the windowed square of the tower he spent many hours looking at the city fall away to the river, only to rise again on the bank opposite, a series of streets perpendicular to the river. Streets where he seldom roamed nor visited. It was the other side.

He never was bored by the vista, especially when the steel-grey clouds lifted their shroud to shed some weak light.

Like most of the O'Donnells, Harry attended the Christian Brothers primary school, followed by 'The Tech', the secondary school above it on the brow of the hill. It became known as 'The Brow'. It played second fiddle to its neighbour, Saint Columb's College, the local Catholic grammar school. When Harry taught at The Brow, before being stationed in a modern secondary college on Foyle Hill; he had seen the gas yard below and smelt its gaseous effluence, often stuck under a blanket of cloud, with no escape. Even in those days, Harry recognised that music was in the air amidst the stinking smell of coal-gas, kids sang and danced. Many children went to Irish dancing or played the piano or sang in choirs. It was natural to them, genetic. His two kids were testimony to that fact – the musical talent that the city bred, flourished.

In front of Harry's tower lay the Christmas hallucination – one created by the season of goodwill and whiskey. It was a temporary respite, a temporary illusion, from the bitter northern wind and the violent reality of another year of the Troubles.

A gust blew a smattering of snow in through the window, cooled his hand and scattered cigar ash over its skin – stinging slightly. He enjoyed the discomfort knowing he would soon be ensconced by his fire side, glass in hand. The comforting snug – his wife on the sofa, knitting, and the kids stretched half-asleep beside her, watching, with millions of others on the islands the traditional television highlight of the Morecambe and Wise comedy show.

Having a laugh is essential to staying healthy and comedy makes life more bearable; simply having a sense of humour helps people survive. Indeed the blacker the better in chaotic places like Derry. Art in its all forms provides that escape or knowingness too. But having a doze in the bosom of his family couldn't be bettered, even in front of lightweight comedy like Morecambe and Wise. Home – where your family is nourished and can flourish, where you feel safe and fulfilled, where you matter to the people around you, where you belong. That is home. That is home in Derry.

The Stain

Oh for a cigarette, thought Pauline – the slow drag of a cigarette – the smoke going down, down. Smoke going out, out, out through the nose. Let it take its toll, beautiful, lovely on a frosty night like tonight. She remembered hanging out, smoking up a wintry lane with some mates. They were chilled to the bone. Wintry enough to see your breath. Breath and smoke intermingling, such a long time ago, innocent days. Dermot didn't smoke. Just as well.

Pauline settled by the fire, a coffee in her hand, switched on a lamp by her side and found the remote control. She turned up the television's volume as the Morecambe and Wise show started. She wiggled her bottom deep into the chair and drained her coffee. A well known orchestra conductor was made look a fool by the comic duo, a familiar face, but she couldn't put a name to him – predictable Christmas fun.

The next thing, she almost jumped out of her chair. She had fallen asleep watching the comedians fumble their way through the manhandling of each other and their guests. Something on the mat caught Pauline's eye. The mat had little stains – six little marks. She put on the centre light to look and then went to the kitchen to fill a jug of hot water and washing-up liquid.

Carefully, she rubbed the spots with a nail brush until suds formed and went out again to find a towel to dry them. Still the stains remained. They needed to dry, she thought. Her eyes kept darting back to them as she tried to distract herself with the buffoonery on the screen. She couldn't relax. Her stomach was beginning to rumble. Pauline felt hot. Shit. This is nonsense, she repeated to herself. What torture, she could easily explain them away. Guilt seeped through her. She couldn't get rid of it. She had betrayed her husband, her kids, herself. She didn't care about herself. She wondered if Sean ever noticed – the betrayal. It hadn't happened before in the house, Dermot was the first. Sean was away in the States training. Their physical relationship at that time was as cold as her maiden aunt's love life. The kids were on a weekend sleep over. She was bored, simply bored. She wanted more, than her life could offer. Dermot appeared with a letter wrongly posted to his house. She asked him in for coffee.

She got up, glanced at the spots as she walked around the room, and dragged her finger over the modern furniture, looking for comfort. She didn't get it.

The stains were still there. She went to the kitchen cupboard under the sink, still open and the wrench on the floor inside. The memories of her liaison that evening flashed through her head. Stop. Relax. Nausea passed over her. Turning on the tap, she splashed water on her face and dried it with the tea towel.

She put the wrench into the potato basket and covered it with potatoes, and retrieved a cleaning spray. She sprayed the stains on the mat and wiped gently. Using the towel again she dried the area. Wait. Patience!

Pauline went upstairs, switched on the radio and lay on the bed. She tried to sleep, tried to relax. Fuck! She couldn't. The radio played classical music. She tried to concentrate on the flows and ebbs of the music. It didn't work.

The bed cover annoyed her. It was the wrong colour for the room. It didn't match the curtains. She got up and looked out the window – still the snow covered all recent imperfections. If only it could do the same for Pauline.

After coming down the stairs, the living room was still warm, the fire's glow-holes beneath the black heap slumped. The stains were still there. The area around them seemed discoloured. Had she removed the colour from the mat? She was annoyed at her overreactions, her silly anxiety and failing to curb them.

Where was the hairdryer? She dashed upstairs and returned with it. She unplugged the lamp by the chair in the living room and plugged it in. The spots dried but still bloody noticeable.

She was furious with herself, for letting it happen. Turmoil in her guts, confusion in her head and stains on her expensive new mat. She should have had tissues handy but then it was a moment of recklessness – something she craved for. Now she paid. Sean's moaning insistence that everything had its price was neon lights in her head. If she wasn't careful she would give herself a headache – a migraine.

But it was only a few marks on a mat. She tried to convince herself. Nobody will notice. Pauline will! Sean will!

She went to great lengths to get the right shade to match the colour on the wall paper. The whole city had been alerted to her needs – now the whole city will know about the stains and who they belonged to. She imagined the worst. She knew she was panicking. What could she do? Calm down. This is silly. Still the marks remained on the mat, but the greater stain remained inside Pauline. Sleep would be impossible. Someone would ask. Somebody would make a remark. This would be a constant reminder of her affair within her own home, by her fireside, by Sean's fireside. A constant reminder.

To get rid of the stains she would have to get rid of the mat. How and what reason could she give Sean? Her hands were beginning to shake. Think, come on, this is silly. The panic was not evaporating.

Rusty licked her finger, and for the second time that night she jumped. He sat looking up at her with his pleading eyes. Rusty was not allowed in the living room – his place was his mat under the kitchen table. He was surprised and delighted he had got that far.

Pauline petted his head, and feeling more confident he lifted his paw onto her lap. Pauline continued to stroke his head. Confidence surged in Rusty, he turned and sniffed at the mat, ignoring the cleaning fluid and turned around on the mat a few times before settling himself in front of the fire. It must be Christmas. Pauline thought that was what Rusty must have been thinking.

Pauline, confused and indecisive, sat there looking at the dog and the fire and occasionally glancing at the television.

What to do?

Rusty, you are a good boy, good boy, well done. Rusty looked at Pauline with expectant eyes, his tail clipping the mat.

'Out.'

She yelled at Rusty who didn't have time to be confused any more but reacted to his training and the sound of Pauline's excited voice. He got the message immediately and ran for cover to his bed. Pauline followed.

Outside the kitchen window above the sink, the white powder still fell. She pulled on her wellington boots and coat in the back porch and called Rusty outside. He jumped and ran about in the snow and Pauline pretended to chase him. Under the protection of the trees at the rear of the garden where the snow didn't settle, it was a little mucky. Pauline called the dog over there and made him roll in the mud. Rusty enjoyed the attention, even if it was icy and wet.

They both went inside and into the living room. Rusty sat on the mat in front of the fire. At first unsure, but he stretched out, lounging by the fire side. The trail of dirt from the backdoor to the yellow mat provided the evidence of the mud bath.

She cleaned it all up, and threw the filthy muddy mat into the garage for further cleaning. Wasn't she silly for using that chemical spray on the mat after Rusty made a mess? She chuckled inwardly as

31

she showered the dog in the bathroom. She had an answer, an excuse, at last. It was a small but expensive sacrifice to pay, but she did it without further recrimination to herself.

Memories

On a casual wander through the communal garden a couple of weeks before Christmas, Harry had noticed the overgrown vegetation. It needed tidying for the festive season and he needed the exercise. There was always talk about a communal Christmas tree but it never happened. One Sunday morning while kneeling and ripping out weeds he overheard a conversation outside the garden wall, in the street. He wasn't sure who it was, but it sounded like Dermot and another young man. It was not good news. The whispered tête-à-tête fuelled his enthusiasm for the season of goodwill – a sojourn before the potential and unspeakable dread of the New Year. He had knelt and held his breath for so long as they spoke that when he eventually stood up he was dizzy and his knees and chest ached, but it was his heart that ached the most.

Harry had grown up in Cillefoyle Park. He enjoyed reading in his sky-room – always an escape from family and everyday routine. He was so small that no one saw him, and he had watched unseen. Later he created a space made of carpet and cushions in the corner to sleep, think and ponder his inside and outside worlds. It was his 'lonely impulse of delight'. As he grew, his legs flopped over the hatch for the ladder. In his pillowed recess he could only see the sky. That was enough. His world was the adventures in Gulliver's Travels, Treasure Island or the maroon set of Mee's Encyclopedias or wherever his imagination took him. Sometimes, homework had been completed there, but not often as it was his refuge from reality.

Even as a small boy, he loved day dreaming up there and it was an indispensable part of his life. As a teacher, like most adults he frowned upon children who day-dreamed, especially in the classroom, and were not attending to the task prescribed. The doubleness of life. The ambiguity of life. The tower was a channel to the world outside the thin veneer of translucent sand; too much reality took place – the overheard conversation had foreshadowed a grisly New Year.

In a curious way, the tower unlocked the external world, thwarted his natural insularity, his introversion, and his own self-obsessed worries. Life went on outside the security of his sanctuary. He saw it.

After a few glasses of Guinness in the local Rock Bar, a regular haunt for Harry and his neighbour, he had admitted to Dermot that he went to his tower to think and meditate. Dermot replied, 'Don't believe everything you think'. He was always good for the one-liners, but Harry needed to ask his neighbour about his conversation outside the park, if it had been him.

Harry considered himself a contented man, with no major health or money worries, and friends aplenty. 'So far so good' was his throwaway motto. He had cast his if-only thoughts aside a long time ago. His life in Derry, he reckoned, was fine, grand as they say – content in his routine, punctuated with births, deaths and marriages – his was a reflected life, one marinated in his tower. He felt his was a lived life. Montaigne said 'the greatest thing in this world is to know how to belong to oneself'. They say the male species should have a shed, Harry had his tower. Many of the natives escaped to their front rooms, to escape the Troubles, Harry escaped to his tower, his life, a dull contentment, a work in progress.

Looking out at the troubled city, its reality was at least postponed during the festive season. The blanket of white hushed the bomb and bullet. The IRA normally had a Christmas cease fire over the northern province of Ulster: no riots in William Street, no booming of bombs, only the jolly cacophony of shopping and carols in the city centre. Silver Bells echoed within the stores and houses in the panic and the rush – a childhood memory of Jim Reeves, his mother's favourite. An atmosphere of good will to all men pervaded the city, momentarily suffused, sometimes, even to the stalking boys in camouflage.

Raising children in a violent environment was daunting, as it was for most of the families of Northern Ireland, although it depended upon where you lived. The O'Donnells smoothed their family life, where possible, continually anticipated issues and problems, protecting them from the reality, teaching them decent values. Harry tried to keep his own counsel – not easy for him – and help the youngsters find their own solutions, or at least think they did. Of course, their daily conversations were littered with subtle prodding and hints. Christmas Day in Ireland for them was one of home detention, too boring for their youthful energy. Harry and Marie agreed that there was more to life than speeding it up, they tried to maintain a tranquil family home, but that didn't appeal to their teenage children.

American television portrayed a technicoloured Christmas: the all-American happy family, lush Christmas trees and carols around the piano. A life quite alien to Harry's childhood where an abundance of gifts, spacious homes and understanding adults where children were seen and heard. His childhood was not one of poverty or abundance. It was one of being seen and not heard.

His earliest Christmas memory was eating a Bounty chocolate bar one morning, taken from his Christmas stocking. Another one, going shopping with his mother as a child when she bought a new electric razor for his father, an embossed drawing on the box carrying its name – Phillips. It united his image of sparkling American life with his ordinary life in small town Ireland. It was the pulling power of Christmas television programming. Harry shaved his father most Saturday mornings in the range-heated, soup-smelling kitchen. The electric razor was heavy in his small hands. Its metal cover was light and flexible. Soup and stew simmered on the stove, always available for snacks or dinner. Harry and his mother often walked to the city for shopping, and he often saw her return home from the city looking out from his tower.

Harry used to comb his mother's hair on a Saturday night, her fine long hair that smelt of Clinic shampoo, before she went out socialising with his father. He watched her from the tower as a child walking down the street, and sometimes imagined seeing her there. Hearing the song 'Raglan Road' as a teenager took him back to those days – capturing those delicious memories:

'On a quiet street where old ghosts meet I see her walking now.

Away from me so hurriedly my reason must allow.

That I had wooed not as I should, a creature made of clay.

When the angel woos the clay he'd lose his wings at the dawn of day.'

Dermot called one evening to the house to organise a Christmas drink with Harry and left a bottle of whiskey and a present for Marie. They were wrapped in Christmas paper and placed under the tree. Harry looked forward to that particular present. He did not look forward to asking Dermot about what he had heard.

Christmas Drink

'I think I saw you, years ago, with your parents at St Columba's Long Tower Chapel. Was Frank with you? Christmas mass was always packed, but I am sure I saw you and Frank one year.'

'Well that's where we went. We stayed with my Granny around the corner. I preferred a Derry Christmas than an Edinburgh one. We had more family here. Why did you go there, Harry?'

'We were always connected with that church. It's a lovely one. Midnight mass for the family was always in the chapel, such an atmospheric place at that time of year. My great-grandmother Josephine had a cousin who was an influential priest at the Long Tower chapel.'

'I remember the thronging church but the air inside was a real odorous mix. Damp overcoats, aftershaves, body smells, perfumes, alcohol breath and thank God for the incense. It was a nice time for everyone as much as for those that had religious fervour.'

'Dermot, do you remember how dim the back of the church was? You had the bright, imposing altar of gold and blue at the front, but the rest of the church was almost in darkness. I loved the music. The musical director was always outstanding, was usually well known, as were the choirs, the soloists and orchestra. The traditional carols were great. Were you there for Handel's Messiah? A very popular oratorio for the choirs. The Hallelujah Chorus was just stunning. Almost raised the roof. That's a cliché fit for that place. Your grandparents and parents would have listened to it. It was a fixture of the Christmas calendar. First heard in Dublin, 1745 I think, when it was premiered. Such a long time ago.'

'The spirits rose alright, not just the living and dead but the tipsy too. As the carol goes – the voices rose in unison that night of nights. Goodwill to all men. God bless us one and all. There were many who imbued the spirits in my pub before going to midnight mass.'

'That's true enough, I suppose.'

'Anyway, they talk about Mother Church. It is Father Church. Only interested in sin, soil and sex. Men rule the roost.'

'Dermot, you're a cynic.'

'A spiritual one! An apophatic one!'

Both sat back and drew heavily on their drinks and sat silent for a while.

'Well, how did the year go for you, Harry?'

36

'Good, not bad. So far, so good, as they say. I have had my successes. I have some trepidation for the New Year, though.'

Dermot continued despite Harry's hook for him to ask why.

'Success is but quiet accumulations of small triumphs. Measured over time. It's a culture of innovation, being open-minded, curiosity, creativity and getting out of your bed every day. Just getting out of my bed every day is an achievement for me!'

'Which positive thinking book are you reading now, Dermot?'

Both laughed and drained their glasses.

'Another?'

'Yes, please?'

Harry decided he needed to raise the topic. So after Dermot returned from the bar, he asked:

'Do you think the Troubles will be bad next year?'

'I can't see any end yet. It's a continuing violent backdrop for this city. As you know the Troubles are centuries-long, the armed Irish Republicans who want to eject the British from Ireland aren't going away. So no change there. Fortunately, for you and I it hasn't brought too much misery to our extended families. We have survived its excesses yet we know plenty of people who haven't.'

'Derry is a small town really, a village of villages. Most people know each other. I am happy here, happier if all that stuff would stop. People talk to each other, plenty of gossip. Have you seen Frank in the pub?'

'No, I haven't seen Frank. You know it has its advantages living in a wee town, I suppose. And you have got to be careful with that gossip. Remember, 'whatever you say, say nothing'. That's Derry's omerta. We have a Republican poster in the pub toilets that warns people about loose talk. It's like one of the British posters used during the Second World War.'

'Yes, Dermot. What about this war? Can you break that omerta code?'

'Business as usual for the Brits and the IRA, I would say. Enjoy Christmas, Harry, I would say.'

'Christmas is all about family and kids and eating and drinking. Time to forget all our troubles and the Troubles.'

'I think it was the Two Ronnies's comedy show. One of them is buying half the stock from the off-licence. All the bottles lined up on the counter. He says to the shop keeper: 'Christmas!, we wouldn't bother, but for the kids.'

'True enough for some. It is a binge. How were your Christmases in Edinburgh?'

'Thankfully we spent most of them here. I remember the bitter biting wind walking to school. The living room was always over-heated at Christmas. The rest of the rooms were freezing. Some of my friends, like Frank, and my parent's friends came over. Frank was always staying with us. My bedroom was like an ice box at times. I survived using a hot water bottle, huddled under the blanket. Always hated the early mornings when I woke up. The cold hot-water bottle was ready to be kicked out. It was great when Frank stayed during the winter. We shared my bed. Lovely and warm. Sometimes, I would crawl into my parent's bed, mostly a welcome sanctuary when Dad wasn't drinking.'

'What church did you go to?'

'On Christmas Eve, when not in Derry, we would walk down Leith Walk, it took ages. It's one of Edinburgh's longest streets, I think. We went to Saint Mary's Cathedral. Despite my mother's antipathy to the church, she enjoyed midnight mass and all the carols associated. I guess it was the seasonal ambience. She said it was a memory of past Christmases, a pleasant connection to her childhood in the old country. The path would be covered in ice or snow and the walk seemed to take us forever. Slipping and sliding. That's how I remember it, anyhow.'

'We had central heating, not many had that. During Christmas the heating was cranked up and the whole house was warm. Not so the tower. Christmas is really about being nostalgic, don't you think? That tower is my homecoming. But as they say in Derry – nostalgia isn't what it used to be.'

'I enjoyed looking out from my bedroom window in Edinburgh to the streets below watching the people coming and going. Always something to watch. Sometimes in the winter the windows were covered in ice and the curtain froze to the glass. I used my finger to make a little square window in the ice to look out. My bedroom in the Banana Flats in Leith looked down on the main road; Cables Wynd. Why was it called Banana Flats? Because it was curved like a banana.

'Ah! Memories. Mostly good. Thank God. I used do that with my finger in the tower. All the windows were solid with ice. There is a little copper pipe to collect the condensation with a little plug that drains out. I wonder who designed that. I used to leave the door below open to melt the ice. If my parents found out, all hell was to pay. Wasting heat. Still the same with Marie. They never go up there, never. Don't know why.'

'They know it's your place, I suppose. You must worry about them especially in this city? I don't think you need to. They are good kids.'

'I do worry about the kids. Where they could end up, but they are good children. Enjoying life as best they can and Marie is a blessing. She's the pillar. Subdued and unemotional. Keeps them on the straight and narrow, just like me and you too. Like all of us she has contradictions below that calm. Her greatest talent is cutting to the quick of a problem. Niall has tested the boundaries, but always pulls his head in after a chat with Marie. His peripatetic creative curiosity never ceases to amaze me. Some of his ideas or drawings reflect a depth that is rarely shown. He is quiet, a bit of a dreamer. Sinead is a studious girl, good looking and lives in her own world of friends and school. More lively than Niall. Both, like many Derry ones, were born with natural musical talents and play piano and sing a fair tune. I am not so distinguished.'

'Nor I'

'I worry about next year.'

Again Dermot didn't respond to the hook.

'I don't blame Marie or the kids. I wouldn't go near that glacial tower of yours. What's the attraction?'

'Marie warns that I could be regarded as a nosey pervert. She never comes up. Any time she did she claimed she felt a shiver. Said it was haunted or something. My family's skeletons, maybe buried in the walls. She warns me constantly that reading up there in the twilight would destroy my eyes. There was a story that one of my great uncles, a bachelor brother was accused of being a pervert, but that was just a story. Down below, I see many spectacles within my neighbours' homes. Most windows are shielded against the penetrating chill. Most of the rooms have vacant grates. I know what she is saying. But I do my serious thinking up there, have the odd cigar, but it is almost impossible to remain there without being seen. I have to sit very low, and lie against the corner wall. To see anything one has to stand and be exposed from below, except of course at night. This is the beauty of night viewing, no one sees me unless I have a glowing cigar in my hand. The city looks good. I enjoy it, especially with the window open.'

'I suppose you watch me. Thank God you can't see into my joint. What about Pauline's? Do you see in there?'

'Only if they leave their curtains open, and the light is on and if I use the binoculars. I can't see your place. It's set back from the main house.'

'Good.'

'Did I hear you talk to someone outside the park a couple of weeks ago?'

'What?'

Harry decided to ask directly. He needed to know. The few pints helped his candour. Maybe a whiskey chaser would be needed.

'Did I hear you speak to someone outside the park about the town being blown up next year?'

'No, don't be daft! Harry, you're being daft.'

'Are you involved?'

'What do you mean involved? Were you drinking before we met? How much have you drunk? Of course I'm not involved with the IRA.'

'I heard you. I think it was you. Talking about some big visit from Royalty or the Prime Minister. And they are going to level the city centre. Inside the walls.'

'Hold on, hold on. I know now. There are two mad lads I know who are involved. Well, one is really crazy. The other one is just a follower. He's nuts and heading for a fall. He hates me. I met him outside of the park. He wished me a Happy Christmas and to enjoy it as there wouldn't be anything left after next year. He is a mouth. Showing off. He really is heading for a fall. If they knew about this he would be knee-capped and chucked out. They won't listen to me. They think it's a personal vendetta. Look, forget about it. He's a mouth. A dangerous mouth.'

'Okay. Okay. Let's get back to festivities. Tell me a Santa joke.'

'What do you call people who are afraid of Santa Claus? Claustrophobic.'

After a couple of whiskeys they went home, childish and giggling, sliding their way home. Harry fell on his rear end twice, Dermot was more surefooted. Each perilous step, a soft crunch underfoot. At Dermot's house the handshakes melded into an embrace. Harry reminded him that his home was open to Dermot any time and that his presence was expected on the twenty-eighth with promises of a meal free of Christmas tinsel. Harry and Dermot both preferred the celebrations to terminate at midnight on Boxing Day night.

View from the Tower

Harry returned home. His wife sat dozing by the fire, an empty wine glass by her side. The television murmured, flashing a dim light across the room. A cursory greeting indicated a 'Do Not Disturb' state. Harry went into the kitchen, fixed an ample measure of Jameson's, decanted some nuts into a plastic bag and picked up a cigar, hidden in the bedroom on the way up to the tower. He ascended to his perch and switched on his little radio. Pete, his ex-teacher friend was on the radio – his programme displayed his esoteric range of music. Thankfully Harry hadn't removed his jacket so he opened the window. He lit up, sipped on his whiskey, listening to Pete's agreeable selection, placed a cushion on the window sill and settled across it, sniffing the night chill.

Derry was settled for an evening by the fireside and television – the snow had covered the highways and made the byways impassable. It had got worse as more snow had fallen since he had come home from the pub, but the sky cleared to a display of stars. Most of the locals had journeyed during daylight and returned home before the darkening blizzard, having completed their seasonal duties. Of course, some hardy souls didn't let a bit of snow put them off. They were determined to get to their destination. Harry saw that Dermot was one. He left his home and disappeared to the left outside the park. Dermot Lavery had always something to do.

Dermot was resident in an apartment, attached to Mrs. Jenny Doherty, at number five. Cillefoyle Park had been built years ago as a gated community. Samuel O'Donnell, a prosperous plumber from London Street was behind its construction. Five houses, large homes for the newly-wealthy merchants of 1920's Derry. Mrs. Pauline Laughlin lived at number one, Harry at number three. Mrs. Doherty's husband had died years ago and his enterprising widow turned her home into a boarding lodge – a part of her ground floor was Dermot's apartment. From Harry's glass tower he had a few insights into his neighbours' lives, mostly only suspicions that he kept to himself. Dermot frequented the Laughlin household on a regular basis. He saw those that came home drunk and on what nights, he saw those couples that quarrelled when they thought no one was around. Their routines, he could describe – their clothes, their cars, their children – he could tell a lot about them by his distant observations.

To his right, the historical centre, the spires of the two cathedrals: Saint Eugene's Roman Catholic and, further inside Derry's Walls, Saint

41

Columb's Cathedral, silhouetted in the bright star-lit night. Doire, the oak grove, as it is sometimes known in old Irish, is an ancient settlement. The monastery founded by Saint Columcille in the sixth century was then known as Daire Coluimb Chille and situated near Harry's family's church; The Long Tower Chapel.

Derry's Walls are a complete example of a walled city – the only set found in Ireland. Derry City is a little enclave surrounded by the county of Donegal and because of the historic significance of the city walls to 'The Planters' – the Scottish and English settlers during the Plantation of Ulster – the treaty signed by the government of the Irish Republic in 1922 allowed six northern counties of Ireland to remain part of the United Kingdom. Derry was granted a royal charter as a city in 1613 and renamed Londonderry in recognition of the London merchants who built the walls to protect those inside and the settlers from the area. Their aim was to develop the city into a modern business centre, being one of the first planned cities in Ireland. Thus, Derry was linked with its near neighbour across the Irish Sea – England – whose colonising forces spread across the island of Ireland. Those forces brought strife over the centuries to the native Irish and Derry was always in the middle of it.

To his left were the rooftops of the Argyle area, to the north he saw the spires of Magee College, its grounds rolling down to the docks at the Strand Road. He viewed the roof of an old mill at the bottom of Rock Road, and across the sparkling river to the equally snowy Waterside and its Saint Columb's Park. From his vantage point, further to the north he saw one of the many shirt factories converted to a supermarket, a garage and some houses in Aberfoyle Crescent and a cul-de-sac known as Dill Park, where his Uncle Dougie lived. A print in his uncle's hallway, possibly one of the earliest of the city, showed the view in reverse, taken from Saint Columb's Park on the waterside, over the river to Magee College, then, a training college for Presbyterian ministers. The houses stretched up the hill to Culmore and left the city borders into the hills of Donegal. On the twenty-first of May, in 1932 Amelia Earhart landed in one of those border fields after flying solo from North America – the first female aviator.

The rear of the tower overlooked the back garden with its red-roofed garage – a huge building that housed his great grandfather's plumbing business. Behind that a mini forest of tall poplars draped in white. 'Wind shakes the big poplar, quicksilvering' – a line from a Seamus Heaney poem came to mind, which one, he couldn't remember nor did he really care. A little bench was erected against the rear of the glass tower. Harry and his two kids could just about fit into the tower's viewing platform, but neither child shared their father's enthusiasm for it, or at least pretended not to. The front and rear windows could be opened and secured with latches.

Below his house, the neglected communal garden of Cillefoyle Park was barely seen in the white-out. Once hedges of privet stood six feet tall, arches carved into its three sides that had been heavy-gated. The gates had been taken away, two lay in his garage, and the third, God knows where? The privet hedge had been chopped to a mere two feet high, preventing trespassers and their ilk seeking privacy for any nefarious activities that a tall thick hedge could provide. The fourth side, still tall with patches of bare bark, created a degree of privacy. They grew behind a high wall, blocking views of the garden from the street. Harry occasionally managed to control the errant growth, being the unofficial custodian of the park. To his occasional delight, the kids from the surrounding houses played footy or whatever in the mucky patch.

Nerdishly, for a few years he recorded the daily weather in a little school exercise book. The book had belonged to a young Irish Australian visiting for a school term. His first written work for Harry had contrasted Derry to his home – a country town in Victoria. To Harry's pleasant surprise the work was nicely illustrated with the boy's observations: birds, buildings and people. Full of grammatical mistakes, but it was pages of swirling thoughts and ideas, free and bright. He told Harry they were encouraged to write and illustrate it with drawings. Harry asked if he was taught to edit. It was as if he had asked him to play the didgeridoo. Though Harry was sure the young boy would have made a fair attempt at playing it if Harry had produced one. The student's writing and behaviour became more formal as he succumbed to Irish schooling. He left after a term to return to Australia, his mother's adopted country. The boy had potential and the school system stifled the boy's natural creativity. He loved the drawings and the sense of fresh wonderment of the writings. Harry kept the book in the tower. Sometimes, he set written work which allowed the pupils to create suitable illustrations.

The snow was an exquisite opportunity to enjoy the shimmering glint of an ice covered city. Normally the view was blocked by the interminable heavy clouds, sitting on the roofs, accepted as a local immoveable burden. Up there, in the clouds, where the sky met the buildings, he marvelled at the changing smeared light. If one waited long enough, one was repaid by a transformed sky-scape. That moment when the sun broke through the woolly quilt would pleasantly surprise Harry, and even the city, with a multiplicity of rays and light. The sun shone more often than thought.

Not a soul moved on the streets below. A car passed on the Northland Road leaving tracks in its wake. Harry's cigar crumbled between his fingers; he couldn't get any more drags from it. He tossed it through the open window and watched as it landed on the snowy roof and died a solitary death. Harry closed the window.

After enjoying the chill of his viewing cube, the smoke and his mellow sup, he descended the steep stairs to the second floor landing and into the warmth of the house. Down the stairs to the comfort of his snug fireside, he was in a reflective mood and settled for a nap – 'Happy, Happy Christmas, that can win us back to the delusions of our childhood days, recall to the old man the pleasures of his youth, and transport the traveller back to his own fireside and quiet home!' Was that Dickens? That was his last thought before the pleasant quiet of sleep took over.

Frozen Childhood

Despite a childhood of freezing winters in draughty apartments, Dermot Lavery loved the silent white obscurity of the snowy landscape. He loved the hushed white-out. It was the white-out of peace. Heavy rain often killed the riots as the youngsters sought refuge in front of the television. So too, Dermot mused, the continuous snow might curb the Troubles on the street. Blurry snow scenes, winter landscapes, weather snow reports, snow blizzards – he loved watching it all on television. The sugar-covered pavement in front untouched, and the few tyre tracks disappearing fast under the latest storm. Peace and quiet. Alone in a frozen urban landscape.

Most houses were hunkered down, their windows heavily curtained, flickering light sometimes escaping. Some occupants sat in the unearthly glow of their television sets with their uncovered windows allowing them a festive vision of blanketing snow behind their sparkling Christmas tree, waving to anyone passing by. It was an alternative to the goggle box in the corner or perhaps it was loneliness, hoping to see a familiar figure.

The obligatory Christmas trees, flashing in the window or set in the corner of the living rooms. From inside the warmth of the room, eye-catching colourful illuminations contrasted with the external white and black night. He avoided Lawrence Hill. It was too dangerous to traverse. A car passed leaving double lines of tracks. They ran down the centre of the Northland Road as far as the eye could see. Passing the fire station, he slowed. Will something have been dropped? The drop-box in the fire station's garden had been used for years. He had overheard Mick and Brendan talk about it in the pub. He overheard too much but Cathal knew he would keep his mouth shut. As he stepped into the garden he wondered who was at the pub. Why was he asked to do some stock control on such a night? Not that he minded!

He ensured no one was watching and went to the glistening icy bench. Taking off his leather glove, he swept the snow off the top of the bench and looked behind it. Carefully, walking around, he nudged the bottom of the stone wall with his foot. The brick hadn't been moved. Simply by kicking it, he knew by experience if it had. Re-gloving his hand he resumed his journey to the city centre, his curiosity satisfied.

He felt he could keep walking for miles and miles onto the next towns – to Strabane or Lifford. Just keep on walking in the complete anonymous white-out. He remembered there were seventeen hundred and sixty yards in a mile – the benefit of those days of rote-learning, of rote-chanting in his Scottish classroom. If only he could have a complete black-out in his mind and stop worrying. Yet his mind drew him back to Derry and the New Year and what Mick had suggested. Was he bullshitting? Likely, but maybe he knew something. What were they planning? Would it all go according to plan? He knew he wouldn't ask Cathal. Maybe pick up something at the pub. If he thought too much about it he would walk on and on, get away from it all, leave it all behind. Go anywhere – Australia or Spain. He thought about it often. He would winter in their snow fields or at least have a cool holiday in the mountains.

Edinburgh, his childhood city, held little attachment anymore – maybe a bed for the night in his parent's house or in the home of fellow activists. Most of the houses of his childhood were blatantly unheated. He wondered where his parents would be. They spent most of their time back in Derry, anyway. New Year was a big occasion but this year he wasn't going over to Edinburgh as his parents were coming to Derry. They had moved from Leith's Banana Flats on the Cables Wynd Road where their home was comfortably heated. He wondered if they still went to midnight mass on Christmas Eve in Saint Mary's Cathedral. He enjoyed the service as his mother sang along to all the carols. His thoughts turned to Frank. He wondered where he was on a night like that. When Frank stayed, it was always warmer – when both shared a bed or built a tent of sheets in his bedroom. It wasn't always ice and snow, during the summer he played at The Shore or at Leith Links in the playground but summer or winter they went to cowboy films at The State picture house.

The drone of the engines and tyres flattening the hardening snow drew his attention to the two army Land Rovers by his side. Dermot broke into a sweat. Where the hell had they come from? Dermot's mind had been elsewhere. The driver slowed down, and out of the corner of Dermot's eye, he saw a smiling face and a wave offered him Christmas salutations. Dermot imperceptibly nodded his head, the typical Derry salute, keeping his hands pocketed; his tight-fisted acknowledgement was due to the inclement weather, that's what Dermot hoped they thought. Picking up a little speed the Land Rovers turned left, down towards the river.

There was nothing on him to implicate him should they have decided to stop and search him, so no need to have worried. He felt he must have appeared an odd lonesome sight, trudging through the snow-pacified street. It was too harsh to be outside, even for the army. He suspected something was going on in the pub. Still it was a shock to see them, without warning, without his usual readiness.

Dermot Lavery was always ready, always watching, observing, ruminating, not a person who liked to be caught off-guard. He reckoned it was Christmas, sucking in the softening affects of the seasonal spirit. His usual reaction to such an infiltration of his normal stiff armour would have been severe self-criticism, but he was off-duty, had had a few drinks, so he let himself off lightly. It was this self-discipline that set him apart from most people and provided few friends – indeed it was the fertiliser that grew enemies.

His walk to the pub took him through the familiar streets. He had been reminiscing, when the army crept up on him. The usual flood of memories cascaded at that time of year anyway. His evening with Harry was a trip down memory lane. Skipping along in front of his parents, often leaving them behind as they stopped and talked to everyone and anyone. Dermot and his parents made slow progress through the streets of their city, Edinburgh or Derry but especially Derry – the one they called home. Nearly everyone they met gave or acknowledged the Derry salute – a slight twist of the head, accompanied sometimes with a subdued 'Yes' or a 'what about ye, hi?' It was the same little nod he gave to the soldiers in their sheltered vehicles.

Even though Dermot grew up mostly in Scotland, his parents were from Derry and returned often. To some they were as local as themselves – part of the community. They went home so often many didn't realise they lived and worked in Scotland. Their regular visits made them familiar visitors because they loved meeting old friends and acquaintances. While his parents stopped every five minutes to chat Dermot spent his time studying the shop windows and buildings and learnt the name of the shops on each city street. The adults were mystified by his local knowledge; they were busy chatting as he soaked up the local landmarks: the underground toilets near the police station, Austin's grand department store, a little church here and there, and of course the brass teapot in Waterloo Square.

Trips to the supermarkets were the same, the hours that Dermot glazed over the biscuit or sweet aisles while his parents talked to all and sundry. Often, he was given a few pence to buy sweets. His father was the most talkative. Always neat in his tweed suit, the oily maroon tweed tie on a variety of dark shirts – maroon, green or brown. His Donegal tweed cap, his pride and joy – specially made in Donegal town, woven in shades of grey, sat slightly to the side of his head. He was quite a dapper character who played that vacuous role with gusto, rolling out the usual platitudes and bonhomie – a town saint and a home devil.

Many topics were discussed – detailed analysis of the weather, the football, the horses, the church or the latest rumours. Kevin, his father, saved his ardent enthusiasm for politics – voicing his strident socialist values. His staunch hatred of the British and Northern Irish Labour parties – too meek and middle class – but his most disparaging remarks were saved for the Catholic Church. Or, as his Protestant friends liked to call it, the Roman Catholic Church, with an emphasis on Roman. It was too powerful and controlling, and he dismissed it. When he did criticise the Church and the middle of the road politicians, people usually grew quiet and found a chore that needed doing, so hastily left his company. It was too extreme for them. It was these excitable topics that drove people away from him. When volatile, he tripped over his words, slurred, spittle spraying from his shunted sentences. Always intoxicated by his biased views – his mouth couldn't keep up with his thoughts. Kevin was a card-carrying communist. When he had a few drinks he was even more unbearable.

Clarendon Street, a magnificent street of Georgian terraces, fell away towards the Strand Road and the River Foyle. It reminded him of Edinburgh's grandeur. He wished he owned one of the houses. The first drawing room he saw was in a friend's house, in Westend Park, bordering the Creggan and the Bogside. He imagined it filled with antiques and awash with Dickensian Christmas decorations. It was the prettiest route to the silent city, the familiar shops on the Strand Road in all their Christmas-dressed splendour. To get into the Strand Road he had to get body searched. The security check point of brick, steel and sandbags protected the soldiers on duty. As he entered the dark passageway of the checkpoint he automatically spread his arms out. A boy soldier stepped out, stared into his eyes while Dermot looked at a buckle on his flak jacket. After a cursory fingered roll of Dermot's body, arms and legs, a cockney accent wished him Season's Greetings. Dermot returned the compliment.

His walk took him past the shops, the police station and Waterloo Place with the underground toilets and a popular chain store. A large teapot hung high above a restaurant, topped with a crown of white.

The teapot always attracted him, mysterious and foreign, something resonating from far-off countries – something, alien and fascinating. The teapot was a restaurant sign with its tarnished brass that somehow made him feel uneasy, as if a genie would appear. It just seemed incongruous for Derry. It unnerved him. Why? He didn't know, but then he lived in Londonderry, part of the United Kingdom.

Every time he passed it, this peculiar reaction intrigued him. Was it a symbol of the British Empire – the colonial history of India and Ceylon or the recently named Sri Lanka and their capacity for producing tea? Those who ridiculed the English, gestured by bringing a pretend cup of tea to their lips with the little finger stuck out and then joked – 'anyone for tea?' But there were few houses in Derry or Ireland where you weren't offered a strong cup of tea – dish-water coloured tea was an abomination. Many British films, watched on Sunday afternoon had civilised ladies taking afternoon tea – tea in fragile china cups in fancy middle-class rooms, leading to well-heeled gardens, everyone very polite and slightly eccentric.

Tea came from the colonies. Perhaps, that was it; it represented the colonisation of Ireland and all the countries known as the British Empire. Northern Ireland was just part of that, a little too close to London. The world abroad started opening up for him when he read The Children's Encyclopedia by Arthur Mee, a set of books he repetitively read during his childhood, written from a British Empire point of view, he thought. One particular puzzle presented in the book – how to get to an island using just planks, really annoyed him for some reason, maybe it was that jolly-hockey sticks, 'anyone for tea?' point of view, an English view point. As a child he asked many questions, much to the joy of his proud parents. They fed him stories and supplied books. Later in his life, books became a necessity. Television was a window to the world, to that adult world. While watching cartoons he laughed inwardly, barely audible. He was not emotionally demonstrative.

Over-hearing the heated discussions of politically-active parents around the fireside that often bored him in those long wintry nights or long summer evenings, he realised those socialist ideals had seeped into his psyche. He identified with these colonised people – people from across the world, the same as him, like-minded. The international social movements of the 1960's, the cost in human lives in the quest for civil rights in America, India, Mexico, France, Eastern Europe and his town of Derry, made him realise he was not alone. They were not alone.

The teapot symbolised Dermot's continuous battle for those civil rights and how to achieve them, the double-edged sword of the gun or the ballot box. It rattled with his conscience. There was no easy answer. For some, yes, but not for Dermot. He remembered his mother telling him that it was about power and people were merely pawns, merely assets to be moved around when it suited the capitalists. His father told him the Irish Famine of the mid 1800s suited the powers that be; it coincided with the general movement of people from the rural to the urban. The industrial revolution needed the labour in urban areas to power the new factories. Simply more cogs in the dreary new factories. Karl Marx referred to Tillie and Henderson's huge factory at the end of Derry's Craigavon Bridge. It was world capitalism – Globalisation, as some economists called it in a book Dermot had picked up in a library – the global village. A sharp contrast to the many hidden villages or town lands – called 'Baile' in Irish or 'Bally' in English – pre-famine years where often the only evidence of existence was a little track or smoke from the chimney. The Baile often contained five hundred souls, his father told him. 'Throughother' was a way of maintaining a simple farming life with their neighbours, helping each other in a complex yet disorganised fashion, a method in the madness of pre-famine village life. Even in those days, some powerless peasants rebelled, causing outrages to the ruling classes with maiming of cattle and burning of crops by groups called Ribbon Men or Molly Maguires.

A disembodied voice shook Dermot, bringing him back to the chilly reality of the streets.

'Hey, hey you Mr.. Have you any odds?'

Dermot prepared himself for a mugging – someone out on this night looking for trouble or some poor bastard without a welcoming fireside. Even though, he refused to give money to the drunks and winos. It was a matter of principle. If he had his usual half-eaten pack of polo mints he gave it to them or bought them something to eat – a sandwich. Regularly they threw the sweets into the gutter, or at him, mouthing profanities.

Once, while he was talking with a friend he automatically handed over the mints to a dirty-engrained palm without looking at whose hand it was. The sweets hit the back of his head. He swept round ready to defend himself and there stood Frank in a huddled group of winos, acting as if nothing happened. Frank's eyes were sad and confused. Dermot went over to him and handed him some paper money, Frank took it as Dermot tried to hold onto his soiled hands, but Frank pulled it away and told him to 'Fuck Off'. Dermot was as sad and confused as

Frank. Thereafter, he avoided Frank, if he had been on the streets drinking with his fellow alcoholics.

That night was not the night he wanted to comfort some unfortunate's soul. A figure stepped out of the shelter of one of arches in Derry's Walls.

'Hi Dermot, where are you off to?'

'Hey, Damian, you scared the shite out of me, what are doing out on a night like this?'

'Oh, I'm heading home, I was down in my brother's house and he dropped me off on Foyle Street. All the main roads are open but I have to walk the rest of the way. I stopped for a smoke in the arch, was heading off when I saw someone. I wanted to know what other mad bastard was out on a night like this. What a nonsense all this carry on is – Christmas presents, streets lights, drinking and eating – all this money. What a waste!'

'Well, I am off to work, stock control.'

Dermot thought – doesn't misery love company? He hoped his new-found walking partner would leave soon. At least it wasn't Frank. He didn't want to hear anymore whingeing or see Frank on such a night. He was happy with his own thoughts. Damian asked:

'What? Why can't it wait?'

'Oh needs must, anyway the boss wants to have a little drink for the staff for working over the season. Free drink tonight. He's giving us a Christmas bonus too, but wants us to work for it – tight bastard. I don't go in for all this sentimental Christmas crap. Money is money.'

'All this money and time wasted. Could have a nice holiday. I'll walk up with you. I'll visit my brother on Bishop Street and have a wee drink with him, sure the night's young. Like Santa Claus, I usually only visit him once a year. It's not him, it's his wife. It'll be a quickie drinky if she is in, then head home to the wife, kids and a night in front of the TV. My sister-in-law makes me appreciate my own dear wife. Maybe I should visit her more often!'

'Fair enough.'

They clambered up Shipquay Street. Snow shoes would have been appropriate. Its steep slippy climb reduced any chance of conversation. Dermot was thankful that Damian didn't say anything as the blizzard stalked the centre of the city. The opposite side of the street was unseen in the sheets of white. Still, Dermot loved it, not so much the Christmas lights – coloured rows of bulbs zigzagging all way up to the centre cast adrift in the storm – but the anonymity of it all. The squatted buildings of the city street refused to surrender to the winter gale. No surrender as Derry's streets once again refused to be breached in the mantle of the storm.

'I think I'll leave you here and head home. It's getting worse. God all this bother and then this weather. The struggle up this hill has sobered me up. Quicker and wiser to go home to my own fireside and a few more wee drinks. See ya. Season's Greetings and all that.'

Damian strode down Castle Street towards his home. Dermot was glad it had been Damian, a regular at the bar where he worked and not a wino. It would have been very awkward if it had been Frank, his childhood friend who had become an alcoholic. He could not have left him on a night like that. Memories of his drunken father flooded his mind.

From a young age, Dermot had known that his gaze made people uncomfortable. People looked away. He was told by his parents numerous times not to stare. He overhead them say that more was going on inside his head than that steadfast blue gaze allowed anyone to see. Actually, he wasn't aware of it at that time, all he was doing was just looking, concentrating, and comprehending the world around him – he was being reflexive, self-critical and hesitant. Harry was like him in that sense. He thought that was what most people should be doing and that there would be less suffering in the world if they did. Most people talked to cover up the thinking process, but not Dermot. Talking would have softened his intensity. Dermot didn't feel the need.

He knew not to stare at his parents when being told off – he unwittingly looked defiant, emotionless, uncaring, they said. It was much later that he realised there was power in his emotionless expression. That's why Mick hated him and Cathal was unsure of him at times.

Often, after one of his parent's drunken sessions, his parents had noisy sex in their adjoining room. Dermot was sent to his bedroom, if he was still awake and his sensitive if somewhat inebriated mother would say 'listen to your radio son, use your torch and go under the blankets and read your comics. You like that, don't you'? He could still remember the muffled sounds of the spring bed and his father's groans. Like many sons he felt his father was a barrier to his mother's affections. Often they competed for her attention. Only later, Dermot realised that only for his mother's strength and love for her husband, Kevin, his father would have ended up in the gutter. Kevin was a functioning alcoholic, like Frank. His mother always had a sense of noir and her gallows humour about the plight of her husband's drinking problem was reflected in oft-repeated joke – he could stop drinking anytime as he often drank brake fluid.

One night when his drunken father came home to an unheated apartment: no wife, no food, no comfort, no heat and no sex, he ordered Dermot from his bed to make him some food – fried bacon on toast and tea – and told him to light the coal fire, even though it was one in the morning. His father switched on the electric fire, sat with his head in his hands, and fell asleep.

While Dermot was valiantly attempting to ignite the coal while holding a sheet of newspaper over the fireplace, the bacon started to burn on the stove. His father woke striking fast and furious. 'You stupid wee fucker, the bacon's burning.' Distracted, the newspaper was sucked into the fire. In the confusion the burning sheet fell out of the fireplace and Dermot scrambled to grab it, burning his hands in the attempt. His father floundered and dismissed his pain and efforts to please him.

With rage growing, Dermot turned to face his father, and glared at him – his blue defiant stare. It was met with the full force of his father's hand. Both collapsed onto the floor, father and son, both unable to move, his father, mumbling before finally falling back into a stupor.

Dermot stood looking over his father on the floor, shaking with fear and cold. The fire hadn't lit, the bacon was burnt. His hand and face hurt. He went into the bathroom to look at himself, hand and face, red and aching. His mother had taught him to use dishwashing liquid on a burn. So retrieving the bottle from the kitchen he poured copious amounts on his hands and wiped them on his face – his hands and face dripping in gel-green ooze.

His father had wet himself where he fell in front of the fireplace. Dermot felt confused but not hatred. He loved his father and he knew his father loved him, without a doubt. They had many good times. It would be okay tomorrow, but not before his mother avenged her husband's cruelty. He hated those fights. Bridie's shawl, used when sitting by the fire on a winter's night lay on the back of the chair. Dermot threw it over his father.

Eventually Dermot went to bed, after filling his hot-water bottle again. His hands and face still stung. The Hibernian Football Club flag above it and its year of origin in 1875 was the last thing he remembered.

His mother came home later that night after being out with some of her activist friends and found her husband on the floor asleep. That didn't perturb her too much. She smelt the urine and retrieved her shawl. You are better sleeping there than the gutter, but you will get one hell of a tongue-lashing from me in the morning, she thought as she kicked him in the rear. He jumped, grunted, but stayed asleep.

She went into Dermot's room, bent down to kiss him and felt the heat from his face. Touching it with her hand he awoke. She worked out quickly what had happened. Dermot couldn't answer her, tears welled. He tried to be strong and buried his emotion within. She said she would deal with her husband in the morning.

Bridie got some ointment from the bathroom, covered his face and hands and wrapped him in her arms. The smell reminded him of a hospital. She pulled the blankets over them and stayed there all night.

In the morning, after rising quietly, Bridie went to see her husband. Dermot heard her in the living room and got up to listen at the door. He opened it slightly and saw Bridie's look of disgust for her husband. She kicked him several times as he lay on the floor, shouting at him, but then lowering her voice, woke Kevin and told him to leave and never come back. Dermot heard the determined slow and deliberate voice of his mother. His father said nothing. His downtrodden father realised that he had the potential to lose his wife and child as he left the apartment in the clothes he slept in. He didn't come back that night.

'He's no' a bad man, a bit of a town saint and home devil. It's just the drink, drink and his political obsessions. He feels 'powerless' was all his mother said. Dermot had missed his father who never apologised, but never physically abused him again. Kevin wanted to stay with his family and defying his pragmatic wife was never an option. Bridie came from a long line of strong-minded women who were capable of standing up to the home-devil town-saint breed of Irish men. The next time he saw his father was two months later in Derry. They all travelled back as a family to Edinburgh.

Dermot was born with the strength of his mother. His childhood gave him first-hand experience of the curse of drink and its addiction. He rarely drank himself; he saw the damage it could do every day in his pub and on the streets of Derry. He saw the damage done to his own family.

As a child, Dermot was easily pleased and amused; being an only child he had his parents' affections and attention, even though they were busy with their own activities. Dermot enjoyed accompanying them, sometimes with Frank. He naturally soaked up the political experiences. They weren't wealthy, but had enough – he always had a few toys or a few comics, friends to play with – especially Frank, who often lived with them for days. Out on the walks with his parents he studied the landscape all around, while observing peoples' behaviours. Any television programmes or books that showed how others lived, how their lives could be improved and that explained why people did things, either in history or in contemporary life, was his interest. He was always an observer and later, like his parents, became a back-room activist. A favourite activity of the solitary child, while his parents were engaged in their activities was walking the streets of Edinburgh or looking out of their apartment to the streets below and its many characters. Maybe he had something in common with Harry O'Donnell, observing from his tower.

Austin's windows in the centre of the old city – were aglow with Christmas displays and Santa scenes. Even its radiant tower was lit up. Dermot remembered Harry telling him about visiting his great aunt Kitty, an upholsterer in one of the rooms in the tower – the smell of leather and dust and fabric and machine oil. A musky aroma pungently emanated from the tiny room, much like the reek rising from most great aunts. Harry, as a child, must have enjoyed the view down into The Diamond from her workshop window, perhaps that was where his interest in watching from his tower evolved.

His journey took him to Bishop Street Without – outside the walled city – past London Street, where Harry's great grandfather had his plumbing business, then past the Court House. It was there that his political motivations were finally hewn. While his family fireside discussions and his father's inane obsessions often appalled him, a diminutive Bernadette Devlin, on the back of a lorry when he first saw her deliver a resounding speech, christened his political ambitions. Bernadette was a Republican Socialist like his mother, Bridie, as he was. His mother was the source of his spiritual and political education. She told him Irish fables, myths and legends by his bedside. Indeed, he and his mother had come over from Edinburgh for Bernadette's campaign and both helped her by delivering pamphlets and attending her meetings. She was the youngest Member of Parliament ever elected. It was Bernadette Devlin that sealed Dermot's fate. On the steps of the court house, Bernadette gave her usual eloquent, but fiery speech. Dermot had listened and was energised – Social Republicanism. He started to read the lumieres – Connolly, Pearse, Lawlor and Tone. His parents laid the ground work for his ideals, but it was Bernadette that ignited his passion. They all got to know her and his mother thought she would save Ireland, a new Maeve, the Celtic warrior princess. Maeve's Irish name, Medb, means she who makes men drunk - an appropriate saga for Bridie's life with her drunken husband.

It was the captivating power of Bernadette's oratory and her diminutive size that impressed Dermot. She had punched the British Home Secretary for his remarks about Bloody Sunday. More than once she felt the weight of the establishment when the army and police charged into the crowd at the court house – a mixed bunch of all ages and genders – as Bernadette finished her speech. The vocal youth – with their aggressive chanting 'SS RUC' before everyone rose to a crescendo, comparing the local police force, the Royal Ulster Constabulary to the Nazis. Someone spotted the army Saracen and Land Rovers roar from The Diamond and as always Bridie had Dermot by the hand out in front heading towards Bishop's Gate, the escape route. Unfortunately, the trap was set, a contingent of the security forces blocked the gate, and the crowd had nowhere to go but down Stable Lane, a narrow alleyway onto the Derry Walls. Some stood their ground but received blows from the truncheons and batons as a reward, and decided better to run and fight another day. The Laverys and others sought sanctuary in a tiny house in Stable Lane, one of Bridie's relatives. Dermot often wondered who he wasn't related to in the city. Through the window, Dermot saw a big husky policeman with an asinine face lash out at men, women and children. A sour toothless grimace next to Dermot asked, 'The hallions are fairly laying into us. Are ye alright, son? Call themselves a pleece force?'

Stable Lane was built against the Derry Walls. Looking around amidst all the bodies in the tiniest house he had ever seen, he could see two rooms below – a sitting room, fitted with a sofa and table, and a roaring fire. A flagged hallway led into a kitchen. Upstairs, by way of a narrow twisting stone staircase, were two bedrooms. On previous visits, he remembered, even though the front door was ajar, on arctic winter days the permanent blazing fire warmed the interior.

Dermot walked past the Court House, without giving it a blink, and thought about the comfy fire in Stable Lane. Not a track or imprint in Stable Lane on the virgin white blanket of snow to the walls. He walked through Bishop's Gate aware he was being watched from the security tower at the check point.

Dermot got an ache in his arm. He shuddered, and it wasn't the piercing wind. He got that aching feeling about tonight. It was a physical body signal from his nerves. Just like everyone else he was suspicious as to why he had been asked to work, although he didn't betray his suspicions to anyone. The pub was a known Republican haunt, raided a few times, but his boss Cathal was a shrewd businessman. Members of the Irish Republican Army drank in the pub, that he knew for sure. Some of them dropped in for a few pints, and were known locally as the Hard Men. Dermot was pleased they weren't regulars. They were regulars of another pub in the Bogside, the sort of guys that you wouldn't want to meet up a dark alley, but to have them on your side would be a different matter. With those blokes one exercised extreme caution – political debates and issues of the Troubles were avoided. Cathal's nephew, Michael, and his side kick, Brendan, were occasional visitors. Dermot hated their visits. Everyone knew their affiliations because they mouthed off enough although not when Cathal was around. They did not like Dermot as he had had to tell them to shut up a few times and had reported them to Cathal. Their subsequent reactions to Dermot proved that Cathal often had severe words with them. Dermot believed Ireland had more to fear from the likes of those two than the occupying army. Their impenetrable simplicity and odium never ceased to amaze Dermot. An occasional visitor was Frank, his old mate who had moved to Derry to marry, and looked for a free drink when he had nowhere else to go.

He avoided discussions of the IRA violence and the resultant causalities. He could understand their commitment to an armed struggle, but disagreed with it. Some IRA saw it as an honourable continuity to the men of the 1916 Easter Rising. Harry O'Donnell, his teacher friend told him about seeing the Boys in a fleet of Cortina's in Creggan during the No-Go era, a time when the police force did not enter the Creggan or the Bogside. On the way to educate the youth from that area, Harry had been often prevailed upon to produce his driving licence by a balaclava-headed youngster, armed with a machine gun in one hand and a rifle in the other at an IRA checkpoint. After the customary boot and bonnet search, and with a final hearty farewell: 'See you later, Mr. O'Donnell.' Harry did see the youngster without the balaclava, in his classroom.

Mostly, the horses, footy or her indoors were the topics – politics were barely mentioned except to curse the British – a trip to the bookies across the street to back a horse, the latest football results and how their team was robbed. The unreasonable wives who should know better, their husbands sought solace in the sports and their mates at the pub – the fact that many of them were unemployed made the pub life more necessary.

Cathal and Dermot sometimes discussed if and how the IRA campaign would end. Cathal called them Óglaigh na hÉireann, their Irish name. What was their fate of the Movement, the volunteers, the chances of getting caught, or killed, their beliefs, education or lack of it? Dermot wasn't sure of how best to approach the subject, but it was interesting and he often wondered about fate, its role in his life, where would it lead him? Was he being dragged or led by fate? He was hoping fate would intervene. But to do what? He was still young enough to believe he could influence his own life, his fate, and maybe he could.

In Republican versions of history the IRA were called heroes. Ireland has a long and bloody history of heroes. Heroes were often released from their fate by death, bearing their death for the greater good of the cause they served, for the people they served – the people of Ireland, their freedom, their future, their children's future. Dermot didn't see them as heroes, there had to be a better way than the death and destruction of themselves and the people of Ireland.

Sometimes he found himself skilfully led down a series of arguments about the IRA campaign, indirectly. How do combatants control the irrational savage within, are they counselled or do they even need it? Are the British always painted as some grosser specimens of humanity in order to execute the necessary Dogs of War? Dermot knew this, the IRA commanders knew this – it was a war. He realised he shouldn't be discussing these concepts with strangers, but they pressed the right buttons by introducing the ideas of the Irish Republican thinkers and how they applied to social justice in their time and Dermot's.

These strangers with a variety of accents seemed to know about Dermot and his interests. Often, after the discussion melted away, Cathal asked Dermot if he knew who he had been chatting to, most times he didn't, and Cathal never did say. Dermot thought about how dim-witted he was, talking about sensitive subjects, but the arguments were peppered with the thoughts of the great writers of Republicanism and it was probably through Cathal that the strangers may have known about Dermot's deep knowledge of socialist Republicanism and his general sagaciousness. He was being tested. Or was he being used as a testing ground for ideas?

Dermot and Frank

Frank was about Dermot's size as a boy, small and skinny. That probably was why they hit it off, at first. He was from a big family of about nine or ten, but he would spend all day in their house, away from his mob. Dermot's Mum didn't like kids hanging around and never did cook for anyone except the family. It was a chore to be fulfilled. Frank was an exception. He talked a different language to her or his father. He could anticipate her questions, her worries. She trusted him and was pleased he was Dermot's friend. Perhaps, it was her delight of Frank being his friend that bore a heavier responsibility on Dermot but he didn't understand at that time. She didn't want to hear anything negative about him. Frank would have easily lived with them, as an unofficial adopted child. It happened in many homes. The eldest child often went to live with Granny or some relative. Bridie wouldn't entertain such an idea but Frank stayed as often as he liked and he did.

One day Frank appeared in Dermot's primary school, Bridie was suspicious of his moving from his local school at the other end of town. There was never any objection by Frank's Mum to him staying overnight. Bridie suspected that Frank's mother hoped we would adopt him and lighten the load of her large family. He was in the class below Dermot and when his teacher was away or sick or something and the class had been divided up between the other classes. He went into Dermot's.

A boy called Jack, had sat beside Dermot most days, was very bright and luckily for Dermot, he was moved by the teacher to be placed beside a couple of temporary immigrants. Their education was intermittent and needed someone to help in their daily tasks. Jack was their new friend and mentor. So Frank ended up sitting beside Dermot for weeks before his normal teacher came back. Jack grew jealous of the bond, but even he accepted their close relationship. People remarked that Frank and Dermot were like non-identical twins, inseparable. If they weren't selected to play for the same soccer team they often ran away together after awhile. Frank stayed in the class even when his teacher eventually returned, maybe his mother asked if he could stay, no one really knew.

When Dermot eventually went to the local Catholic grammar school, Frank didn't. Both adapted and met each other where possible, mostly on weekends and holidays. Frank was clever, but as he developed; school and sport seemed too dull for him. He wanted to experience more, he wanted to experience life. He got obsessed with things. No one seemed to mind their togetherness – some made suggestions that they were too close as their teeming adolescence took hold. Physically and sexually Frank jumped at fourteen and left Dermot behind. Body hair poured forth from his pores, his sexual awaking was shared, and soon he was talking about the shape and size of the female teenagers. He was even attracted to the older female, as he looked older when his body filled out. His stubble made him look about nineteen and he matured in every way faster than Dermot, who was enthralled by him. He became more than the older brother and mentor, he had been infatuated by Marilyn Monroe, the glamour Goddess. He became Dermot's idol, in a way.

They planned their escapes from the confines of family and local life, walking around the streets, getting away from the familiar streets had been their constant refrain. During their early teens they were equals, at one time, even though Dermot didn't think he was. Frank had left home, had lived on the streets or had bunkered down on some one's couch and stayed regularly with Dermot's family. They were growing apart but Frank always had time for Dermot, even taking him on some of his dates, but Dermot often left him with his girl friend as he took off to see some other mates. Frank started to drink, had worked part time in a bar and moved in circles beyond his years and beyond Dermot's. He made Dermot feel important and listened to his feeble exploits while Dermot had listened, enthralled about the girls he had slept with, the bands he had seen, the drugs he had tried, and the narrow escapes from the police. Dermot was in awe and loved him. School had become a drag but every time they met as two normal sixteen year old teenagers, obsessed with sex, movies and soccer, he was still Dermot's best friend. When he was with his other mates, male and female, Dermot had been cast to the shadows, not intentionally, but Dermot was too immature, jealous of his super confidence and easy charm.

Dermot started to mix with his own mates from school and they explored their own social and sexual life through dances, girls and pubs, at their own adolescent pace. Occasionally Dermot caught up with Frank, for a few beers and had gone to a local dance with him, but it was a different scene, much older and rougher crowd. Frank had money, good looks and a line of chat that Dermot had tried to emulate. It had worked sometimes.

Frank met Barbara, a real beauty, golden hair, with a Hollywood figure on one of his trips to Derry and they eventually got engaged. Frank was so infatuated, he moved to the city from Scotland. They seemed to have got on well enough. Dermot had met them over the summer while he had been visiting and sometimes in Edinburgh too. When Dermot moved to Derry he started meeting up with them for a few drinks and an odd dance. She had been all over Frank, like a rash, as Frank had once commented. He had complained that her extrovert behaviour had attracted attention from older men floating around to pick up some young honey pot, but Frank had always been big enough to defend his corner. The two young men had continued to meet, in their late teens, ending the evening buying chips in the wee hours of the morning, before wandering home in the quiet streets of the city night.

Frank got married a year later; everyone thought Dermot would have been the best man, but having gone to university, their relationship further loosened. Dermot attended the wedding. For a few years Barbara and Frank had been happy but every time they had tried for a baby, Barbara had a miscarriage. It took its toll on her, on both of them, but worse, her last baby was stillborn. Both were devastated. She became more inward as post natal depression took hold, and became attached to her sister. Frank became a barman and was well known and respected, managing several bars. Little did anyone know he had been drinking heavily and gambling and mixing with a crowd of no hopers that frequented his bars. He had been drinking the owner's profits and started slipping some money to himself to finance his gambling debts. It was discovered and he was sacked. He got another job in a factory but his marriage was all in name only. Slowly, but certainly all had been lost between them. He had debts. Barbara moved back to her family home and some say he got involved with some of his previous crowd bordering on criminality, his drinking and debts led him to the gutter. Some said that was to be destiny, but for another lady, Jen.

Stability reigned for a while and Frank became a manager of a pub, again. Rumour was he still had contacts in the underworld. Jen and Frank had a couple of kids, but drink had taken hold in their lives and they were more or less functioning alcoholics. Despite their addictions, their kids kept the relationship going and provided some semblance of normality between the binges. They lived for the kids and the next drink, often the priority got confused.

Every time Frank and Dermot met, the years melted once again and they could talk about anything, Frank read widely and knew about his life outside of Derry. Dermot still loved this man, his intelligence and wit still sparked, but Dermot encountered a level of drinking and self loathing that had shock him to the core. He reeled from it and Frank had sometimes turned aggressive late into the drinking session. The barrier to their ongoing relationship had developed. Dermot had felt he should have done something to save the relationship and save Frank from himself. Dermot walked away, badly shaken and disappointed by his idol. Frank had the potential to be anything he wanted. Dermot saw it as a waste of his life.

Frank's pub's cliental were full of locals and he had many friends from Donegal. He visited the wild north-western county regularly, owning a caravan in Portsalon, eventually living permanently in Donegal. The two childhood friends had gone their separate ways. Both never forgot each other.

Stocktake at the Bar

Dermot walked past the Inishmore bar, surveying the street and its buildings. He saw a faint radiance at an upstairs window, some movement in a house opposite the pub. A silhouette appeared as the curtain was pulled to look out. Was it just someone looking out at the atrocious weather, but like most people not wanting to get involved in anything they saw, preferring to return to the comfort of their chair and the warm glow of a British comedy on television? He didn't think anyone was watching the bar, but he wasn't sure. He returned to the single fronted local bar, an inconsequential establishment. A Guinness sign, unlit, over the dark bottle-green door, atop of three steps. He could see tracks in the snow leading to the door, left by fellow travellers. He followed them.

Dermot tapped the frosted window three times beside the front door. It was the method used by staff to gain entry. The door opened, an unfamiliar head stuck out, looked up and down the empty street and said:

'Dead as a doornail, quiet as a mouse.'

Dermot kicked off the excess snow from his boots against the stone and stepped in. Stamping on the mat, knocking the snow off a second time, he looked around the darkened interior. No one was there. Where had the stranger gone? Four tables squatted by the unlit fire and a couple more against the rear wall where the dart board hung. The bar stools in a row at the end of the bar. Photographs of old Derry were displayed on the pasty beige walls. The bar light flooded from under its glass shelves – reflected in the sparkling glassware and the mirrored wall behind it – the usual nightly security light. He made his way to the cellar, under the stairs, a dismal glow shone from its open flap.

As Dermot's eyes settled in the twilight of the cellar light two figures came into view, Cathal and the unfamiliar face. After Christmas greetings and muted apologies to Dermot for bringing him out on such a night, Cathal introduced him to the other guy, Pearse with a Belfast accent who had just opened the door. He shook his hands.

'Nollaig Shona Daoibh.'

'Nollaig Mhaith Chugat.'

Pearse responded in Irish to Dermot's Christmas greeting.

'Are ye not at home with the family, Pearse?'

'I am, sort of, they are here with me, visiting her sister in Buncrana.'

'How were the roads? It's getting worse out there.'

'The main roads are fine, gritted, the snow is soft so easy to grip, but I need to get away soon, if that's the case. Down to business, Cathal?'

'We'll be in the back room, Dermot, not to be disturbed, you understand? We are expecting another friend – Joseph. You know Joseph? Don't you? Could you keep an eye for him? Just have a look out every now and again. He will knock on the window as per normal. Go up stairs and look out, if you don't mind, save you opening the door and letting the winter in and do the stocktake as we are opening tomorrow.'

Dermot knew Joseph, an infrequent visitor to the bar. He was also known as the head of the local IRA. A couple of hours later Cathal came out and ordered two Jameson hot whiskeys with cloves and lemon. Dermot had finished his work and was reading a book.

'You know Dermot; I was reading a book the other day. It was about anti-gravity. I couldn't put it down.'

Dermot stared and smiled.

'Joseph didn't turn up. Maybe the weather put him off.' Cathal added before retreating to the office.

When Dermot went into the back room Pearse had gone and the whiskeys were for Cathal and himself.

'Pearse gone?'

'Yes, he slipped out the back way and will probably slip all the way down to Buncrana. Just having a meeting with one of my friends from Belfast. A good opportunity now that he is down our way.'

What was going on, thought Dermot. But he knew not to ask – Derry's omerta. He didn't mind, he was getting paid.

The Class

Harry O'Donnell stared through the condensation on the classroom window at the turbid river below. Its cobalt meandering was a constant pleasure and an arresting meditation. Harry liked his classroom – its magnificent view across the Foyle Valley to the verdant fields of the Waterside contrasted with the verdure wits of the thirty three boys in front of him. The endless emerald patchwork stretched beyond the city – the road to the north towards the town of Limavady and to the south towards New Buildings. A road he had taken many times to visit his relatives in Strabane and Lifford. The ashen clouds tickled the roofs on the hill opposite, light emanating from the breaks in the cloud – shades of red and purple from the bilious shapes, spreading its luminosity. Their changing wind-driven formations were an agreeable distraction from the mundane bell-driven routine of the school day. The swooping birds, envied by Harry: floating in midstream, their courtships, their freedom, their jostling squeals like the boys in his school yard. Sometimes, on cloudless days, unyielding brightness flooded the room through the massive windows.

January, the gloomiest of all gloomy months, winter storms added to the post Christmas depression and a glacial mood settled in the class too. Often, to distract them, Harry focused their immature minds on imagining a world inside their heads, away for the gloom outside. He nevertheless rugged up despite the room heating blasting for all its worth, it was insufficient for the single glazed corner classroom, the butt of the wind and the rain. He savoured the changing illumination, the shadowing light, as if a curtain was slowly drawn. The city below darkened in its own existence and his thoughts of his own fireside were all the more rewarding. Everyone was relieved, staff inwardly, students outwardly, when the last gong of the day singled the finale.

Some activity at the permanent army checkpoint on the Craigavon Bridge caught his eye. Lines of cars queued for their inspection. It seemed another January day in a city engulfed in battened–down homes, combat fatigues, ashen skies and stony countenances. On the street below the school, a group of women clustered around a pram, heads nodding in agreement, coats pulled tight against the unforgiving wind, another pushing a pram, the children skipping along in procession. Above the grassy bank opposite, two men, strolling, their dogs scampering ahead sniffing at lamp posts and corners, oblivious to the winter rawness, unlike their owners wrapped in puffed anoraks. A

Christmas wreath hung forlornly on a front door, an insult to the festivities gone, still colourful unlike the gaunt and forgotten garden.

Winter, at the beginning of the New Year, was a dark season, the cool damp penetrating to all that ventured out beyond their car or home. The money spent on Christmas celebrations and the reality of future months in payback. Some fortunate inhabitants escaped to warmer climes for a week or two, but for the majority it was the routine of their work, fireside and television. He felt like taking his binoculars from his desk drawer, but that wasn't possible. The school for some local boys was a refuge from the Troubles on the streets and from their own troubles in their homes. Sometimes, for a distraction from school work, Harry let the students ask questions about anything. The topic usually focused on the latest football match or news item.

The Troubles affected most of Northern Ireland, in one way or another. Yet, in many places, it seemed as if it never existed, people went about their lives. Even in troubled cities like Derry, people led normal lives, well, as normal as bombs and soldiers would allow. What else could anyone have done? The schools were refuges. People took refuge by their firesides too. A different matter outside the school gates, where Harry spotted an army patrol walking into view.

Suddenly his mind spun on the overheard conversation outside his home between his neighbour, Dermot and someone else – what did it mean? Was there to be a major escalation of violence? Some spoke of a civil war. The Troubles. What a feeble idiom! His mother, like many, referred to someone who had their 'troubles'. It usually meant some health problem or an errant child – a serious matter for the individual or family, enough to deal with. They had enough of their own troubles without worrying about the Troubles.

As if to remind Harry of the nature of the Troubles, a red Ford Cortina drove past the school and down Southway, the road running past the school, with three young men inside. It stopped. It was the Boys. It was the same red Cortina that had blocked his return from lunch. Except this time one of the lads that had stopped him was sitting staring into the corner of the ceiling in Harry's class. A youngster dressed in a combat jacket, a black scarf over his face, a hand gun by his side, got out, shot several times at the patrol. He threw himself into the car and was out of sight in a matter of seconds. The car was gone before the army realised it was in the firing line. Some pupils stood up shouting 'that was gun shots' and moved to look out the windows. Harry stopped them, saying it was a car back firing, but they disagreed with their teacher and they were right. They had grown up familiar with the sound.

Harry remembered the tiny brown eyes of the youth now settling back to his classroom work. After lunch time on his return to school, Harry was stopped at an IRA check point, not far from the school. The same tiny brown eyes stared at his teacher, his rigid stance, the clipped pronunciation asking: 'Licence, Sir?'

He handed his license over, the boy made theatrical gestures flipping through the pages, probably looking for his date of birth, thought Harry.

The machine gun resting on his hip bone, 'Could you open your bonnet and boot, Sir?' trying to sound as officious as possible. Harry bit his lip to prevent himself laughing but held his composure and said nothing.

The aim of getting through any security checkpoint, lawful or otherwise was to get through it as hassle free and as speedily as possible – it required subdued composure, subservient compliance and minimum conversation.

Harry got out of his car and let out a resigned sigh. The boy rebel said 'Sorry, Mr. O'Donnell' in a moment of confused sympathy. Harry opened his bonnet and boot and stood back looking at the school gates a couple of hundred metres away. The boy was enjoying himself. He said half heartedly:

'Thanks Mr. O'Donnell. Sorry for your troubles.'

There it was again, that word, 'troubles', inconsequential yet deadly for Northern Ireland.

He heard the murmurs gathering apace, as the boys realised their teacher was absorbed elsewhere and they lessened their interest in their written task. Having one eye out the window and another on the class was Harry's usual escape, but he got lost in his thoughts and the class knew it. Looking at the river for a final time, he took a mental snap of the view before going back to his duty. It suddenly occurred to Harry it was his turn to make dinner. Did he leave the mince out of the freezer this morning, he pondered?

As he faced the class he caught a glimpse of Davy O'Carolan, his hand down his pants massaging its contents. Unwillingly, Harry drew himself back to the reality. Most heads looked at him. Davy was otherwise pre-occupied. Summoning up as much enthusiasm as he could:

'Stop writing, pants down, sorry, pens down, everyone, hands on the desk. Everyone, that includes you too, Davy.'

Harry tried to distract them and pressed on as the class roared with laughter at his pants mistake. He ignored the laughter as best he could, and attempted to re-direct the student's attention.

'Right, quiet please. You should have finished the paragraph on the Old Man and The Sea. For your homework, and you can start it in class: what was he thinking about, out alone, on the boat? Imagine, someone on a boat fishing on the Foyle, on a nice summer's day. Maybe further up the river, away from the city. Using the same thoughts and words written on the board, imagine your father, your uncle or older brother out there for hours sitting, waiting for a catch. What thoughts would be going through their head? What contemporary issues would be going through their head? A list is on the board. Family problems, how much they lost on the horses and they have to tell their wife? Look at board for some ideas. You add your own. Imagine looking at the boat on the river down below!'

To add to further mayhem, desks and chairs scraped on the floor and the classroom filled with noise as they all stood up, clamouring towards the windows.

'Sit down everyone, you have seen the view of the river many times, and if you haven't, imagine it.'

Harry bellowed at if talking to a dog half a field away and thought himself a fool for daydreaming and not keeping an eye to the class.

'Sit! Start the paragraph now and finish it off for homework.'

The boys sat down disappointed. Their opportunity for silliness dashed. All heads slowly glanced from the board to their jotters; pens glided unwillingly across the page. Peace again reigned and Harry drew a deep breath and relaxed. He wandered down towards Davy, the student at the back of the class – the page in his exercise book was mostly blank.

'Okay, Davy?'

'Aye, no bother, Sir.'

Harry picked up the exercise book and flicked through its pages. Not a lot of evidence of written expression within. On his current page Davy had written – And the dour granite sky wept.

'I see you managed to copy my sentence from the board.'

'It's very good, Sir. You should be proud, thinking up a line like that. Isn't it good hand writing? I took my time, Sir.'

'What about some self-expression?'

'Some what, Sir?'

The exercise book's cover was a piece of abstract colours and swirling line doodles. Harry showed the cover to Davy:

'What is that?

'That, Sir, is art.'

'Maybe. Who am I to judge art, Davy? There is no must in art, art is free, as some Russian artist said. But your time in my class is not free. I suggest you get started.'

'Yes Sir. Ah damn, my pencil lead just broke. Sir, did you know broken pencils are pointless?'

'Daveee!'

Davy's left arm covered his book and with slack jawed concentration he made demonstrative movement with his writing hand. Harry was sure little was happening in Davy's book.

Harry thought Davy was in jaunty form, not his usual querulous self. The numerous years Harry had spent in the classroom, teaching every day. The same stuff, just new faces. He felt he was getting tired of the whole experience. What else could he do? The children seem to be getting more cantankerous and vigorous, more assertive. They needed more hand-holding, more spoon-feeding. As Harry told new teachers – spoon-feeding taught nothing, but the shape of the spoon. They needed explicit instructions, control of their physical movements, and awareness of their shortened activity time. They were less willing to give things a go or were they simply behaving stupidly with boredom and anxiety? The days when they sat and listened to him or listened to each other with surly respect were gone. At least they had the good manners to fall asleep or daydream, instead of confrontation, thought Harry.

The bell tolled the end of the school day, the final joyous day before the weekend. Harry delivered a few final words on homework, then a short prayer. He used prayer to focus the boys – it settled them. The chairs were placed on the desks before the final orderly scramble for the door.

Harry stared out the window once again, breathed deeply, another day, another dollar as his thoughts turned homeward. The brightening murkiness lit the cars on the Craigavon Bridge. The grammar school on top of a hill, tree entrenched, the ancient Round Tower just edging above them. Harry's old school, just behind. The late afternoon mist drifted over the city. Smoke staggered from many of the chimneys and dissipated into the mist. The houses outside the school ran down the hill towards Lone Moor Road, flowing to the riverside, and lines of terraced streets rose again on the hill opposite. Harry opened the window a crack, wafts of moist fresh air roused his weary eyes, the window's security feature preventing it opening wide so no one could fall out, intentionally or otherwise. After a few moments he closed it, creating a plume of dust as he wiped the blackboard and gathered his stuff from the desk, closing the door behind him.

In the French store room, Seamas, the Head of French and Irish sat reading Friday's Derry Journal, the local newspaper. A few colleagues gathered to have coffee there, sometimes for lunch or just for some collegiality. Seamas had a frown permanently etched on his face, hard to see sometimes in his abundant facial hair. He sat with his back to the window, the view of the Foyle winding towards the city behind him, and he kept reading the paper, without lifting his head.

'Any news? Are you calling into the Castle tonight?'

'Naw. We're having Elma's sister and hubby round for drinkies tonight.'

Seamas answered, the usual mild irritation in his tone.

'How is Elma, Seamas? Did she survive the fall?'

'My wife, Harry, is the great survivor. Within days she was back to work, organising my life and the kids.'

'Good on her, you need someone to sort you out, I'll see you Monday. Have a great weekend.'

'Same to you.'

Harry left and on the ground floor stepped into the staff room, a palpable mood of sociable relief pervaded the remnants of staff. Friday afternoon was usually devoid of good company, but he saw Eamon hanging about the foyer, looking for a possible drinking partner. Eamon was set for an after-school drink any day of the week, but Harry decided to skip Eamon's company and slipped out to the car park. A few teachers were already driving out and with a meek salute to them he plopped into his car, and as he eased his aching back into the driver's seat, he thought about getting into his car more mindfully in the future. The slick wet hill for home lay ahead, he pushed the Horslips tape into the slot. 'Dearg Doom' blasted his ears as he cranked up the volume. What would his wife and himself do on the Friday night? Perhaps catch up with some friends after he made dinner; there was usually a party, somewhere. He wondered if sex was on the agenda. He was mulling over his possible sexual encounter as blood started to pump into his crotch; Friday night deserved sex, drugs and rock and roll as soon as possible. Totally absorbed in Celtic rock music and the thoughts of sex and booze, he drove home to start his weekend.

He made slow progress along Park Avenue – always a delay, one of Derry's traffic jams. Lorries were pulling in and out; two were double parked, unloading onto the pavement. It was simply too narrow for cars travelling in both directions with many parked cars. Harry lived at the end of the avenue – a row of terrace houses on either side, many with little walled gardens. He sat behind a white van with a shamrock on its rear door. Horslips pumped out its electro music and Harry was oblivious to the world and its troubles, tapping his fingers to the Celtic beat on the steering wheel.

Going for a Drink

Suddenly Dermot Victor Lavery was in the passenger seat, waving a bar of Fry's Chocolate Cream – Harry's favourite.

'Jesus, Dermot, you're going to be the death of me.'

'I'll give you this bar of chocolate if you take me to a pub.'

Dermot laughed, showing his perfect teeth, his blue eyes aglow and staring into Harry's, never withdrawing.

'I smell something in this car. It's a funny car smell. Very pungent. This isn't new? Is it? I smell a bar of chocolate.'

Dermot held it under Harry's nose. Harry smiled at the happy smell of his favourite chocolate bar.

'You'll be here awhile. It'll not be moving. Someone bumped a car and they are swearing at each other. Some poor lady is in tears. I suggest you turn before you get trapped. Fancy some chocolate? Have you time for a pint? I'm paying.'

'Yes, to both questions.'

Harry did a U-turn causing a few cars to reverse, but luckily he was beside someone's driveway and managed to reverse out of an awkward position. Dermot laughed at Harry's antics to turn the car around, his face erupting, enjoying the circus. A few other cars started to follow him. Dermot thumped Harry's knee as he clutched and geared his Ford Escort.

'Jesus, this is great craic. Why does your car smell like a teacher's car? Where can we go that smells like a pub?'

'Shut up or you are walking or, worse still, you are drinking on your own.'

Harry first met Dermot in the Rock Bar, both having a quiet Guinness at the bar and they got chatting. Dermot was looking for accommodation and Harry recommended his neighbour's boarding house. Dermot had settled there ever since, they became good friends and had the odd drink together. Although he was quite a few years younger than Harry, a serious lad with an awesome steely stare, they enjoyed each other's company. Harry was one of the few who saw an intelligent sensitive young man while others saw a rod of emotional-less emptiness. Dermot's severe gaze was transformed when he smiled. Here was a young man craving intellectual debate, thought Harry. According to Harry's wife, others saw a rod of iron and that glare scared the wits out of most people. There was a compulsive personality at work – tension and light, sternness and charm. Harry felt he was chosen to be Dermot's peripatetic companion. Dermot reserved his friendship for a select few and Harry was one of them. Yet he never socialised in Harry's network of friends. It was often meeting on the street or the odd phone call or jumping into Harry's car. It was as if he needed to talk, to impart some great tragedy, but every time Dermot sat in Harry's company he drew comfort from it and said little. Both enjoyed their silences and Dermot always insisted on paying for the drinks. That was the only thing they argued about and he often departed as hastily as he arrived.

Harry was knocked out of his reverie by the man sitting beside him.

'Tough day, Dermot?'

'You could say that. Two little gob-shites gave me some hassle.'

'Punters at the pub?'

'Yip, something like that.'

'Tough day, Harry?'

Both laughed as Dermot copied Harry's question and tone.

'Oh, let's have a quick one in the Rock Bar.'

'Great idea, Harry. My treat.'

Harry and Dermot never drank or socialised in Dermot's bar. He parked in Aberfoyle Crescent, just above the Rock Bar. As Harry passed the corner house on Aberfoyle Terrace and the Rock Road, Bob, another teacher from another secondary school stood distracted at his window, cup of tea in one hand and the Derry Journal in the other. Bob absent-mindedly stared at Dermot and Harry, his countenance telling them he was miles away– the stresses and strains of teaching borne on his face. Harry just walked on by to the bar. One old guy in dungarees, a thick yellow pencil behind his ear had a half of Smithwicks beer and a whiskey chaser in front of him on the bar. He nodded to them and reverted his attention to the swilling colours of the nectar sat in front of him, anticipating the potency soon to be enjoyed. John, the old barman, looked like a grammar school teacher – dark grey flannels, mousey v-neck jumper, blue shirt with a maroon tie, not even loosened for comfort. His pale face, sharply shaven, his hair short, a slight annoyance across it when he saw the two men enter. It took him away from the horse race on the television in the corner of the bar.

'What'll you have, gents, the usual?'

'Two pints of Guinness, thanks. Any luck on the gee-gees?'

'Naw, not a good day for me? Do you know the origin of 'gee-gee'?'

'No, I don't'

'After a Chester city mayor; Henry Gee started horse racing because previously the field was used for football and that tended to end up violent, so he replaced the football field with a racecourse.'

'You are a font of all knowledge. Don't tell me you are a quiz boffin?'

'Never miss it. I'll bring over your pints.'

The barman warmed as he exhibited his quiz knowledge, a popular pastime in the city's pubs. It was obvious they had interrupted a race where John had lost and he wanted to watch the next race.

Both settled in the corner watching the door. The pints arrived. Each toasted the other with a sláinte when they clinked their glasses. Dermot dumped his chewing gum into the Sweet Afton ashtray. It was five minutes before Harry spoke.

'Did you ever see the cigarette advertisement for Sweet Afton? This pub used to have a great advertising hoarding for those cigarettes – a bucolic scene with: 'Flow gently, sweet Afton, amang thy green braes. Flow gently, I'll sing thee a song in thy praise.'

'You are a poet, Harry?'

'Nope. It was Robbie Burns and that's part of his poem Sweet Afton. Most people thought it was all Irish. There was a connection between Dundalk, a town across the border where Robbie Burn's sister lived and where the cigarettes were made. I remember coming up the Strand Road and seeing the advertisement after a day's outing with my parents. I knew I was home from wherever we had been: the beach, from Belfast or just out shopping.'

'Well, who would have thought I would learn this trivia just by going to the pub.'

'Trivia and gossip make the world go round. Why do you chew gum, Dermot?'

'Because one of the nicest things in life is fresh breath, for myself and people I am chatting to. All you need when travelling is a toothbrush and clean undies.'

'Why? Where are you going now?'

'Nowhere.'

'Thank you, Dermot for your simple wisdom. Though I thought you more profound with all your knowledge. They should be written on stone. Send them into the Readers Digest, all those one-liners.'

'Are you taking the piss?'

'Yes.'

'That's okay then. I shall continue with your education for a lived life. Clean teeth and clean undies that would do for starters.'

'What about a clean mind?'

'Well, that leaves you out. Someone to share your up and downs, keeping a dream alive, a hobby you love would help, planting stuff in the garden, enjoying small daily stuff, a child's smile, or something. Having something to look forward to the next day is important, even a cup of tea with friends or something. You have all that with Marie and the kids. I have no one.'

Harry smiled at Dermot, but wasn't sure if he was being too serious.

'Dermot, you have got me. You are a bit of a nomad, a bit of a traveller, a traveller of the mind and the world. I am happy in Derry. I ain't moving. I am travelling through life in this town. You are travelling through life, God knows where! I think you will move on. I hope not. So, tell me what would you recommend for the traveller? I mean anyone who is travelling on this earth, whether spiritually or physically, even someone who never leaves Derry, like me?'

Dermot instantly responded, as if ready with his answer:

'Work with your hands, in the soil, especially cultivating something, or a hobby making something, creating something, and for those competitive types and the need to prove themselves, running a race or something, either in work or in sport.'

'True, so true, having some sort of dream. Keeping it alive. Imagination is also important. If I just ignited the imagination of the boys today in class, I would say that was a success.'

'What if you are stuck and poor and can't afford to dream?'

'Well you know the French peasant saying: good food, good fuck, good shit and a good night's sleep is all you need or something like that.'

They roared with laughter, Harry spitting out some of his beer, narrowly missing Dermot.

'If you had a list, what would it be? I know you read these positive thinking books. Didn't you try to pass me that one – Your Erroneous Zones, by someone called Dyer?'

'Yip, those books can be interesting, mostly full of common sense, and mostly could be condensed to a hundred pages, but then they wouldn't sell. For what it's worth I think a cosy home like yours, Harry, is vital. A solace from the world.'

'Something I wonder about you, being a nomad, and a dark horse, will you ever settle?'

Dermot's pupils seemed to grow dimmer, but otherwise not a facial expression changed on his face. This was as much a reaction he got from Dermot. Something was odd about Dermot. Harry knew not to query too deeply. He always answered any of Harry's questions about his background, but it always seemed abbreviated in explanation.

'So Mr. Wise Guy Teacher, teach us your home truths for a happy life.'

Dermot tumbled his words as if he was exhausted. Harry reckoned, he wanted to change the subject, but still asked a direct question.

'Are you happy, Dermot?'

Dermot drew heavily on his pint of Guinness and his eyes darkened again, his pupils dilated but settled, and his cheeks freshened. Harry had learnt to concentrate on Dermot's expression to note these minute muscular tensions. Dermot forced a smile to hide his discomfort.

'Hmm. That is an elusive subject. I just batter on and leave it to the philosophers. Let me tell you, my bar is often full of them, night after night, and as the night wears on, they would soon tell you what life is all about. Bar stool philosophers. Mostly shit, of course, but good craic. The best ones are the wise ones with the great one-liners. Some punters get excited and certain in their ideas, forgetting about life's vastitudes. Needless to say, they get happier the more they drink but as the night wears on and home beckons, they become more sullen. For some it's all part of the craic. They are the wise ones. Life is ironic. Just being alive is ironic.'

Dermot grinned.

'But seriously though, did you never give it much thought?"

'Very serious thought, actually.'

Immediately Dermot realised he had given too much away as Harry's eyes widened in surprise and Dermot drooped a little. Dermot felt committed and to hide his slip he pretended to be serious, so carried on. It was one of the few times Harry saw Dermot lose his shield.

'Freedom is vital, the freedom of one's country, the freedom to get jobs, to go as one pleases.'

'Oh, a political statement, why am I not surprised. I suppose that's them Republicans you mix with in your bar. Gide said, getting your freedom is one thing, but having it is the more difficult part.'

Dermot immediately followed up his thoughts trying to deflect Harry.

'I am a Republican and agree with them on many things. Brits Out! You know they will never leave. I like the idea of a United Ireland, but I have problems with how it can be achieved. All this bloodshed leaves me cold. There has to be another way. The Brits will never leave, so the only way forward is some form of negotiation, I suppose. Everyone involved, the governments, the people of all persuasions and the gunmen. They need to be brought into the negotiations. How, I don't know?'

'Wow, I knew you were a socialist, believed in social justice and had to be a Republican to work in that bar. You really are deep, thoughtful, even. Politics is something we avoid except at the ballot box. We slip in a few thoughts to close friends and colleagues, but really we have emigrated to our front rooms. We see more watching the London or Dublin news to find out what trouble is happening down the town in William Street or in Belfast.'

'When you say we, you are talking essentially about the middle class.'

Dermot's cheeks coloured imperceptibly. Harry thought Dermot was worried he offended him by classifying him as middle class.

'Oh I get plenty of it at work. All the fuckin' bar-stool politicians and Republicans at the pub. I just agree with them. There are some cute whores at the bar sometimes, not regulars. They try to provoke me, but I have learnt to button my lips. Just agree with them all. They know I have read all about the Republican struggle through the centuries, know the history of their own town better than them. Sometimes they tap into that, but mostly they try to wind me up. Somebody must have told them about me because they ask. I try to keep a low profile at work. I suppose I am too serious at times.'

Dermot laughed to lighten the air. He had given too much away already but his acuity was plain for Harry to see. Both were unsure of each other's divergent political views, wary of testing the waters and not wanting to muddy their friendship – a normal stance for Northern Irish people. Whatever you say, say nothing. They both lived too close to each other to fall out. Harry remembered his grandfather's motto in business and personal life – always keep a civil distance. Dermot added:

78

'Years ago, maybe they still do, but I loved the way the Irish used the only weapon of the weak: throughotherness. They pretended to be dumber than they were. They doffed their caps. They agreed with their masters. They looked befuddled with their feigned deference. The Irish realised the landlords controlled their destiny and their labour, but they weren't getting their souls or their mind. They had their own way of doing things – throughotherness. I guess peasants across the world did the same?'

'Indeed, Dermot they didn't have much else to give. The bosses weren't getting their spirit, but their outward demeanour was one of a broken spirit – a grovelling acceptance of the crumbs from the master's table. They depended upon the paternalism of the landlord. I wonder what they would think of the idea of freedom to live one's life as desired. But can we here in Derry?'

They both sipped their drinks and Harry continued:

'I think enjoying the moment, day in, day out, little things, family by the fireside, petting the dog, a Coltrane track, a Horslips concert, sex.'

Harry added, both grinned boyishly as the topic turned lighter.

'Well, you would know more about that than me.'

'Oh, I don't know about that. You are getting your share.'

Dermot's eyes darted to Harry's, and it confirmed Harry's watching brief from his Tower, he had suspected his liaisons with Pauline.

'That book Erroneous Zones, sexy title by an American, Wayne Dyer. He says you got to love yourself before you can love anyone else.'

'I do see people's self-obsessions, Dermot. They seem to be getting obsessed with self-obsession, but I guess like all these things there is some truth in it. I think it is not just self-love, it's self-knowledge, that's key. Plato or one of those ancient guys said something like – an examined life is a lived life. A life lived with virtue and wisdom. They constantly tell you to 'wise up' in Derry. They must be so wise by now in this town. Wisdom flows out of any man or beast you chat to. Tell me some of the wise craic from the pub, if you remember?'

'I don't think I want to scrounge around my past life, it was happy enough. Like most it had some not so happy bits. I lived here most summers with my Granny. She was lovely if somewhat unfathomable. She went to Mass every morning, and dragged me along. All the other boys lay in their bed while I went to the altar rails. Yet, she was stinging in her attacks on the church, the male domination etcetera, etcetera. You know, I think she liked the routine, the ritual and of course the social side – chats with all and sundry afterwards. The memories I have of waiting for her while she gossiped. My parents were the same. No wonder I keep to myself. I used to bang a stone or a piece of wood on the church railings to get her attention and she would give me the sternest look. I stopped immediately.'

'Somebody said wisdom is like a butterfly, not a bird of prey. Was your Granny a butterfly or a bird of prey? She sounded a bit like you – a bit of both, yet unfathomable? The unfathomable Dermot!'

'Maybe, a bit of both I suppose, like my mother. Aye, true, a bit like that. What about health, wellbeing, jobs? I mentioned: good housing, good opportunities. That's the stuff my mother was on about, preached her socialist ways in Edinburgh, floated like a butterfly but stung like a bee, like Mohammed Ali.'

'Surely, that all left a mark on you, Dermot Victor Lavery? Those strong ideological women.'

'That's why I am a barman. Too much stuff in my head. Our Seamas Heaney, the poet says it's the imagination pressing back against reality. I need something to hold back reality – Guinness and poetry – just so fuckin' Irish.'

'Happiness for me: the family, the kids, the opportunity to flourish, to live your life well, to have respect, decent jobs, good health and as you say freedom to follow that through, a dream, to imagine is so important. To daydream, using your imagination to dream that path you might like to follow. Music is great for that process, it helps.'

'Granny Ellen used to say the best music of all is the music of what happens, and I happen to be a barman.'

'So you just let it happen?'

'I don't want to get caught up in all that intellectual bullshit. Intellectual masturbation. I just want to be myself, nobody else and that is not an easy option. Oscar Wilde said: most people are other people; their thoughts are other people's opinions, a mimicry, their passions a quotation.'

'You could be much more, Dermot. You are clever, handsome, all that wit and wisdom. God, I have such witty friends, clever, intellectual friends, like you. Now tell us some Derry wise crack from the pub.'

'I'll tell you a dirty joke.'

Dermot rubbed his palms together and smiled into them and poured forth:

'A man goes into a restaurant and is seated. All the waitresses are gorgeous. A particularly voluptuous waitress wearing a very short skirt and legs that won't quit came to his table and asked if he was ready to order, 'what would you like, sir?' He looks at the menu and then scans her beautiful frame top to bottom, then answers, 'a quickie'. The waitress turns and walks away in disgust. After she regains her composure she returns and asks again, 'what would you like, sir?' Again the man thoroughly checks her out and again answers, 'a quickie, please.' This time her anger takes over, she reaches over and slaps him across the face with a resounding – SMACK! – and storms away. A man sitting at the next table leans over and whispers, 'Um, I think it's pronounced 'quiche'.'

Both chuckled.

'You know, I wouldn't be surprised if I woke up one morning and you were gone. That nomad in you, that restlessness will explode sometime.'

Dermot smiled at Harry's understanding of him. Harry worried about his constant needling and knew that Dermot wanted privacy, needed privacy, yet Harry couldn't help himself. He was inquisitive and genuinely wanted to know about people – what made them tick. It wasn't just nosiness. Well, maybe a little, but he wanted to gain a better understanding of Dermot. It would never happen, he would remain inscrutable. Dermot befriended Harry, one of the chosen few, always would be. If Harry needed help he would be by his side, telling dirty jokes, if need be. Dermot could extemporise on most subjects, a great memory, whereas Harry needed some prompting or notes. He could never remember jokes, even dirty ones.

'Yep, you are probably right, but nothing mysterious. Just travelling really. It would be simply sun, sea and sand. I want to break free and become a beach bum. Feel the sand skittering under my feet. That really appeals to me. One of those tropical bars you see in the advertisements. Me serving the cocktails on a tropical beach. All them girls clad in little to nothing. Maybe even break free of this place, break free from Ireland. I heard a group of my parent's friends talk one night. Somebody called it the CRAP of Ireland – Catholicism, Republicanism, Alcoholism and Poverty. Shat upon by our colonial masters – The Brit'

'Very good, Ireland summed up in a piece of shit. The crap that fuels the drunken poets, one on every corner. Sometimes I would like to break free. But what responsibilities have you? You're only a barman! I have a family to rear; thankfully the house is mine, built and paid for by my great grandfather. I'm a lucky bastard, good wife and good kids.'

Dermot went quiet, his eyes softened. Harry tried to lighten the conversation.

'There is a fine line in slagging, having the craic and insulting people or winding them up. Perhaps, there is too much slagging, putting people down. That type of humour is a fine line, preventing people to flourish. However there is so much stuff going on in this town and I want the kids to flourish. Education is one of the routes.'

Before Dermot could speak, Harry rolled a question:

'Why don't you go to university?'

'Beach bum in the sun, that's me. I tell you what, when we get our own university in this city I might consider it. They have discriminated against us enough putting the university in Coleraine and not here. We are the second city.'

'Plenty of beaches here, that part is right, but little sun. Magee College should have got it in 1968. I know, just another example of the Northern Ireland Government's discriminatory policies. They didn't want to give the Catholic city of Derry a university.'

'Harry, unfortunately underneath it all I have that certain Irish malaise – accepting our lot. Perhaps one day I might do something about it, but if not it was nice thinking about it. I have the best of intentions. Anyway I got my university education at home, all the discussions by my mother with her cronies, no wonder I escaped into Enid Blyton. I had enough of working class solidarity. She was furious I was reading such English middle-class jolly-hockey-sticks stuff. She hoped it was a phase. Although reading anything was important to her.'

'Would you really move to sunnier climes, Dermot? '

'You bet. Some old guys come in for a pint, home from Australia or South Africa. Their stories intrigued me. You can have your pubs and rain. I'll take the sun. Spain, Australia, here I come!'

'You need to be in the tropics to get away from any cool weather. Talking about the icy weather, we better brace for it.'

'Yeah, I need to go too, Harry. We should have some hot whiskeys. My treat.'

After John brought down the whiskeys, Dermot said:

'As we have discussed life and its meaning all evening perhaps I will try and remember some home-grown wise words.'

'Well, you are a good listener.'

'Well one fellow, referring to the Brits, said everyone is sociable until a cow invades his garden.'

'I like that one, Dermot.'

'The one I tell some of the oul fellas that come in for a chat with me and sit over their half pint. Well, I say to them – in order to find his equal, an Irishman is forced to talk to God. And I'll accept being second choice.'

'Not bad at all. I like Sean O'Casey's: All the world's a stage and most of us are desperately unrehearsed.'

'My favourite one is when they get into an argumentative state and you can see the temper brewing, I tell them: a good time to keep your mouth shut is when you are in deep water.'

'So enough of these proverbs, Dermot. Let's go home. The future starts tomorrow.'

'A proverb is one man's wit and all men's wisdom.'

'Aye, no more wisdom please. I have had enough. Call round some night this week. I believe it is to tumble to minus four one night. Grand excuse for hot toddies. Not a bad idea. I'll leave the light on if I'm not in bed.'

With a nod to John, the barman, they both left, Harry went to his car and Dermot to his work.

Allen Wells

Allen Wells sat in the corner booth reading the Derry Journal. Fresh-faced and tanned, close-knit cerulean eyes, thin nose bridge, pencil-line black eyebrows, narrow mouth within near-perfect lips, cleanly shaven and his hair neatly coiffed yet touching the blue collar of a soft button-down, perhaps a Ben Sherman, a tilt to the fashion of the day. His thickly-woven navy v-neck jumper and matching fitted trousers were off the rack of Marks and Spencers. The laced-up brogues shone in the mild light of the bar, a testimony to quality bought somewhere else.

In front of him on a low dark table sat a pint of Guinness, barely touched, and a shot of malt whiskey in a crystal glass. He sipped the malt.

The salt-and-pepper haired veteran barman John was neatly dressed with a soft worn face. He served Allen a twelve year old Jameson and the Guinness, and kept an eye to the door while watching the horse racing on television. Allen lifted his pint regularly, sipped it, but consumed little and also glanced at the front door. He hoped John didn't notice his studious analysis of everyone in the bar.

He had read the Derry Journal quickly, but it deposited little knowledge or lasting impression on him, but for the dark print smudges on his finger tips. Allen had read the same page for the past twenty or so minutes.

John had asked him if he was on holidays as he was tanned. Allen answered he had been in Spain and was waiting for some work friends to turn up. They planned a game of golf at Redcastle Hotel in County Donegal or at the city's golf club the next day.

Allen had followed Harry from school. He had nearly got mixed up in the traffic jam in Park Avenue, but had sensibly held back and parked. He noticed Harry had picked up another man so when they turned, he followed them. Allen thought Harry looked more like a manager from the local insurance office or a local shirt factory than a teacher. He thought the barman was dressed similar to Harry. It then occurred to him that John, the barman, Harry, the teacher and Allen, the MI6 agent were all dressed in Marks and Spencers clothes.

His clothes had been bought in Oxford Street, London, and he assumed the others probably bought theirs at the Desmond's factory outlets in the local villages of Claudy or Dungiven, clothing manufacturers for Marks and Spencers. Marks and Sparks, as it is affectionately known, is a British High Street chain store, and many locals purchased the same clothes from the factory outlets. Allen thought his clothes were a perfect cover for surveillance in Derry – a stroke of luck initially that then developed into his cover as an agent.

His clothes and his accent didn't expose Allen. Perhaps the accent was a bit anglicised or educated, but many locals had gone to Great Britain and returned with their Derry accent modified. Allen's cover story while undercover in Northern Ireland was that he worked for Marks and Spencers as a buying manager. He had identification and paper work to prove it. He visited Desmonds, the Northern Irish clothing manufacturer with several factories across Northern Ireland. This meant he spent his working life between Northern Ireland, visiting his clients, and head office in England. It would explain his mixed accent. It would explain his travelling all over Northern Ireland. Allen was careful with his accent, it easily changed to being distinctly local or it could carry the weight of authority and a clipped tone when talking with his fellow officers and comrades.

Allen in fact was a local, born in the city, just around the corner from the bar in Aberfoyle Crescent, then, mainly a Protestant middle-class area so he knew the city well. He was named after his Scottish forebears the McAllen's. Allen had attended the local grammar school – Londonderry High School – an established college of several hundred years, for the Protestants of the city.

He spent most of his early life in Derry before moving, at the age of eighteen, with his family to England. This was before the civil rights marches made a lot of his people uncomfortable and the violence followed. Many of his Protestant neighbours moved to the Waterside for the same reason. His father was a retired British Army Officer who had worked for the Imperial Tax Office, located a street away after being bombed out of the Embassy Building in Waterloo Place.

His past social life took him to all parts of the city and he still had many friends in the North West. Allen joined the army after university and trained as an officer. As the Troubles developed, his local knowledge was in demand by his superiors. During leave he often visited friends in the Waterside, but once he ventured into the Bogside, a Republican stronghold, with a couple of his British colleagues.

It was sheer bravado that took them there. They spent an hour in a Republican pub in the Bogside. He told the barman he was home on holiday and was reassured by him that his mates with English accents would be safe enough, providing they kept their mouths shut. The story he gave was they were just accompanying him to find where his father grew up in the Bogside, having moved to the London in the fifties looking for work. The bartender was familiar with the story many times – a common occurrence for returning emigrates or visiting English relatives of Derry people. Allen introduced himself as Padraig, telling the barman he was named after Padraig Pearce, the famed Irish rebel executed by the British for his role in the Easter Rising in 1966 in Dublin when a group of fellow Republicans attempted to overthrow the British Administration in Ireland. When his comrades heard their mate's story about his name they erupted with laughter, bringing untoward attention to themselves from the locals.

Allen's nerve in that situation reflected his suitability to do intelligence work, if somewhat fool-hardy. His current assignment in his native city was an interesting challenge that might do some good.

Allen had studied the history of Derry as a school boy, a town in North Western Europe also known for its harbour, and proud, but little-known role in the Battle of the Atlantic. Its position was key for the defence of the Atlantic route to America. Indeed, a strategic Western Allies bunker was installed underneath Magee College. It was behind the college where Allen's father took him to see two canons from ships of the Spanish Armanda. They were kept in concrete baths of water to prevent them from disintegrating, The galleons belonged to a failed Spanish invasion of England in 1558 that were shipwrecked by storms off the North Donegal coast.

Allen's eyes rested on Harry, who was having companionable fun with another fashionably dressed young man in his twenties – all Wrangler denim and Ben Sherman shirt, courtesy of one of the many shirt factories that Derry was famous for. Londonderry, as Allen called it when talking to his military comrades, was known as a city of shirt factories. In 1902 there were thirty eight factories, four years before the landmark department store was built – Austin's of the Diamond. In 1857 the five-story Tillie and Henderson factory on the city side of Craigavon Bridge – the largest factory in the world at the time – was built. It was a gateway to a female-based shirt industry producing some of the finest in the world. Employment was mainly women in the thousands coupled with many more thousands as outworkers in their homes or out-stations making collars or sewing buttons.

Allen noticed that his own brogues were very similar to Harry's mate's, both pairs shone, except Allen's were much newer. Harry constantly slapped Dermot's knee or punched his shoulder showing the ease of their conversation. Sometimes he saw Dermot's eyes momentarily flinch as each slap or punch landed, but tolerated each blow in a spirit of friendship.

Harry's photograph sat inside Allen's jacket pocket, wrapped in an A4 piece of white paper, which contained a few scant details of Harry's personal life, his family, movements and interests. It revealed little of the man's suitability for the project. His friend was not mentioned. Allen made a mental note of finding out about Harry's Wrangler-dressed friend.

Allen was a British subject, reared in Ireland yet part of the United Kingdom. He liked his birth city, and the people in it – Protestants and Catholics. As a boy, Allen went to the local cinema every Saturday for the cowboy matinee double bill, like many boys of his generation from both sections of the sectarian divide, in a city that once had seven cinemas. He never felt the need to denigrate any of his neighbours nor did he buy into the racist slurs of his British comrades. His ease at switching from his Northern Irish accent to an English one never brought much attention to himself in England. When his mates found out he was Northern Irish, they teased him about being Irish, but he accepted that Irish jokes from the British Tommies were part of his life in the British Army. He took it all in his stride.

His enemy was the IRA. He felt they were tearing ordinary peoples' lives apart with the fear, the bombing and the killing of his neighbours and military comrades. The battles were fought on the streets of Ireland and England, something he had accepted. He believed the British Establishment was not going to abandon his people, the people of Northern Ireland. Most Northerners were decent law-abiding people, Protestant and Catholic.

The fact that there was an accepted level of violence by the British Government frustrated him – decent policemen, soldiers and citizens of Northern Ireland on all sides were caught up in the spiral of Ireland's violent history. He wanted it to end. Allen could have served outside Northern Ireland, but this was an opportunity to be deployed in his home country and city. He wanted to be part of the solution.

His current assignment was simply observing certain individuals and making contact with a few individuals who might be interested in initiating a peace campaign through dialogue.
Allen had already spent a week observing Father O'Regan – a well known peace campaigner – in Belfast, and noted his regular contact with priests in a local monastery. The authorities thought he was just

administering to his flock as the monastery was in his parish. However on one observation he followed Father O'Regan and an unknown monk to a village in the Republic of Ireland – Carlingford across the border. They went into a church belonging to the Church of Ireland and the doors were shut behind them. Even after waiting and then searching for to see where they went, Allen didn't see them again. He had been aware that some Protestant clergy men had approached Sinn Fein in Belfast in an attempt to talk directly with the IRA.

Father O'Regan was introduced to Allen in Derry at a Police Community liaison meeting during the tea afterwards. The police commander had suggested to Allen that Father O'Regan may be able find a suitable contact. O'Regan knew a teacher, Harry O'Donnell, in his brother's school that may be able to help. Just leave it with him and he would be in touch, he told Allen. The agent then collected details of the staff at the school and started to watch Harry as soon as possible after that.

As soon as Dermot and Harry left the bar, Allen followed discreetly. Only John looked at him and noticed his quick exit, the unfinished pint and the clean whiskey glass left behind on the table.

Allen followed Harry in his Ford Fiesta with Northern Irish registration plates, and although he would like to have followed Harry's mate out of professional curiosity, he followed Harry up to his home, a five minute drive.

Allen noted Harry was probably over the legal limit. He filed that away for future reference – could be useful to bring him in for interrogation sometime and make contact.

Allen parked his car in Northland Street and walked up to Cillefoyle Park. He decided to park further away from the park as Harry may have seen him in the pub. By the time Allen got to the entrance, Harry had parked his car and was inside his home. He noted the number of the house and its glass tower, and as he walked around the park made a mental note of its layout for his notes.

Allen wondered about the lives of Harry's neighbours, and why this Derry school teacher would be a contact. He needed to pick up more intelligence.

A major story was going to hit the media. A few other intelligence officers were working on an IRA man to become a Supergrass. A disgruntled IRA man could provide information on a huge number of his fellow activists and supporters. The MI6 handler felt it was a matter of time, sooner rather than later. If a dawn sweep on their homes and raids across the city were imminent, the Supergrass would be exposed. A few school teachers were mentioned, and certainly one from Harry's school, but Allen knew little about that intelligence and wondered if Harry knew or was directly involved and how it would affect his assignment.

London

Allen entered the heavily-furnished darkened room and the secretary closed the door behind him. It took a moment for his eyes to adjust to the light emanating through the drapes on the covered windows. The room were encased with books – three walls of soft teal and stacks of reds of various hues. As his eyes adjusted he saw an oak desk in front of the three windows, clear of any papers, but for an antique pen set. Allen looked out the window covered by silky net curtains. It looked like another square in Whitehall with a dry fountain and a bit of grass underneath, the proverbial pigeons making themselves at home on the fountain head and the window sills. His fellow officers had described these rooms to him since he had become involved in intelligence, and here he was getting instructions from his Whitehall masters. It seemed his politically-driven role was sanctioned from the high echelons of the government. Was he about to meet his political master?

He moved to another window. The heavy curtains hooked onto brass bud-shaped tie backs. He lifted the nets that clothed the glass, allowing dappled light to enter and saw the River Thames in the distance. A few pleasure crafts glided through the murk taking the tourists on their sight-seeing trips. From the bookshelves he lifted a book on Parliamentary minutes, dated 1954 and sat down. He replaced it, shortly after. After waiting for about thirty minutes, he spent some time wandering around the room and noted there was nothing personal in it and started to search for dust - no dust anywhere. He checked the ivy-patterned folds of the curtains and again found no dust. He wondered if the cleaners came after midnight, when most of the staff had gone home. The boys down in the basement, of course, worked around the clock processing information.

He looked outside again and saw a tourist guide holding aloft a union jack topped umbrella, guiding a group of Asian tourists along the street below. He thought he could be a good tourist guide: wear the perfunctory British outfit – bowler hat, three piece pin-stripe suit, an umbrella with a little union jack on its tip, and shepherd the hordes of sightseers around the major attractions of Central London. He imagined himself striding around Trafalgar Square – his little flag-emblazoned umbrella held high, waving in the breeze, pointing out the lions and the columns as required.

The door behind him opened and in came a man of average height. White hair on top of a round face, chubby red cheeks, dark suit, shiny shoes and a military-type tie on a white shirt - an average civil servant–looking type, thought Allen.

But, unknown to him, the man who entered, Ian Blackthorn, had been involved in more skirmishes around the world supporting British interests than Ian would have cared to remember. He had a fierce reputation for getting things done – successful or not, something happened.

'Ian Blackthorn, Mr. Wells. Or should I address you with your rank?'

'Allen will be fine, Mr. Blackthorn.'

'Ian, please call me Ian. Please sit down. Sorry for the delay. Like all of us you are a busy man, so I will get straight to the point, if I may. Tea or something?'

'No thanks, I am fine.'

Allen sat on one of the bloated couches; the gilded table in front of him contained a magnificent figurine of a boy on a branch. He was surprised at seeing a possible Hummel in such a place.

'I am sure you know who I am and what this is all about. You were mentioned to me a few times.'

'Oh, I think I only met you once.'

'That may be so. Sorry I don't remember, but we have your file and watched your performance in Africa very closely. The way you worked with the French, eradicated any resistance from the locals, kept the local government on side. That took a lot of nerve. How you got our troops in and out, quelled that rebel force in the mountains and still kept the mines in British hands. Fantastic job. You know the government there is eternally thankful to us. They are providing security for the mines now, right down to exporting the stuff out. Of course they wouldn't say, but they did indicate a new export tax was in the offing. Typical, we save them from insurgency and they will be asking us for money, not to worry. The French got roasted in the UN for dabbling like an old colonial power.'

'Well, the pieces came together Ian, and we came out smiling.'

'Full credit to you, old chap. We need someone like you in Northern Ireland. It's a new dynamic role for us. The Prime Minister thinks we need intelligence: just what are they thinking, more covert operations, recruit more of their own crowd, more spies on the ground. We need an MI6 supremo for Northern Ireland. We want you to lay the ground work and we have been approached by some clergymen about the possibility of some peace talks. What do you think?'

Allen raised his eyebrows, thinking of what to say to stall an answer, but before he could speak, Ian continued:

'It's a tough one, no mistake about that. You will liaise with the Northern Ireland Secretary's advisor on this particular job, but also report directly to me. No doubt you have your plate full with other stuff working over there, but we will let you run with this one on your own. Any issues on the ground contact the usual. Who is your boss over there? Never mind, it's all on your file. Budget is not a problem, at the moment. As you know the PM will visit NI soon and wants to announce a new security initiative to the world, especially before the President visits Ireland to celebrate his Irish roots with the obligatory Guinness in Bally-go-something-or-other. The Irish-American lobby is getting vocal. They are getting good ammunition from the heavy-handed tactics in Belfast. The child that was run over by the Saracen was only eight and an American citizen. His Irish parents had returned home to bury some parent or other. Ted Kennedy wants the President to call in the British Ambassador to rap his knuckles. What do you think?'

Again Ian continued:

'This will happen very quickly, so we need to know very quickly, and the PM wants to have some sort of war cabinet meeting on Londonderry's City Walls. The Apprentice Boys, the Protestant Orange men that march around them every year, have meeting rooms there. Maybe hold a meeting there, overlooking the bloody Bogside. Then, go to the Magee College to announce a major investment or something. Carrot and stick sort of thing. We need to contain the insurgency over there. As I say, we, the PM, that is, would like to announce a few sweeteners when there, on a visit, see if we can get the blasted place off the news. People on the mainland accept that the Irish are a tiresome bunch. The local people always wanted their own university established there. The PM may just do that. Well, have you identified the contact? I need to know ASAP because this will happen soon.'

'I am very grateful for the opportunity. I haven't met the bloke yet, but I think I know who it is. It will take time to establish trust and rapport. I need to consider...'

Before he could complete his sentence, Ian again blurted out his thoughts.

'You were born in Derry, or was it Londonderry?'

Ian stared directly at Allen, his face lighting up.

'I need a cup of tea. Tea? Please wait a moment.'

Ian left the room. Allen wondered as usual if there was more to this contact than he was being told. It seemed straight forward. Someone would let him know if the IRA were ready to talk and let him know what their thoughts would be. Allen sat staring at the gloom for fifteen more minutes. The door opened.

'Mr. Wells, Mr. Blackthorn has been delayed. He would like you to wait. He shouldn't be too long. Tea?'

'Yes, please.'

The secretary had come in and stood at the door. Allen could barely see her in the shadowy light. A few seconds later tea and biscuits were delivered by another lady, in a black-skirted business suit. Nothing was said, but with a little nod and a smile she deposited the tray in front of Allen. He ate a couple of oatmeal biscuits as he waited. Twenty minutes later Ian Blackthorn returned.

'Sorry about that but I was getting a report from Belfast about our little project. It seems it's all systems go. There was a query about who the contact was, but it seems to be the teacher you were observing. There was a cautionary note to wait until they made contact, but by the time you get over there I am sure it will be sorted.'

'Where will we meet?'

'Good question. I don't know, but I'll let you work that out. Keep an eye on him and pick your time. You know better than I. You have been there for a while. I'll let you decide when to send me a report, but not too long please. Let me know if anything worthwhile may come out of this.'

'Okay. I'll do that.'

Before Allen could finish his sentence, Ian was on his feet.

'Good, I see you got your tea and biscuits. Well, thanks, Allen. I look forward to your first report.'

Ian was surprisingly nimble on his feet: he skipped across the room, opened the door, turned to face Allen, his hand extended to shake, and a smile waiting.

'Good luck, old boy.'

'Thank you, Ian.'

Behind the Savoy Hotel

Allen was glad to get out to the air, London-fresh. He had always liked London and had worked at the Savoy hotel as a student. The most interesting aspect was seeing the stars of Hollywood and television and exchanging short chats with the likes of Charlie Chaplin and Robert Morley.

He took a walk to Cleopatra's Needle, the obelisk from ancient Egypt, as he had done when working as a porter where he had arranged to meet another contact. They had met initially when observing the home of a policeman, a farm house in South Armagh, who had known ties to the Ulster Volunteer Force, the UVF. South Armagh was a corner of Northern Ireland that had been a hot-bed of IRA activity. Allen had worked with the local special branch in Northern Ireland on this operation and had met Mike Moran. They had arranged to meet behind the Savoy Hotel, after Allen's meeting with Ian. Mike had been based in London, after moving from Northern Ireland to London on a major promotion. Allen had asked him to find out what was going on regarding a member of the Royal Ulster Constabulary who was based in Derry. He also wanted to know any general intelligence of what was happening across Northern Ireland including Derry, as his contact was abreast of most of MI5, MI6 and other operations. They had met again on an operation in Belfast and once enjoyed a drunken evening with a few of their colleagues in Portrush. As it had been a glorious summer evening, both went walking along a moon-lit coast line to sober up. Their sense of humour jelled their friendship.

Mike paced up and down past the Needle. Allen saw Mike on the embankment, looking agitated. Both shook hands and smiled, recognising the camaraderie in each other.

'Nice to see you, Mike. What's up with you, given up the cigarettes again?'

'You're not an intelligence officer for nothing.'

'How are things anyway?'

'Great, I'm enjoying London, Allen. You should join us.'

'Oh, I get plenty of R and R here. How's the family?'

'Grand, the wife misses the family and friendly faces, but all is well. The kids like their school and we're all planning a trip home for the summer. They'll go over at the beginning of the school holidays. I'll join them later. All we need is the weather.'

'So why am I watching a police officer?'

'Probably passing information to the UVF or using his farm as a safe house or for weapons. But I've been informed that Special Branch have set up a special squad to look at a few rotten apples in the RUC. I think they brought over a few from England to work with them.'

Mike's story wasn't totally untrue. There was talk about a team being set up to look at collusion, just not at this point.

'So where does that leave me and the operation?'

'I believe you are being taken off the surveillance as we speak. I think you will be told. Special Branch will take over.'

'Well, I have enough on my own plate, Mike. Thanks for your help. Do you still keep contact with the boys in Belfast?'

'Not really, we catch up when over there, but they see me a bit like yourself now – a Brit. Not sure if they can trust me. I had to push for this information. I don't think I'll be of much help in the future.'

'Don't worry Mike. I'll not ask unless I am desperate.'

'You are always desperate. What are you doing in London? You're not based here.'

'Just business, but will be flying back in a day or two. I was in Spain for a week's holiday with the lads.'

'I thought you were a good colour, but then I thought you had spent a week or two out in the Irish countryside being weather-beaten by all that wind and rain.'

'Very good, Mike. Have you time for a beer?'

'Sorry mate, got to go, work calls.'

'Thanks for your help. Anything else to let me know about?'

'No need to worry about that Armagh Operation, at least. No other news really, except there are moves to instigate some peace talks. You are assigned to something like that.'

'That is true enough. Any whispers about that, me in Derry, Mike?'

'No, you are doing your own thing there. It could be useful. All the best, Allen. We'll catch up again for a pint.'

'All the best, Mike. See you again soon.'

Allen walked off but felt he hadn't been given the full story of the operation. They had just been assigned to it and now they were being reassigned. He expected to get more information about a RUC officer. Allen and others had suspected the policeman was passing information to Loyalist death squads. The police investigation surmised that an intended target hadn't shown up so the death squads went on a trawl of a Catholic area and kidnapped and murdered an innocent Catholic at random. Mike, like most in the security services of Northern Ireland, would be happy to see the IRA blown away with their sympathisers, but there was a limit to killing innocent Catholics. Many had been tortured. Allen and his colleagues in army intelligence suspected collusion between some members of the RUC and the UVF. They were told it was under control and that the RUC Special Branch would now take over the operation. It smacked of a cover up, but Allen was being assigned to another role and Mike wasn't giving anything away. He knew Mike was not happy because Allen would have perused the operation and reported back to his superiors. Mike knew that the Loyalist hit squads killed more innocents and if there was collusion he didn't want to be involved, even if he lived in London. He was glad to get out of the madness.

Allen had twenty four hours to get back to his base and fly to Northern Ireland. He planned a visit to a friend in Maida Vale for a pint or two and would go to the base in the morning.

Father O'Regan

Brother O'Regan, the principal of Harry's school called into his classroom during lunch time. Harry was working at his desk, his lunch sitting wrapped in a brown bag to his left. Sometimes, he ate his lunch on his own, enjoying the peace and quiet of his own company and the view towards the city. Normally he ate in the French store room or staff room, otherwise it was considered unsocial. That day he planned a lunch in the store room where the coffee was freely available and the river view towards the south was very pleasant. It was unusual for his principal to come to his classroom at lunch time as he usually caught up with staff on school business after school or communicated the least important business in a note passed on by a student.

If Brother O'Regan happened to be passing the classroom, it was a wave, a social nicety referring to the weather or something inane. But on this occasion he strode in, smiled and in his husky voice, he unusually got straight to the point:

'You know my brother, Father O'Regan, the peace campaigner in Belfast, is coming to Derry. Would you like to meet him?'

Not giving Harry a moment to reply, Brother O'Regan pressed on:

'The Bishop is having a reception for him next Thursday at four thirty. I would appreciate if you came with me to it. Nothing too formal. Just an update for the Bishop.'

Harry looked at his principal, stunned:

'I am sure he would have something very interesting to say, Brother. Travelling all the way down from Belfast, I am sure many would be very keen to hear him speak, especially those in the peace movement. Isn't John O'Kane involved in something like that? He would love to hear and talk to your brother.'

Harry was talking, attempting to say something constructive yet wanting to opt out of the invite. He was quite surprised. He wasn't even in the principal's inner circle, but they had talked about general things like education or life in Derry, and a few times he was invited to the Brother's residence for an informal school meeting and a malt whiskey.

'I am sure John would love to come, but I heard you say how much you admire my brother and his valiant attempts to get all the parties together. I was speaking to him last night telling him I have an admirer on the staff. He said he would love to meet you.'

97

Harry didn't want to contradict his boss, but that conversation had never taken place, or if it had, it was a passing comment on Father O'Regan's gallant peace initiatives.

'Well, if four thirty on Thursday afternoon is okay with you I'll meet you at the Bishopric. I'll talk to you just before we leave. We'll go in our own cars. Then you'll be able to slip home, unless you want me to drive? Thanks, Harry. See you on Thursday.'

Without a word from Harry, Brother O'Regan left as quickly as he entered. Harry had been railroaded into the meeting, but thought it might be interesting. He hoped Marie hadn't any plans for him on Thursday.

When Harry went home he told Marie that he suspected his headmaster's reasons regarding the visit to the Bishopric. They discussed the possible reasons and both concluded it involved some type of joint school project and Harry was being set up to lead it. Maybe his boss wanted him to invite his brother to the school. If the principal had invited him it might be seen as a personal favour. The local IRA – whose sons attended Harry's school, as indeed, did some of the Boys themselves – would have objected to the presence of a well-known peacemaker. It smacked of political overtures. Harry was being used. He was sure of it.

Harry did pass the Bishop's residence on the way home so it wasn't too much of a hassle, but then so did many other staff.

The week flew by as usual. Thursday arrived and Brother O'Regan caught up with Harry as he made his way to class. Tugging gently at his cuff, Brother O'Regan whispered conspiratorially without breaking his pace:

'See you at four thirty. The Bishop serves a decent malt.'

'Okay, see you there.'

After school there was no sign of the principal in his office so Harry went ahead. He parked in the Bishopric's grounds assuming he would see a few others dressed for the function. His principal hadn't arrived. Harry waited a while in his car for him.

At four forty he decided to enter the house on his own. After being greeted by the housekeeper at the door he was shown into a large dilapidated book-filled room. The bookcases appeared as if they were seldom opened. A grand fireplace held a tiny two-bar fire. The well-worn table and matching chairs occupied the centre of the room. Frosted windows on the lower panes allowed the interior to be unobserved. Heavy crimson curtains hung on either side of the large window dropped thickly to the floor. Above the windows, a matching pelmet. Underfoot a richly patterned red and gold carpet, threadbare in little patches – at the door, in front of the fireplace and circling the table. Harry stood at the most worn spot – in front of the fireplace. He automatically walked there when the housekeeper opened the door for him, warming his bottom at an imaginary fire, as did most people, Harry surmised. A very tired and cheerless room.

A few tattered Catholic magazines sat on the table in front of him, obviously for waiting visitors to peruse. Harry studied the heavy brass crucifix on the mantel piece and on the left side of the window a life-sized statue of Our Lady smiled down at him, resplendent in blue and white, still failed to lift his apprehension.

Harry heard voices – whispers outside the door. He was tempted to listen, ear to the door, but common sense prevailed. In a while the door opened and Father O'Regan entered. Harry immediately recognised the familiar figure from the television news. Any time there were outrages caused by the IRA or the British Army, he was on the media criticising the actions. He called for negotiation between all the parties involved in the Troubles. He introduced himself none the less.

'I am Father O'Regan. The Bishop has allowed me to use the room and my brother did me the favour of luring you here under false pretences. My apologies. It will be worth a few free classes I am sure! Unfortunately I don't have much time for discussions on whys and hows, but I want to talk to you. Would you like a cup of tea? Annie is bringing in some. You know, Harry, we find it easier to talk about our big faults than our small faults. Yet it's our small faults that trip us all up. I would like you to help us with our small faults to solve our big faults.'

So much for my malt whiskey! As for free classes, forget it. I have a well-known peace-maker talking in riddles in front of me, when I could be at home having a nice cup of coffee and a chocolate digestive in my own kitchen, contemplated Harry.

'You know what I have been involved in. My brother says you do and you have discussed your feelings about the Troubles with him.'

'Only in a very general sense.'

'But you voiced your suspicions about Dermot Lavery?'

'I don't think I have any suspicions about Dermot. He's a barman.'

'Yes, yes, but Dermot is very well-read, self-educated, I think, and fairly active on the community front. He is involved in the civil rights movement and yet he is much respected by Cathal, his boss and family friend. Cathal's brother, Conor is getting out this week after serving five years. They say he transformed himself from a hawk to a dove. He might even finish an Open University degree. A history degree, I believe. He read widely about Irish History. I visited him several times in prison. We had great discussions. Dermot and him would get on well.'

Before Harry could answer in the affirmative, the priest continued:

'I know you and Dermot are friends and go for a drink or two. Do you know what he does?'

Again before Harry could answer Father O'Regan pressed on. Just like his brother, thought Harry, he answered his own questions.

'Our Dermot is a man of many colours and his dealings with the Republican movement have been pretty distant, despite the fact he mixes with them daily in his job as a barman. I am in Belfast most of the time, as you know. I am down here on Church business with your Bishop's blessing. Do you know what Dermot does?'

Harry's head was spinning, what was this man talking about, but he answered quickly before the priest could answer for him.

'He's a barman.'

'That, he is.'

The priest replied. The southern brogue broke into his tame Belfast accent.

'We would like you to help us. Putting it bluntly, we want you to continue your friendship with Dermot and give him a message from me. First of all I want you to test the water to see if he is interested in what we are trying to do.'

'And who are we?'

'We are people who are interested in peace, building peace. We can't run before we walk and we can't walk before we crawl. So there needs to be negotiations between all parties. Before that we need some contacts to explore paths of negotiations.'

'Paths of negotiations? What do you mean?'

Harry's head was still spinning. The man was full of riddles. The priest continued:

'Look the British Government state that their position is they will not talk to terrorists. The IRA will not talk to the Government until they state that they will withdraw from Ireland. Two intractable public positions. Myself and a few of my fellow clergy of the Protestant persuasion have been ferrying messages between the two parties for years and we felt Conor might accompany us on that path. He said no, but that he would be supportive. We want you to facilitate the process. To talk to Dermot. That's all. If you say yes, we simply want you to facilitate the meetings. We want Dermot to see if there is any chance at all of talks. Test the water. Get his feet wet. Talk to Conor. Hopefully, Conor will get involved at a later date. We feel Conor will be the man to facilitate the real negotiations between Sinn Fein, the IRA and the British.'

Harry had sat in the nearest chair to the fireplace, stood up and warmed his bottom again at the imaginary fire. When the priest came in, he sat in the nearest chair, across the table from Harry. Harry turned towards the fireplace, paused and turned to face the priest, holding onto the back of the chair in front of him. His mind was overwhelmed by the priest's suggestions and he didn't trust his body to remain upright unaided.

'Are you okay, Harry? You look pale. Do you want to sit down again?'

Harry shook his head. His legs didn't buckle, nor did the priest's flow pause.

'Basically, Harry, we want you to explore the possibility. Would Dermot act as middleman between the IRA in Derry and the British Government? The government has already indicated indirectly they might listen. I have met a man who would be the contact for the British. I wouldn't be surprised if he isn't in place already, watching me now and maybe you. Your role is simply this: if Dermot is prepared to help, then you tell me and that's your role finished.'

'Are we talking James Bond stuff? Are we talking code words and all?'

'They will probably use code words, but don't worry about that. They will approach Dermot. You will not be involved.'

'Why me? Why Dermot?'

'Simply, Dermot has the potential to have the ear of the IRA via Cathal. Hopefully Conor will be a good ally. He is respected by most of the people that matter in the movement according to our research, though not all. He knows his boss is the head of Sinn Fein in Derry, all part of the Republican movement with the IRA. Whether he is an IRA man I don't know, nor do the authorities.'

Harry began to digest the situation. His legs weakened. He sat down.

'It really is one simple thing, something important, almost vital. We would like you to ask Dermot to work with us as a contact. No one must know. No one knows now, only a few here and a few in London. Once Dermot agrees, someone will contact him. My role is finished as is your role. Pretend it never happened. Reconcile yourself to the fact your minor role could save countless lives.'

'What are you on about?

'We are attempting to establish a line of contact between Downing Street and the IRA. We think the Derry command will talk to the British indirectly. Belfast and Dublin may follow, but this is all in the future. Baby steps. Your name was put forward to me by my brother. You had mentioned your connection with Dermot. Dermot has been to meetings where he voiced his opinion regarding negotiations. He attended the housing action group, actually instrumental in its development. He is seen as a potential leader. An activist, yes, but maybe more of a thinker, a bit like yourself. The more I know about him, which is little, the more I can see an important role for him. Quite suitable, in fact. He has brains, a good understanding of the situation, and it seems, from what you said, an abhorrence of violence. Dermot is a political activist rather than a militant. I was talking to a leader of one group where Dermot attends and he would be happy for Dermot to take a leading role, but he never seems to step forward. He is a good talker, good at speeches, seems intelligent and committed. It's a wonder he has never gone to university.'

'I have said that to him. He could easily disappear tomorrow.'

'What do you mean? I don't know, but it seems when the time is right we will approach the IRA through these contacts, these intermediaries. The risible attempts by the British at coming to the table aren't very positive and the IRA command is an unlikely mendicant. Whether this is the right time or this is the right approach I just don't know. We have to try. Perhaps you may just need to prime Dermot and the whole thing will take a life of its own. He will do everything. All I need to do is tell my friends in the Church of Ireland that we have made the approach to Dermot and they will do the rest. My understanding is that Dermot feels the British should be more politically active and negotiate some sort peace settlement. They need to approach the IRA. They have no shortage of volunteers and resources. Now is the time to try to stop an escalation. There is a feeling that a major IRA offensive will be undertaken here and on the mainland. Some big ticket projects like getting the Prime Minister, or a member of her cabinet, or a Royal. Something that will put Northern Ireland on the front page, some outrage, bringing Northern Ireland again to the world. Something that might make the IRA think that the British have paid enough and will force them to a withdrawal plan. The reality is that the Brits can't win and the IRA can't win, but neither will go away, so some sort of path for negotiation is needed. We need to start somewhere. Publicly, both sides won't show any weakness – that is, anything to show a weakness in their commitment. My feeling is that Dermot is the right guy for the job. He will need to earn the trust on both sides and that will take time. You and I will have to wait on the sidelines and bide our time. We hope something positive will develop out of this. You were put forward because you are a neighbour and a drinking pal of Dermot's. You must have told my brother. My wee enquires, and I mean wee, but discreet enquires bore that relationship out.'

'Jesus. Oh, sorry Father.'

'I've heard worse, Harry. Put it like this, in the bigger scheme of things, you could be instrumental in bringing peace to this country. If there was a ceasefire, think of the lives saved, the Irishmen, our fellow Ulstermen, our neighbours across the Foyle? They are not going away, either. I don't want to build the expectations. It's a bloody tragedy we have on our hands. Remember a scholar's ink lasts longer than a martyr's blood. Those young men on the streets in military garb, youngsters from the housing estates of the UK. They are only youngsters, boys, up for a laugh. Some laugh! But they are the instruments of British power and we must struggle against its misuse. It is a struggle of memory against forgetting. You, we as teachers must remember that.'

'I see older faces in my class at school than those manning the security check points.'

'As for those that want to die for Ireland – enough is enough. Can we make a start to build a path for peace, for negotiations? Get these warring parties around the table.'

'Paisley and the Unionists won't agree to this, or the UVF or whoever.'

'One step at a time. Remember, baby steps.'

'And you want me to say to Dermot – 'you work with the Provos! Have a chat with them and see if they want to chat to the Brits? Tell the Brits what you think! You are mad!'

'Maybe. But you'll never plough a field by turning it over in your mind.'

Father O'Regan sat back in his chair, stretched his legs and crossed them, proud of his little axioms. He did the same with his hands and laid them on his lap. Harry thought the priest had relaxed and basically was saying 'over to you'. The tea was hot and required, although Harry wanted that malt whiskey.

'Look, Harry, you will have many questions should you accept my request, but I don't want you to phone me to discuss them. I do not trust the phones. We can go to my brother's house or, if I don't hear from you, that means you will proceed. Just leave a message with Peter, my brother, simply saying all is well. You can update Peter, if you wish. He is very diplomatic with me on the phone. I will find out if Dermot makes a contact or rather the British agent will contact him. Anyway, I need to go. I have a special mass to attend in Saint Eugene's in ten minutes. Thanks for your help. God bless.'

'Well, it will make my viewing of Top of the Pops as my usual Thursday evening highlight seem very tame. Good bye and I'll say to your brother at school that my friend is willing to act as a contact as soon as I have worked out how to do it and if he agrees.'

'Very good. Could you let me know in two weeks if it's yea or nay? God bless you. Blessed are the peacemakers. You are doing Christ's work.'

They both struggled to their feet. The weight of their purposes hung heavy. Father O'Regan left him to the door and wished him good luck. The evening was dark but dry. Harry was looking forward to his dinner. He wanted to walk home to clear his head, but the car was there. A little wander up to his tower and a malt after dinner would have to do.

Harry goes Debating

When Harry returned home, he had a shower and changed into a tracksuit. He wanted to rid himself of the heavy weight placed on his shoulders. It didn't work. Harry, like many, did not want to get involved. Dinner was the usual Thursday night fare, bacon and cabbage. The kids ate rapidly and had disappeared before Marie said:

'How did the meeting go? You are very pensive tonight? Fancy going out? Do you fancy going up to the Debating Society? Haven't been there for a while.'

'Is it raining?'

'No, it's clear, but cool and crisp. A nice night really.'

'What about walking up? Joe will be there. He'll give us a lift back. It would be nice to have a walk and a drink? We can chat on the way.'

Harry went upstairs and changed his clothes and on the way down called to the children:

'Hey, you two. Your Mum and I are going out for a walk and we'll not be back till ten-thirty. Can yous tidy up the dinner stuff please?'

They heard muffled sounds from up the stairs and shouted bye to the children.. Harry spoke and kissed his wife as they closed the door after them.

'Let's take our time.'

Harry and Marie had got wrapped up against the chilly, but pleasant winter's night. Hats, gloves and scarves, their seasonal coats snugly fitted and the starry night perfect for a refreshing evening walk. Marie detected Harry's preoccupied mood despite his attempt to hide it. After a few pleasantries and some family news, Marie asked:

'Is there some problem at school annoying you? Are they asking you to do some sort of peace project or joint project with a school in Belfast?'

'Unfortunately, it's a little bit more complicated than that.'

Harry answered in his usual understated manner.

'It's a good night for a riot. Have they any excuse tonight?'

'Not sure, there were a few raids today. We'll avoid William Street.'

They crossed Waterloo Place. The burnished teapot reflected the bright moon. Its echoed rays bounced off the windows in the surrounding buildings. A few police stood at the foot of Waterloo Street, their colleagues inside a Land Rover, parked on the pavement in front of a chain store. Harry passed the military patrol, the police's backup, tucked into doorways on his side of the square, and ignored them. An officer called to Harry.

'A lovely night, Sir.'

''Tis indeed.'

He usually spoke to the police and army when spoken to. Many of his non-violent fellow nationalists chose not to, their way of showing their displeasure about the British Army on their streets.

Marie and her husband walked up Shipquay Street, the strenuous hill to the Diamond.

'God, is this street getting steeper?'

'No, you are getting older!'

'Do you want a thump, Harry O'Donnell? You can buy your own drinks tonight.'

Marie laughed at her joke.

After getting to the Diamond at the top of the hill in the city centre they quickened their walking pace. As they walked towards Bishop Street Gate they slowed and Harry explained what Father O'Regan asked him to do. Marie remained silent throughout.

'What do you think, Marie?'

'I don't know, bit of a damn cheek!'

'Hmm.'

'No wonder you were quiet at dinner tonight. What happens after you ask Dermot? I didn't know he worked in an IRA pub. We should call in. We'll be passing it in five minutes!'

'You are joking?'

'Of course I am. What happens after Dermot tells you 'F-off'?'

'Not sure. I tell my boss whether it's a negative or positive response. He tells his brother in Belfast and that's it really, as if nothing has happened.'

Harry and Marie didn't usually attend the club every week, but were glad for a bit of distraction as the debate was: 'Should Greyhounds become a Derry Icon'. It was full of the usual witty repartee exhibiting Derry's black sense of Olympian humour at its best. The debate was little to do with the topic, more a vehicle for showing off a few of the society's egos. It was also a great means of honing one's public speaking and indeed a few went on to further careers in media or other public offices. Pauric, Dermot's cousin, was a regular at the club and was on the winning side. It distracted Harry's mind for a few hours as they socialised with a few of Harry's colleagues, one of whom gave them a lift home and refused the obligatory coffee afterwards.

Harry didn't get a good night's sleep, waking several times. He woke at four and decided a cup of tea was required. The central heating was off. His overcoat was hung at the bottom of the banisters and he wrapped himself in it. After making his tea, he climbed to his tower, grabbing a hat on the way. He wanted to smoke, a cigarette or even a pipe would do. There was nothing in the house that he had secreted for such an occasion.

The night was still clear and triangles of ice covered the streets. A murky yellow light hung around the street lights. Below, a Ford Escort was parked in the street outside the park. Harry was sure the driver sat inside, as the car's bonnet was clear of any frost yet its roof was simmering in its icy coat. The houses were closed up for the night, protected from the sub-zero night air, a mantle of frost on the roofs where the attic insulation prevented the heat escaping. A solitary car came up the street as someone returned home. After they parked they hurried into their house. Harry could see a few cars' lights somewhere on the Northland Road. An army patrol drove down Northland Drive as Dermot walked up it. He arrived at Cillefoyle Park. He stopped and stared up at the Tower. By that time Harry had sunk to his knees, eyes peeping over the window sill, hoping Dermot hadn't seen him. Perhaps he should have stood up and waved, called him in, asked him directly and then got on with his life.

Allen Wells Follows

Allen Wells had been following Harry and his wife. He got out of his car on Northland Drive as they passed. He kept a solid distance from them. As he passed his military and police colleagues in Waterloo Place he nodded and smiled, giving the impression he was just a friendly Derry man, for a change. He had prepared a dossier on Harry and nothing further had presented itself. He had spotted Dermot; Harry's drinking companion and neighbour, leaving the park. Perhaps he thought he should place him under surveillance. When they arrived at the Bishop Street premises of the Debating Society he hadn't wanted to be noticed and so hadn't followed them in. He observed others arrive, a few faces he recognised from Harry's school, from the intelligence photographs he had gathered on some of Harry's fellow staff. He asked a passerby about a nearby club that a friend had told him about where he could get a drink. He was told it was the Post Office Club. When a couple was going in, he asked them if there was music on tonight in the club. They told him they didn't know, but the Debating Society was having their usual Thursday evening debate and it was always a bit of craic. Allen decided to investigate the Debating Society – perhaps it was a Republican cover. He still wasn't sure if Harry O'Donnell was the contact, but his name had been given to him. Allen's observations were that he was a school teacher and family man, but maybe he met his Republican contacts at the Debating Society. Further investigations were required, he thought.

The Next Morning

At the morning break, Brother O'Regan stopped Harry in the corridor, a smirk on his lips and his eyebrows risen in anticipation of Harry's greeting.

'Thanks very much for organising yesterday's meeting. I appreciate it.'

Brother O'Regan's eyes narrowed, his cheeks coloured a little and his face set sternly at Harry's sarcastic remark:

'Don't mention it, Harry, but I owe you a wee malt.'

It was obvious the principal's serious countenance indicated he did not want to discuss the meeting.

Harry O'Donnell couldn't decide how he was going to broach the subject with Dermot. He had seen Dermot once since returning home. That evening Father O'Regan had phoned to encourage him to make contact. Everything was in place on his side to contact Dermot. Father O'Regan assured Harry that the British government and someone in the Northern Ireland administration were aware of the plan and wanted a contact. He said phone calls to him from a group of Protestant clergy confirmed this.

Harry wondered if his name had been mentioned throughout this network. Or was he known only to the Belfast priest? Did the British Intelligence know him? Was he being watched? Something had spooked him. That car parked in the nearby street, its bonnet always uncovered by frost, that had drawn his attention. There was nothing that unusual about it, but after the meeting he was ultra aware of everything. His major worry was; he might put his family in danger. Perhaps they were watching him from the Waterside where they had a military encampment. He could see their watch towers from his tower. He was sure they could see him. The watcher was being watched, perhaps. Why couldn't they make direct contact with Dermot, if that was what they wanted? Why involve him? It never occurred to Harry that Dermot knew more than he said. He was sure he wasn't involved with the IRA, but he was a dark horse.

The priest had used the term 'baby steps'. It was a sensitive situation. No one wanted to show their hand. No one wanted to reveal who they may or may not be talking to. The British Government would not talk to terrorists, publicly. The British Prime Minister stated that at every opportunity, used the word 'emphatically' repeatedly. The IRA would not talk to the insidious British Government without a statement of intention to withdraw. The whole thing was in a state of stasis. Harry was involved simply by mentioning informally to his principal that his mate Dermot worked as a barman in a Provo bar. That was all or did he say more than that, pondered Harry? Was the church involved or simply Father O'Regan acting on his own? The well-known peace campaigner was known to have established connections with the IRA and Downing Street. Why didn't he act as a go-between? He wondered why him, why Harry O'Donnell?

Harry asks Dermot

Harry and Dermot sat enjoying the warmth of their hot toddies, even though it was after midnight. Harry had to get up in the morning for school so didn't want to spend too long with his mate on the subject. He decided to state the case, ask him to think about it and not get into a discussion on the merits or otherwise.

Dermot had been lamenting the quality of his patron's debates before his journey home after work, when Harry turned to Dermot and said hesitantly:

'I have something to say to you that might make you want to run away. But it was put to me and then you ended up in my house tonight, but fate and all that. Anyway, I need to get to bed as I have work tomorrow, so I'll ask you now.'

'Sounds ominous. Hope you're not looking for money cause I am skint, mate.'

'No, nothing like that. I was up at the Parochial House at Saint Eugene's the other day and met a priest.'

'Well, if you ever want to meet a priest, it would be pretty certain it would be in a parochial house.'

'Oh, shut up, a minute, Dermot. Please let me say my piece and say nothing until I have finished. Please Dermot.'

'Oh, serious boy, Harry.'

Harry glared at Dermot making him see that he was serious. There was barely a frown over Dermot's face. The unfathomable Dermot, as quick as anything, had switched modes. Harry looked at Dermot's set jaw, waiting, to be told something important. His eyes, icy blue, bitterly sharp as outside, his mouth dipping slightly to the left, an expression that was anticipating some bad news – as if a close friend or family member had died.

'It is because of your pub, I think that I have to ask you something. The owner of your pub is Cathal, I think his name is. Well, his brother has had some sort of Damascus Road transformation and the Brits want to talk to him. Now how I got involved I will never understand and why they can't let someone else already in the field contact him. I don't know. I don't know if this comes from Downing Street. Cathal's brother's name is Conor by the way.'

'Oh, I know Conor as well as I know Cathal. We were childhood friends.'

'Let me say this and then we'll take it from there. Do you a fancy another hot toddy?'

'No, no, I'm grand.'

Harry looked as Dermot moved his lips, but his expression was one of bewilderment.

'Okay, I think the sequence of events went something like this. A group of Protestant clergymen were chatting to Father O'Regan, the peace campaigner. They feel it might be time for some peace initiatives, directly with the IRA. At least they may have got some overtures from the British and Father O'Regan had talked to Conor in prison. Father O'Regan felt this was a good time to make contact as they may be open to a ceasefire at some point. If the contact in prison gave him that idea, I do not know. They want to make contact, but with who? Brother O'Regan and I had a few drinks one evening. We were discussing the Troubles and I chatted about you and your analysis. He put two and two together and his brother in Belfast, Father O'Regan, must have been interested and the result of that is – me and you chatting now.'

Harry stopped, sipped at his empty glass and studied Dermot's face. It hadn't changed much. Harry thought, quite correctly, that he had ruined Dermot's little sojourn into Harry's comfortable world of toddies on a winter's night.

'Basically, they wanted Conor. He has stated that the armed struggle may not be the only route for Republicans. Father O'Regan contacted him and sounded him out. I think he said no. I think they want you to sound him out, maybe they know he is a friend of yours. But if he still says no they want you to be a contact. Don't answer now. There, I have said my piece. Just think about it, please.'

The 'please' sounded like a child asking meekly for a lolly pop. Harry folded his arms as he did in the classroom to show he was finished and serious and wanted a response. He wanted an oral one from Dermot. Dermot just looked at him. After a few minutes Dermot responded:

'A thousand thanks, Harry.'

Dermot got up, went into the hall and put on his coat and hat. He said:

'I'll be seeing you.'

Dermot moved to the front door, and stood, waiting for Harry to open it which he did. Dermot stepped out into the early morning. He did not look back.

Harry's Alarm

Harry's alarm jostled him from his dream. In that world, his imagination ran riot – as he floated above the towns and villages of Northern Ireland, casting a spell over the men of violence as they too floated trance-like to join him hovering over the countryside.

Marie had left the bed and he heard clinking discordant sounds from below. The house had thick doors and walls and Harry was grateful that his great grandfather had built such a solid home. He listened to the rattle of the radiators and the gurgling of the water pipes carrying hot water to the shower next door.

Dawn was rising outside as he rose, pulling on his robe, making it float across the chilled room, falling around him. He tied it with the cord. At the window he faltered, barely moved his head and glanced at the garden below, cobwebbed in the morning points of frost; a lazy blackbird snuggled in the crook of a bough.

After using the adjoining bathroom, his wife returned to the bedroom, lifted her black veneered hairbrush and pulled it gently through her hair, looking at the mirror and watching Harry in the reflection.

With deft movements she stepped beside him at the window, still brushing absentmindedly, and saw Dermot standing in the communal garden. He looked up to the house before walking down Northland Avenue.

'What is he up to? What were you two up to last night? Did you ask him?'

'Yes, I did. He was not a bit pleased. He walked out without a word.'

'I am really uncomfortable about this. I wonder where he is going at this hour. He looks well, nice tight arse in those jeans.'

'Marie, will you stop it, at this hour.'

'Well, what's going to happen?'

'I don't know, it's too early. We'll talk about it later.'

'Who's in the bathroom next door, Marie?'

'One of the kids must be showering, Harry.'

The bathroom had been a dank place for ablutions even though a shower cabinet had been installed a couple of years ago, with a fan. His great grandfather's white ware had stood the test of time – the Florentine mosaic floor was impressive and was the nicest feature in the bathroom.

Harry's draught-proofing efforts and Marie's penchant for heavy drapes ensured the house was comfortably warm most of the year. However the radiators produced a heat that still required pyjamas, house slippers, and a hefty dressing gown, but with thick carpet, all possibilities of heat loss were excluded, where achievable.

Still, Harry, having only woken up after a mere four hours, felt the cool air of the room. The room was dark; the only light came off the luminous alarm clock, so he pulled the curtains. He went onto the landing; it too was in the dark, shielded by the well-fitted curtains, a light from under the bathroom door lit about two feet of the carpet.

Harry's bowels told him he needed to evacuate as soon as possible. He heard the shower in the bathroom so went down stairs to the toilet below. He really didn't want to use it, but needs must, preferring to awaken in his own toilet, the one next to his bedroom he considered his own. The kids used the one downstairs mostly in the back hall, but it wasn't heated and didn't have a shower.

As the children became adolescents they wanted a lock placed on the bathroom door. Harry refused and while the argument resurfaced now and again, he always won the argument. The house rule was, if the bathroom door was shut, one knocked on it and did not enter if someone was using it. Privacy was to be respected in the house, the bathroom and the bedroom. It was his rule so he had to adhere to it.

He returned and the bathroom was still being used. He tapped the door. No answer. He tapped it again and gently opened it. He was met with the thunderous voice of his son.

'Dad, close the bloody door. I'm in here.'

'Sorry, sorry. I never heard anything.'

Harry lied and closed the door. Lying further:

'I'm not feeling well. I need the loo, please.'

'There's one downstairs.'

The door swung open. A dripping, red faced, towel-wrapped boy emerged from the fog of steam and brushed past his father, leaving Harry's arm wet, sending drops of water over the hall carpet and in little pools in his foot prints.

Harry rushed in, closed the door, delighted with the sauna-like heat of the bathroom and resigned himself to his pleasant shower. Harry remembered his dream, but the details escaped him. All he remembered was floating with people above the country side.

Then, he remembered the conversation with Dermot. Well, he tried to reassure himself that he was just a messenger. That was all. He

114

delivered it. He hoped Dermot wouldn't fall out with him. Dermot didn't quite storm off, but he left without any friendly goodbyes. He didn't want to think about the reason why.

Shit, shit, thought Harry.

Dermot's Promotion

Dermot looked at Harry's house, he was sure someone was at an upstairs window. Harry would be getting ready for work, doing his best for the kids in his classroom. Good old Harry, a sterling guy. Genuine family man, dedicated teacher, always ready for a bit of craic. What was his last aphorism – everything is important but nothing very much, or something like that? Dermot thought Harry must collect the proverbs, maybe used them in school. He saw how he often would memorise some of his sayings, even writing them down. Dermot knew Harry thought highly of him, constantly goading him into trying to do a degree, and his face always lit up when he saw him. But he always seemed to want more, to be his friend, a confidant, a confessor, or a counsellor. He couldn't think of another description. Maybe a priest. He wished he would just fuck off, and leave him alone Just enjoy the few pints together, nothing more, nothing less. Dermot was not impressed by Harry's approach to him. He must have said too much to his boss. He was disappointed by Harry. Who knows what they knew about him? He didn't like it and certainly didn't want the responsibility of talking to the IRA or a British agent. If Conor wanted to become a peace campaigner so be it. Leave him out of it. He was just a barman and a social activist, happy to play his part behind the scenes.

He had come into work early for a special delivery. It didn't arrive. He was in an agitated mood when he met Cathal in the pub.

'We should be busy tonight, darts competition, a semi final or other. Benny was in organising it. He asked me about hosting the final. It might put the regulars off their routine. We would have to stack the tables to make room. What do you think, Dermot?'

'Hmm, I don't know. Why this place suddenly?'

'Well we host a couple of games during their season and we supply a bottle or two for prizes. The usual place got flooded or something and I think the owner fell out with the players, not enough drinkers. I know Benny doesn't drink but the rest do, I think. Anyway, we are a community, we should promote community activities rather than being known as just an old man's pub, a place of drinkers of a blood-pressure hue.'

'What are you on about?'

'I was thinking. There's a large room upstairs, with toilets. A few prints on the wall and some lamps, it could be used as a meeting room for community groups. Those strip lights are too stark. Have a look?

Maybe even move the dartboard up there sometime. I want you to develop that. You are now officially the Development Manager of the pub.'

'What the hell are you talking about? Development Manager, any money in it for me? I am a barman.'

'We'll talk about that if there is an increase in trade, a commission, that's right, a commission. If you get groups in here that's community service, sure you are all into that. The time you spend here organising upstairs, I'll pay you, within reason and time constraint.'

'You have lost me.'

'Look, phone Benny about the Darts Tournament. We will host the finals and contribute to the prizes and we'll see how we go. You mentioned a while ago one of the groups you go to – Socialist Alliance or something – needs a new meeting place. Why not here? Upstairs, I mean.'

Dermot's mind was floating. He sat down, disconnected from his surroundings and Cathal.

'Oh, Dermot, the early morning delivery didn't come. I phoned you, but no answer. It will arrive later on this morning or lunch time. Something about a bomb scare at the yard. Can you take care of it?'

'Yeah, no problem. I left the house early this morning.'

Dermot and Conor

Dermot usually let the drunken bullshit float over his head, but it was a bad day, thinking about his meeting with Harry and he was letting the customers get to him. Bernie, a fellow barman sensibly had taken a step back and was polishing glasses behind.

The punters harped on about their church, their God and their sense of entitlement after what the British had done to them. They were younger than the usual crowd, the older boys had more sense most of the time, or until they got drunk. They were even quoting the bible – to prove that their sanctuary in the church and Derry entitled them to the dole. They felt they had the burden of their world and colonialism on their shoulders, and like good pious Irish Catholics would bear that burden drinking themselves stupid, while on the dole and going to mass on Sunday.

There was a couple sitting at the bar that Dermot could have done without.

The two were trying to get Dermot to engage with them and then wind him up so they could argue and maybe start a fight.

'Hey Dermot! Do you like my beard? I wasn't sure meself, but then it grew on me!'

Both of them nearly fell off their stools laughing at their pun. The bearded one had carefully told the joke, spitting out each word so that all could hear it.

Dermot smiled, after all they were customers. Pat, the un-bearded one started up:

'Sure didn't Jesus say something like – Come to me with your heavy burden and I will give you rest. Sure that's what we are doing, resting.'

'I think in some bibles they say refresh rather than rest. In other words, you do not stop, but get energy to keep going. Jesus didn't mean to sit on your arse all day and do nothing. You can't take the bible literally.'

Dermot's answer didn't provide an excuse to do little with their lives, but instead it goaded them even further. Pat, a short stumpy curly-haired eejit, came in to the pub now and again. Some of the more thoughtful regulars usually ignored him or cut him to the quick. He usually moved on but he had the field to himself and Dermot, normally diplomatic and agreeable, wasn't in the mood.

The other one asked:

'And why not?

'Well, if you did, you would be burning people at the stake and stoning people and owning slaves. And anyway you would be just like a Paisleyite.

Dermot replied, his fingers gripping the edge of the bar. These were gobshites. Why argue with them? Pat demanded:

'Your head's a marley! What did you call me? A Paisleyite?'

The spotty-faced moron reared from his seat, not much bigger when he stood up. Although Dermot could easily win the argument, he stupidly wound them up further.

'Paisley and his crowd are fundamentalists. You would be a fundamentalist just like Paisley.'

'Are they fundamentalists? Sure there is no fun with that crowd, they don't even drink. They aren't fundamentalists; they're fuckin' mentalists. All mental cases, marching up and down them hills like the Grand Old Duke of York.'

The pair fell about laughing, feeling they had topped know-it-all Dermot.

'Aye, it's a heavy burden we carry for the sake of our people and our church.'

Dermot knew he was being caught in their web of ignorance and cynicism and he knew he should have just kept quiet. They were customers, paid their way, usually kept their opinions to themselves, cowed by the other regulars, just their moronic sense of vocal loyalty to their church and country irritated Dermot more than he wished. Letting his irritation get the better of him, he said:

'Sure, which bible do you believe?'

'What do you mean?

'As I was saying, you hope for rest in the arms of Baby Jesus, what he says in another bible is that he will refresh you, allowing you to revive, give you more vigour or help your spirit to continue the tasks in front. In other words get off your fat arses and do something about it.'

They didn't like that at all. They weren't sure how to react and Dermot knew he had overstepped the 'keep the customer happy' line. He retreated to the store room. Bernie called to him later for help as the place got busier and when Dermot came back the two drunken partners had left.

'What happened to the two eejits at the bar?'

'They drank up and left. What rattled your cage tonight? It's as well the boss isn't in tonight or you might be leaving too. They pay their way and your wages. By the way Frank, called in, but I told him you were away.'

Dermot was in a mood alright when Conor came in. He was on his own. Dermot was mindful to be the dutiful barman.

'How's it going Conor, what'll it be?'

'Oh, the usual, Dermot. Thanks. Isn't it great? You are away for a while and you drop by your local and it's as if you were only in yesterday.'

'We aim to please. Welcome back.'

'Thanks, Dermot. Hey, don't you give talks to the Young Socialists?

Dermot was unsure if he was being baited again by the Provo, just out of jail. He thought it was going to be a tough night. He knew his activities and politics were known to his boss who respected him for them, although was somewhat suspicious.

His politics weren't talked about to the wider Republican fraternity that frequented the bar. Perhaps his boss had said something to Conor. He was sure he was being discussed in certain quarters.

'Yeah, I go to some of their meetings.'

'That's what I thought. Would you mind if I tagged along with you to the next meeting, especially if you are speaking? You have a reputation for being knowledgeable, a good talker, and full of bull. Hey, only joking.'

Dermot wasn't too sure how to take Conor's jibing, but decided to play along:

'Well you know me Da was the biggest socialist bullshitter this town had, so it must rub off somewhere.'

Conor smiled at Dermot's nonplussed expression.

'If you don't have a sense of humour, Dermot, you probably have no sense at all. But seriously Dermot, give us a shout and we'll go together to the next meeting. Let's have a drink some night. I would like to chat with you about your thoughts.'

'No bother, mate. The pint is on the house. Anyway, welcome home.'

Dermot did not like the idea of having a drink with a Provisional IRA man, just released from jail. What was he up to? Was it time to move to warmer climes? Dermot pondered again.

Conor lifted his pint to Dermot to acknowledge his free drink and moved to an armchair beside the fire, taking out a book from his bag and settling in to read. Dermot couldn't see its cover and didn't want to ask, but felt he should have asked Conor what he was up to and how he was settling, after years in prison. Time enough for that. What a night! What a day! This town was getting too hot. Dermot just wanted to be left alone.

Dermot thought it couldn't be a coincidence that Conor had wanted to meet him for a pint and discuss his politics. Perhaps, as Cathal had said to Dermot many times, his knowledge of the Troubles and his astute analysis of them were wasted behind a local bar in Derry.

He did get the feeling he was being interrogated, at times by some Belfast or Dublin IRA commanders sometimes in the pub. On those nights Cathal was always there at the bar and had bought them drinks all night. They were introduced as business associates from Belfast or Dublin. Cathal said they were interested in how the Troubles were affecting their businesses, much in the same vein as Cathal always discussed with Dermot. Dermot always felt there was more to those discussions, but couldn't put a finger on it and it was something best left unsaid – 'whatever you say, say nothin'.

Why did Conor approach him only shortly after Harry had spoken to him? Dermot was always looking for a reason to walk out of his life, to start afresh.

Everything seemed pre-ordained. His early life in Edinburgh, in Leith with his parents, his knowledge of the devastating effects of alcohol. And yet here he was, a barman serving it to many functioning alcoholics. In the bar, publicly, they sang the praises of the Church, the Republican freedom fighters, the family, their working class community and origins. Privately, in a drunken state, they scorn it all: the power and influence of the priest, the fear of speaking out against the militants and possibly worse still – the physical and sexual abuse of their wives and children that was happening across town.

Dermot heard it all as he escorted them to a taxi, unfit to walk, true or untrue, men burdened with their past, trapped with their own vile secrets or vices or another's, unable to break free. Their missed opportunities to work in good jobs – here in Derry or in England, or take the chance to play for a sports team or emigrate to a new land. Dermot's job was to serve and listen. He was shaken from his thoughts by Cathal:

'By the way, I was talking to Conor. He was telling me you and him are going out for a night on the town. Some night, the two of yous will be talking shite all night instead of enjoying the craic and chasing a bit of skirt. Mind yous, you two might get on. Conor is becoming a more thoughtful person these days. Jesus, I don't know where it will end. He's chatting about getting a job – a proper job? Talk to you later.'

'Okay. Goodnight, Cathal.'

Shit, shit, thought Dermot.

No

Dermot went home. He had decided to see Harry that night, but he usually called much later. Should he wait? Maybe Harry was out, gone to bed or watching his favourite television show. Dermot decided to call in.

'Hello there, surprised to see you, Dermot'

'We were a bit slow tonight and I came home, actually came home early to see you.'

After the obligatory cup of tea in the kitchen, Dermot had explained everything to Harry.

'So even there is no contact they still want a contact, or think there still is one? Very confusing. Do they think it's you?'

'Sorry Harry, it's not me. Do you want to do it?'

'No fucking way mate. I am only the messenger, don't shoot the messenger. I wish Brother O'Regan hadn't mentioned me.'

'I wish you hadn't mentioned me to Brother O'Regan.'

'You were in the papers, again. You are always good for a succinct and articulate comment. We were just discussing your newspaper story and I happened to mention we have a pint now and again and you're a neighbour.'

'I know, I know. The boys have a poster in our toilets about loose lips. I think I might take it. I like it. Maybe I'll give it to you to put in your bog.'

'Honestly, Dermot, I didn't say anything about you, just you're intelligent, a committed socialist, too handsome to be single. We discussed your sexuality, though.'

'Fuck off.'

'Marie thinks you have a tight arse.'

'Fuck off.'

'Sure I fancy you meself.'

'Fuck off.'

Dermot pulled his seat back, scraping the newly varnished floor.

'I'm only joking, Dermot. I guess I did paint myself as a fan of yours. He must have put two and two together. I bet he has his own contacts, maybe through the clergy. They have their own network.'

'I know, I know.'

'I was a useful contact myself, Dermot. What will I tell him?'

'Buggered if I know. They want a contact. Just not me. We might get Conor.'

'Did Conor suggest you?'

'Well, they did meet, in the prison, so that is a possibility.'

'Indeed, that is a possibility, Dermot, but why ask me to ask you. He could have approached you directly. Anyway, Brother O'Regan said he would understand, as his brother has been involved in this stuff for years. I'll tell him no and find another contact. Father O'Regan probably knows someone anyway, probably has a Plan B.'

'Yeah, go for it, Harry. I think I'll take advantage of an early night and go to bed with a good book.'

'Fine, I'll tell Brother O'Regan tomorrow.'

'Seeya then.'

After Harry left Dermot to the door, he went into Marie and the children.

'I am having an early night. Good night, kids.'

Harry nodded to Marie that he would tell all upstairs.

As Harry pulled into the school car park the next morning, the principal was chaperoning children whose teacher was absent. He hurriedly walked past him and said he would see him at lunch time.

Much of the morning Harry was distracted, glad he had his classes organised well in advance. At lunch time he ate his sandwiches and gulped down his coffee. He went to see his boss.

The principal was standing at his desk, keys in his hand.

'Are you off out?'

'Yip, have to go to Belfast, and funnily enough will be seeing my brother this evening after my meeting this afternoon.'

'Well it seems my reply is no.'

'Walk me to the car.'

After Harry explained all, Brother O'Regan responded:

'Leave it at that. We have done our bit. I'll pass on your message. We'll have a malt.'

Harry stood as his boss drove down Southway, not knowing what way his life was turning. As he returned to class, he was glad to get back to routine; the Foyle looked drab as ever, but the sun shot thin rays through the clouds to add sparkle here and there. Now what was for dinner? It was one of his favourites, chilli con carne and to mark the start of the weekend, a bottle of wine. As Bedders, an old Hopwood weed said, 'Thursday is the start of the weekend'. Harry didn't care what night of the week it was; he was opening a bottle with his dinner.

Cafe on Sunday

Harry O'Donnell walked to his usual cafe on a bright, cloudless Sunday morning, almost perfect in the warm sunshine. Harry liked nothing better than to rise, shower, have a drink of iced orange juice and head out the door to walk to the Italian café on the Strand Road – a contemporary cafe with shiny, easy-to-clean surfaces. Its origin was reflected on the photographs of the original cafe in Derry with its owners in white aprons on the street in front of it. An unmistakably similarly-posed photograph of a cafe in Italy was hung next to it, with its owner in front of an open door, a shade cloth hooked to one side of the door, a canopy over the window, and underneath, its patrons at a table smiling into the camera. A pyramid-shaped mountain rose behind, bleached in the Italian sun.

Old black and white photographs of Italy and Derry ran the length of the cafe on the wall above its tables. The Italian owner co-ordinated the local young female staff who served plates of breakfast to older men or ice-cream and chips as birthday treats to children. It was owned by one of the Italian families that had come over to open ice cream parlours and cafes in many of the towns and villages in the North of Ireland and beyond. Harry's wife, Marie, was taught by one of the daughters of such an Italian family, and remembered her classroom experiences with admiration and fondness for the Derry-born daughter of Italian immigrants. Indeed, the mother of Harry's old school friend, Liam, was part of that Italian connection. A fond childhood memory for Harry was Claudio's birthday party, his Italian school friend held it in his father's cafe. It was a feast of music, chips, sweets and of course, lots of ice-cream. Claudio's family had returned to Italy and, like many Italian families, they were 'pendolares' – families who moved back and forth between the two countries. Harry thought they had returned to Lattina in Italy, but wasn't sure and often wondered what had happened to Claudio.

His regular Sunday morning walk to the cafe passed the Ford Escort that had aroused Harry's interest. He had noticed it a few times parked. A local man who lived in the street where the car was parked was washing his car beside it. Harry asked:

'How ya doing? Who owns that car? Do you know?'

'No idea. He must be visiting someone around here. It's only in the last few days that I have seen him. Sometimes I see him sitting in it, talking to himself or writing. He comes at all hours. I think he must be visiting someone from your street cause that where he heads.'

'Thanks, it's going to be another nice dry day.'

'So long as it doesn't rain after me washing the car.'

The journey took Harry past a corner shop on Asylum Road where he bought the Sunday papers. Many people were on the streets on that fine winter morning, out walking, buying their papers or simply enjoying the winter sunshine. When he arrived at the café, his friend, Pete, was already seated, head buried in his paper. Harry sat down and spread his own on the table beside him.

'I ordered for us.'

'Well, done.'

'Any craic?'

'Nope.'

They had their short conversation without raising their heads. Pete was an ex-teacher who had worked with Harry. With his extensive knowledge of music and public performances of his own songs and music, he presented his own show on the local radio station. He left the teaching profession and it wasn't long before he got enough work to make a living from his radio shows and performances.

Little was said on these mornings, just gossip about family and work. Possible holiday itineraries were discussed for the summer as they frequently went on holidays together with their families to Europe. Pete had a holiday home in Donegal. Culdaff was the village on the coast where he liked to go: rain, hail or shine. He had found his muse there, on the dark wintry nights – songs flowed although he missed his piano for developing them. The Donegal weather, his melancholic humour, the isolated house and the dwindling creamy wake along the beach were his inspirations. Pete was also a great teller of jokes and stories – a natural performer.

After a fulfilling, if somewhat unhealthy, Ulster Fry intertwined with a pleasant couple of hours of reading and chatting, they both parted and hoped they would meet again the next Sunday or one soon after that for more of the same.

Harry returned home, slowly enjoying his streets and the people he met, full of the joys of his full stomach and the world put to rights by Pete and him. The day was still clear and cheery and only marred by the thought of some late afternoon homework marking. He planned to tend to his garden that afternoon as the pleasant weather allowed. The ground had dried up nicely despite the poor porosity of its soil and the winter storms had brought lots of debris into his back garden. He thought he might tidy it up, even tidy the front communal garden with a bit of vigorous raking – a pleasant way to work off his greasy fry.

On his way back home he noticed the Ford Escort was still parked there. At the front gate of Cillefoyle Park he surveyed the front garden and mentally noted the work required. The children were out and his wife Marie was sitting dozing by the fire, a book fallen from her lap. As far as Harry knew she had planned few activities for that Sunday. The television was on and turned low.

'Do you fancy a brew?'

Marie quickly answered yes without opening her eyes and both were soon sitting by the kitchen window discussing the condition of the gardens.

'I think I'll start at the front. It only needs a quick rake and I'll put the stuff in under the tree for later removal. Some of the grass is long in parts. A wee clip is all that's needed. It'll not need cut till spring. The front ground is drier than our back garden. Good drainage, I suppose.'

'Well, enjoy yourself. I'll make dinner for six o'clock. Anything planned for tonight?'

'No, I'll just do some marking before dinner.'

'Fair enough. I'll pop out this afternoon and be back after five. I'll start dinner then.'

Marie drained her cup and was off up the stairs to get ready to visit her family. Harry stood daydreaming, looking at his back garden through the kitchen window.

He loved working in the garden, he would say it was his hobby, but in reality the garden needed little attention except for his several vegetable beds: potatoes, cabbages, peas, and carrots. He had thought about a green house and growing some tomatoes or some more exotic fruit, but that was for the future, maybe for his retirement. There was something meaningful in working in the clay and seeing things grow, cultivating for one's family. Still it had its problems – the constant battle with weeds, plant-eating snails and other insects. The masses of midges in late summer always provoked an irrational angry response and he had attempted a number of remedies to get rid of them. Some battles were won, but many lost. Then he resorted to a dram of whiskey in the Tower – a small consolation.

After changing into his gardening clothes, worn trousers and jumper that were stored in the back porch, he went to face the challenges of the front garden. He had wellington boots for the wet

127

days, but preferred his old hiking boots – still comfortably solid. With a rake in his hand and clippers in the other he strode to the front communal garden. Lots of twigs and other debris had fallen over it, some of the grass needed clipping and the paths needed brushing, including the driveway around the park.

Harry started the raking and became aware that a man had walked past the entrance a couple of times. It was someone with good posture and wearing well-fitted casual clothes. He recognised them as Marks and Spencers, similar to something that he would wear. Harry raked the debris into a pile.

Allen meets Harry

'Excuse me. I am looking for someone called Mickey O'Donnell. I think he lives in Cillefoyle Park.'

Allen lied, always aware someone might be listening or watching.

'No, I am Harry O'Donnell. No Mickey here. Unless he may be staying in the guest house, over there.'

Allen checked again to ensure no one was listening or watching, but there was always that possibility, some one behind the curtains or behind a wall, so he whispered:

'Actually, Mr. O'Donnell, it is you I would like to talk to if I may?'

Harry's mind went into overdrive, but immediately realised this may be something to do with being asked to relay messages by Brother O'Regan. His knees buckled, but he leant on the rake and hoped it wouldn't be noticed. He studied the man standing before him – well-dressed, sunburnt, in his twenties, maybe older. He talked with a Derry accent and yet didn't sound local. He had a bit of an English accent and, or had lived in England, sounded educated and looked neatly groomed. His clothes were fairly new and his hair, although slightly long, was also well cut. He looked and sounded middle class and had the bearing of someone who kept fit, perhaps an old fashioned teacher in a posh school or a manager from one of the companies dealing with Northern Ireland. Harry concentrated on the man's eyes. While his face was youthful, his eyes looked intent with purpose.

'I am sorry to spring it on you like this but may I come into your house? Are your children in?'

'No.'

Harry automatically answered the truth and regretted it immediately.

'Look, it will only take a few minutes of your time. I just want to make contact and get your immediate approval of our contact. We can play it anyway you want it. Here or anywhere.'

Harry's head was starting to spin again and he spurted out:

'Would you like a cup of tea?'

'Yes please, that would be kind of you.'

Harry again felt daft and out of control bringing a stranger into his home, but he felt it would give him time to think about the situation. He wanted to tell the guy to go away but felt he should at least listen to what he had to say and point him in another direction – towards Dermot.

They both went into the kitchen; Harry removed his boots at the door.

'Please sit at the table. Never mind Mickey O'Donnell. I think you are taking the mickey!'

'No. Mr. O'Donnell I am serious. I apologise again for coming like this, but I thought maybe now was the right time. I am sure you were expecting me.'

'No, I wasn't.'

Harry stated emphatically. Harry was stalling for time to get his thoughts into words, worried he might say the wrong thing or indeed that he might mention Dermot. Let the guy sort it out himself.

'Hold on a minute. Let me get the tea ready.'

After a while both sat looking at each other across the kitchen table, steaming mugs of tea in their hands. Harry said:

'I didn't get your name?'

'I didn't give it. I just want to check if things are okay and then we can get to the niceties.'

'What do you mean 'okay'?'

'That you are Harry O'Donnell and you are the Contact?'

'Yes, I am Harry O'Donnell and no, I am not the Contact. I am a teacher.'

Harry again felt foolish at his outburst, but he felt bewildered despite all attempts not to. He continued:

'Look, my boss asked me to ask another person, a friend of mine, regarding certain individuals, if they would like to talk about stuff in a very indirect way. You are aware of this?'

'Yes, I am and here I am. Allen is my name. I have been watching you for some time. Indeed I followed you to the café and went in myself for some tea and toast. Did you notice me? You were too engrossed in conversation, eating and reading. I left the café earlier and made the right assumption that you were going home afterwards. I went up to your house to make contact by simply ringing the bell, but I noticed a sun in the stained glass above the vestibule door and walked on by. It was very apt as 'Sun Hill' is my code name. I didn't want to make contact with your family around. When your wife left and when you came out, clearly intent on gardening, I was delighted.'

'You, the guy pacing up and down the street? Do you have a Ford Escort?'

'Oh dear, I am obviously not very good at this, Harry. You have caught me out. Your observational skills are excellent.'

'I do watch people and the streets. I know all the locals, their routines and their cars. I spotted yours a few times, but never saw you. I can easily spot strangers or strange cars.'

'Your tower? I have seen you there. You are the Contact.'

'Hold it. Hold it. What the fuck are you on about?'

Harry again felt he had lost it, trying to stay in control, but not very successfully.

'I am sorry for dropping in on you like this, but I thought it would be best. We don't have to meet here. I want to let you know that even though we know you live here we are not a threat.'

Harry immediately rose to his feet, screaming:

'Not a threat! That felt like a threat. Not a fucking threat! Get out of here you bastard and I don't want to see you or anybody like you again.'

'I am sorry, Harry, really sorry. I didn't mean to scare or intimidate you in any way. Please, please let me explain. Please. Give me five minutes and I'll leave. You will never see me again. I promise. I give you my word. Let's keep this sociable.'

'Sociable, you say. Everybody is fucking sociable until a cow invades his garden and it's not just in my garden, it's in my fucking kitchen.'

Harry stood looking at what appeared to be a mild-mannered man in front of him, but he was a spy, speaking meaningless words. Harry realised he was in a dangerous situation. He glanced around the kitchen for something to defend himself. Nothing was at hand. The knife drawer wasn't too far away.

'Look, Harry. I'll leave now and we can have this conversation somewhere else more public if you like, to make you feel safer. I can tell I am frightening you. It is all too important and if you don't trust me then it's over before it started.'

Allen laughed and Harry smiled.

'Okay, five minutes. You have five minutes, Allen.'

The tension of the situation relaxed and Harry sat down, staring intently at Allen.

'We will meet whenever you want; anywhere you want, for as long as you want. Once a month, once every two months.'

Harry couldn't believe his ears. What the fuck was this guy talking about? Harry was lost and, as was typical in such situations, he burst out laughing. Allen sat looking at him smiling.

'What the hell are you talking about?'

'We need to set up some form of periodical contact and build up a rapport, to trust each other. I think I read the situation wrong here. You are obviously shocked at the way I approached you. I got it wrong, sorry and maybe I should have approached you in a public place, to avoid any risk of offence or fear. Trust is the most important thing at the moment. I haven't made a very good start in that way. Don't you think? Surely, you were expecting me to contact you.'

'Wait a minute! You think I am the Contact?'

'You are the Contact.'

'No, no, you crazy bastard, I am a simple teacher, keep me out of it.'

'I know that. You would make a good contact. I can tell from my observations. You are good at watching people.'

'I don't want to be the Contact or anything like it. You are a buck eejit, so you are. What the hell do you mean observations? Have you been watching me? Of course you have? You are a buck eejit.'

'I haven't heard that in a while. Yes, I have been watching you. I was Harry O'Donnell's shadow for a while.'

Allen laughed and both giggled like two school boys. Harry noticed Allen had relaxed, his jaw slackened. He seemed at ease. There was something about him that seemed familiar and local. Harry had the instinct that this guy was genuine and was being honest.

'Look, I am not the Contact. I don't want to be the Contact.'

Harry enunciated the words 'The Contact' in a way he did many times in school to ensure his pupils understood what he was instructing them to do. He continued:

'I was just relaying messages. That's all. I wish to God that Brother O'Regan had never mentioned it to me. I wished to God I never mentioned Derm...'

'Look, I have been told you are the Contact and you relayed the message that it was on. The idea was on. It was a go.'

'No, I relayed a message that it was a possibility. No one was willing to be the Contact.'

'By the way who is Derm, something or somebody or other?'

'Nobody.'

Harry had said too much.

'No, not me. I am not the Contact. It's a great idea and I wish you luck. Anything to stop this spiral of violence is worthy of trying, but I am happy with the refuge of anonymity.'

'Well, that is strange because I honestly thought it was you. Our lines have got mixed up. Is there any chance you might be interested? We need someone who I can talk with, someone you know and who can be trusted. I can guarantee anonymity. I would not be following you or anything. Your life or family would not be at risk. I wouldn't let it happen. Only one or two people know about this. Do you know people?'

'That would be the problem. I don't know you and don't know if I can trust you.'

'I understand that. It can be developed.'

'Count me out. It's too dangerous. I know nobody. That stuff is for the films. Not me!'

Both men stared at each other.

'I am sorry, Allen.'

'Well that's that then. I better go.'

The door bell rang. Harry ignored it. It rang again and Harry still ignored it.

'Aren't you going to answer that?'

'Nope. If it's important they will come back.'

Harry heard a knock at the back door and in walked Dermot Lavery.

Dermot meets Allen

Allen and Harry stood up quickly. Harry's chair fell to the floor adding to the sudden tension of Dermot's arrival. All three stood looking at each other for a few seconds as Dermot's eyes seemed to work out immediately what was going on.

'Allen, meet Dermot, my neighbour.'

'You're the Contact, Dermot?'

'Are you the Contact?' Dermot asked Allen as Harry switched on the kettle to make more tea and said, 'Look, gentlemen, let's sit down and I'll make some tea. A cup of tea soothes most situations according to my grandmother. She was a grand old dame who had the airs and graces of a wealthy lady before she was wealthy. This is all very confusing.'

'Well, I finally meet the Contact.'

'We'll see about that. I haven't said yes yet, but I am willing to listen to you Allen. God, Harry, you should see your face! Confusion reigns.'

The three men sat down and had a discussion about the Troubles and the role of the current protagonists including Allen, Dermot and Harry. Copious cups of tea were supplied and many comments for something stronger dotted the conversation. All three wished the cycle of violence could end. Their discussion was brought to an end by Marie coming home and doing an 'Auntie Lila'. Auntie Lila was Harry's mother's youngest sister who visited his childhood home, almost daily and Auntie Lila's first port of call was the toilet.

Marie's arrival terminated the discussion with Harry agreeing that Allen would contact Dermot again discreetly. Harry and Dermot agreed to talk later that night if Harry was in his Tower at twelve thirty. As Allen stood by the table, he said: 'Look, we are not going to stop the operations on both sides. Hopefully the talks will start a process. The bombs will continue'.

They heard Marie flush the toilet. It was time to leave and both men left by the rear door.

'Who was that?' Marie asked on entering the kitchen and seeing the three mugs on the table.

'Oh, just a British emissary asking me for advice to solve the Northern Irish problem.'

'That's good, so long as you have it sorted before dinner because I want you to peel the vegetables. Has something been sorted?'

134

'No, I am as confused as before. I don't know what's going on.'

Harry was glad to do the routine peeling as a way to keep active, to keep his mind off what had just taken place. Had he agreed to consider acting as a go-between or at least provide a place to facilitate the meetings at one of the most enervating moments in his life? He felt Dermot had agreed to be the Contact and had been convinced it was a useful operation. From what Dermot said there was a growing movement within the IRA for a peace process. Some comments by Cathal that his brother Conor McCaffrey felt a political process was possible and relevant for the Republicans. Dermot felt there was a possibility. Well, if so, then Dermot could be the Contact and leave him out of it.

'Did you do any work in the garden today? I thought I heard voices. Have you spent the afternoon boozing while I am nursing my sick mother. Was it that eejit, Dermot? You and him seem to be getting rather fond of each other, or is it the Guinness again?'

'Actually, he did pop round and we had a long discussion about things so yip, the garden got a bye.'

'I haven't seen any bottles about or glasses.'

'We drank tea.'

'Yeah, pull the other one.' Marie scorned as she basted the chicken.

'By the way, I was looking for your fountain pen for Sinead in your office at the back of the garage. She wants it for school. That's quite a cosy place. You've sealed it up, carpeted it and a wee heater would be all you need. Maybe Sinead might use it, though her desk in the bedroom is up against the radiator and she is quite comfortable there. She is on the bed with a blanket most of the time anyway.'

'You know, Marie, I might start using it again. A man has got to have a shed. My own little back shop. Maybe I'll put a toy railway around it.'

The garage was huge. It was his great grandfather's workshop and office. Harry thought it might be a good place for Dermot to meet Allen. At the rear, the small office had a built-in desk with numerous little drawers. It was a piece of quality workmanship from the 1920s, probably completed when the house was built. Harry enjoyed opening all the drawers and still got a velvety pleasure from it. He had found a secret drawer a few years ago. It reminded him of Cicero's comment – no old man forgets where he has hidden his treasures – but unfortunately nothing was inside.

If he was to facilitate the Contact, then maybe that was the place to hold the meetings. He had pulled out a drawer once, and there, inside was a rolled-up A4 sheet, discoloured with age. He took it out and unrolled it. Printed in landscape it said: Dig a Well with a Needle. He remembered he was doing some handouts for his pupils on a school printer and printed off this Turkish saying. He had meant to stick it up above his desk as inspiration for his writing. Neither happened. Marie and the children didn't use the office and it was quite accessible without going into the house. Some pipes and plumbing odds and ends still littered some of the shelves in the garage, but his pride and joy were the various stationary items belonging to the business. One or two items had been framed.

Harry was in his tower, having a final goodnight to his city. Everyone was in their beds as midnight approached. His mind was spinning with the thoughts of his role in the future conflict of Northern Ireland. It was a dangerous role for an ordinary family man. Dermot was the activist, but wasn't interested, or so Harry thought. Perhaps the conversation with Allen may have changed his mind.

As Harry was about to leave, he saw Dermot come home. Harry stayed. The barman waved several times to ensure that Harry saw him. When Dermot came up the drive Harry was standing in the shadows. Harry motioned to him and both men went towards the garage. The side door took Harry and Dermot into the office of the plumbing business. A curtain hung over the door for insulation and Harry turned on a Superser. Instant heat made the little den comfortable. Harry withdrew one of the many drawers from the desk and produced a bottle of Jamesons. He poured two tiny measures into each glass. Dermot took one, who was not a drinker in the sense of regular consumption like Harry. Possibly, why he made a good barman. He always took the money if a customer offered him a drink and if some insisted he drink with them he accepted a little nip of whiskey.

'Well, Dermot?'

'It's dangerous, but it might work.'

'You can use this place, Dermot, if you want. I'll tell the kids that you want to write a book and are using it, so stay away. That you'll be doing it after work so they will not worry about your odd hours during the night and come and go as you please. Wells can slip up my drive, mostly hidden. He can bring the car up too. I'll tell the kids that he is a fellow writer. Maybe that he's your gay partner!'

'Piss off.'

'I suppose it could work. It will take time. Do you trust him, Dermot?'

'Yes, I do. I just get that gut feeling he is genuine.'

'Look Dermot, do what you want. If I can help, let me know.'

'Harry, you'll be sorry you said that.'

'Yeah, I know. Slainte.'

Both clinked their glasses, swallowed, stood up and left for their beds.

Big Polo

Phil O'Doherty was sick and Harry was asked to take his class in Phil's classroom. Business Studies posters and other related topics peppered the walls. Most of their corners had curled up with time and pupils' irreverent thoughts on the subject were scrawled on some of them. Business Studies was always a comfortable option for the pupils as Big Polo was an easy-going teacher and his classroom was always the first to empty at lunchtime. He had a propensity for polo mints, almost six foot six, hence his nickname, Big Polo. He always had a lengthy discussion of the previous night's televised soccer match at the beginning of his classes. His height helped curtail any class indiscipline; his teaching strategy flowed from the horizontal position, his bum on the seat and legs on the corner of the table, the polo mints positioned in front of him. He was famous for his open debates of any topic depending upon his mood: history, literature, current affairs. Often he would simply say to his class – 'Ask me any question, boys, anything you like.' Something Harry did too.

His red Business Studies book was the prescribed text for his subject and he got the students to read a number of pages during the class in silence. It was followed by a discussion. When finished, the pupils simply dozed in a reading position, in silence too. While this worldly contemplation took place, Big Polo read his thriller, the latest John Carey, but he was a passionate Raymond Chandler fan.

His teaching strategy, his question-and-answer sessions where the kids fired questions at him, often unrelated to the text, soccer being a favoured topic. The boys liked the easy predictability of that routine. He always encouraged the interested soccer players in the class to shoot a question at him, the pupils hoping someone would ask another before his attention went to the textbook. His paradigm in the classroom worked. Teacher and students were happy and many passed their examinations. Big Polo was well-liked by staff and pupils. His proclivity to work his finger up his nose or up his bum added to his notoriety. He loved his shoes and wore buckled shoes in silver or brass, leather piled on leather with carved intricate patterns. 'A buckle is a great addition to any shoe' was an apt Irish proverb that fitted him well. His well-shod feet matched his bejeweled fingers. Silver, gold, and stone rings enfolded them. Celtic filigree produced in silver over emerald worn on his lanky, aged fingers, etched silver bands on his little ones. Different rings appeared frequently. His tight silvery beard covered his thin face; his mouth, almost lipless, and tobacco-stained teeth were dominated by his sharp protruding nose, famous for enjoying frequent excavation. Only on close inspection did the surprising discovery of his deep set, beady eyes, betray those determined pupils. His preponderance for saggy cardigans transposed him from a dapper dresser, a man about town, into a work-a-day teacher, a man with a hidden passion for baps, a locally-made muffin.

Most days Big Polo sent a student for fresh baps to the corner shop. Usually he sent a local lad, John for his lunch. A mature-looking boy, John regularly got out of bed ten minutes before school started and still arrived on time by wearing his pyjamas under his clothes. A bap and a cream finger from the shop across the grassy slope was Big Polo's usual requirement. This errand was against the school rules and the student had to avoid the roving headmaster and other prowling staff. The bread and pastry had to be acquired by stealth, even though everyone knew it happened. Down three flights of duplicate stairs, the boy hoped for a quiet exit. Getting past the foyer and the headmaster's office was particularly challenging. The approaching flap of the headmaster's soutane sent fear into the boy. John hid until the coast was clear and then flew through the front door and up to the shop.

The corner shop was across the soggy grass embankment, opposite a square of houses, where the proprietor stacked the vegetables outside in wooden boxes. Big Polo warned him to carefully count the change. Another rule was keeping the bap and cream finger in good condition on the return journey. Such antics from Big Polo made him a legendary character.

Big Polo's room faced the fields on the other side of the school, away from the grand view of the Foyle River.

Harry decided to use the Big Polo's experienced errand boy and had procured himself a fresh cream bun for lunch. John had once again managed to escape the notice of the headmaster, but Harry believed he ignored the mischievous duo, teacher and pupil. On his return, John explained that after coming out of the shop he had seen several men in long overcoats, with rifle barrels sticking out at the bottom. Harry thanked John for the errand and stopped him explaining what he had seen. The teacher did not want the boys distracted by John's stimulating tale.

Through the windows on his right a couple of open fields lay beyond the school's playing fields, each bounded by tightly grown hawthorn hedges. Harry spotted a group of men gathering under the hedge alongside the school's grounds. It was not unusual to see groups using the field for target practice. Harry looked at the class; they too were looking at the men below. Harry called to them to ignore the men outside; they were used to seeing them and just get on with their work.

Harry had continued Big Polo's tradition of reading from the red class set of the Business Studies book. He tried to remain as calm as possible as the obvious intent became clear. The men outside milled around the edge of the field below. John put up his hand and called out:

'Sir, Sir, I saw them. They are going to shoot.'

'Calm down. What did you see, John?'

John recounted his journey back to the school after getting the cream bun for Harry. He told Harry and the class that when he crossed the embankment again, on his return, a familiar person stood beside him, curiously wrapped in a large duffle coat. From within its huge hood came a grunting salutation. John did not reply, but it was a familiar voice, John informed the class, but he knew not to identify the gunman. The person in the duffle coat hid his hands in his pockets. However, something about the flop of the elbows did not look right. John noticed the sleeves of the coat were tucked into the pockets. Underneath the long coat was a thin rifle barrel, exposed just above his ankle, positioned tightly to one side of the trouser leg. This was the purpose of the oversized duffle coat. John watched the bloke waddle into a lane next to the school. He scurried downhill towards the school. By the time John got to the gates, he had disappeared. That duffel coat was moving weapons for the session of target practice.

Mostly the group of men stayed close to the hedge, hiding themselves from view, while a couple of them placed targets in the centre of the field – one a round target and the other a dummy. The unreal movie unfolded outside, through the dirt-smeared windows of Harry's class, and captured their full attention. They could not see the precise movements of the men, but knew what was happening. Only the staccato blasts echoing through the sunny morning indicated something amiss. After a while, Harry drew the class back to his discussion of the text they had been reading.

Suddenly, all heads turned to look through the windows to determine the source of a great rumbling outside. It was the whoop-whoop of a helicopter's blades, flying outside the school's windows. After hovering over the fields, it rose swiftly, the pilot realising what was occurring below. The helicopter dipped again, flew at speed over

140

the field and headed towards the school, leaving the windows vibrating in its aftermath. Whop, whop went the helicopter as the sound dulled in the distance.

Harry sighed:

'Ah! Where were we, boys? Write your questions and we'll start.'

Five minutes later, the thunderous whirring of three Wessex helicopters came into focus. They hovered over the fields next to the school until, one by one, they disappeared beyond the hedges and rose sharply again. The helicopters came down so low allowing their cargo of British soldiers to drop into the field beyond the hedge. The teacher and his pupils could see unmistakably their camouflaged garb as they moved along the upper hedges. The IRA collected in a bunch by the lower hedge. A stream of shots rang out. An IRA sniper had climbed a tree and let off a volley towards the newly-arrived troops, who returned fire, scattering the top leaves of the trees and hedges where the Boys positioned themselves. Two fields and a hedge separated the warring parties.

Further rattles of guns erupted beneath the classroom's windows, as the British Forces attempted to move towards the gunmen, but they held their defensive positions. From their grandstand view, Harry and his boys could have advised both parties how to advance given their strategic position above the opposing fighters.

'Boys, I think we better make a move, leave your books.' Harry said, just as a bearded teacher stuck his head into the room, shouting:

'We will evacuate to the Quad, NOW!'

The evacuation bell rang too, and hundreds of boys filled the corridors and stairs leading down to the quadrangle, a sanctuary from the gun battle above, and below the surface of the main part of the school. The Quadrangle housed the metalwork room on one side and the woodwork room on the other. A pond had been sculptured by the metalwork teacher, and the woodwork teacher planted a garden of vegetables and other various plants. As the boys streamed into the safety of the Quad, they trounced everything – the garden pounded by hundreds of tiny feet. The metalwork teacher stood astride his pond, attempting to save the newly-installed fish by pushing away any errant boy. Escape from the quadrangle was through a side gate, into a square of houses and down a winding hill.

As the boys evacuated to the local square people outside were going about their daily business, unaware of the life-and-death battle a few minutes away. The students got some unexpected freedom and flowed downhill away from the mayhem on top.

After the students left for home, Harry and the staff discussed their exit with the headmaster. The car park was below the level of the front door of the school and the staff easily and safely got into their cars and drove off home. Like the boys, they had been glad for a few extra hours away from school, but burying their anger at the reality of life in a Derry school.

Allen's Phone Call

Allen was about to go on holidays when he got a phone call from his boss, Ian Blackwood.

'How are things in Londonderry?'

An authoritative voice at the other end of the phone, composing his breathing.

'Oh, hello Sir. What can I do for you?'

'Well, we think we are making headway. It's not Harry O'Donnell. It's his drinking friend and neighbour. A chap called Dermot somebody or other. We will send a file on him to you A.S.A.P.'

'Sir, I know. I met him. I was told it was Harry O'Donnell. I am booked to go home today.'

'Fine, fine, it will be a few days and probably a week before you should contact him, as soon as he agrees. Has he agreed? Anyway the point is we want you in Londonderry to confirm by next week. The rest is up to you.'

'Sir, I will be in London next week with friends.'

'Okay, take the week, but after you read the file, contact me and start the Op. on this boy Dermot.'

'Should I still watch Harry O'Donnell?'

'As your report said I think you are right, he's not our man. He's not a teacher who frequents these bastards' company. If you think it is worthwhile then do so, but that is your decision. I don't think a week will make much difference and we don't want anyone to know what we're doing here. Might come to nothing, anyway so we don't want to spend too much time and money on this. Come and see me before you go over again. Enjoy your R and R. Bye.'

Allen stood in Foyle Street, staring into the phone, taken aback and annoyed. Annoyed at the fact his trip was now for one week. He would have to change the flight back and tell the lads he would have to curb his holiday. Allen climbed into the car taking him to the Belfast Aldergrove military section of the airport to fly to the mainland. As he passed Altnagalvin Hospital on his left he said to himself – Shit, shit.

Conor Meets Dermot

Conor Mc Caffrey sat staring out the window, looking at a bird, a sparrow, its head twitching, alert for food or enemies. Not much different to us, he thought. It was perched on a stone in the city walls, a small ledge on one of them. The defensive walls were built to keep the natives and anyone else out of the London colony and were high above the bog below. That bog below became known as the Bogside where Conor ran as a boy, playing Cowboys and Indians and then as a boy-man where the wooden stick became a real gun and the Indians were replaced by the foreign British soldiers on his streets of his city. He intended to drive them from his country by force and thought it was only a matter of time. 'Tiocfaidh Ár Lá' – our day will come. By bombing and killing the British Imperialist Forces, the enormous cost to them to stay in Northern Ireland in terms of bloody bodies and pounds and shillings would force them to leave. It would be just too costly to the British Government and its people, the British taxpayer. Yet, they didn't leave, certainly their public statements were not to be trusted. Conor had talked to Loyalists and British journalists who had been briefed by the British Government and Military hierarchy who said they were not leaving Northern Ireland. One of those journalists had told him recently at a peace rally he attended, that the British Government classified the Northern Ireland situation as an acceptable level of violence.

Unfortunately for Conor he was identified at the peace rally in Belfast a few days after he got out of prison. His conversation was reported in a British tabloid with his mug-shot supplied by the Royal Ulster Constabulary, when as a young 19-year old, he was on his way to prison. The other newspapers picked it up – the angle being that he was a hawk-turned-dove – he was a peacemaker.

Five years after his sojourn in Long Kesh prison – the University of Terrorism – he sat looking at the little bird, envying its freedom. Thoughts of leaving the Troubles behind enticed him, going somewhere warm and gentle, where the sores of history had been put to bed, more or less – Southern Europe, Australia or America. Some of the IRA's problematic members were shipped off to Uncle Sam, an escape route for them. There was a real option for him to go to New York or Boston. He could work there, on a political level, on a community level, gathering support and funds. Conor wasn't sure what he would do. The Movement was giving him time and space to work

144

out his future in Derry and Northern Ireland. He didn't want to leave his family and friends. He had told them he might become more politically involved. Being the brother of Cathal, the Derry Sinn Fein chairman, helped and Cathal knew his younger brother had an intelligence that could benefit the cause. His publicity at the peace rally did not endear him to his brother, but as Cathal said to the media it showed that Republicans wanted peace.

He heard Dermot before seeing him, as he stood in front of the window and the light blinded him. Dermot apologised for being late and had offered to buy Conor a drink which he declined. When Dermot went to the bar, Conor studied his old friend: a slim man, younger looking than his age, hair to collar length, blue wrangler jeans, and a checked shirt under a navy jacket. The back of his shoes shone, as usual. Dermot always liked to dress well, even when Conor had known him as a boy. A few minutes later, Dermot joined Conor in the corner seat.

Both sat looking out the window, no birds, just the city walls, and a church spire ascending into the brightening sky.

'Thanks for coming.'

'No bother at all.'

Dermot replied, taking another swig from the glass of Guinness.

'What have you been up to?'

'Oh, the usual, working away, nothing really to report.'

Dermot answered as if they had met on a regular basis and Dermot's life was routine. He had to think about how he would tell Conor about his potential meeting with an MI5 agent. Both sat back and stared out the window.

'Can I ask, how are you enjoying your freedom?'

'Fuckin' magic. I love it. Just being here. I am quite fluent in Irish now. Ní fhaca mé le fada thú. Plenty of time in jail. I learnt to meditate too. I think I am more calm, not as angry, I guess.'

'Are you a different man than the one that went in? What do you think of your newspaper story, you, only a few days out?'

Dermot wasn't sure whether he was stepping on thin ice, but he was intending to step on thinner stuff soon so this would gauge Conor's reaction.

'Aye, could have done without that. Now I am hailed as the new Republican peacemaker. I have seen the light! You know I always was a bit of a pacifist, maybe more of a thinker, but like many others after they murdered us on Bloody Sunday. I was outraged. I have thought

145

hard about staying active, but I still feel it's not for me. One of the lads was at the University in Coleraine, on an operation. They pinned stealing a car on him for a shooting at a cop's house in Portstewart. They had nothing on him, but he got five years. He came out the same time as me. It was him that helped me become fluent in Irish. He is thinking about going to America. They organise pen pals for the prisoners and I think he might go out and see his female pen pal. I thought about escaping there.'

'How fluent are you in Irish? Labhair Gaeilge liom?'

'Íocfaidh an fear seo as gach rud. Not bad, I had a thing with languages, could pick it up. My teachers at the Brow were proud of my skills. I was one of their best students. Even Brother O'Regan was proud. We conversed in Irish. Do you speak Gaelic? Labhair Gaeilge liom?'

'No I don't, but have thought about it. What did you say anyway?'

'That you will for pay everything.'

Dermot smiled and said:

'We are setting up some Irish classes above the pub. I need a teacher. Would you like to participate, even teach there? I might get a few, how shall I say, non-political students. Some potential students would not be happy with the Republican thing and then throw in ex-prisoners and a Republican pub. Well we may as well say: 'Republicans only'. I would like to open it up to anyone. The location of the pub might be a help.'

'Excellent. Yes, I don't see why not. I'll help.'

'My friend, Harry, the teacher, he had to evacuate his school. A fire fight with the Brits and the Boys outside the school. They say the school should have stayed in their old site, the Brow of the Hill, behind the College on Bishop Street. As soon as they moved to their new school the whole Troubles blew up and the school is in the middle of it. It was bad craic. Harry O'Donnell's class could see the Boys were practicing their shooting down below in the field. The Brits came in with helicopters and all sorts and what a battle they had. Harry, easy going as usual. Took it all in his stride. The evacuation alarm went off.'

'It's not fair to the teachers and the kids. You're involved in some young socialist groups, aren't you?'

'Yes, I am. Sure they want me to run the groups, but I am happy being a barman.'

'Bullshit. Your intelligence and knowledge of Irish history and the Republican Movement has people in awe. People consult you.'

'The first I knew of it.'

'Well, Cathal holds you in great regard. He's not sure about your socialist views. But Cathal and people like him realise the movement is a broad church. There was much debate in The Kesh. I think that debate is extending to the leadership especially in Derry. They see a political struggle and an armed struggle. Cathal suggested I stand for the local council in the up-and-coming elections.'

'I can see where you are going: a political process, but the armed struggle goes ahead.'

'The political process has sort of, already been flowing. I might just join it, give it momentum. The prolonged martyrdom has to stop, Dermot.'

'Which ties in with something I would like to ask you. Somebody asked me to ask you something, something off the wall actually. I prefer not to be doing this, but here I am. No names. It didn't come from him directly, but somebody asked him who had asked him. As far as I know it is genuine. I believe the guy who asked. I want to ask you something in complete confidentiality.'

There was a touch of sarcasm in Dermot's voice. Conor turned to look at him and raised an eyebrow and smiled a small smile, as if both seemed to understand each other. Conor continued:

'I think I know what it is. This just isn't just a social drink? The answer is probably no. Time for another. Same again?'

Conor lifted an empty glass and went to the bar as Conor returned with his Smithwicks.

'Your Guinness is on its way. Look, spit it out Dermot. You look like something is up your ass. Unless you are fucking with me, messing me about. I don't think you are. You have my word this is confidential.'

Dermot looked around to see if anyone was close by that might overhear.

'Okay. I have been asked to ask you to act as intermediary between the IRA and the British Government. There I said it.'

'For fuck sake Dermot, are you serious? Father O'Regan put you up to this. No was the answer I gave him and no is the answer I am giving you.'

Conor looked at Dermot, his face serious, eyes intent. The barman delivered Dermot's pint, nodded to Dermot and returned to his bar. Both said nothing.

'Look, no fucking way mate. I am not getting involved. It might be a good idea though. But not me. You do it. It's not a good time for me,

Dermot. I need to get my head sorted and have some relaxation after the last years. No way. You do it. I'll support you, if you need it.'

Dermot sat looking at his pint.

'Don't look so worried Dermot. Say no, if you must.'

'I think my bowel contents are turning to liquid. My sphincter muscle is as tight as can be. Jesus, what now? So Father O'Regan approached you?'

'Yes he did. I said no. I tell you what mate. I'll think about this and test some waters, if they think it's an idea to run with then do it. I'll talk to Cathal who'll chat to people. Let's meet again, in a day or two. Don't worry. I'll keep your name out of it. Leave it with me. Now tell me about your communistic policies'

Dermot relaxed a little and added:

'Okay. I'll wait for your answer, but I am not interested. If the thing goes belly up, what then? Fuck Harry O'Donnell. He got me into this mess. If you won't do it, why should I? I trust you Conor. Did you by any chance suggest me? We go way back.'

'Fuck who?'

'Never mind, Conor! Well, Marx said 'Reason has always existed, but not always in a reasonable form'. Are you suggesting we develop a reasonable form?'

Conor smiled and said:

'Well, I will support you and help in any way I can, but enough politics. Perhaps we should talk about something else. How's the footy going?'

'Before that, Conor, did you mention me to Father O'Regan?'

'Your name may have come up, but I didn't suggest you as an intermediary or anything like that. The O'Regan brothers maybe put two and two together to make five.'

'I wish people would leave me out of their conversations.'

'What do you mean?'

'I have had enough, thinking about this, Conor. Do you still support that useless London team?'

After their short chat on the British soccer results they finished their beer, Conor said:

'I'll call into the pub or leave you a message. When are you working there? Or we could meet up another time? Look, with regard to the Irish classes, count me in.'

'Nothing organised yet so will let you know, thanks.'

'Okay, I'll call in for a pint, but it's not for me, Dermot. I need time to work out my future. If you want to do it, go for it. I'll check it out for you.'

'I am only a messenger. Please don't shoot the messenger! That's what I am afraid of, they might shoot the messenger.'

'Relax, you have me behind you. You have Cathal, and a lot more than you realise. Talk to you later.'

'Dia Duit. Conor'

Both left the pub, neither looking back.

Two days later Conor called into the pub. He eyed Dermot as he cleaned glasses. Two white-haired men sat at the bar supping at their usual half pints and whiskey chasers. It was four in the afternoon. No one talked. They glanced at the races on the television, one had a paper in his hand, one fiddled with a cigarette.

Dermot asked one of the customers at the bar to call him if he was needed as Conor and him went upstairs. The room was newly painted, some old Derry prints sat against the wall, ready to be hung. The shades of the central candelabra sat on some tables, with some table lamps. A tin of varnish, with its lid, off centre, allowing its fumes escape to fill the room. Dermot opened a sash window with a great deal of effort. Lozenges of paint spotted the windows.

'Must scrape the paint off those windows. I am painting the upstairs bar as you can see. It will look good with a fresh coat of paint. There is no heat up here, but Cathal says he'll organise a gas heater. A Superser.'

'Looks good, Conor. As I said to you earlier, count me in for the Irish classes, but count me out for the talks. I had a talk with Joseph who expressed great surprise, if not shock. But I told him I fully supported you, should you wish to pursue it yourself. I am happy to be the vehicle to Joseph. We will be seeing each other at the various meeting and pubs. I want to tap your brain. I say go for it. People have great certainties. They believed in Victory 1972. I did. Then it became Victory 1974. I started to have my doubts. We believed we could do it on our own, force the Brits out. But now, let's see what a channel could bring.'

'I know what you are saying. There is no such thing as a certainty. People are quick to judge rather than understand.'

'Somebody said that already – people prefer to judge rather than understand, to answer rather than ask. Foolishness of human certainties.'

'I'll think about it again, but really I do not want to get involved, Conor.'

'Well, you have my support and a cautious one from you know who. He doesn't believe in certainties anymore. One thing though, Dermot, the British Empire will never beat us. There are over twenty-two thousand British troops here. There are over five thousand in the Ulster Defence Regiment and there are, what around twelve thousand local police including the reserve, and most are locals, our fellow Ulstermen. They will never beat us. The problem is we will never beat them so we need an alternative path to a United Ireland. You and me together, we could do something about that.'

'Do you mean, Joseph?'

Conor saw Dermot's eyes dim a little at that final comment. They both went downstairs without saying a further word.

Dermot meets Joseph

Harry had a free period after lunch every Wednesday and often went to the city centre for some personal business and then had a sandwich in a café for lunch. He had been to the bank to deposit a cheque and as he stepped out into the street he literally bumped into Dermot.

'I am going to have a quick sandwich for lunch. Care to join me, Dermot?'

'Sure why not.'

It was a cool dry day, pleasant enough to enjoy a walk to the cafe in Austin's department store that overlooked the Diamond, the city centre. Both men sat by the window to enjoy the view after the lunch was ordered. Dermot wanted to discuss his thoughts on the possibilities of a planned contact.

'I am glad I met you because I think this whole thing about the contact might crash and burn. I don't see you usually during the week, so maybe this is foreshadowing a disaster. It's a warning.'

'Well, it will be risky, no doubt about that. Though I don't have too much time to talk about it now, Dermot.'

Their sandwiches and side salads arrived. Harry started to eat, but Dermot sat pondering, looking over the Diamond and the War Memorial in the centre. Harry looked too. People were meandering across the road as if it was a pedestrian precinct, avoiding the oncoming cars.

The overheard conversation before Christmas between Dermot and an IRA man outside Cillefoyle Park as Harry had done some gardening had really un-nerved him. The young man Dermot had talked to, promised some sort of major offensive by the IRA. Harry was worried about the potential threat to the city and its inhabitants. Perhaps, as the contact developed, it would alleviate that possibility.

'Look, Harry, I don't want to get involved in the dodgy and dangerous business of relaying information to one side or the other. I know the importance of such a possible contact cannot be underestimated. The possibility of laying down the path to talks, to peace, to a ceasefire. I know there would be limited involvement on both sides. Few would know about this, but if someone discovered the contact was happening, someone down the chain, on either side, they might think I was a spy. I could get hurt very easily.'

'I understand. Don't do it then.'

'Victory '74. Victory '72. These were the Republican mantras. Conor told me they were confidently predicting a victory, but the fact is, it's not happening. Conor seems to be going the political path but he is aware that there are still strongly held views in the Provisional Irish Republican Army – the Provos – that the only option is the military option. The bombing of commercial premises and the shooting of the police and the army, both here in Northern Ireland and England, will continue. That means more death and destruction. What worries me is that it could be my death and my destruction.'

Harry shook his head and grimaced in sympathy.

'You know my views. Harry. Yes, I am a Republican, a socialist Republican. This is my way – the slow pull of politics. Make people aware of the vested interests of the powerbrokers. The issues of the working class are exploited by these conservative forces in the British Government, in the government of the Republic of Ireland and of course within the Republican Movement. I live and work with these boys daily, most think I am a communist. But it's these conservative forces that take advantage of the disillusionment and lack of opportunity in terms of housing, jobs and equality of citizenship. The brute force of the so called British Empire is met by the brute-force of the IRA. The working-class English from their working-class estates in England are cannon fodder for the British Army, as is the unemployed Catholic youth for the IRA. It is a class war, Harry. This is a clash that I avoid with Cathal.'

'Hold it, Dermot. I know you are passionate, but keep your voice down. I am having my lunch with a friend not with Bernadette Devlin. You should marry her. Plenty of political pillow talk.'

Dermot ignored Harry's attempt at wit and continued in a whisper:

'Maybe I could plough a furrow for some sort of dialogue, or maybe, as I said to you, Harry O'Donnell, many times, I just want to get the hell out of here, away from the brutality, the sombre climate, and the narrow-minded attitudes of the people. There are many decent people here. I know that, even those that are blasting their way through life. They need leadership, just not me.'

'It's the moral ambiguity that we all bear in Northern Ireland. Dermot. The murder of a British soldier or policemen, a fellow Ulsterman, would bring cheering and celebration in your pub. Each time, we would walk away and try not think about it, but it was somebody's son, brother or husband. A little of you dies too. The savagery of fellow beings, yet life goes on within minutes: births, deaths, marriages, the footy, the horses, the everyday concerns of people.'

'Yes, the very same concerns as the people from across the water in England, or anywhere whose boys were sent to the Derry streets to patrol and create more havoc yet they are supposedly the peacemakers. I have that ambiguity now. Is it time to change and follow another path? Time to get out. Or is this a time, an opportunity to alter the course of violence – the course of the Troubles.'

'Simply run away to the Donegal Hills with me, Dermot. We have done that too many times. Unfortunately the hills were too wet, too windy. That westerly wind goes right through you, carrying all that damp. I love the place though, Dermot. But like you I would prefer a bit of heat and blue skies. Is it time for you to leave this place, Dermot? Perhaps? I don't know, but what I do know is I need to get back to work.'

'I need to get to my work too.'

'A wee malt helps the thought processes on these occasions.'

'Not tonight, Harry.'

'I wasn't inviting you!'

No further discussion on the subject took place as both finished off their lunches in silence. They were about to go when Joseph and Conor walked in. Both sets of men saw each other immediately and nodded the Derry hello. Conor and Joseph took a table by the window a few feet away from the other two. As Dermot and Harry were about to rise from their seats, Dermot saw Conor shake his head and gestured to them with his hand to remain seated.

'Jesus, I'll be late for class. Brother O'Regan will not believe me if I tell him who I was waiting for.'

Harry whispered to Dermot.

'This gets more complicated by the day, Harry.'

Harry thought Dermot's impenetrable composure was about to crack.

Conor leaned over to Joseph and they were in close conversation for a few moments with Joseph nodding his head. Conor gestured to them to come over.

'Dermot, I'd like you to meet Joseph. I have been telling him a few stories about you, how you lived with your Granny beside us and the time we had on our night out together.'

'Pleased to meet you, Dermot. I hear you had a good night's craic. I have read about your activities in the papers and seen you in Cathal's pub. I want you to know that I think you should begin a long and fruitful friendship with Conor. If Conor wants to continue as a political activist I am happy. I am sure he can learn much from you and if you see each other regularly, he can update me on all the news. Go for it.'

Harry knew Dermot had met Joseph a few times in the pub and he had turned up at various community meetings, but they all continued with the formality.

'Thank you Joseph, I am not sure if Conor would want to associate with me. I might be a bad influence.'

'Dermot, it's me who is the bad influence. If you want to be a good influence maybe you should associate with Conor and he can be a good influence on me.'

Harry was standing slightly away from the other men, but heard the conversation. Were they encouraging the contact with Dermot?

Harry and Dermot got their answer from Conor.

'As Joseph says you could be a good influence on both of us. I will tell Joseph all the craic after you have told me. That is, if there is any to tell.'

Dermot introduced Harry.

'Conor, Joseph, do you know Harry O'Donnell?'

'I have heard of you. You teach in the school in Creggan and teach the kids of many I know. A good job you are doing, too.' Joseph replied. Conor spoke next:

'I remember you at the Brow, but you didn't teach me Harry. I'll be seeing you Dermot. I'll give you a call.'

Joseph held out his hand to shake and spoke directly to Dermot.

'Hope to hear all the news from Conor if things happen. After all we expect them to leave once and for all, so whichever method that gets them to do that, I don't mind.'

They all wished each other a good afternoon and Harry said to Dermot when they got outside:

'I better dash, teaching in 20 minutes. I have changed my mind. Come round tonight to chat about all of this stuff, if you wish.'

'I'm working late so maybe another night, but I'll be in touch soon.'

Conor Confirms

Dermot walked up to the bar, a matter of ten minutes. Lots of thoughts flew about in his head. A few regulars were already perched on the stools. All eyes were on the television showing the afternoon racing in England. Cathal was working behind the bar reading the paper as Dermot emerged from the street.

'G'day mate.'

'What?'

'G'day mate. Skippy, the bush kangaroo was just on the telly. Dermot, you must have seen it?'

'Yeah, I have. We all grew up with it.'

'Those kangaroos are some clever two-legged mutes, not like our four-legged mutes we have here.'

'Cathal, they are not kept as pets and it's a television show.'

'I know. I know. Smart arse. Are you under control with the room upstairs? I have put up the prints. The bar has been painted. It looks well. Will we ever use it?'

'I'll take a walk up stairs and have a look at the progress. The boys from The Housing Committee sounded positive and an Irish group are interested. They think it's the town centre location that might attract more from across the city rather than just locals. I have just thought of someone. The barman in the Rock Bar, John, is a quiz organiser, and maybe he might be interested or knows someone who might like to host a quiz night here. Again, we could put up some prizes.'

'Thanks, Dermot. I might get a few pints out of them and sure it will help the place. It will raise its profile. A bit of more life about it rather than just the locals or the usual crew. A bit more culture, as they say. The darts crowd said they will definitely use it for the next tournament. Now that's the sort of culture I like. The fact I sponsored a trophy helped.'

'Have you a dartboard upstairs?'

'Good point, Dermot. They can use the one down here.'

'We don't want to upset our regulars so best get one installed upstairs. So where does all this social concern come from, Cathal?'

'This is where capitalism meets socialism. You're the socialist and where does that leave me? I'm the capitalist. No harm in making a few bob.'

Cathal chuckled as he left the pub in the hands of Dermot. It was a quiet afternoon. Dermot switched off the television and put on one of his Bix Beiderbecke jazz tapes, made a coffee and settled down to a book on Australian history and settlement. He thought of having an Irish coffee later – the essentials of life in one wee glass – alcohol, caffeine, sugar and fat. He needed one after his experience during lunchtime.

Dermot's music and books were buried deep in a cupboard under the bar, kept for quiet times. Harry had given him the Bix Beiderbecke jazz tape. One of Harry's students, Pat, had achieved an athletics' scholarship to Southern Illinois University in Carbondale – the home town of Trumbaur – a saxophonist who played with Bix. During their previous liquid rendezvous, Harry introduced his passion for jazz to Dermot.

He sat in a comfortable seat facing the door and dozed off while reading his book. He awoke and saw a figure of a man standing in front of him; the light from the windows obscured his view. When Dermot stood up and walked behind the bar he saw it was Conor.

'Having a drink?'

'No thanks, Dermot. Just thought I would pop in to clarify a few things. I hope I didn't wake you. Joseph is fully supportive of establishing a contact. It will not be me. I suggested you and Joseph agreed. Not the right time for me. Okay, Joseph and I will go our different paths. I am convinced politics is the way forward. Joseph doesn't see any conflict with my view and his way. Gun in one hand, handshake with the other. If the contact happens, he will have to convince Belfast, but that may mean he will take responsibility for it to a degree and that, likely, will be only if it is you.'

'No thanks, I don't want it.'

'Think about it? Please. Dermot.'

'I will Conor, but really I don't think so.'

'What about the guy who contacted you? Is he suitable?'

'Let's keep him out of it.'

'I tell you what, let's go forward with this and tell your guy the contact will happen, but we will let them know. It will take years before anything happens, I think.'

'Maybe Conor, maybe you hope it will default to me?'

'Maybe you are right Dermot. You are the guy for the job. I think we should grab the opportunity. I know you agree with me, Dermot.'

'I do, but I don't want to be involved.'

'True, but no one knows.'

'I tell you what Conor. I will tell my guy, yes, but let's see what happens.'

'Okay Dermot, talk soon. See you at your Irish class.'

'Bye, Conor.'

Dermot was more confused than ever. Did he agree to something he wished he hadn't? It would be good to talk to Harry. At eight o'clock, Cathal returned. The bar was quiet.

'Do you fancy staying for the rest of the shift, Cathal?'

'Why, you got a date or something?'

'Yeh, a date or something.'

'Sure, why not? I want to fix the lights upstairs. Paddy, here can you give me a shout if someone comes in.'

'Okay, I'll be off then.'

Guns

'What have we got there, Mick?'

'Half a dozen armalites, an assortment of small arms, all the ammo we need, a couple of shotguns, some detonators and a box of explosives over there. I believe there's more fuckin' stuff on its way from Stranraer where it landed, but stored up there.'

'We have moved all the stuff from the fire station's garden. Not a problem since we met that bastard Dermot and then the Brits appearing. Then, the bollocking from Cathal. We should deal with him someday. But first we need to decide what we will do with this stuff, Mick?'

'What is this stuff exactly? We will be told where to put it and don't you worry, Dermot Lavery is on list. I will deal with him.'

' Good, will look forward to that day. Anyway, I thought you knew everything going on and more, you always had eyes and ears beyond these walls.'

'Don't be a smart arse, Brendan. What are you talking about? I'll keep to the decision that the less Cathal knows the better, am sure you will find out soon enough.'

'So how did it get here? Did it come from America?'

Mick screwed up his simian face like Steptoe from the television comedy. He wasn't sure how much to say to Brendan, but wanted to demonstrate his knowledge.

'It comes over on the QE2. Some of our boys in the States carry the stuff on to the boat without anyone noticing cause they work on it. At Southampton, they carry it off. All, of course, wearing long coats. The boys from Belfast collect it and drive the stuff to Stranraer in Scotland and take the ferry over here to Larne. It's all hidden inside coats and cars. They have done it before. Some of our lads are bringing a car or two down to Derry. That's why we need to move this stuff A.S.A.P.'

'Mick, does Cathal know about the stuff here in his cellar?'

'Of course he knows, but doesn't want to know. He hasn't seen anything, so out of sight, out of mind. This is only temporary anyway. We need to move this stuff to the dump in Lone Moor Road, the one near the graveyard in the back shed. It will be split up and some will be shifted to the dump near Cillefoyle Park.'

'We can't take it directly to Cillefoyle Park?'

'Good point, because this stuff is here I think we should move everything else out. To where I am not sure, but I want you to take the papers with you and put them in the shed in Lone Moor Road. No more meeting here, we need to get this stuff shifted around town too. Actually we have to mothball this place after we shift the stuff. Cathal isn't to be compromised especially now the elections are coming up. You take the papers, anyway. I'll sort the rest of the stuff.'

The look out, the stager Pat came running in frantically into the back lane:

'Mick, there's a Brit patrol in the street, seems just routine. I'll watch from inside.'

'We can't. The pub is locked up. We only have keys for the back yard gate and the cellar. Cathal doesn't trust us inside. Keep an eye, if they stay on the street we are okay, but if they come up the lane we might be buggered.'

Mick gave Brendan a small case. Brendan lifted it.

'It's light, Brendan, just the papers.'

Mick scoffed, his lips curled like a satisfied priest and said:

'Head out the back way, down the lane, over the little park and store the suitcase as planned. The days of this place are numbered. Cathal is starting to use the upstairs for the various groups. A great cover for all sorts of activity.'

'I heard that. I might start some Irish lessons myself. This is a handy place though. We will miss it. The back lane is very handy for the Bogside, lots of lanes and places to hide stuff. It's not overseen by the Brit watch towers on the walls.'

'God Almighty, you are fuckin' well informed. Maybe too well informed, who told you that, Brendan?'

'Sure, I have my ways.'

Before Mick, his forehead a mass of rippled contours, could articulate his scowl, Pat stuck his head in, sweat dripping from his brow.

'There's another patrol coming down from Bishop's Gate. They seem to be staying in the street.'

'Right, Brendan, you have all the documents. Hide them in the shed. Pat, you stupid eejit, are you still here? Go to the corner of the street, and stay put. We are leaving. Hang about and come back immediately if there is a problem. I'll follow Brendan in five minutes and secure down here. Go, for fuck sake! Go!'

Brendan tried to climb the cellar stairs with the suitcase, but Mick shoved it hard through the hole and it went flying out onto the yard.

Brendan bellowed something like 'it wasn't made of metal, take it easy' and went into the yard and looked out into the lane. Mick came past him and waved the 'all clear'. No one was in view. Brendan walked towards the Bogside. Mick waved again and a car across the street flashed its lights.

He walked back to the pub on the cobbled lane. The redbrick walls had seen better days, many with missing bricks and cement, leaving peep holes into the yards. Some of the wooden back gates had fresh paint and recently pointed walls, renovated by new shop owners or occupiers. Mick stood in the pub gate doorway as a Ford Cortina reversed up to the pub. The driver came into the yard, a young guy who had just joined the cell. Within minutes they had the armaments out of the cellar and into the boot. Mick had locked up and they were on their way to the dump near the City cemetery. At the end of the lane Mick saw Pat and give him a thumbs up. Pat walked off down Bishop Street. As Mick sat in the passenger seat, the driver, Sean asked what the problem was. Mick replied they were worried the pub might be raided. To Mick's right he saw Brendan walking alongside an elderly lady.

Brendan

The street in front was empty, but for an elderly lady with some shopping bags. He slung in beside her. She glanced suspiciously and he smiled, wanting to be friendly.

'What are you up to, son?'

'Oh, just coming home from Belfast and spent too much time in the pub.'

'Are ye a student?'

'Yes, I am. Where are you going?'

'Just down to the Bogside.'

'I'll walk with you then.'

'If you want,' she replied.

Brendan thought – a great cover. He saw another patrol of soldiers drive towards them. He asked her:

'Do you know where Abbotts Walk is?'

'Just keep walking on down here, down the steps and you should come to it, just ask anyone there.'

'I know. I was born here. Just wondering if you know my family.'

Brendan had asked a typical Derry question regarding family acquaintances, but hoped that from the soldiers' view it would appear as a mother and son going home and chatting. Brendan felt something was going on. Were they saturating the area? Maybe, there was a raid.

'Looks like a shower of rain?'

'Well, there's no news in that, son.'

'Are those bags heavy, would you like help?'

'Naw, son. I have the wisdom of years. I know what I am fit for. Sure that big suitcase of yours must be heavy enough?'

'It's pretty empty, I'm returning it home. Too big to keep in the flat in Belfast.'

In fact, its contents could probably have compromised some of the Derry operations of the IRA. The lady and Brendan walked together as he planned, down the slight hill where it bent at his old school, and there at the bottom was a check point. The British must have thought something was happening. A tip off, perhaps. There were just too many around for it to be a coincidence. Brendan said his goodbyes to the old lady and made his way to the steps that took him down to the Lecky Road. It would be quicker to go straight up the street in front of him, but that would leave him open. He would go through the side streets and alleys that would provide protection and a chance to hide his case, if need be. He decided it was best to stay on the streets, and could call into a house with an open door. If he went down a back alley, there might be no way out.

He made it to Lone Moor Road and went up the lane to the drop. The gate to the yard was open, and he silently placed the case in the coal shed. He threw old coal bags over it. It was to be picked up the next day.

He went back onto the main road and saw his old neighbour from his childhood days across the street, walking towards him. Brendan strode away ahead of him, not wanting to meet anyone. He turned the corner to head up the hill, towards the Cathedral; its dominance against the inky skyline gave him a stifling feeling. He felt like dipping into its dim and musky interior, but it would be locked up at that hour. He loved wandering around old churches and their graveyards. It had an atmosphere that the newer ones didn't have. The history and the people that were interred there, he believed strongly a spirit was left behind either where they spent their lives or embodied in their offspring.

To his left the empty shell of a terraced house: the front exterior exposed the gaping holes that once were the windows and doors. Inside scaffolding supported a new roof and beams supported the walls of the houses on either side. The lives lived in that little space. Others living maybe several feet away separated by a brick wall, perhaps never really getting to know each other. Yet they lived beside each other for many years. Melancholy descended upon him, like a plague of pigeons settling on the cathedral roof. He would have been moved to tears only he noticed the traffic queue in front wasn't moving.

Someone was directing the traffic at the junction. It was a soldier. Thankfully he had got rid of the stuff.

Just as he was about to turn and stroll uphill away from the soldiers, someone poked him on the shoulder. He nearly shat himself and his legs grew weak, so weak he grabbed the wall, next to him.

There before him stood his neighbour from the past.

'Are you alright? You look like you've seen a ghost.'

'Yeah, you caught me unawares. I was relaxing after avoiding those guys down there.'

'Ha, the great Brendan caught unawares. Me too, so I came up this way.'

'Where are you going?'

'Home sweet home, Brendan.'

'Me, too. Remember we used go through the graveyard when we were neighbours. Will we go through now?'

'No fuckin' way mate. I'm off home this way. The mad Brendan, you haven't changed.'

Brendan laughed, he still could create a bit of fear, just another ten minutes and he would be sitting at the kitchen table, having a beer and maybe, fry up some chips.

Allen on the Walls

Allen Wells stood on the Derry walls overlooking the heartland of Republicanism – the Bogside and the Creggan. Down below was 'The Town I Loved So Well', a well-known local song written by Derry-born Phil Coulter. Was it the town he loved so well, thought Allen, having been born here and living through those early nurturing years with his parents and extended family? He used to visit his Granny in the country on the outskirts of the city, near the Faughan River: the sweet cups of steaming tea, the cream buns served in front of her range, the kettle never off the boil, the stew in the corner, flavours mellowing in the pot, perhaps a lamb bone thrown in or an extra spud or more onions, and in the oven the daily bake, sometimes wheaten scone, sometimes a sponge cake. It wasn't that long ago when Phil Coulter also won the kitsch Eurovision Song Contest with Dana, a local schoolgirl, singing 'All Kinds of Everything' and with Cliff Richard's 'Congratulations'. All recent musical memories.

The gas yard smelt malodorous as usual, the smoking chimneys lazily lifting their exhaust fumes into the rank air blowing gently towards him and the city walls. Oh yes, that old gas yard wall. How did that song go? He certainly didn't play ball against it, but played ball against many walls and then went home in the thin rain, ran up many dark lanes and, yes, he did walk past the old jail in Bishop Street many times. Dermot Lavery worked opposite the old jail. Yes, he still loved his old city, it was his childhood memories: his parents, brother and sister, now resident in England, and of course his school and the friends he had made. In his memory, he saw the streets of women going to the shirt factories as the men walked their greyhounds. Allen hummed the tune. He just didn't want to live in it and wished that the Republicans would realise that they couldn't and wouldn't bomb people like him into a Republic.

The Creggan Estate on the far hill, the Bogside below and the Moor to the left – the cobweb of streets that were full of kids and dogs and IRA men and women yet so full of life, in apparent normality. He saw Ball Park where he used to play in soccer competitions. Now, he saw the army, his army installed, in their reinforced concrete bunkers and cages of barbed wire.

He was installed in the city, as the army was. They were on the streets and he was in the shadows. In his civvies, and one wrong move, he could be dead. He was reconnoitring for a meeting place for the

164

government officials, even possibly for the Prime Minister. There was talk that they wanted to visit and have meetings with all sides, some on the Derry walls, in the Apprentice Boys Hall. Allen was told that if they had high hopes of an IRA ceasefire, the Prime Minister's visit could be groundbreaking. There were many groups attempting to mediate. The hall wasn't neutral ground; it overlooked the Bogside, looking down on it. It was symbolic for one side of the community. They needed places to meet, important to both communities. It was what the Prime Minister wanted, but the people below might not agree with the venue.

The laden sky broke into blue patches – a distant sun threw its weak rays over Celtic Park, highlighting the plush grass of the pitch. Allen strode past the tiny church of Saint Augustine, its neat graveyard, cut and trim, the trees bare, spring buds yet to appear.

Behind him an army patrol of four soldiers in combat gear scattered across the top of the walls. Would they challenge him? He felt safe in the town of his birth. His Derry accent had never really left him; he never let it be smothered by his day-to-day Oxford English. He often went into a news agency and bought a newspaper to test his accent – the shopkeeper frequently asked if he was home on holidays from England; they could trace a rounding of his vowels and a precision at the end of his sentences. He answered by saying he was working in Belfast after a few years in England – an explanation that went unnoticed. Thousands of Northern Irish left and returned after a few years, happy to be home.

Allen had enjoyed the relative solitude of the parapet, before the soldiers arrived, the fully-enclosed city of medieval walls that was never breached. Derry, the Maiden City, with its total of eight gates, many with security barriers or check points. The soldiers ignored him and he walked down towards the river and stopped at Waterloo Gate, looking down at the locals scurrying about their business. To his right, the Castle Bar, to his left, a couple of shops: an estate agent and a wool shop.

He remembered a raid on the bar one night, a few weeks ago while he was there as an observer. Twenty soldiers had raided the place. They had information that a few of the Boys were there and had grainy photos of their targets. Most locals ignored the imposition and provided personal details, when asked, with a resigned indignation. With intelligence from Allen's unit the searchers had some idea who drank regularly in the pub on Thursday nights. Sure enough the drinkers' details matched the intelligence gathered, but the wanted men

165

were not there. A group of youngsters sat in their usual corner, four or five of them, pints of Smithwicks or Harp on the tables in front. One decided to provide flippant answers, giving his name as Charlie Chaplin. Allen remembered his name well, when he did provide it – Des. The young soldier was getting red-faced and embarrassed by this small bloke making fun of him. The brazen young lad could easily have been pulled outside, beaten up or arrested, but perhaps Allen's presence prevented it. His mates told him to wise up and provide his details as they had plans to go dancing that night and didn't want the night interrupted.

From the corner of his eye he saw another youngish man, emerge from the gateway arch in the walls underneath. He was well-dressed and looked like someone out on the town. This guy was striking, something about his strident posture, his denim coat and black jeans and shiny shoes. Allen recognised the clothes – Wranglers. The guy was too far away to see his face or eyes.

Allen wanted to see the face, but he seemed to slouch as if keeping it tight to his chest against the sharp wind. Allen stood up from leaning on the walls and noticed the guy perceptibly tighten when he saw the patrol emerge from the street opposite. But then anyone would if four soldiers in combat gear suddenly appeared. Yet they should be used to them in this town. The guy kept on walking, his slick black hair brushed back, his head averted, looking down. Just as he walked alongside the soldiers, he stepped up through a door. Damn, thought Allen. He didn't see his face, but recognised his gait. His suspicions were aroused. Why would Dermot Lavery have slipped into a door just as the soldiers went to pass him? Was he hiding something?

Allen went underneath the arch of Waterloo Gate and followed Dermot who had entered the side door of the Castle Bar. Allen followed down the steps from the Walls. Momentarily he gathered himself by the side door of the pub, unsure what was on the other side. Allen opened it and looked around. A couple of old guys sat with their half pints at the bar. He went up the narrow stairs – no one there. The barman looked at Allen.

'What can I get you?'

'Have you seen a couple of young blond girls? I am meeting them here.'

Allen lied in his best Derry accent.

'I thought I saw their brother just come in.'

'No, I haven't seen anyone come in the last half hour.'

'Thanks, maybe I got the wrong pub.'

Allen left the pub by the front door. Where had he gone? Perhaps he had called in to meet someone and they were not there so left by the same door as Allen. A simple explanation. Why had the barman lied? Maybe that's what barmen do? Dermot was a barman. Tell strangers nothing. Again, a simple explanation.

Meet in Ballymena

Conor was sitting at the bar when Dermot arrived back with a crate of mixers from the cellar.

'Can a man not get any service here?'

'What'll you have, Conor?'

'The usual, but it's not a social call. The Belfast mob wants to meet you. Nothing sinister or anything like that. They just want to put a face to the name. It will be Cathal's counterpart from Belfast. I said I would go too for a bit of support.'

'Jesus, are you serious?'

'Look Dermot, you have the support of the right people. Nobody knows. Maybe a half a dozen at the most, and some others know it's happening, but they don't know who's involved. It's all pretty secure. Go meet him and then everybody is happy.'

'Where, Conor?'

'Ballymena, of all places. Bible belt country. It saves them coming all the way to Derry, I think.'

Conor supped his pint as Dermot pondered again the consequences of Harry O'Donnell's mentioning his name to his principal. The whole thing had taken a life of its own.

'Dermot, I will phone you, when and where. I will meet you there. You don't want me with you in the car when you are travelling up there. Cathal will lend you his car and I'll buy you lunch. Can't say fairer than that.'

'Okay. Let me know the details. Let's do it!'

'I will. I'll phone you. See ya later. And don't look so worried.'

A day later Dermot got his instructions from Conor to go ahead with the meeting in Ballymena. The instructions told him where to meet and who to look for, but that they would recognise him. Dermot reckoned he had met some of the IRA from Belfast in the Inishmore pub, with their Belfast accents, and accompanied by a few of the local Boys. He generally didn't like them, cock-sure, as if they were ready to swing their six-shooters in the High Street. However, it was the head of Sinn Fein and his driver that they were going to meet in Ballymena.

The arrangements were to meet them in the Swimming Pool car park and they would go for lunch in McKinley's, and to dress like business men.

It was a bright morning after a few showers, the sun slipped through the breaking clouds, and reflected on the black glistening tarmac. As usual, Dermot made his way along the Strand Road. Harry's wife had offered him a lift, but he preferred to walk. She queried his movements at that time of the morning, as he normally didn't rise till nearer midday, after getting home late from the bar, the previous night. He told her he was stock-taking without losing his stride.

The early-morning shoppers were out – women with wicker baskets, sometimes their husband alongside, trotting down towards the city's centre. Some men walked their greyhounds, others with little white bags of baps for the mid-morning breakfast, some returning from mass, the newly-baked muffin still warm in their paper pocket. Most did not pause for a morning hello, instead gave the Derry greeting with a twitch of the head.

Before work he walked through the town to get batteries in Woolworths as he had been told by someone in the bar the previous night, they were on sale. Sometimes, he avoided the town: too many security patrols where everyone was body-searched. That really narked him at times, being touched by a pimply faced lad from Lancashire, or the East End of London. Unfortunately it was the way of life in the city. As he was body-searched, Dermot's face was as relaxed as possible, eyes to the ground, ignoring the encroachment of his personal space. He went up Waterloo St, past the Castle Bar, where he would go with a few mates for a jar after an occasional game of soccer, or across to the Gweedore Bar when he wanted some live Irish music. He had dropped into the Castle the other night, but no one was there that he knew. His favourite spot inside was against a bit of the exposed Derry walls in the Castle's snug. At the top of Waterloo Street where it joined Faughan Street, at the Castle Gate, the walls continued their imposing ramparts overlooking the Bogside and the rising hill to Creggan. Below, in the Bogside, the smoking terraced rows and the modern expanse of the newer housing in Creggan. To his right, the blocks of the Rossville Street flats. He didn't like them, but needs must and there was a resigned acceptance by some of its residents. Dermot thought the residential blocks wouldn't last long before they became unfit to live in. The flats had a special significance where a red-headed Republican named Josephine Riley and him had a delicious weekend in her abode on the top floor. He saw her once again in a pub slobbering over a big bearded bloke. Their eyes flitted several times and each time the same message: stay away.

The Castle Gate provided access through the walls and into the city centre. It had become a security check point: its thick fortification with a corrugated iron wall, sandbagged entrance and a narrow pedestrian alley that led into a darkened arcade, that created a natural shelter for its inhabitants. Further protection was provided by a heavy net of wire. A rifle protruded in a slit in the metal above their heads.

As soon as Dermot stepped into the reinforced cloister, he regretted it. A ranting paisley head-scarfed woman roared into the face of a youngster in combat green, his face red with anger and embarrassment. The tension was palpable. His comrades ready with pointed guns. The lady's extensive posterior shielded two bewildered children. The soldier confronting the hefty woman was joined by another, slightly older, with a stripe on his arm.

The officer roared two inches from her face.

'Lady, open your bags, or go back where you came from.'

Within a second she hacked up a cobweb of phlegm over the young face. The bag lady erupted into a cacophony of banshee wailing and the children pitched in with screaming howls. Snot and spittle wiped on the lady's coat as they tugged.

'You fucking bitch.'

The soldier boy used his striped sleeve to wipe his face and pushed her into an elderly man's chest, knocking out the little air in his lungs, but managed to grab Dermot for support. Two women behind joined the melee, shouting at the soldiers to leave the lady alone, and, what the hell were they doing in their country anyway and stop abusing women with children. Dermot was powerless, pinned by supporting the old man, as the two women behind crushed him in the narrow passageway. The old man was supporting the bag lady who was struggling to find her feet. Meanwhile the younger soldier panicked and raised his rifle within inches of the civilians in the little cave, as his senior bawled:

'You Fenian bastards can fuck off. I'll arrest all of you.'

More people were crowding in at the entrance and exit. A soldier managed to close the heavy reinforced door at the Bogside end. Shouts and bangs reverberated on the corrugated fence as stones pelted making any communication impossible.

A big police man appeared and stood between the lady and the two soldiers, ushering them outside as Dermot lifted the man onto some sand bags. The bag lady with the two children tootled off, still cursing the British Empire and the world, her bags unsearched. The two children skipped in front of her, unperturbed. The winded man needed to rest. The policeman, in a broad Ballymena accent, came back urging the small crowd gathered to move on. He ignored Dermot,

170

asking the old guy if he was okay. He replied he was and he sauntered off too. Like Dermot, they were glad to be free and away. The stones continued on the other side. Now Dermot knew the reason for the wire in front of these fortifications, it was to stop the stony reverberations as much as stopping more deadly fire.

Dermot walked through the Diamond, leaving the commotion behind, passing the lady who caused it, as she wiped the nose of one child, and discussed her shopping needs to no one in particular – her potential spark for deadly confrontation forgotten.

Dermot looked at Austin's tower, where one of Harry's aunts was an upholsterer and where the fateful meeting with Harry and the others had taken place. Its windows stocked with the latest spring fashions, as the locals felt the brunt end of winter, coupled with the freeze on finances, the aftermath of the Christmas celebrations.

A tartan umbrella caught his eye, an expensive-looking handle of smooth blond wood. The display in the umbrella shop window was always worth a look. Next door was the fruit and vegetable store with its round corner step, and a display window that faced sideways onto the pavement rather than onto the road.

Dermot bought a bulk pack of Everready batteries in Woolworths. They should last him all year. Unfortunately the plastic bag supplied by the perfunctory acne-faced girl, not much younger than the boy soldier, wasn't strong enough, so Dermot rolled up the bag and put it under his arm.

Some nuns came out of the convent in Pump Street and nodded to him as he walked by, maybe off to buy the value-pack batteries, he thought. Ahead lay the fifteenth-century cathedral of Saint Columb's. Its ancient walls and windows still standing, keeping out papists and ne'er-do-wells. In London Street, Harry's great grandfather had made a fine living in plumbing. Dermot tried to identify the house, but the shop fronts were all shuttered and he had forgotten the number Harry had told him.

Dermot heard a bang followed by a ping, several that sounded like ricocheting bullets, from the end of the street. He stepped into a doorway. A joint army and police patrol ran into London Street for cover. Not again, Dermot thought. A soldier gestured for him to stop and not proceed. Dermot turned, and walked back the way he came. The soldier ran up to Dermot and pushed him against the wall saying: 'Up against the wall, Paddy.'

The Geordie accent echoed in the narrow street. Dermot did as he was told: he left his batteries on the damp ground, and stood, feet apart, hands on the wall. Dermot studied the textures of the brick, its mossy-green blanket showed the lack of any sun, a permanent feature in the shadow of a narrow street. The solider bent down and pushed the bag with his rifle.

'Some ID on you, Sir?'

A Ballymena accent bellowed into his ear. Dermot produced his driver's licence.

'What's in your bag?'

'Some new batteries from Woolworths,' replied Dermot.

'You're the guy that grabbed the old man at the checkpoint. That was a good move.'

'That's right. Those old biddies fairly pack a punch.'

'If they had guns we'd be in a pile of shite.'

'Did I hear a shot?'

'No, I don't think so. Maybe a car backfiring.'

The burly policemen answered without cracking his composure. He stared at Dermot, looked into eyes, inches away from his face. Dermot smelt his sour breath and looked down at his feet and said:

'I hear the Ballymena sales are very good this year.'

'I don't know about that. I leave that to the Mrs. It's a good wee shopping town, all the same.'

Dermot broke into a widening smile as the policeman responded with an encouraging hint – 'Off you go.'

Dermot walked off at a pace, glad to get away from them, especially if some Republican boy-soldier was thinking of taking another pop shot.

'Hey, Paddy, hold on,' shouted the Geordie accent, again reverberating in the narrow street. Passersby looked around. Not again, thought Dermot, but as he turned around the British soldier had good-naturedly walked towards him, his hand held out, holding Dermot's batteries. As they met, Dermot thanked him with a 'Cheers, mate.' 'No problem,' replied the soldier. Dermot pondered whether he put on an English accent when he talked to the soldier.

After getting to the bar, Bernie, the other barman was already there. Bernie was Dermot's mentor, taught him about bar-keeping, knew everything about anybody in the city, could talk politics, greyhound racing, and football in Ireland or the UK, Gaelic, and not insult a soul. He knew when to add a word or piece of wisdom as the

172

customers told their stories, or repeated them for the 'nth' time. Importantly he kept his own counsel, called himself a Professor in the University of Life. Dermot learnt a lot from Bernie and he, like the rest, listened to the few words he spoke. Dermot pottered about, tidying up and shone more glasses.

The owner of the bar, Cathal, came in, stood at the door and nodded to Dermot to come outside.

'Are you going shopping in Ballymena?'

'Aye.'

'The car's outside. Here are the keys and bring it back in one piece.'

'Thanks, Cathal.'

Dermot got into the car, waved to Cathal and drove off. As soon as he got past Altnagelvin Hospital on the outskirts of the city, he relaxed and selected a rock music station. On a straight stretch of road he sped off and put the car through its paces – a powerful Ford Granada. He swept past cars, narrowly pulling in on time on the Glenshane Pass. On the last manoeuvre he faced an on-coming police Land Rover. He was sure he had plenty of space to overtake, but it pulled over to allow him clearance.

Dermot slowed down to the permitted speed and looked in his mirror, expecting a blue light any moment.

Nobody would be happy about bringing unwanted attention to himself, especially after making the effort themselves coming up from Belfast. Dreaded consequences spun in his head. Dermot was not usually so foolhardy.

On the mountain through Glenshane Pass, snow still covered its top and the forest's branches weighed in frozen ice. The countryside was spotted in snow, in sheltered spots and nothing moved. The roads were clear and the sky was blue.

He turned off the main Derry-Belfast road to drive through the back roads at a more leisurely pace and hopefully avoid any police coming after him. He put on a classical music station and enjoyed the barren scenery.

Dermot let the car freewheel down a little hill, when at the bottom a blue flashing light caught his eye in the mirror. Shit, thought Dermot. He slowed down to let it pass, but it stayed behind him and he slowed to twenty miles an hour, but it still stayed behind him. He drove at fifty, suitable for the country conditions, but they still were behind him.

As he turned another corner, the police flashed their lights. He pulled over at a field gate. They overtook him and parked in front, twenty feet away. It was at least five minutes before their back door opened. Four officers got out and positioned themselves at each corner of his car, guns pointing. After a further few minutes the driver's door opened, a policeman stared at the number plate and returned to the vehicle.

Dermot focused on each sweep of Beethoven's Ninth Symphony on the radio. It was an obvious ploy to intimidate or un-nerve him, but externally he was composed as if cut from stone, his eyes focused on a cow in the distance. The armed policemen stared at him while he sat in the car as relaxed as possible.

Eventually, the driver came over, the pointed guns relaxed a little and Dermot wound down the window.

'Licence, Sir?'

Dermot gave him the licence. He took it away and showed it to a colleague. Again, it was an attempt to intimidate Dermot.

'Mr. Lavery, is this your car?'

'No'

'Who owns it then?'

'My boss.'

'And who would that be?'

'Cathal McCaffrey.'

'Out please, bonnet and boot.'

'Where are you going?'

'Ballymena'

'What is the purpose of your trip to Ballymena?'

'Shopping.'

'Are there no shops in Londonderry?'

'Yes, but a friend told me McKinley's has a great suit sale.'

The police searched the car and when they finished, they all relaxed, leaning against the field's gate.

'Do you know Cathal well?'

'He is my boss. Well, I suppose I do. Enough for him to lend me his car.'

'You are a barman? Are you a Republican? Are you a Fenian? Maybe a Fenian bastard? Surely you need to be a Republican to work in a Republican bar?'

Dermot stared out across the fields, trying to resist the provocation. The policeman continued:

'If I was you I wouldn't borrow that car, and maybe get another job in a non Republican bar. You have been arrested a couple of times for a breach of the peace.'

'I was never charged.'

'We don't want any troublemakers up here. If you were a Fenian troublemaker, then you might be a big problem.'

Dermot's mind was swimming. They hadn't mentioned the improper overtaking manoeuvre so perhaps this was a different crew. He was in the middle of a country road and no one was around – he was on his own. Thankfully Conor was right, if he had come with him, it could have been very difficult and dangerous.

There was nothing in the car or on him to show the true purpose of his visit, but he would need to buy something in Ballymena, something for his return journey, in case he met the same policemen again.

By coincidence a gentleman had recommended Ballymena to shop. He lived in Perth or Fremantle in Western Australia and was back in Northern Ireland for a visit, but was from Ballymena. He was touring the country on his holidays. Dermot reckoned he was a Catholic with the ease he had wandered around Derry and the nerve to visit a local bar. He called where he lived in Australia – 'Ballymena-by-sea'. It was a conservative area, mostly white, bright and breezy, where they exported tens of thousands of sheep. In the warmer seasons, the 'Fremantle Doctor' lent a cooling breeze in the heat. He spent an hour discussing Australia with Dermot and it had further stoked Dermot's interest in the place, once again.

The police had kept Dermot waiting outside. He heard the crackle of the radio in the Land Rover and saw the driver gesture to his colleagues. They retreated into the rear of their vehicle. Dermot guessed they had something more important to do than toy with him. The driver came back to Dermot.

'We will let our colleagues in Ballymena know you are coming so they can keep an eye on you. We don't want any Fenians up there. I would borrow another car if I was you.'

The police Land Rover drove off at haste and Dermot drove off at ease, the classical radio station with a Mozart symphony in the background.

Dermot pulled into the car park of the swimming pool. He saw a couple of cars drive past, the passengers looking hard at him. He had been told to park furthest away from the door of the pool and when he

175

saw a car flash its lights he was to move as close as possible to the car. A red Ford Escort drove around the car park, flashed his lights and Dermot moved his car. The red car exited the car park. Dermot waited and placed a newspaper on the steering wheel as if reading it. He saw many drivers park and walk to the town or going into the pool.

The houses around the swimming pool had their curtains pulled or partially opened to avail of the dreary winter light. It was getting close to mid-afternoon and the temperature was dropping again. Dermot surveyed the car park as best he could. He saw a man walking towards his car in the wing mirror. The man got into the rear seat and Dermot removed the newspaper from across the driving wheel.

'So, it's Dermot, is it?'

'Yip, that's me.'

'So Dermot, my name's Jackie. What's this all about?'

'Not too sure. Are we meeting Conor?'

'We are. Let's go for lunch.'

When they found McKinley's restaurant it was emptying of the lunch-time crowd. Conor sat tucking into a lasagne and salad. The other men joined him, exchanged greetings, then went and ordered some food and sat down again.

'How did you get here, Conor?'

'Oh, Dermot, by flying carpet. No, by train.'

Dermot decided not to tell Conor about his dealings with the police. The meals arrived and Jackie started the conversation.

'Cathal has explained the situation to me. Have you met the guy yet?'

'Yes, I have.'

'And?'

'They want somebody to establish a line of communication with you lot.'

'Is he MI5 or MI6?'

'Not quite sure, but I am sure he hails from this part of the world.'

'Ballymena?'

'More from the North West by his accent, although he can switch to the English accent quickly.'

'Well, Dermot, Cathal has explained everything to me. Not many know about it and it's probably best to leave it like that. You'll keep your mouth shut, I'm sure. This is more of a courtesy call. I just wanted to meet you. Your bona fides have already been checked out. I don't think anything will come of this, but we have to start somewhere and the sooner they let us know their intention to withdraw the better. That's what I want to hear. Well, good luck, son. Conor here seems to think it's a good idea. Don't you?'

'Yes, I do. Dermot has my support.'

'Okay, that's fine.'

After a few casual comments about the weather, Jackie finished his lunch and said his goodbyes.

Dermot wondered if Jackie had come to Ballymena just to see him. That surely was a risk. Maybe he lived locally. There were Republican pockets throughout County Antrim. He decided to tell Conor about the police stopping him.

'Just as well I didn't come with you. I was thinking of going back with you, but now that's been decided for me.'

'Probably safer to go back by train Conor, for you and me. I might buy something in case I get stopped again.'

'Didn't I tell you it was just a matter of them meeting you? The rest is up to you now. Okay, see you later.'

'Fair enough. See you in the pub sometime.'

Dermot relaxed when Conor left. The restaurant was part of McKinley's clothing store and Dermot went down into the store and had a look at the sale items. He bought a shirt and drove back to Derry without incident.

Harry meets Johnny

The bus from Strabane stopped at the end of the Craigavon Bridge. A prosperous-looking middle aged man got off in front of Harry and Johnny, wearing a black coat almost to his ankles, and strode off goose stepping in time with his fine black umbrella, precisely wrapped. Harry and Johnny had just met on the bus from Strabane . They watched the man with a burnished wooden umbrella handle that shone like his black shoes. Harry didn't notice much about his face except the firm fortitude in his eyes. The man waited at the traffic lights with them until the bus passed and when the lights changed he crossed and walked up Spencer Road. Harry and Johnny went in the opposite direction, over the bridge.

Their eyes followed the man walk up the street opposite, his erect posture and precise gait, in time, with his umbrella. He looked like a pall bearer at a funeral, or dressed like an Orange man who marches on the Twelfth of July, but without his sash, when the Protestants of Northern Ireland celebrate the Protestant King William's battle over the Catholic King James in 1690. Harry wondered if he was part of the British establishment, as he would not have been out of place around Whitehall in London. Johnny said he envied the man's surety, he seemed to have someplace to go, something important to do, so confident, so intent. Perhaps that's what comes with age, with responsibilities, with a job and a family, with experience, Harry suggested. They both decided he was probably a very senior bank manager.

Johnny seemed to have been preoccupied during the journey so Harry guessed he had something serious on his mind. Harry told Johnny a little about himself, being a teacher, but having spent a lot of time in Strabane and Lifford visiting his relatives on his mother's side. He loved taking the bus, as he did as a child. Johnny knew some of his relatives. The real purpose of Harry's trip was to buy his wife a birthday present, but he had failed to purchase a suitable gift. Marie had gone to Belfast for shopping with their daughter and had taken the family car. Harry had visited his aunt, and had stayed overnight with her. Harry's mother was from Lifford, so Harry walked there from Strabane to visit some cousins, across the hump-back bridge, as he had done many years ago.

The two men had discussed their recent family Christmases and Johnny had mentioned his mother got her Christmas tree from the

Abercorn Estate – the Duke of Hamilton's residence. Johnny told Harry he didn't like the idea of buying a tree from the landed gentry. Harry agreed that the Hamiltons had close ties with the English royal family. One of them, possibly the third Duke of Abercorn, had been the godson of the King and the Unionist Member of Parliament of Derry in the early part of the twentieth century. Johnny corrected him – 'you mean Londonderry.' They both laughed.

Harry told Johnny that his family, the O'Donnells, may be connected to the Hamilton family. The story he was told was that Samuel's brother was a music teacher and had tutored one of the Hamilton daughter's. They fell in love and one day they eloped. He didn't know what happened to them after that. It was said that the Duke was canvassing in London Street where Samuel O'Donnell had his plumbing shop. Of course, Harry said, in those days the voting process was gerrymandered – even though the Catholics were a majority in the city they were never a majority in the local council. Most Catholics lived in the South Ward, having only eight seats. The North had eight and the Waterside had four where most of the Protestants lived so they had the most seats.

As Samuel O'Donnell owned property he could vote. The Duke of Hamilton asked Samuel for his vote as they were related.

The Duke had another daughter Cynthia, the grandmother of a certain Lady Diana.

Johnny asked:

'So you have royal connections?'

'This is not a city to advertise them, is it?'

'Maybe at this British Army checkpoint, Harry? That would be okay. I hate being searched.'

'I am not too fond of it myself, Johnny.'

While the aristocratic roots of the family's Christmas tree troubled Johnny it was the checkpoint on the bridge that Harry noticed Johnny's nervousness. Steeling their nerve, they walked gingerly towards the city. There was a queue at the sandbagged checkpoint, a soldier inside pointing his rifle at every one, following the walkers on the bridge – his face unseen, only a dark shadow within. The soldier outside checked bags and did occasional body-searches nonchalantly, barely registering the people he searched. Like most locals they looked towards the river or their feet as they approached the deadpan soldier. They needn't have feared. They were waved through.

Johnny had told Harry he was going to see some man in the Inishmore Bar in Bishop Street, but he wasn't sure where it was. Harry suggested he would be happy to show him as he was going that way and didn't mind the long walk from Craigavon Bridge to home via the bar. Johnny readily accepted and pointed out:

'I always liked the old-fashioned lamps on this bridge. The fancy balustrade, all painted up.'

'Yeah, it's a nice bridge. I love looking at the river too, from the middle of it, especially if it is a sunny day, like today. The sun reflects off the water onto the windows on the riverside factories. It's very sparkly. Look over there, the rippling water. There, see the stars weaving off the currents. But it's a fast river and dangerous. The currents are well known for their danger. See that swirling? That's evidence of a fast current, but often it can be just as dangerous under a calm surface.'

Harry answered, as the blue sky reflecting on the water provided a summery glint. The cyan-mottled waterway snaked its way towards Lough Foyle. He leaned over the railings on the side of the bridge, glancing at the river sweeping underneath.

Johnny paused and leaned over too, looking at the river. The winter morning was clear and crisp. Johnny recited:

'Earth hath not anything to show more fair
All bright and glittering in the smokeless air.
Never did sun more beautifully steep
In his first splendor, valley, rock, or hill;
Ne'er saw I, never felt, a calm so deep!
The river glideth at his own sweet will:
Dear God! The very houses seem asleep;
And all that mighty heart is lying still!'

'I am very impressed, Johnny. That was lovely. Where did you learn that?'

'I learnt the poem in school, at Saint Columb's College. I remember my teacher making a fuss about the romantic poet William Wordsworth's unusual poem based in a city – On Westminster Bridge rather than some pastoral scene.'

Harry was astonished Johnny remembered so much of the poem. He told Harry that reciting the words always calmed him. He recited it any time he was nervous. Johnny talked about how much he enjoyed the beauty of a sparkling river and how very exciting it was when as a small boy he enjoyed watching the River Mourne flood in Strabane, the never-ending rain producing a torrent – trees and sometimes, an unfortunate cow, getting caught under the bridge in the deluge. On nice days, he would drop a twig on one side of the bridge and dash to the other to see it float on the current toward Lifford. Harry told him he remembered seeing houses and shops flooded in Strabane on television.

They discussed the trip to Derry from Strabane, Johnny's journey to school, the same one he had taken with Harry on the bus. He walked across the old bridge, over the river most days to catch the school bus to Derry. The boys were all dazed in the morning, a sleepy stupor as the little villages of Ballymagorry, Maheramason and New Buildings passed by through the condensation on the windows. The River Foyle flowed alongside the carriageway after New Buildings, where a wintry mist sometimes hovered above the river and created a mystical world. He told Harry it was like entering another world, an escape from every day, but his dread of certain school teachers, in a place he mostly detested, brought him back to reality. In the afternoon, going back to Strabane, the noisy rabble, it was all chat to their fellow pupils.

'You are a very thoughtful sort of person, Johnny? Are you okay?'

'I think so. To be honest it reminds me of going to school and getting a certain teacher when I hadn't done my homework. I knew then I would be strapped. I am seeing a man who owes me money. Well, it's my father's money and we need it. I think there could be a bit of bother. I think he is one of the Boys.'

'Is that who you are meeting in the pub?'

'Yes.'

'Well, I know the barman there. If he is there, you should be okay. His name is Dermot.'

They left the river and walked up Abercorn Road to Bishop Street. Johnny thanked Harry for his company and for taking him to the pub even though he was familiar with the city streets, having taken the same route to school for years. He told Harry plenty of Strabane people worked in Derry. The Derry Road was littered with people looking for lifts. Buses left packed with workers and school children on the thirty-minute run to the big smoke. As a child, he told Harry, he pestered his parents to go on the famous Derry Walls every time they visited for shopping. When he was a bit older they would allow him to walk there on his own, while they shopped.

There was much banter between the citizens of both places. Harry agreed and Johnny told Harry the old joke – the best thing about Derry was the road to Strabane.

Johnny explained further to Harry about what was worrying him. His opponent for the day was a Michael Toal. Harry wondered if that was the same guy as Dermot's arch-enemy. Johnny's mother had told him to go to the Inishmore pub on Bishop Street, just outside the walls and she also told him that he was related to the owner of the pub, but that was not unusual as the city of Derry was full of people related to each other, like his mother, mostly immigrants from Donegal. Recently his father's drinking and gambling had mushroomed and his mother found it difficult to make ends meet. Johnny was coming to Derry, to a pub, to meet a man he didn't know, to collect money. Two hundred pounds, money owed to his father for work rendered, according to his mother. Johnny suspected it could be more likely a gambling debt. Harry was beginning to doubt his offer of walking him to the pub, as Johnny seemed to have a big problem and it could get ugly. The story Johnny told had a serious possibility for violence and Harry didn't want to be caught in the middle of it.

His mother, Johnny continued, that morning had been in a tough mood, and was not one to argue with. Most days she was fairly easy going. She would need to be, he said, to be married to his father. Despite his father's faults, his parents loved each other, but his father's earning capacity was getting less and less, and money was becoming intermittent. His father had been on an alcoholic bender in the recent days. It was the breaking point that resulted in an almighty row. Johnny saw the fear in his mother's eyes and in a fit of uncontrollable shaking she ordered Johnny to Derry to get the money. She needed the money.

Harry thought he was ready for a drink after that, and that Johnny was right to be worried. Having found the pub, they looked inside before entering. They stepped through the door, their eyes adjusting to the dimness of the room, to see a solitary man sitting at the bar, nursing a glass of beer.

Dermot was lighting the fire when they came in.

'My God, Harry O'Donnell. You, in a pub at this time of day. What would Marie say? Disgraceful. What brings you here? Is it to do with you know who?'

'No, no. This man, Johnny, sorry I don't know your second name, is looking for Mick Toal.'

'God help him then. No idea where he is, sorry.'

182

'I have made an appointment to see him here this morning. Can I wait?'

'Sure, make yourself comfortable by the fire. It will get going soon.'

Harry and Dermot moved to the bar. Harry explained quietly what Johnny wanted as he had a lemonade. Dermot told him it sounded like trouble. As Harry left he went over to Johnny and wished him luck, waved to Dermot and left to walk home to Cillefoyle Park.

Dermot helps Johnny

Johnny waited by the fire. Dermot asked if he wanted a drink, but Johnny declined.

'I am making some tea, do you want a cup? It's on the house.'

'Sure. That's kind of you.'

Dermot came out with tea and toast for the customer at the bar, and a cup for himself and Johnny.

'I have to provide some breakfast for your man over there otherwise he won't have anything in his stomach. Did Mick say what time he would be here?'

'No, just sometime this morning.'

An hour later Mick and Brendan came in. Johnny stood up and Mick nodded for him to go out the back. Dermot followed and stood listening, out of sight at the rear door. When they got into the yard, Mick pinned Johnny to the urinal wall, and Brendan stood alongside his mate.

'Look, Strabane man, best advice I can give you is to leave now. I don't have your money. I might get it next week, next month. Come back next month. Better still don't come back at all.'

'You owe my father two hundred pounds. I am not leaving until I get it. I would also advise you to take your hands off me.'

'Your father lost the money on the Lifford dogs. He's a no hoper; he was pissed as a newt. I suggest you just go away now and we'll not say a word.'

Johnny pushed Mick into Brendan causing a crate of empty beer bottles to crash onto the yard and glass to splinter everywhere. Dermot jumped over the steps at the door and saw Mick land a glancing blow into Johnny's chest, but Johnny gave a right hook to Mick's cheek. To Dermot's eyes it looked like a right hook that was practiced in the boxing ring and it caused Mick once again to land on Brendan.

The smashing bottles brought the only customer to see what was happening, he stood at the door for a second and then retreated into the bar. As Mick and Brendan attempted to get Johnny, who had grabbed a shovel for his defence, Dermot stepped between.

'Enough of this shit. Look at the state of the place.'

'Fuck off, Dermot. This has nothing to do with you.'

'Calm down Mick. You don't want to do this. What's it all about anyway?'

'Fuck off, you dumb socialist barman bastard.'

Mick tried to circumvent Dermot and dived to his side to get at Johnny. But Dermot managed to push him and he fell against another crate of bottles. Brendan stood waiting, unsure what to do.

Cathal came in the back gate, pushing Johnny and Dermot in his path.

'What in under Jesus is going on?'

'Dermot's putting his big nose into our business again.'

Mick blubbered, holding his side of his face, a reddening purple developing under his hand.

'And who the hell are you? You can leave that shovel down.'

'I am here to collect my money from Mick.'

'He is causing problems. He's from Strabane. What do you expect from Strabane bastards?'

'Cathal, I came out here to find these two fighting with this fella from Strabane. I tried to stop it.'

'Okay, Brendan and Mick, with me now, in my office. You, Strabane man. What's your name?'

'Johnny Carlin.'

'Are you anything to Eileen Carlin?'

'She's my Mum.'

'Holy God, don't you move. I'll get to the bottom of this in a minute.'

Mick and Brendan went with Cathal to the office. Johnny and Dermot went inside the pub and came out with yard brushes. There was much shouting from Cathal. After five minutes Cathal came out, told Dermot to return to his duties and told Johnny to go into the bar. Cathal sent Mick and Brendan into the yard to clean up the place and called Johnny into the office. By the time Johnny had come out, the other two had left by the back gate. Johnny left by the front door after thanking Dermot for his help and as he left Dermot called to him 'There's always someone ready to throw a brick at a stranger, in your case a Strabane man'.

Cathal came out of the office and said to Dermot as he left:

'That Strabane boy is my cousin's son. I have given him a job.'

'Hope it's not mine.'

Walkabout

It was the usual lazy Sunday morning, found everywhere with breakfast and newspapers in bed or a local cafe. Dermot liked to have his breakfast in bed, but hated the ink deposited on his fingers by the cheap printing, consciously avoiding rubbing it on his sheets. If he had money he would always have clean sheets every day, crisply made-up every single day.

This was the city he liked: quiet, subdued, friendly. The obscured sun on the ill-kept streets - an ideal time to walk down the memory lane, of his childhood, after his languid breakfast on a Sunday on his way to work. He already twisted his head in familiar greetings a few times, grateful the pedestrian traffic was light and remotely familiar. Small-town life was familiar, but sometimes the unfamiliar happened and became embedded memories. Anyway, he had buckets of memories, perhaps too many, perhaps too heavy to carry in the future.

It was a dry afternoon, shortly after midday. The weak sun attempted to warm the streets and their occupants in the city. Dermot was on a mission, as if he had a bus to catch. He needed to be there, his old street, his playground of yesteryear. Those days seemed endless, the summers long and full of play, the years folded into one melancholic haze. He wondered how had it happened, how did it come to this, caught in the middle of surreptitious deeds? He was happy in the nostalgic glow of childhood and didn't let himself dwell too much on the present and recent past. These were his streets, his memories.

He touched Mrs. Brown's windowsill, still painted cherry red. The line of terraced houses, front doors directly onto the street, twenty of them, were opposite sets of semis with their prim little gardens. Most were cemented with a bush in the centre, The O'Callaghan's at the end of the row, was slightly bigger, better kept, a neat privet hedge around the tidy garden, shiny black gate, and irises in their window box.

Dermot was a familiar figure, often seen walking the streets, spotted gazing down the 'bankin' – the sloping space littered with cardboard and decimated bushes, the communal playground of his childhood. Nothing pleased him more than taking visitors over these old stomping grounds, mixing the city's history with his own. Indeed, because of his local knowledge, old neighbours and others asked him to give their visitors – relatives and tourists from England, USA or even Australia – a tour of the city. What charmed Dermot the most was the recognition that he was one of them – a local.

Dermot glanced at his grandmother's door, and her neighbour's, both now occupied by other families. Next door to his Granny's, where he had spent many childhood summers was once occupied by the McCaffrey's. He stood staring at the houses, lost in melancholy thought, when the neighbour's door opened, and out hopped a young man in a three-piece navy suit, white shirt, purple tie, hair carefully cut to collar length, but enough of it to hide his ears. He almost stumbled over Dermot, but quickly recovered and with the Derry twist of the head, acknowledged Dermot before climbing into his dark blue Ford Capri. The McCaffrey's, his other family, was home to his playmates – Conor and Cathal. He was treated as one of them, even had a bath with them and slept over regularly. Now Cathal, Conor and he were in the middle of a clandestine project. Dermot feared this was one of the last times for his walk to their old stomping ground.

Across the road, the Quinn's gate opened, a boy of no more than eight dashed up the street, ignoring his surrounds. Another man on a mission, thought Dermot. On the same gate, Dermot and his childhood friends, Conor and Frank had swung, a pleasurable micro-second of a memory. Dermot was fascinated that it always shut itself. The gate was positioned with a slope and closed naturally, a piece of rubber prevented it from clanging. Despite all its rough treatment the gate never broke, at least not in Dermot's memory.

No doubt Paddy Malone, another neighbour who never left the house, would be sitting at home, watching daytime television, a big brutish fellow that had tormented Dermot's childhood and many others until he fell off a coal-shed roof three streets away. He never really recovered. Dermot remembered his dog, a fevered hairless thing that had lived on the street. Oftentimes since then, he would stand at his front door, watching, his eyes desolate, but reflecting his frustration at his unfortunate fate.

People used to stand at their doors: smoking, gossiping, watching children playing outside, the usual squealing and running, adults chastising the kids, a child crying somewhere, often pacified with a sugar-coated slice of white bread. One summer before Dermot came to Derry on holidays, when he lived in Scotland, a child had died on this street and when he came over, no children had been allowed outside for almost a week. They played inside or their yards until frustrated parents' patience wore thin and the kids reclaimed the street again. The dead child had come from another street, a milk cart had reversed into him. Speculation had the boy hanging on its back, as was the custom, and falling off under its back wheel. The street was seen as relatively safe for playing children as one end of the street narrowed into a lane.

Dermot passed the large stone wall and entered the thin lane, the wall topped with barbed wire to keep out the unwanted. The joke was that the wire ensured its daily occupants on the other side of the wall stayed in – it was a reputable school.

Behind the wall was a fortified Round Tower, centuries old. Here Dermot would gather his tourists and display his motley history of the city. Some of the neighbours came out to listen; however, one neighbour, the recalcitrant Mr. Morgan would correct Dermot on some piece of historical detail, or grammatical error, or add some piece of fact, insisting on its importance. Sometimes, Mr. Morgan was right.

Dermot touched the wall, spread both palms on the cool damp stones. He felt at home. Girlfriends had been brought here, up the dark lane. He kissed them with his back against the wall at his favourite spot – the flattest bit. Determined youngsters climbed it, often after being dared. Numerous times they got stuck and Mr. Morgan's ladder was retrieved to bring the stuck child down. The children thought he was always grumpy and borrowing the ladder was an excuse for the children to irritate him and amuse themselves. Eventually Mr. Morgan got rid of the ladder, he got fed up with the nuisance of being asked.

The wall provided security for a ball, however, being so uneven, the ball ricocheted everywhere. Cricket and football were played up against it. The gable wall of the last house in the street, owned by a crotchety old spinster, sometimes got a thumping. Luckily, she was deaf. This was an inner-city street. It seemed bleaker, despite the brighter paintwork that had illuminated some of the houses, less lived-in, the cars parked on either side of the street leaving little room for the kids to play. During his childhood many families moved to the suburbs with their modern houses and gardens. Sometimes the street looked the same as his memories – the wall, dark and damp, where the sun never shone. The walk down memory lane was becoming more memory and less of a walk as the city landscape changed.

He drew deeply from the well of memories, of his life in those streets of his childhood. They possessed security and belonging. The dank streets under the oppressive sky, his current life and work, while providing meaning, really imprisoned him. He yearned for expanse, for freedom, for an endless sky, for boundless opportunity.

Dermot stood with his back to the wall, looking at the slate sky, and up the street, devoid of playing children, it looked rather sad. He glanced at his watch and realised it was time to get to work. As he turned into Bishop Street he saw Frank with a few of his street friends who appeared to be drinking. Dermot took a side street to his pub.

Robbery

'I am fed up waiting for those bastards to tell us what to do and give us our pocket money. We are volunteers. We deserve a wage. Instead we get a pittance, at their pleasure. I fancy a new coat and jeans. Wranglers from Mc Laughlin's in Strabane or maybe we take the bus to Belfast for the craic.'

'I know what you are saying mate, but we do what we do. We will just have to wait until a big job comes up and we'll get paid for it. We have to just wait and see. The Rosemount Post Office job might turn up. We have been scouting that place for ages. Something must be going happen. Do they plan to rob it or what?'

'Brendan, as I say, you dumb twat. We are on wee jobs, just message boys. That bollockin' Cathal gave us, said it was our final warning. He was not going to protect me any further. Who the fuck does he think he is? My family and them before my grandparents have a history of Republicanism. I am blue-blood Republican, with my pedigree. I should be a unit commander, not a message boy, a gofer, for Jesus sake.'

'Mick, blue blood is the Royal Family, and Jesus, you are not one of them. Are you?'

Brendan started to laugh, but saw Mick's anger rising in his reddening cheeks and ceased his amusement before Mick thumped him, as he had done on previous occasions. Mick roared:

'Blue blood, damn the blue blood. It's green blood racing through my veins, and don't you doubt my loyalty to the movement! It's solid, it's forever. Not a doubt!'

'I'd never doubted it for a minute, Mick, me oul son, but we are who we are and you'll get promoted soon enough.' Brendan offered in a way of calming the fury in front of him. He didn't want a punch in the face just because Mick wanted to vent his frustrations.

'I know, I know, but it's not soon enough and we need some money. He said I was bringing disrepute to the Movement. Fuck him!'

'Let's steal some Mick.'

Mick stared into Brendan's face, squinting his eyes like one of those bubble-eyed dogs, his face contorted like a child trying to open a bag of sweets. His arms raised as Brendan readied himself for defence, but, instead Mick grabbed Brendan by the shoulders and hugged him. Brendan turned red in the confusion.

'Jesus, Brendan you surprise me at times. We have been scouting the post office. We know the routine. Let's do it. We'll disguise ourselves; wear one of those Mickey Mouse masks. Nobody will know.'

'You are crazy. If they find out they will kill us. Kneecap us. Don't fuck around with them. We have already got too many warnings. We are on our last warning.'

'Nobody will know. We know the job like the back of our hand. They must have expected something big to happen. We might be lucky and grab something big. We should get thousands. Nobody would know. The plans are in place. We have cased the joint loads of times.'

'We couldn't, we couldn't. They would know. It would be a disaster, Mick. Someone would recognise us and if we were caught we would be dead men walking.'

'We'll plan it to a tee. We already know the routine, the plans, everything we know – the escape routes, the delivery of the money, could be thousands? I think Woolworths do the masks. They have a fancy-dress section. No one will know. We will spend it quietly, out of town, not show off. Head off to Belfast or Donegal and spend a couple of days, say we are visiting relatives. Just don't spend it here in Derry, in the pubs. We will go on the tear in Dublin. Yer man, your mate, whatever his name, lives in Galway. We will go down there for a few days, then onto Dublin. Need to wait a few weeks before we go off and the heat dies off.'

'My Uncle Brendan, my godfather and the man I was named after, lives in Manchester.'

'Once again Brendan, my wit and wisdom is rubbing off me and onto you. Brilliant idea. Don't fancy those Brits though.'

'He's the president of some Irish Club. We could mix with them. Me Ma is always telling me to visit him. He's always asking about me. Don't know him from a bar of soap. It could work if we went there for a while. Let's sort out a plan.'

'Brilliant Brendan, me oul son. We could say we are off to Manchester for a week or two. He's dying or something. And visit Galway and Dublin. Isn't there a ferry to Holyhead or something? You are just brilliant.'

Mick needed Brendan to agree, be part of it and help him with the plan. The plans were already in place for a robbery by the IRA, but had never been given the go-ahead. He thought it was possible that they may be suspected, but with cunning and careful planning they could get away with it. Mick and Brendan could plan to be in Buncrana and be seen by someone known to everyone, their alibi. A couple of the lads lived down there and could give them an alibi. They could say they were in Buncrana, be seen there the previous evening and come up to Derry during the night. After doing the robbery in Derry, they could go back there. Ideas were flowing around Mick's head, the more he thought about it, the simpler it seemed. They could get a car and be over the border in no time. They could disguise themselves and return on the Buncrana bus, pretending to sleep so no one would talk to them. Nobody would know. They would split in Buncrana, be seen in a few pubs for a day or two and get the bus back, stashing the proceeds for a few weeks and then off to Galway or Manchester or wherever.

They met in Mick's sister's house to plan the possible day and details for the robbery, as Mick had arranged to baby-sit his nephew. According to their information the social security cheques and family allowance money were usually delivered on a Thursday morning. Sometimes there was a queue of people waiting for the post office to open. A lane opposite could provide them a little cover and an escape route, and they would rob the place early as soon as the queue had reduced. Mick would buy the masks in Woolworths and escape up the lane they came from, then dump his mask and hoodie and get the bus to Buncrana or get a car. Brendan would lift a gun from the Cillefoyle Park dump and return it immediately after the heist. His escape route would be down a lane into Northland Estate, in the opposite direction of Mick, and hide the money in his elderly Aunt's coal shed in the estate. After putting the gun back in the dump he would get the bus to Buncrana or meet Mick and travel over by car. When they felt it was safe to do so, they would take the money and go on holiday.

On the chosen Thursday morning, a week later, Brendan picked up the gun from the dump in Cillefoyle Park. It was in an old overgrown toilet at the bottom of a garden that was neglected and unused. The access was through a hole in the hedge from the lane, and the old waterless cistern contained hand guns and ammunition. It caused much laughter amongst the volunteers that knew about it – they went to have a dump to stash or pick up arms.

The damp, dreary morning saw a queue of old-aged pensioners line up and Mick scanned the group to ensure there would be no threat to challenge them. The security van came early at eight-thirty with a police escort. They delivered the goods and left quickly. One problem was that the police patrolled the Post Office frequently on Thursdays. Generally, they would return almost immediately after opening time and then come back within half an hour to an hour. Before they came back, then was the time to rob the place.

At nine thirty-five, Brendan walked across to the Post Office, a small queue of customers were inside. He nodded over to Mick. They both entered wearing Mickey Mouse masks. Mick shouted while Brendan blocked the door and waved the gun.

'IRA. Stay calm and nobody will get hurt.'

An old lady fainted. Mick was pleased as that kept some of the customers occupied. Brendan pointed the gun at the grey-haired female server while Mick told her:

'See that gun, Lady. It's pointed at you. Don't be nervous and we won't be and nobody will get hurt. Now dump everything from the safe in there, and I mean everything because we know what should be there. If you don't then someone might get hurt. All of it from the safe.'

Mick shoved an empty black bag under the counter hatch while holding on to it. He now shouted angrily three times, 'For fuck sake, fill it or somebody will get hurt'. It was filled with money and cheques. Mick and Brendan were out of the Post Office in several minutes. There was no car for their getaway. Both ran to their escape routes. The street was quiet.

Mick ran up the lane and walked down a side street to Creggan devoid of mask and hoodie top, dumped at the bottom of someone's bin in the lane.

Brendan went down the lane towards the estate and shoved his mask and hoodie in the bag with the money. Within five minutes he was at his aunt's house. He went through the back lane and her rear gate and took the hoodie with mask wrapped inside out of the bag. The gun was in his waist band. On the way to Cillefoyle Park he dumped the jacket and mask at the bottom of someone's bin. All was normal in the streets of the Estate. He jerked a second when he heard a police siren and crossed Park Avenue to the lane alongside Cillefoyle Park. He noted no unusual activity in the streets. Five minutes later he placed the gun in the cistern and walked down the Rock Road to get the bus to Buncrana.

Mick walked towards Creggan, but a security check point at the Rosemount roundabout made him double-back. He went into Brooke Park, a thoroughfare to Northland Road. He walked through the park, a few people were there, some like him using it as a short cut, an elderly man walking his white dog. He noticed a queue of cars at the bottom gate, maybe stopped for a security check point, so he went to the park's side gate, but that was shut. He ventured on to the bottom gate. Everyone was being stopped – cars and pedestrians. The security forces had been alerted to the news of the robbery. Two more army Land Rovers appeared and soldiers flooded the streets. It was too late to turn back into the park as that would bring attention to himself. All the cars were being searched, the pedestrians were being body searched and identified via a radio check. Mick was third in the queue for searching. At his turn to be searched, Mick held out his arms and produced a driving licence. The soldier casually searched him until he checked his name by radio, and immediately he nodded to another soldier who came to stand behind Mick. The soldier said:

'Up against the wall, stay there, mate.'

A few minutes later a police Land Rover came down the middle of Northland Road, lights flashing. Two burly police officers grabbed Mick and placed him into the back of the vehicle. Mick was arrested.

At the station he was led to an airless interrogation room, with one table and four chairs. He had been sitting there for what seemed like hours and questioned twice about his involvement with the IRA and the robbery. The first time was casual and friendly.

The second time he got a smack on his face that knocked him off his chair and pinned him against the corner, his arm up his back, his hair pulled back. He expected that treatment. He said nothing.

The final interview, a thin policeman, friendly with red cheeks, talked about his arrest record showing him what they had on him. This time, the policeman said he was spotted by a patrol coming out of the post office and going up a lane. It was the one he had planned as an escape route. They had produced the mask and hoodie that he had worn on the robbery, all displayed in plastic bags in front of him. He was going to prison, he said, and not leaving the station. He was caught.

Mick wondered if he had been followed, or more likely, someone had given the police information and spotted him putting the stuff in the bin. Maybe the police had worked out the same escape plan as him and searched the bins. It was possible they just searched the surrounding streets and found the stuff in a bin, but if a person saw him they would be too scared to give evidence against the IRA. The policeman was conciliatory:

'Look son, we have you. Admit it, you will get five years, serve three with your comrades in prison. Although I don't think this was an

IRA robbery. We could keep you away from your people. Tell us who your partner was and you will serve less. Make no mistake, you are going down. IRA membership at least. Armed robbery. You were spotted. The evidence is in those bags. Sit here and think about it. I'll be back.'

Mick wished he smoked because they offered him a pack of cigarettes. His alibi for the robbery was blown. He wasn't in Buncrana, in the pubs, seen drinking with mates and fellow Republicans who live down there. It was up to Brendan to give him his cover, if he got out of police custody. He was a dead man walking if the IRA caught him, therefore he desperately needed Brendan to give him an alibi.

He was allowed to go to the toilet and afterwards a detective with an English accent came in with a Kit Kat and a bottle of Fanta.

'Hi Mick, you remember me?'

'Sure, you asked me to tout the last time I was in here. I told you to fuck off and still do.'

'I am Ben. I want to tell you straight the dire position you are in. Okay? I am being honest with you and you, Mick, are in a pile of shite. Sinn Fein's Cathal McCaffrey has condemned the robbery, outside the Post Office to the local radio. He said it was a crime against the community. What he means, Mick, is his comrades in IRA/Sinn Fein didn't get their dole today because of you. When he condemns the robbery so quickly I think it wasn't an IRA job, so Mick, you were a solo enterprise. You and the other Mickey Mouse. Was he a member too?'

'Do you think you can bribe me with a Fanta and a bar of Kit Kat?

'Can I Mick? Christ, that would be magic.'

Ben laughed.

'Look Mick, we have had this chat before. It was only a matter of time before we met again. You have put yourself in a dangerous corner and I can help you out. Prison, or work for us. I don't think you can survive out there anymore. We will release you pending further enquires. Some of my colleagues you met today would be happy to hand you over to your comrades, letting them know you provided information to us. Could you survive in prison? I doubt it. They have ways of getting at you. I suppose we could send you to England to serve your time. What about your wife?'

Someone came in and signalled Ben to come out. Mick was left on his own again to his own thoughts. When Ben returned a little later he had a charge sheet with Mick's record and some photographs.

'Look at this, Mick. Who wants you now? You are known to us. You are known as a petty criminal to the IRA. You have been warned by them to keep your nose clean. You have robbed a post office against the wishes of your organisation.'

'What are you offering me? A year's supply of Kit Kats and Fanta?'

'Very funny. Well, let's see your options. One: prison. That is a cert. If your friends believe you are not touting, not involved in the robbery, then you can languish for five years in Long Kesh surrounded by all those you love so well. Two: co-operate on this robbery and we could put you in a prison in England. Maybe, make a new life with family there, after you get out. They still might be after you. Co-operate even further and we will look after you. After you give evidence, we will resettle you, in Canada, Australia or England if you prefer. You and your family. New name. New start.'

'I can't. I can't.'

'Think about it. We will release you now. Give you forty-eight hours to think about it. If the Boys catch you, what will happen to you? What about your young family? We can get them out at five minutes notice. We can get you out in five minutes too. You have few options, Mick! Look at these photos.'

'That's Brendan Donahue. He is here and here and here. He did this job with you, didn't he? Will he squeal on you?'

Ben showed Mick some grainy black-and-white photographs, some from afar, and some close up.

'We have you Mick, so do your mates. They won't like this. It wasn't sanctioned by your mates in the IRA, wasn't it? As I say, we are letting you go. Will you escape their wrath or my colleagues wrath? I have a way out for you.'

'When do you need to know?'

'Sooner rather than later, Mick. I am saying this for your own safety. The IRA didn't sanction this robbery, did they?'

'Maybe.'

'You are in bother, son. I can help. How long will they take to work it out it was you and Brendan?'

Mick tried to show little reaction to the question. He thought Ben was guessing.

'My belief is the IRA will deny they did the robbery when Sinn Fein came out so quickly to condemn it. It wasn't sanctioned, Mick. I know it. You know it. You are caught. So is Brendan. You could run across the border, but for how long? They will catch you. There will be no safe place for you across the border. With your history, the Gardai will be watching you. We will supply all the information to them, there will be no escape.'

'That's mighty nice of you.'

'It's not me, Mick. It's the rest of the mob here. If you agree with my offer, I can protect you. I can get you and your family to a safe place. Once everything is taken care of, you can settle somewhere nice. Does Bondi Beach sound good?'

Mick stared at him. He knew it could be a way out, but didn't want to let Ben know that he was on the verge of accepting their offer.

'What about money? Can you give me a down payment for thinking about it?'

'Sorry, Mick. You give me something nice now, a little morsel and I'll give you something in return. Confirm Brendan was with you on the robbery and I'll give enough for two week's supply of Fanta and Kit Kats. Sure, don't you have the money from the robbery?'

Mick knew if he did that he would be a tout immediately, no going back. It would be too dangerous. He had stepped over the line. If the Boys knew about the robbery he would be kneecapped or exiled to the Republic or America, but maybe could come back. His wife could visit him there. This was his last warning from the IRA, from Cathal. If the RUC decided to brand him a tout and he was blamed for the robbery, the 'nuttin' squad' could do more than just kneecap him. Brendan was a weak link too. He needed to get outside to think straight. There would be a little time, before the IRA put two and two together. It was just bad luck that he ran into the army patrol. He had talked himself out of bad situations before, he could do it again. If he touted he would end up dead. For robbing the post office he might get kneecapped, but he had history and was on his last warning, could be something worse. His uncle Cathal kept telling him he was protecting him but time had run out.

'Here's my number. Call me any time? Get rid of the card soon. Memorise the number. Just ask for me, Ben. Just say I am coming home. We will sort out the rest.'

'What about my family?'

'We will get them out immediately. Gotta go, bye Mick.'

Mick was taken in a car and released in Aberfoyle Crescent. He immediately went to his sister's house, opened a bottle of beer and pretended to be drunk and fell asleep. He slept uneasily on the living room couch. In the morning he went to his home to see his wife.

'You look as if you haven't slept all night.'

'I haven't, Grainne. I was on the piss all day with Brendan in Buncrana as I told you, but got an early morning lift. Remember you said you might visit your sister in Belfast for a few days? Can you go today? I have some money, but not on me. After you come back I'll give it to you then. Spend the savings. The money in the wardrobe I know you hide. Go shopping. Treat the kid.'

'Why? What's going on? You are not using this house for you-know-what? The Boys! Cathal has been phoning here. I told him you were in Buncrana with Brendan, and even Brendan has been trying to contact you.'

'Honestly Grainne, nothing like that, but you are right that something is going on. I can't tell you now, but I will when you get back.'

'What have you done now? Have you done something stupid?'

'Something like that, but I think you will be safer away for a few days. You know what I do. Just the less said, the less you know, the better. I can handle it. Honest. I was drunk last night and said something I shouldn't have. I think someone will come to the house here. One of them, Buncrana men. Just go away for a few days, will you? I will sort it.'

'Okay, Mick I will. But I want to know what you did after I come back.'

'I promise. Stay away for three nights. It'll be sorted by then.'

'I'll get the bus this afternoon and you better not have used our home for anything, And you better replace my savings too.'

'I promise, Grainne. I got to go. Where's the baby?'

'Upstairs in bed. You have only just arrived and it's pissing down.'

'I'll see her later before you get the bus. Got to see a man about a dog. Bye.'

Mick hoped his lies would make Grainne go to Belfast and he put on an overcoat, pulled up the collar and pulled down a beanie over his head, wrapped himself up against the weather and anyone recognising him. He needed a drink.

Dream

Samuel O'Donnell looked at his new house in Cillefoyle Park. It commanded a view of Derry, with its tower being glazed that afternoon. He hoped to move from his home above the plumbing premises in London Street in the next few months.

Josephine, his wife wasn't too sure:

'I like being in the town. I can walk to Austin's and all the department stores in Carlisle Road in all my finery. I can have tea with my friends. I can chat to the Dean of the Cathedral as he visits his flock, but most importantly I can walk to chapel every day to see my cousin, Father Doherty when he says mass in the Long Tower Chapel. I have to take the newly knitted socks to the Christian Brothers on the Brow of the Hill tomorrow.'

'Shush woman. Who were Mary's parents?'

'I hear you ask, my husband – Saints: Joachim and Anne.'

'Did you know Harry, Northern Ireland is a cold house for Catholics?'

'Who's Harry, my husband?'

'Look up there, Harry is in the tower, Josephine. He is always up there.'

'Oh yes, he's waving at us. Don't wave, Samuel. It's too common. Let's go to mass.'

'Okay Josephine, let's look at the house first.'

'I don't want to see it. We are staying in London Street.'

'I will tell you about it. For our five boys and three girls we need five bedrooms, and you can have the Drawing Room. It looks down towards the River Foyle. The guest bedroom is for your parents when they visit from Donegal. The house has two toilets, one downstairs in the back hall, and one in the bathroom next to our bedroom on the second floor. The bathroom has Italian tiles, the latest design and furnished with the best plumbing money can buy. It's Art Deco.'

'We must have a fashionable Drawing Room.'

'The piece de resistance is the central heating. The thick radiators will heat our home.'

'Would it make Northern Ireland a warm place for Catholics?'

'The biggest radiator is on the turn of the second floor stairs under the stained glass window that runs to the third floor.'

'That's nice.'

'It throws an ethereal light into the hallway, an appropriate churchlike impression. Perhaps, Josephine, with your religious observance we could have an altar there. Father Doherty could bless it.'

'That's nice.'

'My home is a temple to good taste, sensible, homely, a model fit for the modern family habitation.'

'That's nice.'

'Harry, I will heat my home, you sort this country out. We are going to mass and having tea with Dean Stewart of Saint Columb's afterwards.'

'Samuel, is Harry waving again? Ignore him. Let's go to mass.'

Samuel and Josephine O'Donnell walked down to Northland Road on their way to the Long Tower Chapel. They were dressed in fine black overcoats. They turned and gave a light dignified wave to Harry. Samuel whispered conspiratorially to him 'sort this place out'. Harry heard him even though he was at the end of the street. Harry shouted to him that he understood.

Harry awoke, startled, to find Marie pushing him saying he was shouting in a dream. Harry explained to her how his dead relatives had told him to sort out the Troubles. After getting up, everything in the morning appeared different, slightly off-centre. The sky a molten cinereal, the streets oppressive, the people more animated, as if Harry was looking at a new world, as if his sensual radar was overwhelmed. Was it a message in his dream from his ancestors, as if it had meant something? Was his great grandfather, Samuel O'Donnell, contacting him? What did he mean 'sort this place out'? He would have wanted him to pursue any chance of stopping the violence in Derry, in the whole of Northern Ireland. Samuel O'Donnell was a nationalist, a moderate and a staunch Catholic. His wife was the sister of an enterprising priest at the Long Tower who attempted to provide an alternative approach to nationalist aspirations via non-violent religious celebrations. Samuel O'Donnell and his wife had friends and business connections in both communities and prospered by those associations. His spirit embodied the house he built. Harry was certain of that.

Though Harry didn't believe in messages from the grave, he enjoyed his musings. It was more interesting than teaching class 3B on that drab morning. Being early in the school day, the pupils were subdued – the one and only advantage. Teaching 3B the rudiments of adjectives when their own colourful language revolved around several expletives was always prone to failure. They enjoyed copying the sentences from their text books, but that was a non-thinking exercise. Then they were required to fill in the blanks in the sentences from a list of words at the bottom of the page. Some kids put in their own words, not necessarily from the list of adjectives provided, much to the amusement of Harry.

Harry gave his son and daughter a lift in the morning, to his son's school and left his daughter to the bus stop. Her college was close to the Donegal border on the Culmore Road.

As he drove out of Cillefoyle Park, Dermot was standing on the road, waving for him to stop. It was a most unusual occurrence as Dermot worked late nights and was usually in his bed at that time of the morning. Harry stopped the car to find out what the problem was.

'Good morning to one and all. Sure isn't a great day for education, those that deliver and those that receive.'

No one in the car was in any mood for cheery early morning greetings. All looked at the soaking rain outside while they wished Dermot, a muffled 'Good Morning'. All without making eye contact.

'Just a word of warning. Harry, I'll be burning the midnight oil in my literary endeavours tonight.'

'Not a problem. You don't need to tell me. The door will be unlocked and if not, the key is you- know-where, as I showed you.'

'Will you be joining me?'

'No way, I'll be in bed reading my latest best seller. John Le Carre, I think. Escaping from the trials and tribulations of this weather and this life. Snug in my beddy-bys with my dear wife. You are welcome to struggle with your sentences and full stops on your own.'

'Fair enough! Have a lovely day in your respective classrooms.'

Dermot and Pauline

Dermot watched as Harry and his family waited for the traffic to allow the car to exit the park. He wondered whether he should just go back to bed with a cup of tea or go and get some fresh baps from the bakery on the corner. A Derry tradition. He walked to the edge of Cillefoyle Park. The traffic was bumper to bumper in all directions, slowed down by the weather conditions. Dermot stepped back into the park, watching as Pauline's husband Sean drove to work, joining the stream of traffic. He usually started earlier.

Dermot wandered over to Pauline's house. He went round the back and looked into the kitchen window. Pauline was in her dressing gown, cup in hand and magazine in the other. Her hair dishevelled as if the brush was dismissively used.

He tapped the window. A huge smile engulfed Pauline's face. After letting him in, Dermot stood against the radiator for some heat.

'Enjoy it while you can. It's going off soon and I am going to the heat of my bed.'

'Is that an invite? I haven't seen you in weeks.'

'I was waiting for an invite, you mad man.'

'Always ready and waiting.'

'Take off your damp overcoat, Dermot and I'll put it on the radiator to dry.'

'Anything else you want me to take off, dearest?'

'Yes, but not here. Come on.'

'After you, my dear.'

They both went upstairs and dropped their clothes on the floor. Soon, they were enjoying each other's embrace.

Dermot was lying back, sated, in the warmth of the bed. There were voices outside. He got up, and walked to the window, the raw cool of the room gave him goose bumps. He looked out to see Pauline's husband outside talking to the postman.

'Jesus, Sean is here.'

'What? Jesus, no!'

Dermot was semi-clothed, shoes in hand and went down the stairs like a rabbit spotting a fox. He heard the key turn in the front door and just as Sean closed it, Dermot closed the back door, gently. Outside he pulled on his shoes as each foot soaked up the freezing damp. His socks tucked into his shirt front.

Pauline managed to get to the bottom of the stairs as Sean came in. Pauline blushed, her hands wrapped around the tissues that they used to wipe themselves.

'Sean, what are you doing here?'

'Glad to see me?'

He went into the kitchen. She flushed the tissues down the lavatory in the back hall before going into the kitchen.

'Did I wake you, love?'

'Not really, I heard the voices outside.'

'Did you look out? I thought I saw the curtain move.'

'Yeah.'

An invisible wall of damp met them in the kitchen. Dermot's coat that had covered the radiator had fallen and was just hooked to its edge.

'Been drying clothes in here?'

'Yes, Sean. It's a shocking day. Why are you home?'

'I forgot I had a doctor's appointment. I went to work and then turned and went to the doctors, but I was on time.'

'I didn't know you had a doctor's appointment.'

'No, I didn't want to worry you. It is a simple growth, a mole. I caught it on something. It bled and seemed to have got bigger. Doctor said nothing to worry about. Was there somebody here? Funny smell, like perfume or aftershave?'

'No, just the drying clothes. I must have sprayed something this morning.'

Pauline had blocked Sean's view of the radiator, lifted Dermot's coat and put it in the cloak room, under the stairs, hidden deep under other coats. She would retrieve it later in the day.

'What about you and me going upstairs for a quickie?'

'Are you serious?'

'Actually, Pauline I don't have time, as much as it sounds like a good idea.'

'Pity, honey. Where's that kettle? Have you time for tea?'

'Already brewed, Pauline. I also have the baps in the toaster.'

Pauline thought this was too close for comfort and wondered where Dermot was.

Dermot had climbed into the lane that ran behind Pauline's house and exited into Park Avenue. With only a shirt on, he was drenched. A couple of schoolboys, perhaps mitching school, had roared at him – 'grand day for not wearing an overcoat.'

Dermot ignored them and walked through the heavy downpour. He realised his keys were in his jacket. Hopefully Sean would not be home for long. Pauline would realise and bring them over at some point. Where could he go? Of course, he could go up to Harry's garage. It would be available. Marie worked that day. He could think of an excuse and visit Pauline to obtain the keys of his home as a last resort. His landlady was another option.

As he approached his front door, he prayed that it was unlocked. It was. He had initially come out to speak to Harry for a moment leaving his door unlocked. After going in he went straight for a shot of whiskey. The slug warmed his innards. He stripped and showered, putting on warm clean clothes afterwards. He went to his front door and looked out. The rain was bouncing off the road. He didn't fancy any more walking in the rain. Perhaps, he would take the bus to his work.

Thank God he hadn't been caught. The realisation of the risk he was taking in having an affair with Pauline struck him and he took several deep breaths. He eyed the bottle of whiskey as the kettle boiled but sensibly lifted the tea bag from the jar to make a cup. Tonight he might need the whiskey after meeting Allen for the second time.

The Revenge

Mick Toal was walking down Park Avenue in the pouring rain. After being questioned by the police and propositioned to act as an informer, his life was literally hanging by a thread. Cathal had tried to ring Mick at home, to ask him if he knew anything about the robbery, and thankfully his wife had given him an alibi – he was with Brendan in Buncrana on a drunken spree. Brendan was constantly leaving messages, as were others, trying to arrange a meeting with Mick. The last message informed Mick that Brendan was on his way up to his house to talk to him. It was easier to face the Donegal western winds and rain than face anybody. Even at that hour Mick knew a pub on Park Avenue that might supply some solace. So he wrapped up, and left the house, wife and child. If he decided to become a Supergrass, his family would be out of town and easily picked up and taken to safety.

After a twenty minute walk and his overcoat soaked, he found the pub shut. Blistering with rage he walked on only to spot Dermot Lavery, also soaked to the skin, and without an overcoat, sockless and scampering out of the lane, that ran alongside Cillefoyle Park, looking distinctly bedraggled and despondent. It was the same lane that accessed an IRA dump in an unused toilet cistern at the bottom of a garden. Dermot was in such a hurry it was unlikely he noticed Mick. Mick was so well wrapped up against the elements nobody would have recognised him.

With his head down, Dermot rushed through the rain. Mick noticed a couple of school boys laughing at the sight of Dermot. Dermot barely raised his sopping head and pressed on.

Mick followed. Dermot went into a house in the Park, stood at the threshold and looked at the house directly across from him for a minute. Mick watched from the entrance to the park unseen, intrigued. He decided to wait, his curiosity aroused, but in that Derry monsoon, he needed shelter. In the thicket of the trees in the park, a majestic oak provided some degree of refuge and seclusion. After Dermot retreated from the dripping onslaught Mick positioned himself under the tree. It was surprisingly dry and protected, despite the occasional plops of drips from the branches above. Mick didn't have to wait too long. Dermot appeared in different clothes – jeans and jumper, cup in hand at his door. He leant on the door frame, again watching the house opposite. Mick retreated behind the tree in order not to be seen. He hunkered down and looked at Dermot's door. Dermot had gone in.

This intrigue was a welcome diversion to Mick's own predicament. What was he to do? What were the advantages of touting? He didn't have to think too long of the main disadvantage – death by torture. He had a wife and kid. They wouldn't want to leave Derry. They also came from a staunch Republican family. He never thought he would be involved in such deeds, but had heard enough about the penalties for touting from others. Indeed, his leaders made sure the foot soldiers knew the gruesome reality of informing. One advantage that stoked him, that appealed to him, was getting out of this fucking drizzle and into sunshine. The notion of sunnier climes down under in Australia or New Zealand for resettlement had been suggested.

The worry was Brendan; if he didn't keep his mouth shut. He was always a watery disloyal comrade. If Cathal and Joseph got their teeth into the investigation, they would find out, sometime, eventually. Brendan could squeal. What a fucking mess, thought Mick. His stomach ached; tears welled in his eyes as the possibility of death dawned on him.

He remembered happier childhood holidays in Donegal at Tullagh Bay – playing football till dark with all the other children and adults who ran in and out. Running on the lovely beach, jumping into the icy waves – sometimes the brief spell of summer provided a tepid swimming pool. All shapes and sizes appeared on warm weather days. Old fat ladies and skinny pipe-smoking grandfathers wore ancient swimwear to dip their toes in the dazzling water – the sun changing a Donegal beach into a Mediterranean pleasure strand. As his Aunt Sadie used to say 'Sure why would you go to Spain when you have this?' This hot spell for a week or so happened once every ten years, or one day a year if you were lucky to be there on the day. The problem was that most people took their holidays during the Derry Fortnight – the first two weeks in August, so whatever the Weather Gods wished to inflict on the poor people holidaying in Donegal they had to suffer. As soon as his sister got paid employment, she and her girl friends saved in a holiday fund for Spain immediately after paying off the Christmas expenditure, to escape the moody unpredictable weather. It was also an escape for the youngsters from family holidays and the all-seeing eyes of parents and grandparents.

His parents, grandparents on both sides of the family were heavily immersed in the Republican Movement, from the cradle to the grave, and as they constantly pointed out, he was too. However, from an early age he hated the tyrannical nature of 'The Boys'. He knew the Green

Book back to front – the IRA training manual. People feared them, people averted their eyes, and few challenged them. The only solution was becoming one of them. He did. Unfortunately for them they never saw the dedicated and ambitious volunteer that Mick was. He would die for Ireland, but he wanted more, He wanted recognition, he wanted power. Mick was ambivalent about the casualties – they were casualties of war. His pedigree spoke for itself yet he knew he was just a foot soldier, worse than old-fashioned parenting – shut up and do what you are told. Mick was born for leadership, he surmised. Now I'll show them. Treating me like dirt, like a child.

Ben, his 'handler' spoke a lot of common sense, or so it seemed. He empathised with Mick's predicament. He also knew a way out for him. Ben had talked to him previously when Mick had been lifted for questioning. He knew about Cathal, Joseph and the whole movement. Or did he? Did he actually know them or just mention them, trying to tap him for more information than he really knew. He mentioned the Rocking Chair, the Bogside Inn and the Inishmore. Ben showed Mick his arrest record – all the petty crime he committed. Only once had Mick been sentenced, and that had been bad luck – he ran into a police swoop. The police intimated that it wasn't luck – there had been a tout. He had gotten beaten up by the police and by some of the Stickies – the Official IRA because he had bad-mouthed them, and then by his own comrades because the robbery was not officially sanctioned like his Post Office one. Although Mick had said it was sanctioned by the leader of his cell. Mick had been involved in petty crime all his life. This, thought Mick was the story of his life: ill-organised, inconsequential and botched operations. It was only pure luck that there were any successes. They wouldn't take his advice, never did, there were worse than the Christian Brothers. Shut up and sit down. Mick remembered Brother O'Regan marching them around Our Lady's Hall in the Bogside singing the Irish National Anthem in Irish – Amhrán na bhFiann – A Soldier's Song.

It was time to play to Mick's song. He couldn't trust Brendan, Cathal was on his heels, and soon, Joseph would be too. The police threatened imprisonment if he didn't co-operate and they couldn't be trusted either. They would let slip that he was considering informing. Mick was cornered. The rain and weather was delightful – he was alive and reasonably dry inside his coat, sheltered in an oak grove – Doire – but for how much longer could he survive?

As Mick pondered on his problems, a car engine started in the park and startled him from his reverie. At the house opposite Dermot's, a car pulled out of its driveway. A woman stood in the comfort of the porch, shroud-like, and waved to the disappearing driver. She stood staring at Dermot's house for a few moments before going in.

Dermot came out of his house, as if he had been waiting for the lady, stood in his doorway, forlorn-looking, uncomfortable, agitated. Yes, very agitated, thought Mick.

Five minutes later, the lady came out again, wrapped for the fierce day, a neat white head-scarf, her very fashionable, white overcoat matched her shiny knee-length boots, and carried what looked like a coat. She went to Dermot's house, knocked on the door, but went in directly, without waiting. Mick moved quickly. He knew something was about to be revealed. No one was in the park on that wintry day. He scanned the windows of the neighbours, but Mick risked being seen going to Dermot's house. He went to the door, listened, then up the side of Dermot's first-floor apartment. Through the window he saw Dermot and Pauline in the apparent rapture of an embrace. Yes, triumphed Mick, I will get that snobby bastard. He is having his leg over, the dirty bastard. That's a pity, he thought as he savoured the moment. Mick wanted him to be gay, he had him as a shirt lifter, a pillow biter. Maybe he still is, maybe plays for both sides. He would have preferred to have found Dermot with a boy. It would have been a bigger scandal. Mick retreated and jumped over the little hedge at the front, nearly fell with the joy, but felt much better than he had done a few moments ago. Just how would he use it against him? I will destroy him, thought Mick. First he needed to find out who the woman was, but especially who her husband was. He was sure the driver that had left was her husband, and Mick planned to have a word with him. Then he realised that he might not have time to plan his jealous revenge. He would do a double – inform the lady's husband and tell the RUC that Dermot was in the IRA, should he decide to tout. All that extra money would be useful.

Brendan Interrogated

After meeting Pauline in the morning and the emotionally charged decision to quit seeing each other, Dermot's start to his day was not a good one. He still had to meet Allen for the second time, but this was the first important meeting. What would they talk about? Where would the talks end? How secure were they? How secure was he? Mick and Brendan would execute him, with glee in the name of their cause, if they found out, accusing him of being a spy. He doubted if they would wait for orders, they would make up some excuse. Working in a Republican pub, overhearing conversations, an ideal place to pick up information for the British, and of course they hated him anyway. He would be seen as a spy, a tout for the British. Some members of the security forces in the army and the police force didn't want to negotiate – they wanted complete IRA surrender or obliteration. Certainly the loyalists in the UVF and the UDA would think of such talks as a sell out of their position within the United Kingdom. Some of the police with ties to extreme loyalists might set him up for execution. It was a very dangerous situation. It was challenging enough being active on the socialist front – it crossed the sectarian divide – and yet too many in Northern Ireland were suspicious of working together. The working class on both sides had many of the same problems: each community needed access to jobs, better health and education, providing opportunities for a better future for them and their children. Instead, the Loyalist working class was herded into the traditional parties of the Ulster Unionists and Democratic Unionist Parties. Both built on fear of the Roman Catholic Church and a united Ireland. They always emphasised the Roman part and to Dermot's knowledge, Catholics from Derry, Ballymena or Belfast or little country parishes in the Northern Counties, never mind the counties of the Republic of Ireland were all quite different in their own unique way.

Allen had said it would simply be a discussion of their thoughts on the Troubles and if they could help stop the mayhem. He said he would bring a bottle of whiskey after asking Dermot what his favourite was. There had been several phone calls and Allen seemed honest in his endeavours. Dermot did believe, as did Harry and the Belfast priest, that there was a genuine attempt from the British for some form of back-door talks. He believed it was happening in Belfast to some degree. Only Harry and he knew the meetings were actually happening and where. The rest knew there was a possibility it was happening and were waiting to hear if anything constructive was on offer – the IRA wanted a date of British withdrawal or at least the intent for British withdrawal from Northern Ireland. Dermot wondered how many knew in the hierarchy of the IRA, in the IRA council.

The rain eased and a watery sunshine reflected off the broken pavements as Dermot walked to work. A few of the regulars were there when he arrived. Bernie, the other barman, left after a cursory chat with Dermot. Dermot was glad of the small talk of the bar revolving around the latest football and racing travesties or the dire state of the weather or last night's television soap opera. He managed to glean some enjoyment from the television in the bar, alternating with moans and groans from the regulars.

Cathal came in, barely acknowledging Dermot, and, went straight into the little office, that was used mainly as a store room. Dermot could tell he was in a grim mood. A little later Brendan came in, ordered a Club orange mineral and sat in the corner, reading the Derry Journal. He, too was very subdued.

A man in his twenties with short cropped hair entered – tough looking, narrow eyed, short nose, black unbuttoned overcoat, jeans and heavy boots. He ordered a Guinness. The boots were a brand name, but Dermot couldn't remember which. The guy looked like he meant business.

'Wild weather out there today?'

'Indeed, it is.'

'How is it going?'

'Ah, grand.'

Dermot recognised his familiar face with seagull eyes and was sure he visited the bar occasionally. He reckoned he was one of the hard men in the employ of the IRA or Sinn Fein, maybe Cathal's bodyguard, used as required. He did not frequent the pub and moved to the corner chair opposite Brendan, obviously not wanting to talk but as Dermot watched, he would try and catch Brendan's eye. Dermot thought he was trying to intimidate Brendan. Brendan did not look at him, his eyes firmly on his shoes or the newspaper.

Cathal came out and nodded to Brendan to come in to the office. Cathal and the other guy barely made eye contact, but subtle contact was made, Dermot was sure. Was this IRA business? Cathal shouted from the door of the office 'two teas, please, Dermot'. He did not look directly at Dermot.

After Dermot delivered the teas, he stood at the door awhile and the stranger watched him. The stranger stood up, but Dermot moved back to the bar and the black-coated man sat down again, his eyes looking at a magazine.

Nevertheless Dermot knew he was watching him, the whole bar, but especially the office door. Normally conversations could be heard in parts from the office but Dermot just heard whispering.

Brendan was being interrogated, Dermot felt sure of it. Perhaps this was an informal and friendly interrogation, if there is such a thing as a friendly interrogation, about some community or Sinn Fein issue, but then why was a stranger there? As a lookout? But by his demeanour Dermot surmised he was the 'bad cop' and Cathal was the 'good cop'. Brendan looked worried and wasn't his cocky self without his side-kick and mentor, Mick. Maybe Mick and Brendan had stepped over the line once again.

There was much chat over the last couple of nights in the pub and the town about the Post Office robbery on Park Avenue. It was widely condemned, as it had inconvenienced the locals, and many did not get their social security cheques. That included the many Republicans on the Dole, the unemployment register. It had traumatised many of the elderly customers and staff. The monetary gain was little for the robbers. The IRA denied any involvement in a carefully- worded statement released to the Derry Journal.

Dermot wondered if the two eejits – Brendan and Mick were involved. It would not surprise him. After an hour Brendan left, eyes to the ground, his face like a busted cabbage. The 'hard man' went to the outside lavatory. Dermot followed and glanced out to the back yard; Cathal and he were in conference.

The pub was fairly quiet on the mid-week night. Dermot was glad to see Conor come in and order a pint.

'How goes it, Conor?'

'Not too bad, I see you are having a meeting upstairs tonight?'

'Yes, some of my old crew from the Housing Association Action group. You should know them all: McCann, Melaugh. John Hume, Austin Curry and Ivan Cooper should be there too. They say they laid the foundation for the whole Civil Rights movement. There will be T.V. cameras there.'

'Are they being interviewed?'

'You are right there, Conor. They asked me for a place to meet, a fairly safe place for a few English men. I suggested this place.'

211

'A Republican bar? Dermot, are ye wise? Well, hopefully they will be having drinks. That will keep Cathal happy!'

'Might as well get their money and keep it in the family, if the Englishmen are paying. I'll send for you and no doubt you'll have a few yourself, if you are here, Conor, tonight?'

'I might indeed. Are you going up there to be interviewed, Dermot?'

'Well, I was involved in those days too. We were associated with the Derry Housing Action Committee, the DHAC. I dropped in and out. I was in Edinburgh at the beginning. More involved with a loose coalition called the Workers Alliance. We wanted similar ends: workers rights, jobs, houses, voting – all non-sectarian and non-violent and probably within an all-Ireland socialist framework. We were a talk-fest really, first sign of rough stuff and we were away. The DHAC were more pro-active, indeed some of them were arrested. I was arrested. We did lend our support and still do. We will meet here to discuss, support whatever needs supporting. The first meeting to be held here this month. Why don't you come along, Conor?'

'I might, you know. That's what was wrong with you lot. Nice middle-class people affronted by the violence in those early days, and they still are.'

'Middle class, middle aged and middle of the road, one of the DHAC founder's called them. A guy called McCann. I think. He was referring to the supporters of the SDLP, John Hume's party. The Social Democratic and Labour Party. They were there at the beginning.'

'I was too busy doing other things in those days, as you know, Dermot! Mind you, I seem to have changed my mind.'

'That's true, Conor. That middle-class lot would like our meeting yesterday with the local Commander of Police. We are planning a rally in the city with focus on equal opportunity for jobs, housing and anti-discrimination legislation. You should come. When we went to the meeting, the Commander, the top cop, was there. He voiced support for peaceful reform and constraint on both sides. As I left, he drew me aside and wished me luck in my endeavours. That was what he said and also said that his door was always open.'

'Interesting, maybe he is trying to build bridges within the police and the Catholic community.'

'My guess too.'

Dermot also wondered if the police man had singled him out as he may have chatted to Allen, learnt about the meetings and was offering his support. The web of intrigue grew, thought Dermot.

The Contact

Dermot walked home after midnight, leaving Cathal to lock up. He liked to walk through the city centre: down through the Diamond, Shipquay Street, the Strand Road, up Lawrence Hill, over and up Clarence Avenue, another hill to the Northland Road and the next left towards Cillefoyle Park. He fancied a cup of tea in his flat, but thought Allen might already be there. Perhaps, he thought, Allen was already watching him, maybe followed him home. Dermot had glanced behind and looked at the reflected shadows in the shop windows on his way home, but did not get any sense he was being followed.

The O'Donnell household was in darkness as the time approached one in the morning. The door to the plumber's office was unlocked, as promised. It was a very tidy place. The heavy curtains on the doors and windows provided a sanctuary against the outside chill. Another curtained door led to a toilet and a sink. Inside, a window was left ajar and an air fresher placed on a sink. Soap and hand towel were provided. The cistern and toilet were a bland taupe. A thick, black chain attached itself to the old cistern high on the wall. A worn, wooden handle swung in the bitter breeze, its surface unvarnished with age. It was a bleached, usable area of post-first-world-war utility. A conspicuous pink toilet roll sat on a stack of magazines – their topics unknown. Dermot shut the window against the bitter draught and returned to the office. He lit the gas fire.

In the corner of the desk a tea towel covered a mound. The desk was a solid piece of mahogany that ran from one wall to the next. Its surface reflected the scratches and scores from its use of the previous years. Underneath the tea towel – matching teacups, saucers, sugar bowl and milk jug. A see-through tub held some digestive biscuits. Perhaps at Harry's prompting; two narrow glasses sat for the whiskey of the night.

Soon the warmth of the small space became stuffy and he switched off the gas fire. A cube of drawers on the wall above the desk had a tube light underneath that lit the room in a cool glow. The heavy, red brocaded curtains overwhelmed the office. Behind the desk a brick wall was covered in old plumbing posters showing various sizes of pipes and bathroom furniture, some protected by plastic sheets.

In the centre of the desk, beneath the multiple drawers sat a writing pad with a red-and-black sharpened HB pencil. On it was written: 'I make the truth as I invent it truer than it would be', Hemingway.

Beneath that, some typical advice from Marie: 'Bring your own milk the next time!', written beautifully in her own hand.

A kettle was plugged in, behind the tea set. Dermot switched it on. The plug, a later addition to the office – its yellowing cable ran down the corner of the room to the desk.

The water in the kettle hummed as it boiled, a light knock at the door took Dermot by surprise. He opened it. The penetrating chill crept in with Allen.

'A cool night for it?'

'At least it has stopped raining, Dermot. Thank you for seeing me.'

'Tea?'

'Yes, thanks, milk if possible, no sugar.'

'Fine, have the soft seat or the chair.'

Allen sat on the chair, saw the writing pad and read the quote and comment. Dermot saw his smirk as he handed him a cup of tea. Allen produced the bottle of whiskey which Dermot left unwrapped by the kettle after a cursory thanks.

'Where do we start, Allen? Perhaps you can tell me a bit about yourself? I am sure you know me.'

'Sure, I was actually born here in the city, Aberfoyle Crescent, not far away and schooled over in the Duncreggan Road, preferred horse riding, sport, outdoors stuff. After school, average results got me to university in Glasgow. We had relatives there. Fairly average results there too, but had a good time with my rugger mates. I wasn't much of a student. Had too much fun. Visited back here on hols numerous times. Joined the army, took to it like a duck to water. After a few years there, but it was actually here in Northern Ireland at a party in Ballykelly that I met an intelligence officer who encouraged me to join them.'

'You joined MI6, MI5?'

'No, no. Army Intelligence. Served in a few places. Again I liked it. Got commended for work in Africa. Someone noticed me again and asked if I would like to join MI5. My time was up in the army. New horizons etcetera. Spent some time in London and again someone learnt I was born here and asked if I would – as those lads put it – have a look around.'

'So here you are?'

'Indeed, not far from my old domain. I bet you, they still have my initials on the desk in school.'

'You have a file on me, no doubt?'

'Nothing to fear there, Old Boy?'

'Drop the Old Boy, Allen. Otherwise we will drop this relationship pretty quickly.'

'Sorry, sorry. It's amazing what rubs off on you. We are trained to listen, so we pick up any local idiom. I picked it up from my superiors.'

'Pray tell, Old Boy. I guess you will be holding something back. Are you going to tell me everything? So do tell!'

'Everything is straight-forward really. Socialist activist. Parents – Bridie and Kevin. Childhood in Edinburgh and Derry. They too, were activists. Socialist working with other known activists. It's the militant Republican ones that we are more interested in. There are people in Her Majesty's Government, the security services, even the RUC who see the need for social change and anti discrimination measures. There are some who wish to repress any social change in all these places. Continuing with what we know about you. You were arrested a few times, but never charged. Barman in a Republican pub. Owner – Cathal Toal – known member of the Republican Movement, Sinn Fein, possible IRA, but business man that maybe fences IRA funds. Brother to Conor, jailed for terrorism offences. Now a convert to peaceful political means. A bit like yourself, but he found God.'

'Oh, I didn't know that!'

'That Conor was an activist?'

'No, that he had found God.'

Dermot thought that there was maybe a closer relationship between Fr. O'Reagan and Conor, than first imagined.

'Why didn't you approach Conor?'

'Not sure if we could trust him.'

'Why me?'

'Don't know really. Your name was put to me. I thought it was Harry O'Donnell first. That was the name I was given so I started to watch him. Please don't say to him. He was upset when I approached him. I ballsed that up.'

'Have you watched me, Allen? You don't inspire confidence when you got it wrong.'

'Haven't had much time to do that. Your name was given to me not that long ago. I tell you this too because I am human, with failings, as does all organisations, like my own.'

'Are you being honest or is that a ploy too? So you have been watching Cillefoyle Park?'

'Being honest, but you have a right being careful and to be cynical of my motives, perhaps. Yes, I have watched this place.'

'So you would have seen me going about my business.'

'Yes, I suppose I have.'

'Anything to report?'

Dermot got worried about his sexual liaison.

'No, have seen you going off to work and keeping barman hours. These meetings are all about building trust. I believe we want the same thing. For the violence to end.'

'Seen me visiting my neighbours?'

'Yes, I have.'

Dermot didn't want to pursue that line of enquiry any more.

'Where do we go from here, Allen?'

'Explore some scenarios, I guess. Where do you think the Republican movement is heading? Are they in for the long haul? What about Paisley and the Loyalists? What will they do?'

'Look, I don't have those connections with the IRA.'

'You know some in the IRA?'

'Maybe, but I bet you lot know them too.'

'You know a lot of Republicans? They trust you.'

'How do you know that? You lot know them too. I do work in a Republican pub, so can't avoid them. Cathal is a Sinn Feiner as you know. As for the Loyalists, well, as some French guy, Emile Alain, said: nothing is more dangerous than an idea, when you only have one idea. I think that will always be their problem – Ulster is Right, Ulster is British – while the tide of change is swirling against them. I don't think they will keep up. Like all ultra-conservatives: No Surrender and vote for the status quo.'

'My feeling, Dermot, is if we put something to the Republicans, they will react. Positively? Hopefully. What do they want?'

'If they respond, how positive will your side be? How will Her Majesty's Government react? The IRA wants the Brits Out! They will also want power. What is the use of freedom without power?'

'I see 'Brits Out' on walls all over the city, Dermot. Not forgetting the Church, of course. Where do they stand? I noticed the letters INRI on the cross in Catholic churches. It caught my eye once, above Jesus on the crucifix. I found out it meant Jesus Nazarenus Rex Iudaeorum. He is king, and we his subjects. He will look after us if we follow his way. Surely they will follow the Church's direction? This meeting was set up by churchmen, after all. Other churchmen are trying to talk to the IRA.'

'Who are 'they', Allen? The Catholics? Not all Catholics. The church hierarchy are famous for opposing Republicanism as a political and military force. Well, like all institutions, there are many dimensions.'

'Indeed. You know I think that is the challenge. Bringing both sides together, all of them, all strands, to settle for something that some extremists may not like. What about a drop of that stuff I brought tonight, Dermot? It certainly will help keep the insides warm.'

'Good idea.'

'Dermot, I don't know what will result from these talks except that you and me would like to see some end to the violence. I am on the side that wants social change with a view to ending the violence. Politics-wise, I am a middle-of-the-roader. Whatever it takes to get both sides to co-operate. Yes, I was born a Unionist, but let's see if there is room for compromise. You are on the left and I would guess you may want to see a United Ireland. The point is, if we can trust each other, if there is some change of policy, however slight, we can relay that to our masters.'

'Wrong again, I am not acting on behalf of anyone, but myself. The IRA are not my masters, but Cathal pays me.'

'Oops. Sorry.

'I am a messenger and one that doesn't want to get shot.'

'Point taken and digested. How did you end up using this place? It's cosy and seems secure enough.'

'Allen, It will do, as long as you are not seen coming here. Things will remain secret.'

'I don't think people will notice. I leave the car away from the park. The park is badly lit so I can walk up unseen.'

'Harry likes to keep an eye from his glass tower. Have you ever seen him?'

'Is he up there on a night like this, at this hour?'

'No, Allen.'

'It's a good point, but what about other people in the park, Dermot? I'll stay away if necessary, if our meetings look like being compromised. Is there a phone here? I could let you know if things go pear-shaped.'

'There is a phone point. I'll check. Who knows about these meetings, Allen?'

'Maybe two people on my side in Northern Ireland, maybe two or three in London. Who knows here?'

'I would say five or six. Nobody knows when or where it takes place, Harry knows we use it, but not when. Although I guess, all they have to do is follow me or watch me at my home.'

'The need for secrecy is paramount. It is all very sensitive for everyone.'

'Well, the same goes here, Allen. The need for mutual respect and understanding, will hopefully extend all the way up in both directions.'

'Well, I'll agree there. So, cheers, Dermot.'

'Sláinte, Allen. I will savour this mellow Irish drop. Hope you do too.'

Mutual Trust

It was a matter of building trust, through phone calls and meetings – the desire on both sides to stay in contact. Dermot believed Allen to be trustworthy and genuine. What did the army teach for their operations? Plan for success but expect the worst. Obtaining mutual respect and understanding in secrecy was the major challenge but Dermot felt they were making a positive start to understanding each other's beliefs and the goals for their conversations.

Dermot walked in the midnight gloom, a torch and a little bottle of milk in his hands, if both were needed. He ensured no one had seen him on these visits to Harry's garage, to avoid any suspicions from the neighbours on his way to yet another face to face meeting. It was number three. His notes of what was said and his own thoughts after each meeting were written up in Marie's notebook. He was sure Allen also made notes afterwards. One thought that never passed his mind in his entire life was that he would be in this position of mediating in the historic gulf between Ireland and Perfidious Albion.

As usual, tea was brewed and the discussions started off with current events before moving on to discussing ways forward from Dermot's point of view:

'I feel an anti-sectarian movement is the way forward. The realisation that people, ordinary working people have much in common – Protestants and Catholics. The one-handed drum beat of No Surrender on the twelfth of July, the one chant of No Surrender that their party leaders have beaten into them will not get them anywhere. We need to provide non-sectarian opportunities for jobs, houses and education. I favoured the People's Democracy movement based at Queens University where all walks of life and backgrounds joined together for a common cause for a fair and just society, a non-sectarian society. Is that possible now? I don't think so. But I feel our needs are no different from the equal rights demanded by the Blacks in America. We are part of a global social movement for human rights. We are all part of it. Did you know when it buckets down here the rioters are inside by their fireside watching the telly? In America, the same thing, similar circumstances, if it rains or a good film is on T.V. there are less people on the streets, and less likelihood of street trouble.'

'Except we are in Ireland and you know this, Dermot, the sectarianism runs deep. No Surrender. Not an inch. Noble words and noble deeds will not be enough to change what is happening here.'

'True, but that sectarianism runs deep within the British Establishment too. Look at Bloody Sunday. Teach the Paddies a lesson. That ended up in a major recruiting drive for the IRA. The result, the hawks in the IRA push for more operations in the British mainland. They were lining up to become heroes, martyrs for Ireland, happy to die for Ireland. It will be the ordinary working class of England that will bear the brunt of this war, the innocents again will suffer. It is the ordinary British working class boys and girls that are over here, on the streets of Derry. The IRA might even try bombing the Government directly as well as their commercial targets. Do they never learn from history? Perhaps we could try to help them understand what they are doing. Bloody Sunday was a turning point in this war. Rather than stopping the Republicans, it encouraged them to continue. Whatever it takes to get the Brit out of Ireland. We need to go beyond noble words.'

'And do some noble deeds, Dermot. You are doing one now.'

'Ergo, provide a framework or strategy or something to move the situation forward? Try to create an opportunity for talks even.'

Dermot looked at Allen. Was Allen giving a little signpost for the future direction of their talks? Dermot observed him, listening, looking, waiting for some little slip of the tongue or some sentence that gave something away – positive or negative, something reflecting the British point of view. Allen was after all, an agent of the British Crown Forces. Dermot was a Republican Socialist. Dermot felt that Allen had given an indication for the directions of their talks. Did a little breakthrough emerge from their discussions? Perhaps they had a goal for their talks. Did that mean more than just having meetings and passing on messages? Had their role become more of mediator? Their analysis of the Troubles with access to the two opposing parties may now have a common purpose. That idea was perhaps the most Dermot had gleaned from Allen's conversation, so far. They might be able to influence events by providing possible strategies for negotiation to the two combatants.

There was a war going on. People had died and were maimed – psychologically and physically. The carnage had been seen on the television news most nights. The destruction of commercial premises in the towns and cities of Northern Ireland was not just physical, but spiritually damaging for the people who lived there.

The MI6 officer had given little away regarding his Government's current position on how to move forward. Perhaps there was no genuine attempt by them. Perhaps they expected the IRA to say enough was enough, we surrender. It was all just a smokescreen and Dermot had to consider that a possibility. Allen was simply being used to find out anything by the powers that be. Dermot's and Allen's discussion had concluded that neither party could win outright. Perhaps the hierarchy of the warring parties worked that out too? Dermot had got some sort of tacit approval from Joseph to the talks. Anything to get the withdrawal of the British was what he supposed was Joseph's default position. Indeed, was Joseph reflecting the position of IRA headquarters in Dublin?

Already, Allen and Dermot had spent many hours in discussion over tea or whiskey or on the phone, but to what end? Perhaps Allen had concluded that their talks should produce something concrete.

That one little statement from Allen suggested a way to break the intransigence. But how was that going to happen? While Dermot trusted Allen as a genuine force for good, his superiors may have other ideas. The two men knew that many on either side did not want talks – they wanted victory for their side, but that was not going to happen. Of course, the British may offer something, but had no intention to deliver – Perfidious Albion. They were just secretly waiting, hoping for the IRA to capitulate or ask for terms of surrender. Getting to a position of negotiation would not be easy for either side as Allen and Dermot both knew.

It was a complex situation and the two talking in a shed was likely to mean little unless a formula for that coming together was possible. A message or a strategy from them that might initiate some movement, for a ceasefire or more formal talks for a ceasefire was Dermot's optimistic outcome from the talks. He would have to tease Allen to supply more ideas or information to see if both of them were on the same page. It also depended upon any change in government policy, or even a different political party in government could influence their talks. The need for more meetings seemed imperative.

Harry's Midnight Pee

Harry knew the meetings were taking place in his office and wasn't keen to know anything about them. It was simply too dangerous for him and his family. He contributed his office – that was enough. Dermot had told him one evening that the meetings with Allen were augmented with phone calls, but Harry cut Dermot off and said he didn't want to have any conversations on the subject. However, he was convinced it was the right thing to do if it helped bring the violence to an end. Good luck to Dermot. He was the activist albeit a peaceful one, but he had contacts in the Provisional IRA. He worked in their pub. He was the right man for the job. He grew up with Cathal, the head of the political wing of the IRA in Derry. Harry knew that Cathal, Conor and Dermot had played as kids together during the long summer holidays when Dermot stayed in Derry with his granny. The McCaffrey's lived next door to his granny and she was a cousin of their granny. A typical Derry extended family. Dermot was regarded as family and could be trusted.

One early morning when friends left for home after a late night of eating and drinking, Harry went outside to pee in his garden, as was his wont on pleasant starlit nights. As he admired the stars he hadn't heard Allen and Dermot come up behind him and each positioned themselves on either side of Harry and joined him in natural flow. Allen said: 'They say it's good for lemon trees'. 'Oh, is that right?' asked Harry. Afterwards they wished each other a goodnight and returned to their respective duties. Harry decided his nocturnal habit would take place out of sight from the garage.

The meeting in the garden confirmed again what Dermot told Harry: that the meetings were happening and that building the trust between Allen and Dermot was a slow affair, especially with the turbulent history of ancient Ireland and the British Government, it was not going to be easy. Dermot inferred, several times, he needed a friend to discuss the talks and Harry again, did not want to be told about them. Though Dermot did say that he reckoned Allen was reading up on the history of political movements as a basis for their discussions. Allen's name was never mentioned, such was the need for security and privacy. Dermot and Harry still had their own midnight whiskey jinks and the occasional pints of Guinness in the Rock Bar. If the topic ever arose again Harry was going to suggest Conor as a listening ear.

A Major Development

One evening while Dermot was working in the bar, Cathal asked him into the office.

'How goes things, Dermot?'

'Not too bad, thanks Cathal. What's the craic? Are you going to sack me again or not give me a raise?'

'No, nothing like that. Actually nothing to do with this place at all. It's about your political activities.'

'What do you mean?'

'Your extra-curricular activities. Joseph tells me you are having little private meetings.'

'What sort of little private meetings?'

'The ones you are having with a certain English man.'

'Oh! Those ones.'

Dermot didn't know what to think. How many people knew about these meetings? Dermot was worried. Cathal saw Dermot's face and realised what was happening.

'Don't worry Dermot. It's all okay. This is between you and me. No one knows. We don't even know who this guy is or where you meet. Do you trust him?'

'I do.

'Anything useful coming from them? What do you talk about, Dermot?'

'The Troubles from the beginning to now? What he wants from the talks. I am trying to educate him about our view.'

'You mean your view?'

'True enough, but I am aware of your views too, Cathal.'

Dermot felt this was an intrusion into the secrecy of the talks. What was Joseph or Cathal playing at? Cathal's self-importance flickered up in his little domain. That was dangerous. Fear now was exploding inside Dermot's head from the clouds of innuendo.

'Again, Dermot you have nothing to worry about! Unless you are shagging Joseph's wife.'

Cathal laughed at his own joke, but did Cathal suspect Pauline and himself? Did somebody say something? Was he being warned off? Dermot's head was spinning – too close, too close!

'Look we trust you. I trust you. You are family. You know nothing about my activities or Joseph's activities. Only what you pick up in the bar or talking to people. Derry is a village so most people know something. Derry people know that whatever you say, you say nothing. That's the way it should be. Nothing goes on here.'

Yeah, right. Nothing goes on here? I don't think so, thought Dermot.

'As a member of Sinn Fein, I have an inside knowledge of the Republican Movement and Joseph was thinking that maybe I should meet this guy. Just to see if there are genuine steps by the British to come to the table. If he is genuine?'

'I believe he is genuine.'

'Are the British genuine in settling this?'

'That is the big question. I believe somebody there is, but who knows.'

'Indeed what's his name?'

'His code name is Sun Hill.'

'Yeah, but what's his real name?'

Dermot hesitated.

'Look Dermot, it doesn't matter. I know this is making you very uncomfortable. Oh, by the way we have a new barman. Pretty inexperienced, but needs the money. A Strabane man named Johnny. Do you know him?'

'I might have met him.'

Dermot was getting more nervous by the minute. Has Johnny been employed to watch him?

'He can do more nights when you train him up. That means less nights for you. I am doing fewer days. To be honest with you, Dermot – and not a word – I am thinking of building a new pub or buying one down around the Culmore Road. That place is starting to have more housing developments than pimples on my son's face. Everyone wants to live on the Culmore Road and feel middle class.'

'Not a problem, Cathal. Sounds good to me.'

'Do you fancy working in my new place. It will be a while before anything happens.'

'Sure, we'll see what happens. I might join that affluent hysteria running up the Culmore Road.'

'Indeed, indeed. A business opportunity, is that! But listen, back to our little talk about your little private meetings. They will stay private. At the moment best to stay that way. What I am suggesting to you, Dermot, is, at a time when you think it's appropriate. I would like to meet him. Just to give him our side of things and see if there is any common ground. Joseph appreciates what you are doing. Do you think that is a good idea?'

'I never thought about it, to be honest.'

Dermot knew he was being told what to do and not asked for any suggestions.

'Look, Dermot. We will leave it to you regarding the timing. Unlikely next week, but next month, two months. There is only so much you can tell him. I am sure. Just let us know and name the day and time and place and we'll confirm if it's possible and let's see if it happens. Thanks Dermot. Your heart's in the right place. Like I say we are family. Have a double of whatever. I would join you, but gotta go.'

'Cheers Cathal. Catch you later.'

Dermot went back to the bar and had his shot of whiskey. How would this affect Allen? Perhaps that is what he wanted after all – direct talks with the Republican Movement?

Dermot and Allen met several more times over the spring months. They agreed on an undeclared alliance to attempt to gel a framework for moving the two opposing parties together.

The weather was softening. The grip of winter's bleakness eased and buds appeared on the skeletal trees. Daffodils and snowdrops were spotted in gardens. People were less wrapped up. Shorter coats replaced overcoats, gloved hands were less common, heads and necks featured more fashionable hats and scarves. Umbrellas still reigned supreme. Rain under leaden skies still provided the backdrop to the city. Dappled sunlight regularly broke the cloud, its rays brightening the shadows and the Maiden City dried occasionally in the weak heat of the solar God.

Dermot and Harry were having a nightcap of whiskey and cigars. The same cigars gifted to Harry by his son at Christmas. They were out in the back garden, standing on the patio. The bricks underneath edged with an emerald mossy sponge. The low sun failed to fall on that area of the garden. A job for bleach, wellington boots and the yard brush, Harry had said to Dermot. A late spring gardening job. Already, Harry and Dermot spoke of how much they were looking forward to the warmth of summer and the change of season.

'Harry, why don't you join us tonight? Allen should be here, not late, as I am not working this evening.'

'No thanks. I haven't changed my mind. You have my garage. That is all you are getting from me!'

'Not true, your kettle, your cups, your water et al.'

'You are welcome to them. Dermot, have you talked to Conor about your discussions?'

'Not really, only in a vague way. He's like you. Doesn't want to know. Still enjoying his freedom, but he has come to some of my meetings. I think it's in his blood. He'll get involved sometime.'

'Well, good luck, anyway.'

They stared at the moonlit starry night, the gentle cool breeze whistled through the trees, moving the leaves and the tiny branches in a pleasant meditative motion.

Just as they were enjoying their moment of contentment, a massive explosion shook the city. The two men jumped, but relaxed immediately in joint acceptance of the reality of a city at war. The IRA had bombed somewhere, likely a commercial premises in the city. Normally, Harry would have climbed into his tower to see where it came from, but both of them went to the front of the house in search. A plume of smoke emanated from the city centre. Often it was the British news from London that informed the Derry community in their homes, about the source and extent of the explosion.

'Jesus, Dermot. That wrecked our cigar moment and whiskey bonding.'

'Yeah, I wonder if Allen will be coming tonight or else tied up somewhere. He should be here in ten minutes.'

'Well, that's me for bed. Good night Dermot and good luck again and sort out this fucking mess, will you?'

'No problem, sorted by breakfast. I'll bring you and Marie breakfast in bed if so. Good night.'

Harry went inside his house and Dermot went into the office. It was freezing so he lit the fire and switched on the kettle. As it hummed, there was a knock on the door.

'Wow, that was quick. I have just come in.'

'I know. I was watching. I didn't want to interrupt your cigar moment.'

'Where were you? That's what Harry said, but that bloody bomb wrecked it.'

'I was waiting for you by the garage. Then the bomb went off. You two hardly flinched. It made me jump.'

'Ah, you get used to it. Where was it?'

'No idea!'

'I thought you would have had a radio or something.'

'I do. It's in the car. I parked it down around Lawrence Hill.'

'Suppose we should get down to business. Remember, Allen, we talked about moving things forward. Well, how would you be fixed to meet a senior member of the Republican Movement?'

'Hmm, that's interesting.'

'Well, I might be able to get you to meet someone.'

'How did you manage that?'

'Well, I have my ways, Allen!'

'I accept, of course. When and where?'

'I don't know when and probably you won't either, but I guess it might be here, Allen. Shall I tell them okay?'

'Yes, for me, Dermy, Old Boy.'

'Less of the 'Dermy, Old Boy' please! You, I mean, we need to have something on the table for discussion. Will you consult on this with your superiors?'

'I don't think so, Dermot. I think this is for discussion only and testing the water, but maybe they are willing to move.'

'Discussion only, I think, Allen. To explore possibilities. The British position. Both factions have to carry a lot of people with them. Maybe that's a discussion point. It will not happen overnight.'

'Right again, Dermot. Just wait and see, but maybe it's a move on their part.'

They had a discussion on what it meant and the need for the right words.

'I don't know Allen, but whoever you talk to will know more about the issues and practicalities than me. It's a move in the right direction. It validates these talks.'

'Sure does. So we meet up and someone will join us sometime.'

'I think so.'

'Well, let's drink to that.'

After their farewell and Dermot's second drink of whiskey, he heard on the BBC news that the IRA had bombed a restaurant in the city centre. It was not one Dermot frequented.

An Important Meeting

Harry was watching the late night news when he heard a light knock at the front door. Marie and the children were in bed. Harry went to the front door and stood aside, for security reasons, while calling out: 'Who's there?'

'It's me. Dermot.'

'What do you want at this hour? Is there something wrong?'

'I have a favour to ask. Could you pick up someone for me at the cathedral in about ten minutes? It's very important.'

'No bloody way, Dermot, but I'll give you my keys and bring it back tonight please.'

'I can't drive. I have no licence.'

'Yes you can and hopefully you have a licence.'

Harry handed Dermot the keys: 'Anything else, Dermot?' 'No', came the disappointed reply. Harry wished him a good night and closed the door.

Dermot went back to the office. Allen was sitting in the only armchair. The kettle was humming contently in the corner.

'Ah! You are here already. Got a phone call. Tonight is the night.'

'You mean I am meeting someone.'

'You are, not sure who. I am picking him up now. Sit tight!'

Dermot did not own a car and preferred not to drive. He had a licence but seldom used it. He drove slowly to pick up the Republican. Maybe it was Cathal, but he was told the man to pick up was called Bill who would be standing at the Cathedral gates. Dermot's instructions were to park near the gates and Bill would get into the car. After parking near the shut gates, the door opened and in got Bill. It was actually Joseph. Dermot was nervous, hoping there would be no check points on the way.

'By the way, do you want a lift back?'

'Yes, please.'

'Well, this isn't my car.'

'I tell you what, let me phone and I'll arrange my own lift.'

There was no small talk. Dermot took Joseph to his home, where he phoned and Dermot heard him say, 'Pick me up in two hours'.

They went up the Park and into the office. Dermot introduced them to each other, offering tea. Allen had said the water had just boiled. Both representatives looked at Dermot and he excused himself. There were only two chairs anyway. Dermot was glad he could leave it to the two – perhaps some positive movement would follow. He had done more than enough, perhaps that would end his involvement.

Allen and Dermot talked on the phone a few days after and Dermot asked how things had gone. Allen felt it was constructive and that he might send a positive message to his superiors. It was a confidential talk, but a wide range of topics were discussed. The potential for a ceasefire – how it could be negotiated and its impact on Northern Ireland, but particularly on Republican areas: harassment, arrests, raids, self-defence, local security, liaison, and the possibility of troops returning to their barracks.

There would need to be further talks to discuss the ceasefire, public statements needed to be agreed upon, and of course, selling the plan to the internal parties – doves and hawks. It would be a complicated affair to organise. Allen said he had been very surprised as talking to Joseph was like talking to a commander in the British forces.

Pauline

The following day was a Saturday and Harry had decided the communal park need a little love and attention. It was due to get a Spring maintenance from a contractor, but some areas were always overlooked, especially the entrance and underneath the trees and bushes alongside the street wall. Harry took his gardening tools to the park and was cutting some undergrowth when he heard the postman arrive.

He was knee-deep and unseen in between the front hedge and the wall when Pauline stood in front of him. Sobs started as Pauline's body retched in spasms. A letter in her hand dropped and blew into the hedge where Harry was. He got up and gave it back to her. Her eyes glazed in disbelief at seeing him. Her body trembled like a pathetic lost child.

'Jesus, Harry.'

That was all she said and almost grabbed him to hug him or hit him, but then she changed her mind.

'Are you all right? What's wrong? Is it bad news?'

'Oh! Harry. My life's a mess. If Sean finds out, he'll kill me. Oh God. The kids! What a stupid bitch I am.'

'What is it? I am sure Sean isn't like that. He will help you. What can I do? Do you want to come to my house for a cup of tea? Marie will be there.'

'God, no Harry, I can't face anyone!'

'What is it, Pauline? Has someone died? Let me help.'

'It's your friend, Dermot.'

Pauline trembled.

'What about Dermot?'

'Here, take the letter. Everyone in Derry will know anyway. I will never be able to set foot in Derry again. They will call me a harlot.'

Harry took the letter. The envelope was addressed to Sean, handwritten, as was the letter itself. In a large scrawl, in child-like hand writing was written:

> Your wife is screwing Dermot Lavery. I saw them. What will
> your neighbours think? What will your kids think?
> The Provos will knee-cap that bastard and tar and feather your
> wife. I will tell them. You might want to tell them first.
> Take the whore and your kids away and save your family from
> that queer fucker.

231

I am watching.

Harry was stunned. How could anyone be so virulent? Although he was not surprised at the writer's despicable claim, having spotted Dermot several times at Pauline's - he had suspected some sort of liaison.

'That person has a filthy mind. This is just someone getting their kicks. Have you anybody in mind that might do this? Is there a reason?'

'Yes, there is a reason. It's true.'

Pauline stuttered through her sobs and tears.

'Oh dear. Look it could be nothing. Leave it. I'll have a word with Dermot. We'll keep an eye for anyone lurking about. Say nothing to Sean. Avoid Dermot.'

'What if Sean finds out?'

'Well, let's cross that one when it happens.'

'What, if another letter comes?'

'Do you get to the post first, Pauline?'

'Yes, Sean is at work, but usually at home on Saturday.'

'Probably why they posted it yesterday to arrive today so Sean would pick it up. Get to the post first and say nothing. Come up for a cup of tea.'

'No, no. The kids are all in bed. I'll have a shower. Can you take the letter please and tell Dermot to stay away.'

Harry told Marie the horrible news and phoned Dermot, who promised to avoid any more liaisons with Pauline. Dermot had said that the affair was over anyway.

Harry left later to pick up one of the children in the car when he saw Pauline waiting at the bottom of the park.

'You haven't been waiting out here for me?'

'No, Harry. I was watching out my bedroom window for you to leave. I dashed out this time and caught you on your own.'

'What is it?'

'Sean was driving into the park the other night when a young man in a hood asked him to wind down the window. He yelled something at Sean, before running off. He couldn't quite make it out but it was something like: your wife's a whore, read my letter, something about Dermot Lavery.'

'It's obviously the blackmailer. Stay calm. Watch the post and any phone calls. These people aren't very brave. What did Sean say?'

'He just thought it was a drunk? But wondered why Dermot's name was mentioned.'

'I think we need to try to have steady nerves here, Pauline. He might never come back. I'll keep an eye from the tower and Dermot said he would watch around the park.'

'Okay, Harry, Sean wouldn't notice. God, you are never too old to do something stupid.'

'Bye.'

Supergrass

Mick Toal, the dedicated full-blooded volunteer of the IRA from generations of staunch Republicans, but in reality, Mick had always whinged like a temperamental bride, and had been known to be a bit furtive. He had strived for more recognition, like a second son, demanding more, but he had more ambition than he had talent and less dedication that had been realised. His pugnacious personality, and his litany of minor infractions within the movement and with the police force, he claimed, had been due to his alcohol addiction, but Mick was never drunk. It was his standard excuse that was accepted. He swore loyalty and faked sobriety each time, and was allowed to continue within the movement.

However it was recognised that he would never amount to more than a foot soldier. His selfish attitude and untrustworthy behaviour had led him to be ordered out of the IRA previously and he had joined a more criminal Republican group – known for its drug activity and money-laundering ventures until eventually, it was confronted by a force of the IRA. Two executions later, several members were exiled, and some members rejoined the IRA while others joined the Dole again. Mick fell in with the main body of Provisionals, swearing strict obedience to the conditions for readmission as that was his only way forward to remain active.

His interrogator turned mentor was his Uncle Cathal, acting as a mediator between the two groups, but nothing was achieved until the show of strength decimated the other Republican group. Cathal and Mick were not mutual admirers. He distrusted Mick, and as indeed the others that were re-admitted into the Provisional IRA, but foot soldiers were always useful. Mick was mentored by Cathal, and in reality Brendan was keeping an eye on him, on behalf of Cathal, but they became friends, each enjoying the power and status provided by the movement. Mick in the end became the despotic leader of the pair, and Cathal had reported that both were causing a lot of headaches.

Mick Toal grew up at the beginning of the Troubles. A relative was shot dead on Bloody Sunday, witnessed by Toal who was on the march with his family. At an early age Mick was into petty crime and had foolishly robbed the house of an IRA man. He had been warned a few times before, but was confronted by the pregnant partner of the IRA man, who he pushed to the floor, leaving her bruised, but still able to identify him. She miscarried the baby a few weeks later. He was kneecapped by the IRA for the robbery and was generally disliked by all who knew him. By misfortune or someone informing on him he was arrested by the RUC when he attempted to rob a bookies on the Strand Road. He ended up on remand in Crumlin prison, Belfast, with the IRA partner of the woman who had lost her baby, and was badly beaten by him.

Mick caught up with Brendan after being detained by the police:

'Fantastic to have you back with your oul comrade. Where the hell have you been?'

'Just on a bender, didn't quite make it to Buncrana, but you gave me an alibi?'

'Cathal asked me to call to the bar to see him about your whereabouts and discuss the robbery. I told him we were both on the piss in Buncrana. He wants to talk to you. He has been up at your house, no one was in. He has been phoning you forever.'

'I'll contact him.'

'Well, Cathal isn't happy with us, with you.'

'Did he believe you?'

'I'm not sure, maybe. But yer man Paul from the nuttin' squad was at the pub the same time as Cathal asked me about the robbery.'

'It was only to frighten you, put pressure on you. If they thought you did it you would be having a chat with Paul directly.'

'Cathal thought it strange that you and your wife weren't contactable. I told him the last time I saw you, was in Buncrana. Where is she?'

'She's gone to Belfast to stay with her sister. That's all, Brendan. Have you still the money?'

'It's hidden. There is a lot of talk about the robbery. Sinn Fein has declared it's an attack on the community and the Boys have issued a statement saying it wasn't them. I think we don't touch it.'

'You are right. Just take forty pounds and we'll have another smashing time in Buncrana or my sister's house tonight.'

'Great idea, Mick. A nice bottle of Jameson and some beer. Eh! That would be good.'

'We will have a celebratory drink. We need to keep our heads down, lie low for a few weeks, but I tell you what. I am at me sister's tonight, baby-sitting. You bring round a carry-out and something stronger and we'll toast to Ireland's freedom and mine. Best I stay out of the pubs for a few weeks.'

Mick went home to an empty house, his family away in Belfast. He picked up a note dropped through the letterbox. It was from Cathal advising Mick to see him urgently. Then Mick made a phone call to make some trouble for Dermot. After making some tea and toast for himself he went out the back door and down through the back lanes to his sister's house. He was wrapped up, his face barely seen under a hat and a hood.

On the way, he had to walk past Brendan's house. He was using the back lanes to avoid contact with anyone who might know him. Just as he passed the house, he noticed Brendan's back door open and one of the Boys facing into the house. Mick jumped over a neighbour's fence and stood against the shed looking into Brendan's house. The shed's door was unlocked and no one was at the neighbour's windows. Mick opened the shed door to shield himself even further from Brendan's back door. The man at the door turned around and came out, looked about, and motioned for those inside to come out. Paul led the way, followed by Brendan who was sheet white and bleeding from the lip. Behind him the other man from the 'nuttin' squad' pushed Brendan after shutting the back door. As they came down the garden path and into the lane, Mick slipped into the shed next door.

A few seconds later he looked out as the men walked to the end of the lane. Mick was about to shut the garden gate when the man from the house, whose garden he was in, called to him 'what the hell are you doing in my garden?' Mick ran in the opposite direction of the 'nuttin squad' before they realised who he was.

At that point Mick turned informer – a Supergrass.

Sean

Harry and Dermot were having a drink in the Rock Bar. It was a quiet evening, two elderly men sat at the bar staring at their drinks sitting in front of them and occasionally glancing at the television above, in the corner. Likewise, John, the barman, glanced at the flickering box while reading a newspaper spread out on the counter.

The two friends were sitting discussing Harry's harrowing experience with the gunfight outside his classroom.

'It's certainly not the first time it has happened, but was the fiercest. The Boys training and target practicing, we have got used to. We mostly ignore them, but when those helicopters flew so close to the school, the windows and everything vibrating I guess it was time to leave. Too close for comfort. Unfortunately we have got used to it. Pity we didn't stay at the Brow. Safer there.'

'It is a sad consequence of the Troubles that while a school can be a refuge for the boys, it then gets caught up in the middle of it.'

'During the summer holidays the army used it as a look-out post, but the locals demonstrated and eventually they moved out. The state of the store room on the top floor was a complete wipe out. The books were smashed up, bullets everywhere and after the window was smashed, the rain got in. Lots of the English texts, new sets, a mass of mush. Some older sets from the Brow too.'

'Why that store room, Harry?'

'They must have thought a gun man was there! I was talking to James McGuinness, works for the paint shop at the bottom of William Street. Do you know him?'

'That's a coincidence. I met James the other night. He was up at the bar for the inaugural darts competition. He was captain of one of the teams. He was telling me he was into pigeons rather than darts. Well, I told him he wasn't bringing his pigeons into my bar!'

'James was telling me the store room was completely shattered, they had to re-plaster the walls, paint it and of course re-glaze. A few of the bigger windows too in the other classrooms needed replacing. He has been up a few times doing the same thing. They must think the IRA was using it.'

'That day it happened, one of boys in the class asked me did I want baps for lunch as he usually gets them for the usual teacher who was off sick. I said okay. The lad saw them gathering outside the school

– rifles hidden under duffle coats. I suppose they see them all the time in their fleet of Cortinas.'

'Sad business, Harry.'

'I hope your little endeavours prove successful.'

'With Pauline?'

'No, you bloody fool. That episode of your life is done and dusted. Not to be mentioned. Stay away until everything cools down. The other thing that is not to be mentioned.'

'Oh, the meetings in your office?'

'Yes, Dermot.'

'Well, it's early days yet. Just getting to know each other, building trust and hopefully presenting ideas too.'

'Well, good luck with that anyway.'

Both chinked their classes and glanced at the door as Sean Laughlin walked in. He marched directly to the two men, eyeballed Dermot, paused and returned to the bar.

'Oh shit!'

'He looks as if he wants a word or two. It could be anything. Let's stay calm, Dermot. I know you can handle yourself. Deny all.'

'I wonder what he heard.'

'Just wait and see, Dermot. Calm yourself.'

Sean ordered a shot of whiskey. John watched him carefully as he came towards the two sitting.

'I got a phone call at work from someone today that you were visiting my house when I was at work. Several times.'

'Yes, Pauline needed some help with a leaking tap.'

'Several times?'

'Well, once or twice I was over, Sean.'

'Who was the phone call from?' Harry asked.

'I don't know.'

'Then if you ask me, it's someone creating mischief.' Harry added.

'Well, no one is asking you. Look, Lavery, I'll fix anything in my house that needs fixing. Just stay away. Don't come near it again. Ever.'

'Fine with me.'

At that final command, Sean stared at Dermot, walked off; his head erect and with deliberate force of the palm of his hand, Sean pushed the door open and left.

'What was that all about, Dermot?'

'Well, he heard something, didn't he? Someone phoned. He either knows the full story and is pretending to ignore it or he knows little.'

238

'Well, I think he knows little. I also think he doesn't trust Pauline. Pauline is a little flighty, head in the clouds. You should have known better. Keep a low profile, Dermot. Avoid him at all times.'

'Let's have another drink, Harry.'

'Yes, it is too much for a lowly teacher like me, bad enough seeing that fire fight outside the school. I need peace and quiet. I need peace and quiet in Cillefoyle Park'

After they had finished their drinks and walked up the hill to their homes on a cool dry night, they turned into the Park. A man stepped out of the shadows and hit Dermot on the cheek. It contacted, but Dermot automatically stepped back to avoid any further attack, stumbled on the edge of the path and fell. The man went to kick Dermot, but Harry rushed at him and pushed him back. It was Sean.

'Stay away, you fucker! If I see you around and I am driving my car, get out of my way. I don't want to see you here. I am not scared of your Provie friends, just because you work in a Provo bar.'

Sean stormed off in the direction of his home.

'Are you all right, Dermot?'

'I am fine, twisted my knee a bit falling down. He didn't really touch me.'

'You are a bit red on your cheek.'

Dermot got up with the aid of Harry. He straightened his right leg and limped to his front door.

'What do you think, Harry?'

'Stay away. Don't walk past their house. I wonder what he knows. Hope Pauline is okay?'

'True, hopefully she and the kids are okay.'

'Dermot, your reputation for being a Casanova is getting you beaten up. Lie low for a while.'

'Do you have time for a nightcap?'

'No, the only ice you should be having is some wrapped in a tea towel and then go to your bed on your own.'

'Yes, Doctor.'

Dermot went in and Harry walked up to his own house. Everyone was in bed, but Marie was reading in hers. Harry explained all. Marie told him to take his own advice and stay away from people who are trouble, namely Dermot.

At tea time, two days later, Harry was up in his tower looking over the city, just day-dreaming and relaxing when Sean reversed out of his drive. A short time after, Pauline walked up to Harry's house. Harry met Pauline at his door.

'Sorry to bother you, Harry. How are you?'

'I am well. More importantly, how are you?'

'Good, good, just to let you know Sean doesn't know anything. He suspects everything. My over-reaction probably made it worse. He confronted Dermot in the pub. Then came home and we had an almighty row. He stormed out.'

'Did you know he hit Dermot?'

'No, I did not. It must have been after the pub. Probably venting his anger. I am sorry about that. Look, tell him to stay away. The anger of a patient man. That's Sean. It was all so silly. I was bored. Dermot is an inscrutable, interesting character. Sean is a good man, dull, but good and I think he might have a go at him again. Maybe he should move out of the Park.'

'Look, Dermot knows to stay away and avoid meeting Sean.'

'It may not be over. Sean doesn't forgive easily. He is a thick man. If anyone who does him ill, he will not let it be. Just tell him to go away, for his sake, for all our sakes.'

'Okay, Pauline. I will tell him. He knows. Take care, Pauline.'

'Thanks, Harry. Bye.'

Pauline went home as Harry looked sadly after her and thought; will things ever be the same again in Cillefoyle Park?

Another Meeting with Allen

'Hello, Dermot, How are things going?'

'Oh! Can't complain! No one would listen anyway.'

'Yeah, I know what you mean. At least spring is in the air. The days are getting longer. Hopefully I'll be heading back home for a short break.'

'What happened to your cheek, Dermot? Bumped into a cupboard door?'

'Something like that. I suppose where you live, in England, the weather is milder.'

'I have a place in London, Dermot. It can get pretty cold there too. My parent's place in East Sussex, you should see the Spring flowers sprouting. I was chatting to my mother last night: daffodils, primroses, blue bells. They have a small glade that fills with blue bells. Perhaps one day I could take you there Dermot.'

'That would be nice. I was never into gardening.'

'Oh, they are, big time. They have a formal one, a wild English patch and the wood. Dad is ailing a bit so I am going over to see what's what. Dad is your typical stiff-upper-lip. I need to check him out and send him to a doctor. He is too stoic for his own good.'

'I am sorry to hear that, Allen.'

'Harry has a nice back garden here.'

'Oh, I think it's Marie's doing, he's just the unpaid muscle. Last time, we discussed how we could move things forward and present some ideas.'

'Yes. I do. But we need to be careful of the language. We can produce ideas alright, but how do we present them and what language do we use?'

'Like?'

'Some terms are loaded with symbolism. Some conjure up all sorts of outcomes. Surrender, defeat. We need to avoid such loaded words. Compromise is what this is all about. I am not sure we are there yet. But we could sow some seeds. Otherwise, what are we negotiating?'

'It's as you say, sowing the seeds. We need ideas for creating a pathway to the negotiating table. Proposing a strategy to get there is a good starting point. We are not doing the negotiating, they are. We want to lay the groundwork to get there.'

'Maybe, Dermot, but we need a kick start. Something to kick start the process, to put the parties together, to see that something is possible, something that both can live with.'

'The major problem, with any of this is we have powerful forces within the two parties who oppose any deal. You know this. I know this. There aren't just two parties, there are many. Your crowd fear the loyalists, the loyalist backlash. Does it really exist? They all need to come aboard any deal, of course. Maybe think outside the box. What structures that do not exist already might work for instance. A structure outside a Northern Irish context, within an Ulster context, the old province of Ulster?'

'Yes, a federalised solution, maybe become a state of the United States of America?'

'Why not consider it? Get the Yankees involved. Why not? Again, we need to be careful with the language, as you say, Allen. What does that mean? What does American involvement mean? What does British withdrawal mean? It's loaded with meaning for different people. For instance, a withdrawal might mean a withdrawal of the army to its barracks, a withdrawal of the RUC from nationalist areas. A police force could be a joint police force – RUC and locals, RUC, locals and Military Police or even a United Nations peace-keeping force. A withdrawal doesn't necessarily mean an overnight withdrawal of your government from here.'

'I see the possibilities, Dermot. These are all excellent ideas for the negotiation process, but our work here is about getting the parties to the table to discuss such issues.'

'You are right, but it's good that we can brain storm such ideas. I think the wording of even agreeing to negotiate is important.'

'Of course it is. But what would the IRA agree too? They want a withdrawal of Britain from Ireland to create a United Ireland.'

'Allen, I think the IRA realise, at least some who are realists do, that there are more than a couple of parties to this problem. The government in Dublin, the government that was in Belfast, all need to be carried along. The extreme loyalists need to be convinced. Some sort of federalist format might work, with self-government. Disengagement might be a good word for the British to use in this process. Let the people engage and the rest disengage, become honest brokers.'

'This is all well and good, Dermot. The format of the talks, the topics, the possible outcomes are for the parties around the table. We

242

can offer suggestions, but our job, as I see it, is to get them talking. Building mutual trust like we are doing is the first step. So don't come to the table with demands and loaded language. Come to listen to the other side. Listen, build mutual trust and understanding. We need that spark to start the process.'

'I know and agree, Allen. Please listen a second. There are many options for disengagement: an independent Ulster perhaps, a joint Federalist structure between London and Dublin or a dominion status like New Zealand.'

'I think the PM's office would be open to such discussions, but how far they would travel I don't know. Would the IRA accept such new structures? Would the militant unionists agree to such talks?'

'I don't know, Allen. So long as they would be included in such discussions. Some form of honourable settlement, I guess. Any form of honourable settlement, I suppose. Nobody loses face. The way I see it, the unionists have all to lose and the nationalists have all to gain.'

'Perhaps. Are there honourable men in the IRA and UVF, Dermot?'

'I have to accept there are some, otherwise I am wasting my time, otherwise we are wasting our time. Are the British serious in negotiating a deal? I suppose we keep going until we find some honourable men to listen. Are there honourable men in H.M.G.?'

'Likewise, how do we kick start the process, Dermot?'

They smiled as Dermot lifted the bottle of whiskey to indicate time for a dram.

Joseph

Dermot was working his usual shift in the bar a few days after Allen's last meeting. He had been to a community meeting about a security check-point beside a play park with a few of his fellow activists, local councillors and residents. Even Conor showed up. The security forces stationed there attracted stone-throwers and one of the children had been hit. It was impossible to stop some errant youth stoning the soldiers so the locals were trying to get the security forces to move the check-point elsewhere.

The issue with Pauline seemed to have subdued. Allen and he seemed to have achieved an understanding of what their goal was. While discussing possible scenarios was fruitful for them, that was not their principle aspiration. It was to kick start the negotiations by laying down a pathway. Yes, they would relay messages as a trusted channel, but perhaps they could do more. He trusted Allen.

Cathal had asked him if the upstairs room was being used and Dermot answered in the negative. Cathal then asked him to join him after the bar had shut up. He needed to discuss something with him. As Dermot was closing up, the Hard Man, Paul, that was present when Brendan was being interviewed by Cathal came in and told Dermot he was picking up Cathal later on and to just ignore him. Cathal came into the bar and stood in the hallway as three others came in after him and went up stairs. Cathal nodded to the other bloke in the bar, sitting reading a book and said to Dermot:

'Whenever you are ready, Dermot. Come up in five minutes. I have locked the front door.'

'No problem, be up in a minute.'

Dermot had been watching the Old Grey Whistle Test. He didn't watch much television, but enjoyed the Old Grey Whistle Test with its eclectic repertoire of the latest music. He enjoyed some of the American detective shows like Hawaii Five-O, and still enjoyed the cowboys like Bonanza. Some of the British comedy shows like Dave Allen, or Are You Being Served were regular viewing while the British soap set in Manchester, Coronation Street, was a favourite for many, he didn't partake.

He wasn't sure why he was required upstairs. Maybe the new bar that Cathal was proposing was on the agenda or simply, he was needed to serve drinks to Cathal's business pals.

Dermot went up the stairs to the upper bar. Inside were four men: Cathal, Joseph, Jackie, the Belfast man he had lunch with, and a Dublin based well-known Republican – Ronan.

Joseph spoke:

'Come in, Dermot. Sit down here, beside me.'

Dermot detected a fractious tone and immediately became very uncomfortable. Cathal stood in the corner of the little bar. The other two stared intently as Dermot sat down, Cathal's eyes were averted. Dermot remembered Paul downstairs – he was part of the 'nuttin' squad'.

'We know that you have been meeting with Allen, the MI6 agent. Can you tell us here what those talks were about?'

'Nothing really. Just general chat about what is happening. Of course we talked about what the situation was in Northern Ireland. Who were the main protagonists? When will any messages be sent? What are the real chances of any form of negotiations? We didn't have anything from either side to pass on, yet. First and foremost we felt we needed to understand each other, build mutual trust for any possible future discussions.'

'Did you talk about any of us?'

'No, Not directly.'

'Did you talk about your contacts in the Movement?'

'No.'

'Did he ask?'

'No.'

'How many meetings did you have?'

'Joseph, I would say five, six? The last one being a few days ago.'

'And did you two agree on anything? Like a communiqué?'

'What? Only that we would meet again. We have had numerous phone calls. What do you mean a communiqué?'

'Is that safe, talking on the phone, Dermot?'

'We have set up a code.'

'Have you one for me?'

'You are the Butcher, Joseph, because you were an apprentice one. No other reason.'

'I thought you said you didn't talk about me'

Dermot reddened. 'I didn't, only in general terms. Just what might be acceptable to both parties. Anyway, I don't have any direct contact with you.'

245

'You are very diplomatic, Dermot. You have suddenly gone from red to white. Cathal, give Dermot a glass of water. You have nothing to fear.'

'I don't know about that. You are not too happy. I can tell. What is this all about? What are these guys here for? What have I done? I felt you agreed to this. Even Conor told me and you met Allen yourself.'

'First things first, Dermot. Yeah, I am not happy. Secondly, I need to find out what has been said between you and Allen. Have you ever said there was any communication from me and it was to be relayed to the Brits?'

'Never. We never got to that stage. Honest. We were building up trust in each other. He didn't tell me anything about your chat with him. Testing each other's knowledge of the situation. What do you think of him, Joseph?'

'Did you trust him, Dermot?' Joseph asked.

'Yes, I do.'

'Why?'

'He seemed a genuine guy. He wanted a peace settlement as much as me. He wanted an end to the violence, as do I. You know that is my motive. His motive seemed genuine.'

'Would he do something to create mischief? Who was he working for?'

'MI5, he said.'

'Yes, I know that, but who was he really working for?'

'I think he had a direct link to the British Prime Minister's office. His boss talked to one of the PM's advisors. I think there may be a direct link to the Northern Ireland office, too. Not many links in the chain. I felt Allen's role was reflecting the British PM's wish for negotiations, but there are many that would scupper that plan. We discussed who would benefit from a ceasefire and who wouldn't. It was slow, slow progress. A discussion between us. Nothing else. I would say I was at the stage where I could say if he was trustworthy.'

'Well, Dermot. There was nothing slow about the message that Dublin got. It stepped over this channel, with you. You were to funnel any messages through Conor, was my understanding. Look, I trust you, Dermot. You are one of Cathal's family. We just exchanged our views too. However, can you trust this guy for sure?'

'I think so. What was the message Dublin got?'

'That we wish to negotiate how to end the conflict and we need the British Government to handle it so we can save face. That will never be our position. Who gave him that idea? You?'

'Not me. As for him, I never got that impression ever. We were only starting our dialogue. Building mutual trust by discussing our ideas and what words, ideas, concepts to use to explore those ideas.'

'I believe you, Dermot.'

Dermot sat with his eyes to the green and orange swirls of the carpet while Joseph and the others moved to the top of the stairs and whispered.

'Right, Dermot. Tell these gentlemen what you have been doing and what was said. What words you used. Did you ever say the 'conflict is over'? They would like to ask you some more questions.'

'I already told you what happens and what we did.'

Dermot endured another two hours of questioning, going over the same questions and answers. At the end of it, Joseph and the two others again went to the top of the stairs and huddled in discussion. Cathal had left and gone down to the bar. Joseph told Dermot:

'You can go now. I don't think it would be wise to continue the meetings for the moment. If Allen contacts you for another chat, put him off, for now. We will talk again about your role in this channel.'

'It suits me. I wasn't keen in the first place.'

Dermot went down stairs, feeling very relieved. Cathal made a cup of tea for both of them. Paul was still asleep on the chair, his feet on another, but opened one eye when Dermot clinked his mug of tea on the bar. Cathal said nothing about the interrogation upstairs except:

'A taxi is waiting for you outside. Talk to you later.'

When he went out, another man in the shadows opened the car door for him. He was the look out. It was two forty-five in the morning and Dermot was ready for his bed. He was in deep shock.

Allen phones Dermot

Dermot was sleeping soundly when the phone woke him. It was in the living room and the time on the luminescent clock face showed it was six thirty in the morning, and still dark outside. He had only a few hours sleep after getting home from his interrogation in the upstairs bar of the Inishmore pub. His thoughts turned on the potential danger he had placed himself into by talking to an MI5 agent. If Joseph and the rest hadn't believed him, hadn't trusted him, where could he have ended up? His neighbour across the park tried to do him damage. He nearly succeeded, had it not been for Harry. Dermot felt he could have defended himself, but he had tumbled to the ground and twisted his knee. Sean could have kicked him brutally, leaving him worse than he felt now. At least Sean wasn't intent on killing, or so he thought, whereas the potential for him dealing with the 'nuttin squad' had been real and still existed. He wondered if it had soured his relationship with Cathal and if his job was secure. Certainly, the pub didn't seem a welcoming retreat nor the upstairs bar where he had helped Cathal decorate and promote its use. Returning to work for his next shift behind the bar wasn't very appealing.

He had consumed a few whiskeys before falling asleep in his clothes on his bed. The phone had stopped, but rang again. Dermot let it ring off for a third time. He needed to sleep. He needed rest. He needed to work out his next move. What was he going to do? It rang again and Dermot jumped up, grabbing at the door frame to steady himself. He gladly sat down on the sofa beside the phone and answered it.

'Yes.'

'It's Sun Hill here.'

'Who?'

'Sun Hill, can I talk?'

'Yeah, I don't know if I'll understand what you say.'

'Why?'

'I am asleep. I need to go to bed to sleep.'

'Well, waken up and listen up.'

'You got me into deep shit.'

'What do you mean?'

'The Boys had words with me last night about some message they received through a Dublin link that the conflict is over or something.'

'What's happening?'

248

'They are furious. They do not accept that any form of the communication came from them. They thought it was me. Was it you?'

'No. I am sorry. I am not sure what happened, Edinburgh. It gets worse.'

'They probably think it was you. I hope so. They can get at me too easily.'

'What do you mean, Edinburgh?'

'They were serious and seriously upset. No more drinks after midnight with you and me. Stay away.'

'No problem, Edinburgh. Sorry, mate but it gets worse.'

'How?'

'I saw a list from a certain gentleman who frequented your establishment, someone you know. Someone who had daggers for you. I am sure you can guess. It's a major list. I can't meet you otherwise I could explain better. Put it like this. It says you are one of the Boys, running a money-laundering business in the pub. You are also a sex pervert who likes young boys and other people's wives.'

'Shit! Are you serious?'

'Yes. Totally serious. I am serious. Get out. A.S.A.P. The collection is on.'

'What do you mean get out? Who is saying this about me? One of the Boys? Are you talking about a Supergrass?'

'Yes. Not just you. Too many to mention and you are on the list.'

'Shit!'

'Can you go somewhere safe? Do you need help? I could organise a lift for you and you could come to me. Even to London?'

'Sun Hill, I'll be fine, I think. Don't worry.'

'Edinburgh, move out of your flat. A.S.A.P. They are collecting. One last thing. The list has escaped. Everyone including you. You are on your opponents list for extermination.'

'You are not serious, Sun Hill?'

'Get out of your place. I need to go. Bye. Sorry. It's been great. See you in Sussex sometime?'

'Bye, Sun Hill.'

Fuck you, Sun Hill. Fuck you, Harry O'Donnell. Who could he blame for the Pauline mess? No one but himself? Fuck you, Dermot Lavery. Fuck you, Mick Toal, you double crossing wee shite. Cathal wouldn't listen. Mick was bad news from day one. He had warned them. That side kick, Brendan, was just a loser, but Mick controlled him with a mixture of fear and bravado. The lies Mick Toal must have spun – impossible to live like that – mentally disturbed with jealousy and hatred.

Dermot sat staring at his parent's photograph on his mantelpiece and wondered what had happened to his life. He was scared and confused. Allen was talking in riddles and code that he could barely understand. He was warned to leave his flat. He had been warned that he was on a Supergrass list of IRA men and Republicans. Finally, he was also on a Loyalist hit list. He looked around his apartment and thought he had better act. Allen probably knew what he was talking about. An IRA Supergrass in Derry! Jesus, it could decimate their whole structure.

He lifted his parent's photograph and a tear came to his eye. Strange, how deep the emotional bond can produce a tear from nowhere, or was it simply, fear. The tear wasn't from nowhere, he wasn't alone, he had his parents and they had him.

A waste-paper bin was sitting beside the fireplace. Dermot dumped its contents onto the hearth and placed the photograph, and others, into it. He opened the drawers and put in some personal items, went into his bedroom and emptied the drawers plus contents of the wardrobe onto his bed. The suitcase he used for weekends to his parents sat on top of his wardrobe. He couldn't go to Edinburgh as he couldn't get through the ports without being arrested. After putting the clothes, the photographs from the waste-paper bin and other sundry items into his suitcase, he took it up to Harry's office. In Harry's garage he found a couple of large, plastic gardening bags so returned to his flat and stuffed anything and everything that would fit from his apartment and returned with them to the garage.

Dermot was exhausted, mentally and physically. Sleep was needed, but would he sleep? In the garage was some garden furniture. He lifted down a lounger hung on the wall and with some sheets that were drying he made a bed for himself, placing two of his overcoats on top. He was sleeping in seconds.

Dermot fell off the narrow sun lounger as Marie screamed.

'Damn, Dermot. You scared the bloody life out of me. What are you doing here? Look at my sheets.'

'Sorry, Marie. I needed a sleep. Is Harry home?'

'Sleep in your own bed not on my clean sheets. Bloody hell, Dermot, I'll have to wash them again. Are you drunk? Did you lock yourself out?'

'Is Harry home?'

'Yes, he's having coffee in the kitchen.'

'Can I have one too? Please!'

'Why are you sleeping here? Oh why am I not surprised? It's Dermot Bloody Lavery! Oh, Go on! Go ahead up to the house. I'll join you in a minute and you better have a good explanation.'

'Fair enough. You're a sweetheart.'

'Don't you sweetheart me, Dermot Lavery!'

Dermot went to the back door and knocked. No answer. He was shivering, so entered and saw two steaming hot coffees on the table. He took one and enjoyed its hot reviving taste.

'Oh, come on in, Dermot, and make yourself at home, won't you? That's Marie's coffee you are drinking and she will kill you. She will kill me first for letting you take it. She made it with her own delicate hands.'

'Thanks, Harry. You are a gentleman and a scholar.'

'Keep your grovelling for Marie. Jesus, you look terrible. Are you just out of bed? Sick?'

'I am actually. Your garage.'

'What are you on about? Sick of my garage?'

'Will I make a coffee for Marie, Harry?'

'No, sit there and I'll sort it. You need something to eat. Do you want some toast?'

'That would be grand. Harry, you are a gentleman and a scholar'.

'Oh! Shut up.'

Marie came in and over coffee, Dermot explained his predicament. He did not tell them about the previous night's experience with Joseph.

'You can stay here, Dermot, as long as you want.'

Marie eyed her disapproval to her husband with a flicker of her eyebrows.

'Well, stay for dinner anyway, Dermot. My husband will no doubt look after your beverages. From what you say, there may be a few that will be lucky to have a last meal before their incarceration in Long Kesh.'

Dermot was about to cast umpteen compliments on their generosity, but their poker-faced reactions told him it wasn't welcome or required. He was a good friend of the family.

Later after dinner, Harry and Dermot had a whiskey in the office. Harry had seen it before, but never tasted it, though he was tempted. However he had sniffed its pleasant, peaty aroma.

'What are you going to do? Is it all over for you, Dermot? Of course you could stay and fight it. You are completely innocent.'

'Of course I am completely innocent. I can't blame you for this. The bastard never liked me anyway. That boy had a backbone as flexible as a mouse's. Guess how many on the Supergrass's list are people he has held grudges against?'

'How many on the list?'

'One hundred or so.'

'Am I on it? Half of Derry, I suppose?'

'No idea, but they come from all walks of life.'

'When are they lifting them?'

'I think now, as we speak. Allen offered me a lift to anywhere. He could square it and take me to England. The Chief Super of police here knows that I was chatting to Allen, but I have been named and they don't know. I might be in the IRA.'

'Was Cathal named?'

'No idea, but I am guessing they got the names of all the Republicans he could remember and anyone else he didn't like, including me. Imagine, he named me as a child fiddler. He mentioned the other thing. Pauline. He was the blackmailer.'

'You are not serious? How did he find out? Did he name her?'

'Not sure, but I might be able to find out. But I prefer to have nothing to do with yer man anymore. It will look good for a Supergrass to name as many as possible but it will be his word against theirs.'

'It's a right mess, Dermot.'

'I think now is the time to vacate the Maiden City.'

'You should stay. I'll miss you.'

'I'll miss you too. I have been thinking of moving on anyway. Now is the perfect time. Dermot Lavery's perfect storm. Allen said the names have been sent to the UVF. He thinks someone with access to Mick's list has given it to the Loyalists. He said I could be on a death list for negotiating a ceasefire with the IRA. Some in the police and the loyalist community think that is treacherous. Traitors to be burned like Lundy, who wanted to open the gates of the city and surrender during the Siege of Derry.'

'So, what will you do now?'

'Run away to the hills. I have a list of people as long as your arm who want to hurt me or see me dead. I don't think it will be safe to return to my work at the pub. I might pack up a few things, actually I already have. They are in your garage. Might go to the Republic for a few days. It would be unwise to go to Scotland. My name might be on all the police wanted lists at Larne port and the airport. I can get over the border easy enough. Maybe some of the Boys are going that way anyway.'

'Who would have alerted them?'

'Not sure, Harry, but they have means inside the security forces. Someone friendly.'

'Well, let's have one last drink and stay in touch.'

Both refilled their glasses and toasted with a 'Slainte'.

'Dermot, if there is anything I can do, just let me know.'

'No problem, I will. And thanks for your hospitality and friendship if by some chance we don't meet again soon.'

'Where will you go, Dermot?'

'I have a few contacts in Dublin. Some money in a bank there too. If I like it I might stay there awhile, or maybe now's the time to see warmer shores. Australia, here I come!'

'Well, send me a card. I know a few down there and can give you some contacts.'

'Great. Harry, there is one thing I would like before I go. Can I see what takes you up to that tower of yours?'

'Not a problem. Let's go. Be quiet. Everyone's in bed. The stair up is really a ladder. So take your time. At the top, there is a seat behind the opening. Just enough room for both of us.'

They went into the house and on the second floor a door led into a room the size of a walk-in cupboard. It was chilly. On the left, shelves carried the detritus of family life and on the right, a steep stair rose into the glass cube. Harry went first.

'Okay. You saw what I did. Just hold on to the banister. The steps are quite short for your feet. Just hold on and I'll tell you what to do when you get here.'

'Hey, I have climbed stairs, you know.'

'Right, come up.'

Dermot climbed up a few steps and slipped, banging his lips on the rising steps in front of him.

'Jesus, I've busted my lip. I'm bleeding.'

'Are you alright?'

Harry asked hiding his amusement.

'I'm on my way again.'

'Well, slowly, put on the light beside you.'

'Okay.'

Dermot climbed up without further incident, holding a handkerchief to his lip and Harry showed him where to sit as he went down to switch off the light.

'If I leave the light on, the tower lights up like a beacon. You can only see our shadows from down below. It's quite ghostly.'

Dermot picked up the binoculars and surveyed the darkened city. The river twinkled in unison with the few stars that could be spotted between the broken clouds.

'It's quite nice up here. It's a nice night, magical really. The city asleep. Its silhouette against the night sky, very picturesque.'

'It's nice, isn't it? Need our coats. It's not too warm up here.'

'Jesus, look Harry! That's ten Land Rovers I have counted.'

'They must be lifting the Boys on Mick's list.'

Harry opened the window and heard a distant clashing sound coming from the direction of the Bogside. It was the locals banging their metal bin lids on the ground to alert the people that the security forces were raiding and arresting people.

'Get down, Dermot. Down.'

Harry pulled Dermot to his knees while both looked over the window sill. Two Land Rovers pulled into the Park. Soldiers jumped out and went into Dermot's garden and up the side of the house. A policeman banged his door, while soldiers milled around the garden. A window opened above Dermot's apartment and his landlady stuck her head out, hair rollers atop.

'What do you want?'

'Mind your own business, lady!'

'This is my house.'

'Is this Dermot Lavery's house?'

'Did he not answer?'

'No.'

'Then, he's not in.'

'We are going into his flat, Madam. We will knock the door in.'

'No, you bloody won't. That's my door and this is my house. I have a key. Wait a second.'

Mrs. Doherty came down wrapped in her dressing gown, her rollers in a dark scarf. She scolded the security forces as she opened the door. The policeman and two soldiers went in. Mrs. Doherty followed. She came out with a solider by her side and stood at the door – her voice squeaking her objection to the inconvenience.

'Looks like your tenant has scarpered.' The police man shouted to the land lady and the other soldiers. On the other side of the park, Sean opened his bedroom window as a few other neighbours looked out from their bedroom windows too, after hearing all the noise.

'What's going on Mrs. Doherty?'

'Sean, they are looking for Dermot and making me stand out in this bloody weather while they search the place.'

'Hope they find him and throw away the key.'

He pushed Pauline's head back into the bedroom and closed the window.

A clatter of stones bounced off the Land Rovers and a couple of soldiers moved into the shadows, out of sight. One stone ricocheted off the roof of the vehicle, smashed the glass in Dermot's door spraying Mrs. Doherty. Blood flowed from her face as the police man came out to see the commotion. He helped her down to the ground and another soldier got the first-aid kit from inside one of their vehicles. More stones landed close by. Two soldiers ran to the entrance of the Park and shouted back to his officer.

'Three or four fuckin' kids up there.'

'Let one off at them. It might clear them.'

A soldier ran out into the middle of Park Avenue, knelt down and fired a rubber bullet at the stoning youngsters.

'They are running away, Corporal.'

'Good, fuck the little bastards. We have sent for an ambulance for the old dear here. She's bleeding from the face and in shock, I fink.'

Dermot and Harry watched as Pauline ran over to comfort Mrs. Doherty, carrying a blanket. A few other neighbours gathered in their night clothes around her as she lay on the ground. The police man chatted to Pauline for a moment before the security forces left the stricken lady in the care of her neighbours, as they picked her up and carried her inside.

Dermot and Harry looked at each other as Marie called up.

'What's all the noise up there? Some people are trying to sleep.'

Dermot phones Harry

'Hey, Dermot. How are you? Where are you?'

'I am in Dublin and I am fine, Harry. How are you and the family?'

'We are fine too. Great to hear from you. What have you been doing?'

'I have been working in Dublin as a barman, but I am going down under.'

'You mean Cork?'

'Ha, ha, Harry. No, further south. To Melbourne. My friend here has a contact there and will help me out. He works in an Irish pub – the Clifton Hill. My father also informs me he has a cousin living with all the Greeks and Italians in Northcote. According to my father the suburbs are both close to each other. The cousin will also help find me a place to stay and work. I always fancied Bondi Beach, but that is in Sydney.'

'Well, well. My dark horse friend. You will enjoy it anyway. I am sure. What about your Mum and Dad?'

'They said go for it. Edinburgh is too far north, weather-wise and the whole Supergrass thing is still burning.'

'Did you hear the Inishmore bar was bombed by the UVF or UDA?'

'No. I didn't, Harry. When did that happen?'

'The other night. The UVF says the bar was a breeding ground for the Provos. Well, you would know, being the chief barman?'

'Thanks, Harry. Someone listening might think you are serious. Anybody else lifted?'

'No, not that I know of. A lot of them are still inside and God knows where Mick is. He's dead if the IRA gets him.'

'Some were over the border in Donegal at the time and stayed there, Dermot. I think Mick's sidekick Brendan is over the border in a wee pub in Castlefinn called 'The 56'. He was arrested in a raid with a few others by Gardai. I was talking to Pauline yesterday.'

'How is she?'

'She is fine, her family is fine. She said her marriage was saved by you leaving. She thinks Sean would never have been content if you had stayed.'

'Well, Harry. One affair down. Maybe I will have better luck with the females down under.'

'You should have no bother. A big hunk like you. This phone call must be costing you a fortune.'

'Naw, Harry, by the time the owner of the bar gets his bill I should be well away. I didn't tell you about Joseph and his mates calling into the bar. That was the night I stayed at yours. Did I?'

'What are you talking about?'

'Let me just say that the contact thing with Allen went belly up, big time and Joseph suspected me. It was very intense for a while. In the end they believed me. I think Joseph believed me from the beginning, but had to convince the others. One came down from Belfast and one from Dublin.

'Oh no! That was around the time you came for a few nights and stayed on our sofa and we watched your place being raided. Marie thought you wanted to move in with us – a surrogate family she said.'

'She never liked me, Harry.

'Actually Dermot, she likes you a lot, but was worried about you and worse still, your influence on me. She cares about you.'

'What? Well, there you go! Tell her I was asking for her and the kids. I suppose I do see you lot as family.'

'I was coming home from school today and, Dermot I had to drive by the city walls. You will never believe what was written in twelve feet high white letters overlooking the Bogside?'

'Tell me!'

'It said 'I knew Mick Toal, thank fuck he didn't know me.'

Both hurt themselves laughing. When the mirth subsided Harry asked:

'Good luck, Dermot. Will you stay in touch?'

'I will. I will.'

'A Christmas card, at least.'

'Bye, Harry.'

'Dia Duit, Dermot.'

Dermot and Marie

I lay on the bed in the guest room, the dawn light streaking through the blinds, flickering shadows across the bedroom wall. The sough in the trees outside in Cillefoyle Park as they tossed in the wind. I too, tossed about, snug under the blankets, the biting night air in my nose – thoughts of my childhood memories, in Derry and Edinburgh, flooded my fitful sleep. I always sensed my doubleness, living in two places at one time; it had been the two towns of my childhood, now it was Australia and Ireland. I was back in Cillefoyle Park in Harry's house once again, back from Australia, to attend my father's funeral. I woke, thinking about Frank – my one true regret. I felt I could have done more for my old friend. They say as you get older, mistakes get smaller, but regrets get bigger.

I thought about my mother and father and our time in Edinburgh and the little Scottish nonsense song my mother taught me came into my head, 'Wee Hughie'. How did it go?

'Wee Hughie! He's gone to school, Wee Hughie'.

And him not what? What was it? Five? six? no, four. And him not four. That's it.

'Wee Hughie! He's gone to school, Wee Hughie. And him not four. Sure, I seen the fright on him, when he left the door'.

I still had the fright on me, every time I left the door. Most mornings I left for school, I had the fright on me. The fear of being bullied by teacher or fellow pupil or the chance of being strapped by any moody teacher, still lingered in my mind. When Frank was with me, near me, fear did not tread. Those that really were bullied or abused must have nightmares, but not me that night. It was a night of half-dreamt memories, mainly the security of home, the warm memories of tea and toast at suppertime and of course, Frank, my lost childhood friend. It had been stalwart of a mother who had shielded me from the brutality of my father's addiction although it did not entirely erase the good times I had with him. Mostly they were good.

I was a boy once, and in many ways I still was, a trusting innocence. We were boys once – Frank and I. Always together. His dominant presence in my childhood, as if he was an older brother, despite him being the same age. He was a head above all of us yet probably was the same height. Fame and fortune would come his way, it seemed inevitable. His confidence with adults, his chatter to them drew silence, they listened. His confidence with girls at all ages drew admiration from us boys. And I was his best friend. Even, his clothes, cheap as they were, looked well on him, as if they were made for him. His mop-top hair declared this is how I want it, even in those early school days.

I remembered Frank and I, when he had to stay with us, standing on chilly mornings outside the school gates, frost-covered, secured by a sturdy chain and lock. I fiddled with the lock cover, playing with it, frozen to the keyhole, icy even through the woolly mother-knitted gloves. 'Ach, son, you're a bit early for school'. It doesn't open for another half an hour. I was jolted out of my playful trance by a lady walking by. 'Why don't yous come with me to mass? It'll be warmer'. The memories fudged in the reel of my mind.

Her face, searing red cheeks, enlivened by the northerly wind, her eyes sheltered by her hat, neck scarf puffed profusely up around her mouth and chin, deep ruby lipstick springing from her small mouth. A sort of mole on her left cheek despite a layer of make-up powder, and her uncommonly bushy eyebrows contrasting with her glowing tiny-set eyes. I saw her regularly passing the school on her way to church.

One of my earliest solo shopping expeditions was going to the newly-built local chemist to buy Velouty face cream for my mother. Every time I saw a mature female face I wondered as a child what cream they used and every time I saw that lady I wondered the same – what cream did she wear on her face?

She was a familiar figure around the school, living locally and always on the streets, smartly dressed, always on the go, a 'gallivanter' as my Granny Ellen would say. Her distinguishing feature besides her bushy eyebrows was her friendliness. She talked and smiled to everyone, especially the children, admonishing anyone that she thought needed it, as she passed squabbling youngsters or cheeky colourful remarks, she would remonstrate with them all. The school children knew her, as she commanded them daily, 'I hope yous are working hard at your books and you'll have a great future' or as we played in the school yard shouting to us, 'enjoy yourselves now when you can cause your childhood will soon be over!' That frosty morning I went to the church with her, close to my school Saint Bernard's in Edinburgh.

Inside the altar was aglow in gold and blue, a smattering of elderly citizens suitably over-coated, crushed into the front seats. Behind, in the cool twilight, people spread across the remainder of the seats. There was no warmth, but for an absence of the life-sucking wind, the familiar ritual on the altar provided some comfort. I slipped into the hesitant group at the back while my female escort walked to the front seats and sat close to the worshipping mass of her peers.

As I lay in the dark the memories flooded back to me. One Saturday morning, triumphant with a purchase of Velouty cream, my mother had been cleaning the cuffs and collars with blocks of Pears brown soap before putting them into our vibrating twin-tub washing machine where I, as usual attached myself as it spun, sending a thrill through my five-year-old body. The coalmen delivered their black nuggets to the neighbourhood, on most Saturday mornings before the family went shopping. While flicking coal dust in the gutter I waited for them. My mate, Frank, visited relatives in the street. He lived in a terrace high on a hill, on the other side of town. Even when my family spent summers in Derry, Frank sometimes came with us.

I wondered if he would turn up at the funeral. Would he be sober? We met a few times, mostly by accident, on the street over the past years when I came back for visits. Once again the years dripped away, as if life had never happened to us. We were older, but every time we met we melted into the same kids, a raw nerve somewhere touched and flared with old memories and emotions. He never held any grudges.

I opened my eyes, more light dabbled the pine furniture of Harry's guest room, nicely decorated in a slight floral theme, the signature of Marie. I thought if I had stayed in Derry, would I have a room like that? Did Harry have a hand in its decoration? The kids had left, but, even though the house was too big for them now Harry would never move. Harry's soul was embedded in that house and his glass tower.

Normally during a restless night I would get up and get myself a herbal tea or scan the newspapers or read a book. I switched on the light. My book was still stashed in my day bag at the foot of the bed, so I perused the best sellers Marie had left for the guests on the bedside table. Nope, they wouldn't do. I got up.

Pulling on some clothes for warmth and respectability I went downstairs as silently as possible to the kitchen and put on the kettle. Thankfully they had a downstairs toilet. I didn't want to wake anyone using the toilet. Hopefully the water system was quieter than my own in Australia. There, the water came down the middle of the house and then distributed to its requirements, but rattled all the way, a water hammer, especially the hot water, gushing up from the outside water heater.

The day of the funeral was going to be a long one for everyone, it was best to let them sleep. Harry and Marie had kindly stated they would be with me all the way – their welcome and hospitality outstanding, as usual. When they met me at the airport, and we all embraced, both had told me to treat their home as my own, that they were family. It was a nice gesture from Marie, as she was always sceptical of my motives. There was some truth in it when things went belly-up, before going to Australia. Using Harry's office potentially had put the family in the firing line. However, their heartfelt empathy at the death of my father was genuine, but I wasn't sad though. Yes, it was an end of an era, and yes, my father didn't mean to cause all the hurt to me or my mother or the people around him. I had phoned him occasionally from Australia and I talked to Harry many times about my father in his later years. Indeed, Harry had invited him to his house for dinner after my mother died.

I poured a cup of tea and trawled a magazine sitting on the bench when Marie appeared in a quilted, maroon dressing gown. It almost covered her house slippers. She was really a sweet person, older and settled in her ways. Intolerant of anything that would smack of silliness, like me. She was very worried about her husband's role with Allen and had blamed me for getting him mixed up in it. He obviously never told her it had been his fault. She was very aware of her social image and how that must be attended to, cultivated just like her landscaped back garden.

My knowledge of Marie was through Harry and vice versa. There was little need to explain anything to her, she knew about me already, from Harry's point of view. Their marriage was one where all was shared, including my friendship with Harry. Marie was never jealous of me, she was much too critical and did not want to be involved in the secret talks.

'Not sleeping? Me neither. My head is spinning.'

'Here, I'll pour you a cuppa. I made a pot for some reason. Why is your head spinning?'

'No thanks, I'll have a peppermint tea. Oh, you have it poured already, Okay, skip the peppermint tea then, thanks.'

She sat looking at me sipping the un-milked tea I had made and ignored my question. I was thinking about all the stuff that went with the death stuff. The botheration of it all, interrupting their routine. Was her head spinning because of that botheration? Marie's attitude was - you just do it, just cope with it, very pragmatic. Hopefully, someone will do it for me when I depart without too much whingeing, I thought.

261

My father's brother, Uncle John was taking care of the funeral. He had taken my father under his roof, but strictly managed his drinking and it had seemed to work. It kept him off the streets. The man who died was not the man that had reared me. My phone calls to him were short and bittersweet.

'Marie, why are we having a church funeral? Dad hated the church! He was a communist.'

'It's your Uncle John's doing. So be it. He looked after him in his later years. Are you hanging around much, after the funeral?'

'No, I think not. I am booked for next Friday. I might jaunt over to Edinburgh or Manchester, not sure, unless they need me for something?'

'No, no, it's all under control, I was chatting to your Uncle John about it. It's all sorted.'

'That was kind of you. I knew you would do anything that needed to be done and if anything wasn't done and you weren't told you would be furious. I talked to him too and he said it was all under control. Even though he said he didn't need the money I sent him some. He said in that case we'd have steak instead of ham sandwiches for the funeral breakfast.'

We both laughed. Marie was very efficient when she applied herself – perhaps proof of the solidity in her marriage. It's not that she whinged much to me about anything, but any annoyance was written on her face, expressed on her posture. Perhaps Harry got the full force of that. She had lived in the same house in the same town for decades and every time I had talked to her I got the sense that she was about to embark on a new project or expedition to the South Pole or deepest Africa. No sense of the rhythm of her routine. Something was always pending and required diligent project management. While very pragmatic, everything for her required the most complicated planning and thought. Harry was the brake to her accelerator. She knew my father had been dying for years, but listening to her you think it had happened suddenly, that required urgent planning. For me, death was always a shock but life went on, just get on with it. That's me being a realist. Maybe that is the same as being a pragmatist?

I also thought these occasions were an opportunity to renew friendships, relationships, meet relatives, and reflect on life, because routine life stops for a few days. A degree of consolation from a sad business, whereas Marie saw it as a list of things to do. I absentmindedly stirred my tea, spilling some over onto the bench. Marie, within an instant, had swiped it with a dish cloth.

'Are you dozing off to sleep? Perhaps you should go to your bed? If I can do anything, let me know.'

'No, you are being too kind already, putting me up and coming to the funeral.'

'No worries, as you say in Australia. We appreciated all those lovely presents you sent to us and the kids.'

'I am sorry I kept Harry out at the pub last night. We were only going for one, but we met other people and they insisted on buying us drinks in my father's memory.'

'God love him. Harry doesn't go out much to the pub these days since you left. Have you seen Frank? I haven't heard anything about him recently. I think they live in Donegal, Greencastle or Moville, or somewhere in that direction.'

'No, it would be nice to see him. I got a Christmas card, last time. It had a Derry post mark.'

'I happened to run into them in Longs Supermarket, ages ago. Frank looked well. They both looked well. I think they are starting to look after themselves. When I had my operation, Jen was visiting someone else, discovered I was in and came to see me for a chat. She told me Frank was having depression problems. When I meet Jen I found out more local gossip about this town in ten minutes than I had heard in ten months. I don't know who they stay with, it's a wonder they don't move back here. I used to see them often, but not recently. Truthfully I avoid them if possible.'

'I avoided him when I lived here. I guess there is still a hint of guilt. He was an alcoholic, on the streets half the time. Truth be told, I have an awful lot of guilt.'

'No need. Harry told me about your friendship with Frank. Oh! Sorry Dermot. I see it still upsets you.'

'I should have done something for him. He was there for me.'

'There was nothing you could have done. It was an addiction. He would have robbed you as soon as he looked at you.'

'Still, I feel guilty about it.'

'Maybe, he might turn up. He could have given your father's eulogy. Both being alcoholics and all that.'

'Oh, you are cruel, Marie! Frank, Jen and I were out for a drink one Christmas I visited Derry. When Frank went to the bar, Jen laughed at me in drunkenly scorn, 'you know, he always talks about you, as if you were part of our marriage and we're not even married'.

'She had a terrible temper especially when drinking, Dermot.'

'I know. He was like a brother to me, albeit a distant and fractious one. We grew up together. I would love to see him. If he doesn't turn up, I will go and see him.'

'Seems more than that, Dermot. I think you two would have been good together.'

'Oh! Stop it, Marie.'

'She was jealous of the only continuous adult relationship in his life – although it was a peripatetic friendship. It was less complicated if we saw each other on our own. I was married too, with kids living in Melbourne. Frank always said they would come down under, but I was glad they didn't. Too much stuff not washed under the bridge. I wonder if Frank will attend my father's funeral.'

My father had returned to Derry and sought help for his alcoholism. With a few exceptions he managed to live a life with it under control. It was not going to be a restful night, with my mind flitting between the joyous innocence of sunlit play in the streets and escapades of my childhood days with Frank by my side. Importantly, Frank was there during the adolescent rite of passage, through our teenage bumbling, sex-obsessed years and finally becoming young men – a period that bonded us further, even though he had another life. Frank became a young man almost overnight. I spent a few years getting there. I was a bit of a hybrid, a doubleness of man and boy. I continued:

'Even Barbara, his ex-wife, seemed to be jealous of our relationship, our connection. On one occasion Frank and I went out on a pub crawl. Things weren't going well with Frank and his wife then. Things I didn't know about, things I didn't want to know about. Barbara and Frank were having another split. Not surprisingly we visited the same pubs, reliving the old days and found Barbara and her mates boozing too, although I thought she hadn't been drinking too much. When they met Frank tried to play the gentleman and decided to buy a round of drinks, rum and coke, whether they wanted one or not, so everyone got one. Frank must have had his own reasons for deciding that drink. While Frank and one of the other girls went up to the bar to get the drinks, Barbara turned to me, staring, mouth awry, eyes flaring, trying to find the words to say, but all that emerged was a slurring gush. Her purple eye shadow slightly smeared over her left eye, where she had rubbed it. 'Why the foock don't zoo look aft' t'him?' She said it with deep, drunkenly venom, haunting jealousy on her voice. It scared me. Time to leave, I thought, or at least get out of the way, so I went to the toilets. Everyone seemed to laden me with Frank, even my mother.'

'You seem to have that sort of problem: you and Harry, you and Frank.'

'Don't tell me you are jealous too, Marie'

'Don't flatter yourself, Dermot Lavery. Frank went screaming into life with all the attendant issues of alcohol, drugs, people, sex and he paid dearly for it. I know you wish now you could have helped him. We all avoided him; he was a tortured alcoholic. You were on different paths. Little did anyone know that your life was going to explode and that you had to leave the city for your own safety.'

'Funny I don't think about that period too often yet I had never forgotten Frank. But the best was to come that night, when I went to the toilet later on that night, Marie, at the urinal a drunken face turned to me and grinned. I was more concerned where his squirting was going. After a few perfunctory greetings and one eye on the other fellow's aim, I tried to hurry myself, but I had a few pints. My wobbling neighbour again turned his face to me, and thankfully that was all he turned, and he slurred – 'when you get a bladder infection, urine trouble'. At that point I finally emptied my bladder, leaving the pissant, Mick Toal, giggling to himself. Yes, that Mick Toal.'

'No! Getaway! I don't believe you. Well, it's only a wee town.'

Both of us laughed, spilling off the breakfast stools, perhaps it was another case of humour noir. I was transported back to the time when my father had crawled underneath the sofa to get something and I came into the room. Not seeing him, I jumped onto the sofa. He let out an almighty scream and I ran out of the room and into the street, bent in two, laughing. I didn't go back inside until hours later. I recounted the memory to Marie. She laughed and said:

'Good memories, best to remember those, forget the bad stuff. You are always remembering stuff from your childhood. I suppose that's one way of understanding life. Life can be understood backwards but only lived forwards. Anyway, was your Dad hurt?'

She asked with a tinge of scorn on her voice.

'God, Marie, that has never occurred to me ever. If he was it was never mentioned. Maybe I was always an outsider and always looking back, studying people, watching people, a bit like Harry. You know, childhood is the purest well to draw from.'

'Well, don't draw from me, for God's sake, and leave Harry out of it. I keep telling him people will think he's a pervert, looking into houses.'

'He still does it?'

'Yes he does. The fool. It's funny how people still talk about you and Frank, as if you were brothers. All those years ago and neither of you not living here. You two always seem to come up in a conversation.'

'We get on well enough still. We send each other a Christmas card.'

I said, tongue in cheek. Marie wobbled on her stool, spitting back her tea into her cup from which she had just drunk.

'It wasn't that funny. I guess we swim in two different streams, always have done.'

'Oh, Jesus, here you go again, drawing on wells and swimming in streams. It's a wonder they don't ask you to speak at the funeral.'

'They did.'

'Will ye stop, I'm goin' to fall off me stool. Are you?'

'No, I'll let Father Jim do the eulogy. He got on well with John and my father. Uncle John has it all organised. Do you see any of my other friends?'

'Yes, Jimmy and his wife Eleanor. Sometimes she phones. I can't get her off the phone. It's like a long-lost relative. She is the boss in that household – SWMBO – She Who Must Be Obeyed.'

Marie was teetering on the edge of her stool, smothering her giggles with the collar of her dressing gown.

'What are you on about now? SMW... Say that again?'

'S-W-M-B-O, SWMBO, She Who Must Be Obeyed. Jimmy's wife is a SWMBO.'

'Christ, will you stop it, it's four in the morning.'

Tea dribbled down her buttoned-up dressing gown.

'It's four in the mornin' and woke up in the dawnin', just woke up, the wantin' in me.'

I cranked it out rather too loudly.

'Shush, will you shut up. It'll waken Harry upstairs. God, you're a trouble maker. Remember all those chats? All those meetings with you-know-who in the garage? Allen something? He was a Derry man, I believe. Harry told me everything. All in the wee hours in the morning.

266

It's a wee while ago now! What are you doin' with a bottle of whiskey? Where did you find it? God sake it's after four, and don't start singing again.'

'It was sitting above the cups. Going to Australia was the best thing for me. The lifestyle, the weather, a new woman and kids. It's a great place. You know, I met Mick Toal again. One night in the The Auld Craic, an Irish music pub in Melbourne, full of comhluadar, full of craic – Mick walked in. Smiled. Bought me a Guinness, tapped me on my shoulder. He said he was just visiting and that was that. He was with some Aussie bloke and sat at the back. I didn't know what to say. Every time I glanced at him, he smiled and waved, obviously watching me. He offered me another Guinness when he left, but I said I was grand. He bought it anyway. I made sure I didn't visit the toilet at the same time as him, but he seemed very sober this time. That was that.'

'Has he settled in Australia? Anyway you are changing the subject. Are you sure you found the whiskey there? I didn't leave it there. It doesn't belong there. Ah, God! Everything is topsy-turvy these days.'

Marie seemed to be more interested in the whereabouts of the whiskey than the reference to those bad old days.

'Are you accusin' me of rampaging through your drawers?'

'Behave yourself. Do you think it will be a big funeral?'

Marie asked, as usual deflecting any awkward moments.

'I don't know, Marie. Well, my parents were well known, never really left the town.'

'Leave that bottle down, it's late and I don't want you singing again.'

She looked at me sternly, almost wanting to tell me off. Marie enjoyed telling me off, telling anyone off, telling them what to do. She felt it was a given right, but she kept her thoughts to herself this time. We sat sipping our now lukewarm tea.

'We should go to bed, even just to rest, as it will be a busy couple of days. I guess it's today already. It's lovely to see you here. I know you. You would sit all night discussing what life is all about.'

'Ah! The existential scandal of the insignificance! Don't worry I'll not start, but thanks for having me. I guess I should have been at the wake tonight, but I'll stay there all day tomorrow.'

'Well, I'll head up to bed before you do start. See you in a few hours. You're not seriously going to touch that bottle?'

'Here, mark the level. I can always top it up with water.'

'Oh! Get lost. You are still a big kid, just like my husband. Good night for what's left of it.'

She leant over and pressed my hand, smiling yet her eyes were immobile.

'We are all big kids, cause the rules keep changing. Who said that? Was it Kundera?'

Her cool stare was softened by a few weary blinks and off she went. I was left looking at the bottle and my dead cup of tea. It was time for bed, but I wasn't too sure what to do. I heard the toilet flush and Marie stuck her head around the door again.

'I've put on your electric blanket, give it a minute. Night.'

'You're a saint, I didn't even know I had one.'

'I know I am! Please tell everybody.'

I got up and rinsed the cups under a dribble of water.

My wife and kids had stayed in Melbourne. They didn't really know their grandfather and father-in-law. They visited a few times and loved Derry and Donegal with all that craic. A few cousins around, of course, just Uncle John left and he seemed to have got on well with my father.

I went upstairs and climbed into the warm bed. Dad was about to join my Mum in the cemetery. She had died suddenly just after I left Derry and I hadn't been able to return. They say her death hadn't been connected to my leaving. The smoking had caught up with her and her husband lingered on despite his maniac lifestyle. Her death had left an indelible mark on me and burying my father would help to a degree the grief of not attending her funeral.

We were all different, living different lives, just like Frank and Harry, same but different.

The last thing I remembered before dozing off was the dozens of eggs Cathal's parents used to buy from an old couple, up a lane in Donegal on a Friday night. I sometimes went with them. The farmhouse had a sparse kitchen with a picture of the Queen above the back door. It was better than thinking about the other stuff.

The Wake

'God, I nearly wet myself. Right at the foot of the coffin too, and himself lying there. He was a good-looker in his day. He could argue the life out of ye, always did as a wee boy. Do ye want one of these coffin nails?'

He mischievously offered a saucer of cigarettes, as he drew heavily on his and handed it to me. The cigarettes laid out in a neat circular fashion. He continued his story:

'I suppose, I will. It's a bitter night. Jesus, I did wet myself. When you reach my age, there tends to be more dribbles.'

I had just joined him after relieving myself in the corner of the garden.

'Go and borrow a pair of Uncle John's or my Dad's. He'll not mind. I think I saw some knickers hanging on the line. Get one of them. She'll not mind either. Remember the Knicker-Thieves? You couldn't leave your knickers out overnight. They would be gone the next morning.'

His cackle exploded in a cough spewing up phlegm and he spat into the darkness into the flower bed.

'Naw, I soaked it up with bog roll, half of it is still in there.

'Jesus, I don't want to know if you need a nappy.'

I was getting uncomfortable about this bloke's personal hygiene. We were joined by his wife. She was slightly bent, but forced herself erect, a well-cut dark suit hanging gently on her.

'You're not smoking again? You fool, with your lungs. You would think you would know better.'

He wheezed a harsh rattle to prove her point.

'The first time I smoked, was one of yours. You had us heavin' the bloody car engine out one wintry November evening and my father nipped off to fetch a wrench or something. I didn't inhale and blew all the smoke out, but it warmed me up a bit.'

His eyes warmed.

'Good memories.'

'Do you want me to get you a coat? It's nippy out here.'

'No, thanks, son, I'm wearing my thermals. My dear wife looks after me. She had everything laid out on the bed, my clothes with my thermals. I am only out for a breath of fresh air. Isn't that right, dear? I am almost talked out.'

'You're talked out! Me arse! You go out for a loaf in the morning and return at teatime. You two can stay out here and freeze. I am away in.'

I stared into the garden, but glanced meekly at his eyes, the warmth still there.

'I'll head in shortly.'

He called after her.

'She doesn't mind, Like your father, she'd talk the legs off a donkey. All that politics stuff. Look at us now. I remember him at the bottom of the street chatting to all and sundry and hours later he was still there. Your gregarious father on the street: his trademark bow tie, that was in his later years, walking stick as always, the tweed hat supported by his ears. It was great. He would give some nephew or some kid a sixpence and then forget and give them some money again. He was standing in the street for so long.'

'I remember. I had to amuse myself while he nattered on. He didn't give me any money.'

The funeral would take place tomorrow, and it had been decided to sit up all night. I did the first shift from eleven to two with my Uncle John and his son Pauric. Most of his living relatives and friends had turned up for the wake. Uncle John was a stalwart, my father didn't die alone, not that he would have known anyway, but who knows. They say they can hear. The hearing is the last thing to go. I got there shortly after, when the nurses wanted to sort a few things before the undertakers arrived. A crowd was in the corridor, the first time in years, I had seen the familiar faces.

Relatives had travelled from all over and abroad, including me. My father and mother were well known, because of their socialising and political activity – always available for the latest cause. I was looking forward to sitting with Pauric, my cousin. He was always great craic and full of old stories, even his family incessantly said he 'smoked like a chimney and drank like a fish' in a reverse psychology kind of way. Pauric was a bit like Dad and could tell a good story. He would joke with him about his politics, but, while easy-going, he had inherited the family's interests, but was just a little more relaxed about it.

I went inside and sure enough there he sat by the window, puffing out tobacco smoke into the night air – a glass with golden liquid sat near his elbow. He winked at me as I walked in. I hooked my rear onto the window still.

'How ya goin', mate?'

'Not bad, not bad. Your Da had a good innings. He always gave the impression he was younger than my Da, but he wasn't. Never wanted to play the eldest son's role. Boy, he was a character.'

Conor and Cathal appeared at the door, beaming with genuine warmth. Both came over and as I held out my hand, they both threw their arms around me almost at once. Tears felt like flowing but didn't. This emotional bond was absent in my Melbournian life. Pauric piped:

'Dermot, yer man here, Conor, is a leading socialist activist and commentator. He should be President of the Socialist Republic of Doire.'

'Pauric, shut up, will ya?'

'Conor, well done. Carrying the Red Flag in one hand and the Tricolour in the other. I have read some of your stuff in Australia. When is the book coming out?'

'Soon, I think.'

Cathal nodded to me to go outside. Conor pushed my shoulder lightly and I followed them out. Conor started:

'It's great to see you Dermot and that's from both of us. Sad time for you, but we want you to know that what you did in Cillefoyle Park was the right thing to do. Never mind you getting your leg over and that wee bastard that squealed. It laid contacts.'

I didn't tell them I had seen the 'wee bastard' in Melbourne. Conor continued:

'The talks are continuing because of the foundation you laid and you never know what might come from them. The trust you built with your bloke was not wasted. He contacted me after a month or so. Having said that, it's a different bloke now.'

I asked who it was.

'You don't need to know, but don't think you didn't help. You took a chance and we appreciate it.'

'Well, folks I guess it is a consolation. I have a life in Melbourne now. I better go in. Funnily enough I am thinking more about Frank at the moment, who maybe I could have saved.'

'I remember when he came over from Scotland. He used to stay in our house with you. I thought he was settled now in Donegal. Look you did your best. We all tried to help when he was on the streets. I thought he and Jen had gotten back together. See you at the funeral tomorrow.'

'Bye and thanks for coming. It means a lot to me.'

I went in and Pauric was still dozing and I sat down beside him. He stirred, and looked at me with bleary eyes, but his mind was still meandering:

'It was a blessing he gave up the alcohol. He still had some function in his liver. You know they were planning to book the church hall for Granny for her hundredth birthday party, but she didn't make it. She mentioned to me once she was looking forward to the Queen's telegram so she could tell her where to stick it!'

'Your father helped a great deal. All the good genes too.'

He laughed, opened the window, spat, and flicked his butt into the darkness.

'I remember coming into Granny's for lunch. I used to go next door sometimes if she was busy. Coming here from my first couple of years at primary school. We were fed intellectually by a warrior class of Christian Brothers – thumped, battered and bruised for our own benefit, educationally and spiritually. We were young soldiers of the church and Ireland. One pupil got bounced off walls and strapped more than us, because his father was one of our teachers. Us now dreamin' of our lives past, present and what of the future? Growing up in this wee town. What was real and what were just confused memories?'

Pauric was continuing in his philosophical frame of mind:

'Imagined memories metamorphosing into real memories or are these memories susceptible to time and mood? Wouldn't it be great to travel back in time, like Doctor Who? Just wander around. If you could travel back to the earliest memories. Did they happen? Did it happen like that? Does it really matter? Your family, your environment and your culture influences makes you, makes you the person you are. Your community formed your roots, spiralling to the present day. Your memories and dreams collide in a fusion of unreality, yet seem very real, as if they happened yesterday. A flow of motion, emotion. It runs deep. I suppose I won't realise my own parental influences until they have passed away or I'm rearin' kids myself. I do remember Granny's stories though; I am not sure if I should be grateful for her family's help supporting the Brother's school.'

'Are you drunk? Well, they did that, all right. You know about your Great Granny's vision. She was told to work for the parish and develop it. Your Granny continued that work, but it was community work. Her mother, your Great Granny, was walking with a friend through the fields that backed onto the chapel. They were in their twenties and were not young impressionable girls. It was a warm summer's evening and the two ladies were strolling along the path in the fields, at the corner of the church and a blue light shone and supposedly a figure appeared. She was told her role was to help the local church and she devoted her life to it.'

'That's where the grotto is now, Granny never really talked about that, loads of other things, but not that. She never was a great Church supporter. She went to mass daily and supported the priests who had a social conscience.'

'I think it suited everyone, including the church to play it down. It didn't stop the bus loads coming and your Great Granny always had the Bishop's ear. A couple of PP's didn't stay too long cause they didn't like her influence.'

The memories started flowing back to me, small touchstones, like going to mass with Granny. These happy emotions projecting through time, holding with trance-like immediacy, a meditation, pent-up energy of life, transient and momentary – memories of tangible embrace.

'Are ye sleeping, Dermot, or what?'

'Just thinking of times I spent in Derry, at school. She produced lovely meals, traditional fare, followed by tea and special pastries bought that very morning. She would always try to buy me a chocolate coconut finger, my favourite. After tea, money for spending, three pence, the twelve-sided 'three D'. Winter or summer, a very happy and nourishing time was had for those two years at school here. She taught us we were a special breed, always advising, on whom to mix with or not to talk to, a bit rough, she would say. Always believed in fair play and social justice. Catholics wouldn't get it in the state of Ulster. This state of affairs was well known around town, even the way we pronounced things. We were well reared as they say.'

This shroud of security was being formed by the family's closeness and support for each other, a part of your makeup as your genes, sort of laughable in retrospect, but part of my roots, why deny them? Pauric was laughing again.

'Some say they had a posh accent! Ah, many couldn't even write their name. They came to your grandmother to write letters for them, and when they were looking for help, they came and asked. They were well connected. But you can never please people.'

'I guess people don't worry about what people think these days. It was a village then and standards had to be maintained so people thought they were snobs. Just trying to lead a decent life for their family. I think Granny was a subtle snob.'

Pauric was nodding and staring out the window and automatically took a sip from his glass.

'Next door to Granny's, McCaffrey's was full of life, steam and heat. Girls and boys, half dressed, bra-chested girls. Great fun. That was great, a glimpse into someone else's world. Even the tea and toast tasted better, real life, comprising of hot, strong tea and toast and half naked men and woman. It was cacophony for my eager senses. What a feast! I loved it. They were my other family.' Pauric shut his eyes, but I could see the upper lip rise a little, maybe nodding off. It was late. Most people had left. There was no one around. Someone was in the wake room. Pauric woke up:

'Granny lived with us towards the end. You take people for granted, just like your parents. She was always there.'

Pauric's lower lip quivered:

'Granny was tiny, always wore dark clothes, always neat, hair in a bun, with a small wrinkled face. She always was pleased to see you coming over on your holidays. She had shining eyes, set well in with a narrow pointed nose just like mine. Her hair was long, but always in a bun. On occasions, if I saw her in the morning, her hair hung over her shoulders of her dressing gown. She wasn't the granny I knew, but some younger shadow. I too loved my granny's dinners, always followed by custard. This was an emporium of custard. It couldn't be bettered. You must remember all this stuff? Every lunchtime I ran to Granny's from school, skipping over the cracks and edges of paving stones. A warm blazing fire in the little backroom was a great welcome. The cat ever present outside on the window ledge perched beside a blue ceramic potted plant of ill-determined health. She had a huge dresser littered with silver plates and bowls. It occupied one wall. A television and radio sat in the corner above the bookcase. A broken tile in the hearth drew my eye every time I went there. Why was it never fixed? A fat leather sofa filled the remainder of the room leaving a narrow passage on a threadbare-threatening carpet.'

'Yeah, I remember all that, Pauric. You paint a great picture. They always seemed to have money yet their house was never fancy. It had an air of decaying wealth and respectability that also hung around Granny. Grandfather had an army pension and a shock of thick white hair. He would appear at lunchtime, often dressed immaculately in waistcoat and bow-tie. He always suffered ill-health caused by the gas in the First World War, after joining up at sixteen, lying about his age. A horse-riding general was looking for a batman and he volunteered, thinking he would be working with horses. He had no idea what a batman was! Later, he was shipped home after being gassed. He loved the horse racing, often listening to the results on the radio or nipping across to the bookies. On good days he simply chatted to anyone passing his front door. When I came in, he commented about the weather, pointing out the wind vane at the local church. He liked custard too. Daddy liked custard. They all liked custard.'

'They always gave us money, despite my mother complaining and asking them to stop.'

'My mother was the same, almost scolding me for taking it. Within the dresser lay my money box. Granny kept it for me. I remember the one penny glass of lemonade in a shop lined by bottles of boiled sweets. It was run by two old maids. I had a friend in Limerick and when his Granny died, they had a party, that lasted more than a weekend. We should have done that for my father. Got you to organise it. Had a big party for family and friends instead of a wake.'

'It's not too late, is it?'

Pauric laughed at this and whispered to me.

'Well, that subtlety wasn't passed to my Dad nor yours! Maybe it was a reaction to their upbringing. They like to think they were down to earth, no airs and graces, common men fighting for social justice and I suppose they were.'

'Did you know that some got away to Australia like you?'

'What do you mean?'

'Two went to Australia, my Great Aunt Maggie and her husband, a policeman, William. They must have bought a farm because we have photos of them at it, with bullocks in the background. That was a long time ago, maybe the 1920s and another relative joined the navy and went to Sydney. They did send letters.'

The funeral was the next morning and we had been joined by the next group sitting up overnight. It was going to be a big funeral. Such is the joy of being part of a family. These people, my family, aspects of remembered characters and captivating memories; the custard, the childhood extended family, in essence, my roots, were the Guinness of my Childhood. I got a lift to Harry's and Marie's house in Cillefoyle Park.

The Funeral

It was a huge funeral and a short walk to the old chapel. People stood on the pavement and many of them followed the hearse too as the road meandered like a question mark to a full stop at the Long Tower Church. Many of the groups that he had had a political association with turned up. I saw some Red flags, Tricolours, and a couple of Trade Union banners lining the route. The remaining family joined me in the final walk to the priest at the church door. After the prayers at the entrance, the coffin was negotiated through the porch before being set up on the trestles in front of the altar surrounded by fresh flowers. I saw Peter, my Dad's friend place a Red flag on top of it.

The cedar aroma of the pews mingled with the perfumed congregation. How many times had this church featured in my life? Maybe it was this church's graveyard that seeded my fascination for them. I love churches – the plain and the ornate, but it's the graveyards that fascinate me the most. Another graveyard spreads on the other side of the Bogside, where most of my relatives are buried and where Kevin will finally rest beside his wife. Walking here for mass with Granny on those damp and dreary mornings, the damp coats and musty interior, at least out of the wind and the rain, getting close to the hot pipes or, better still, beside a radiator for comfort of a secular sort. Peeling paint bubbled here and there on the inside walls, despite many attempts to maintain an even surface.

It hadn't really changed. The family gathered in the front pews with friends and extended family. I saw Harry and Marie and a few old faces. I waved to Cathal and Conor. Anyone's death provided a jolt to think how time passes and our own mortality, a time for reflecting. Kevin, as they all said at the wake 'had a good innings'.

The priest wore purple. I remember we were taught that special occasions required special colours like violet on Passion Sunday to show the shedding of the blood. Some things were omitted for the Requiem mass, like the Alleluia which is regarded as an expression of joy. They also chant the prayers for the dead.

It wouldn't have felt strange to go back to Granny's for Sunday dinner – three vegetables and a piece of chicken. There wasn't much room in the pews, in those days. We were packed tight bum-to-bum. I did a bible reading – 'There is a time, Ecclesiastes 3'. Pauric did one too. We smiled at each other as he returned to his seat.

The priest spoke of Kevin's passion for social justice and the many bumps on the road to sobriety. After the service the coffin was carried out to the entrance. Pauric, Uncle John, Peter, two other cousins and I were pall-bearers. At the door the coffin was manoeuvred onto a trolley where once again it was escorted by relatives to the hearse before being taken to a grave in a corner of the old part of the graveyard. It was also close to his parents' grave. They had purchased it years ago. Uncle John, the relatives, Harry and Marie and friends stood wrapped against the elements and supported on both sides by their children.

When the coffin was lowered, Pauric murmured to us – it's the end of another era. We nodded in agreement. Hooking Uncle John under his arms, Pauric and I walked him to the car at the closest gate. He needed a rest before the funeral breakfast.

Pauric and I stood around talking, shaking hands to all, who came to give their final condolences. Quite a few of the people were faces I recognised, but whose names I couldn't remember, expressing their sympathies; most by saying simply the old adage 'Sorry for your bother'. Many others added 'he had a good heart' or something similar. Their faces gaunt and firm, and many holding their eyes to mine to ensure their seriousness of their sympathies, an unusual gesture for me. Pauric and I got a few internal chuckles when some old lady wrapped like a Christmas present, wearing a glinting lime overcoat said to me 'the saints are in heaven and the babies are in purgatory'.

'Did you hear that? What was that all about?'

'Ah, she's a bit batty, she's as old as the Guildhall. She was at the wake every day, drinkin' and eating as much as was offered. I bet she didn't make a meal those days. If it had been a wedding, she would have stayed for the christening.'

Both of us laughed. Pauric suggested she would be at the funeral breakfast. Most had departed or were on their way to their cars when Pauric asked:

'Shall we go?'

'Do you fancy a walk around the graveyard?

'I hear you were fond of graveyards. I didn't think you were religious. We should go. They'll be waiting for us.'

'You mean your wife and the rest will be expecting you. I ain't religious, but someone said 'We are not human beings on a spiritual journey, but spiritual beings on a human journey.' I guess there is some truth in that.'

'True, a good one, that. They'll be expecting me and you. Anyway we have the hired horse and carriage.'

'That's right, Pauric. Is there anyone else going with us in our limousine?'

'A couple of the children. I'll tell them to meet us in five minutes. You want to visit a grave.'

Pauric joined me at our grandfather Bill's grave. It was huge. A granite block the size of a small wardrobe. Our Lord perched on top, his finger shortened by a stray bullet. It used to have railing around it, but now like most it was grassed over and kept tidy.

'There used to be a kneeling stone here too?'

'Yeah, they removed them when they grassed everything over, don't know where it went.'

'Look, a girl, Louise, stillborn, was buried here a few years ago. What relation is she?'

'I remember something about using the grave for the baby, some cousin's baby or something.'

Pauric answered. We walked around some of the older graves, some of my relatives and names I recognised from the city.

'We better be going, but come down here. It looks a new grave, with fresh flowers on it. It reads: Caroline Brown.'

'It's not our Mrs. Brown, Pauric, our next door neighbour?'

'Yes, that's her, she, of the newspaper cone of chips and apple pie.'

'I loved them, she soaked them in vinegar and the pies were thin and crusty. Remember the time you went missing, we searched all over for you. You went in under her stairs to eat your chips and fell asleep.' Pauric's face lit up with pleasant memories.

'Come on, they'll be waiting for us.'

We walked to the car, a few still stood chatting and nodded to us as we passed. The boys, cousins' sons, were already inside. We went to a local hotel for the meal. Most were at the bar, and I needed a quick drink. We stood close to the entrance of the hotel and welcomed any one arriving after us. Pauric slipped a welcome and warming whiskey into my hand. I said.

'Cheers, mate. I didn't believe all these people were still alive.

We welcomed a stream of old familiar faces. Most went straight into the dining room. Again more relatives I had forgotten about appeared and numerous distant cousins that I had heard about were presented to me. At last, Uncle John arrived and we went directly into the restaurant. After the grace before meals was said we sat down to a traditional but tasty roast meal. When the meal was nearly over, Pauric and I wandered from table to table thanking people again for their kindness.

I was sitting, having a drink with my father's cousin when Marie came over to me after the funeral breakfast:

'Can I have a word with you, Dermot? I have some news about Frank.'

'God, I forgot all about him.'

I excused myself and we moved to a window overlooking the garden.

'I am afraid it's bad news.'

'What?'

'He committed suicide a few days ago. His funeral is tomorrow.'

I drank my whiskey in one swallow.